TIGER BORN

By M. A. Nilles

Available books by Melanie Nilles:

STARFIRE ANGELS

BROKEN WINGS
(Starfire Angels Book 2)

CRYSTAL TOMB
(Starfire Angels Book 3)

ORIGINS OF DARK ANGEL
(Starfire Angels Book 3.5)

FOREVER DARK
(Starfire Angels Book 4)

LEGEND OF THE WHITE DRAGON: LEGENDS,
LEGACIES, DESTINY (Three Complete Novels)

FIREBLOOD (A Legend of the White Dragon Novel)

METAMORPHOSIS: THREE STORIES OF STRONG
WOMEN AND THE TRANSFORMING POWER OF
LOVE

Coming in 2013:
SORIEL (Starfire Angels: Revelations Book 1)

Book 2 in the Demon Age series by M. A. Nilles

For news and updates on these and other works, please visit
melanienilles.com.

TIGER BORN

M. A. Nilles

Prairie Star Publishing ✳ North Dakota

Tiger Born is a work of fiction. Any resemblance of characters, names, places, or incidents to reality is pure coincidence.

TIGER BORN

1

While leaning against a tree trunk for support, Je'Rol groaned as the pain faded and scanned the gory mess around him. The bodies and their dismembered parts were strewn among the trees and brush splattered with blood. From the darkness, parts of his memory flashed back. Now, he would never know who or why. Who were they? Why had the men attacked him?

In self-defense, the monster within him had awakened and lashed out, the blood rage only satisfied by their deaths. Or had it been?

From the mist of darkness, while he had been suppressed by his demon half, his mind had become aware of someone calling to him. They had tamed the beast, allowing him to regain control, but that control slipped away each time. Soon, he would never return, lost forever among the darkness until the demon side took him into death.

But he was back from the nightmare again, sore and tired, although his eyes seemed to fool him. Through the trees, he saw the edge of the forest, where the cliff fell off into a deep river chasm. There, a cloaked figure stepped to the cliff where he had rested prior to the attack. As a child, he might have thought it impossible or a dream for the stranger to cross the air over several hundred feet to a crushing death on the rocks far below, but in the years since he had left the place he last called home, he'd seen stranger things.

The shoulders on the figure were narrow for a man, and the dark, bare feet beneath the cloak too small. The act of walking on air meant magic. Only two groups possessed such knowledge—the immortal demonlords and sorcerers.

He stood upright, the scent of the men's blood overwhelming him. It covered Je'Rol, unforgiving in its barrage on his senses and masking the scent of the stranger.

"You are mine." The feminine voice came from the shadows of the hood hiding the stranger's face.

His chest burned like fire. A faint glow reached him from beneath his eyes, and he looked down at the strange stone shining green from his chest amid the scratches the beast must have inflicted to remove it. It hadn't been there before. The men who had sacrificed their lives had put something on him, but no matter how much he tried, he couldn't touch it.

It seared him but it didn't. No smoke. No blackened flesh. But it burned as if scorching him in flame. He collapsed to his hands and knees, sweating and panting.

The woman lifted an arm from beneath her cloak, revealing black tattoos writhing over the dark skin of her hand and wrist. "Rest now, Je'Rol."

Her voice coaxed his eyelids shut as the sounds of feet trampled through the grass and brush around him.

He slumped to the ground at her feet, and the burning on his chest faded with his surroundings.

* * *

Memories flitted through his head, carrying him up and down with the currents. The lows dipped into dark territory, moments of vaguely familiar shadows, events he never wanted to see. The highs stung worse than the shadowy dips, reminding him of the rare peace and joy that would never come again.

Je'Rol rode through the dreams, sinking into tragedies he sought to forget in the dark depths of the blood rage and lifting with the few bright points.

An innocent memory faded away, replaced by one of the dark memories, when the beast overshadowed him and left him watching as if through a fog. Its roar drowned out all other sounds except the screams of his victims, which died quickly.

Memories arose of the first time he lost control. In his thirteenth year, when he'd started changing into a man, he'd known he wasn't like the other boys. Only pieces of that first time floated from the recesses of his mind; between standing up to a group of bullies and feeling the rage and desire to retaliate rise with the relinquished control of his emotions until he woke up beneath an old tree, he remembered nothing. His clothes were torn and bloody. He returned home to his mother weeping. She took him in her arms and made him clean and change quickly. They left before the accusers arrived and, from a distance, he and his mother watched their home burn.

All his life, even before the first blood rage, they had wandered from village to village, his mother warning him to leave the other children alone. She had colored his hair to hide the unnatural silvery base with the black "V" segments that, with his icy blue eyes, betrayed his tiger demonlord lineage; his father had been of the Je'Gri clan.

In those times he lost control, all sense of who he was disappeared and instinct took over, but it wasn't survival. Rather, he had inherited an instinct to kill but none of the control.

No matter how gentle or noble the demonlord parent, the human side of the half-blood offspring could never contain the demon side. He had been cursed from the moment he'd been born, but he sought a way out of that curse. The obelisk of Mai'Kari would give him control of his demon half. He could have peace, if he could find the obelisk.

But he couldn't close his eyes to the suffering. He had killed them, each life who dared to cross him when he lost control.

The memories washed past him, stinging his chest with the ferocity to choke him.

It burned through him, consuming him in fire.

"Wake up, Je'Rol." A woman's voice.

The scent of wood smoke surrounded him, riding a blend of spices and cooked meat. His side ached where he lay on the hard floor with his arms behind his back.

The burning faded with the dreams. Je'Rol opened his eyes to shadows dancing around the light on the farthest wall. Soft furs lay between him and a hard stone floor and, at the opposite side of the room, covered two chairs near a crackling fire.

A lithe form occupied one of those chairs. Delicate hands at the ends of tattooed arms held a green gemstone set in gray metal. The light side of the woman's profile revealed dark hair tied out of a face with a small nose and full lips, her tawny skin taut with youth.

She turned partially in the firelight, her cheek curving with her smile.

A smile that mocked him, taunting him to break free from the binding on his wrists behind his back. He wouldn't be there for long. No one could hold him, at least no mortal who had tried.

For what seemed an eternity, she stared at him, the smile slowly melting from her face. "You're so quiet. Surely you desire answers." She spoke the words with the seduction of a lover, stirring up painful memories from the sea of turmoil in his past. "Not even a growl?"

She pouted, but only for a second. A wry grin curved up her shadowed face, and she rose smoothly from her chair and walked to him, her dark leggings hugging her body and revealing her nimble movements.

She was the one—the tattoos on her exposed areas of skin confirmed it—a sorceress, as dangerous as any demon hunter. He'd seen it as he returned from the fog of the beast's control. She had walked across the chasm as if solid ground lay under her feet.

His heart sank at the prospect before him; sorcerers and demon hunters were two sides of the same coin—the Adepts of Te'Mea, those born with the ability to *dispirit* demons, a power only full demonlords were immune to. She had the power to hold him without ropes.

The woman knelt next to him on the fur rug. "You cannot escape," she whispered.

His chest burned with the glow of whatever she used on him. From his throat, a growl rumbled.

"You are mine. Obey me, Je'Rol."

The fire burned through his resistance. The beast snarled but made no attempts to escape.

A soft caress on his cheek calmed him.

"Listen to me..." Her words blew warm against his ear. He wanted to listen.

With her sliding over his side, the scent of her body closed in around him as more than blood and sweat. It erased the troubles of his mind, welcoming him into humanity with the identity of a person rather than a being of flesh.

No. She was a sorceress, not a true human. She had fouled her soul for power no demon possessed. Not a threat to the demonlords, the sorcerers were allowed their ways, considered useful by some rumors he'd heard. What did she want with him?

Je'Rol tried to pull his arm free from behind him, but something in his mind stopped him.

"Your will is mine, Je'Rol. You will obey every word I say. The demon will stay dormant until I ask its release. Do you understand?"

"Yes."

A mocking smile curved up her lips. "Very good, but I expected you to learn fast. Someone who can hide for this long from the demonlords and the Adepts must have some intelligence. You gave me a lot to consider in your capture, but tracking you was the hardest part, until I learned you were sighted entering these lands. Then I had only to wait."

The fire faded from his chest, leaving his head clear with the realization that she had hunted him. Why him? Or was he just one more half-blood? "What do you want?"

"Your cooperation."

"Why?"

"Tell me you're mine." Her breath blew warm and inviting across his neck.

The beast resisted, but it could not deny the seduction of her request. He had one other choice—he didn't have to answer her.

Her face lowered to stare at him, her dark eyes piercing in the reflection of the firelight. "Tell me, Je'Rol. You obey me."

His chest burned again, and he could see only one solution. "I…" The fire seared through him, quelling the beast. He couldn't resist. "I will do what you want."

"What do *you* want?"

Je'Rol blinked and tried to focus, but the fire in his chest consumed him in one thought. "I want…I want the pain gone."

Gentle fingers traced along his hairline and jaw, down his neck to the source of the fire on his chest. "Quiet your mind," she whispered. "Soothe the beast. Give yourself to me."

Something in him resisted, fueling the fire. After a few seconds, the resistance faded, along with the burning.

In relief, he took a deep breath and lay quiet on the fur rug. What did she want from him?

"That's better." The gentle tone of her voice soothed the last of the agony from his chest.

"Liandra," a deep voice grumbled from the shadows opposite the fire.

The woman rose from his side and walked away.

"How much longer will this take?"

Je'Rol twisted on his side for a glimpse of the man who spoke.

"You can't rush the conditioning, even with a half-blood like him. The demonlord side is strong."

"Can you make him do it?" The man sounded urgent, and more than a little upset.

"He will."

"I can't afford to waste my time on trials. You succeed, or we're all dead."

"I said he will." Now she sounded upset. "Give me one day. He's already coming around. He'll complete your task when I'm done with him."

A pause filled the room, broken only by the crackling of the warm fire. Je'Rol let out a heavy sigh.

"One day," the man said.

"One day. This time tomorrow he will be yours to command…Lord Bannon."

In the flickering light, Je'Rol made out a small section of face around the eyes and nose of a man surrounded by shadows. Not shadows. A black beard and hair. Those cold eyes caught Je'Rol's for a second before Lord Bannon marched out the door, which thudded closed behind him.

They must have brought him to one of the fortresses of the human leaders. In a twist of irony, the humans had taken the title "Lord" for their rulers, mimicking part of the reference to the powerful domain rulers, the demonlords. Je'Rol could only guess the humans who sought to rule over other humans wished to copy the true domain rulers, thereby taking at least in rank a part of the highest class of beings on the world of Derandria, since they could never hope to possess the same power. A mind game over the humans they ruled. The human lords were no better than their demonlord masters.

What did they want with him? What good was he to ordinary humans?

Liandra stared after Lord Bannon a few seconds before returning to him. The brief movement of air carried the scent of leather and sweat and a touch of spice. It faded with the woman's closeness and her scent surrounding him once more in a clinging imitation of humanity.

"You must be hungry." Her quiet voice stirred the rumble in his stomach. How long had it been since he'd eaten a descent meal? Always traveling. Always scavenging or hunting. The thought of food made his mouth water.

"You cannot escape, Je'Rol." She leaned over him, her tattooed midriff exposed while she unwrapped his wrists behind his back. He could have broken free. She must have known that he had killed the men she sent to attack him. Who else had sent them? They had planted something on his chest to control him, or for her to control him, although it was too late for the men by the time she stopped his demon half.

"How do you know my name?"

The strap loosened and she sat back on her legs. "Your name is whispered among all Adepts, one of only a few half-bloods to evade the demon hunters."

"I could be someone else." He sat up and rubbed the ache from his wrists and arms.

Liandra backed away in a crouch to her fire, her every movement reminding him of a cat and her dark eyes never wavering from him. "You restrain the demon within you. Surviving this long is a rare feat."

Out of habit, he pulled the hood back over his head, despite the warmth of the room. It allowed him to feel hidden in a way nothing else could, cut off from the rest of the world in a physical way, like his outcast status cut him off from society.

"Yet when provoked—" The statement cut off with a growl.

"Yes. I had to be sure."

His claws grew out from ordinary hands and sliced through the leather strap binding his ankles. "Sure?"

A wry grin curved up her face a moment before she turned to the fire and stuck a poker through the flames to the back of the hearth. She pulled out a small cauldron and set it on the stone before the fire with a clatter of the thin handle, then caught the poker on the lid ring and lifted it.

The scent of spices and meat burst from the cauldron with a plume of steam, luring him forward.

"You must be hungry. Eat. Satisfy yourself." She handed him a bowl and ladle.

He sat next to the hot fire and dipped the bowl into the bubbling stew. Not the scalding heat of the broth nor the burning cauldron gave him hesitation when his fingers touched them. Hunger drove him to the food. Cooked food; better than that, meat.

She handed him a small, hard loaf of bread, which he used to soak up the steaming broth. Too long it had been since he last ate a seasoned, fully cooked meal. The emptiness of his stomach drove him to hurriedly finish off two bowls to her one before he slowed with a third. Then he noticed the flavors in his mouth, a rich blend of spices he'd never experienced, almost overwhelming his palate, which normally savored barely cooked, unseasoned game and whatever fruits and berries he found on his travels.

It was food. That's all that mattered. He finished off the last in the small cauldron in satisfaction and sat back in the second chair near the fire, sated for once in a very long time.

"Are you content, Je'Rol?"

He licked the last drop from his fingers and set the clay bowl next to the cauldron, suspicious of what she really wanted. Only one answer came to him: "How could I be content as a slave?" A tinge of anger growled in his words.

Again the smile, but she held the amulet in her left hand.

His chest burned.

"You are not a slave," she whispered. "You are a tool. Tools are extensions of their masters."

She toyed with him, but he couldn't deny her. The magic overpowered him with the fire on his chest. Je'Rol growled in pain and clutched his chest, but he couldn't touch whatever the men had implanted. Claws grew and shrank with the battle inside him.

"You must do as I say, Je'Rol, or all is lost." Her voice took on a whimpering quality, as if she were about to cry. Let her. He felt nothing for the sorcerers and their dark powers.

"Tomorrow we leave for Dev Nadir with Lord Bannon. I will be with you." Her voice lowered to almost a whisper. The soft rustle of fabric announced her movements. "I'll stay by your side, restraining the demon. Would you like that? Would that please you…Je'Rol?"

The fire faded from his chest, leaving him to catch his breath.

She climbed over him and pushed off his hood. Probing hands slid down his neck, but she knelt over his lap without sitting.

"You have a death wish," he snarled. No one would push him to that limit of losing control, least of all a sorceress. Or maybe it would serve her right to test him and satisfy himself with her at the same time.

She smirked and continued her game, leaning close to his ear. "Maybe. Tell me your deepest desires," she whispered. Although acting as if she wanted him, she never pressed close.

He had no intention of playing her games and grabbed her wrists to remove her hands from their mock caress. If she thought appealing to his sexual desires would make him cooperate, she was wrong. The temptation hardened into a desperate need, but violent memories suppressed that with the need to forget.

"Show me, Je'Rol."

He would show her one desire—how he could fight his way free. Claws extended, pinching her wrists so she winced. Human flesh was weak. Not even a sorceress could survive a demon attack if she couldn't control the demon. He could free himself, if he could fight her control.

His chest burned again.

He didn't want to kill. He hated killing. He hated the monster within him, bred into him by a demonlord father.

The rumble of frustration broke from his throat. He shoved the sorceress away and replaced his hood. "Leave me."

She landed hard on her chair but crossed her legs as if nothing had happened. A few seconds later, the sly smile returned. "I underestimated you. Your desires are not what I expected." She licked the beads of blood along her wrists, her eyes never leaving him.

The fire faded once again, leaving him to think clearly. What would she try now that her first scheme hadn't worked? How would he free himself of this?

For a long while, he watched her treat her wounds and studied her for weakness. The tattoos twined around her arms like snakes, dancing in the flickering firelight. He recognized animal shapes and made out strange symbols among them, likely the language of the sorcerers. They ran across her chest and shoulders and up her neck and around her forehead beneath the short locks of black hair hanging there.

Rumors said they used the tattoos as a source of their dark magic, like the talisman binding his will to hers. Even thinking of escape or disobeying her burned him into submission, a far worse fate than the simple *dispirit* power possessed by all Adepts. Whether trained in magic as a sorcerer or used in combination with the fighting skills as a demon hunter, *dispirit* was control over the demon by the Adept's will. At the most intense, his thoughts weren't his own, or exaggerated his own into a strong conviction. He would have to plan carefully how to escape.

Perhaps he should worry more about what she and this Lord Bannon wanted from him. Dev Nadir was the largest human city in the bear demonlords' domain, a shipping and trade harbor. What business could Lord Bannon have there that required a half-blood? For that matter, why would the demonlords allow a human to control a half-blood rather than killing him outright?

Sooner or later, Liandra's tongue would slip, and he'd be waiting.

She opened the lid of a small bowl and dug her fingertips inside. From it, she pulled out a small pale-green salve that hinted of mint and dabbed some onto the tiny points of blood on her wrists. "You're as beautiful as them."

Je'Rol curled his lip back in a snarl. She wasn't the first to tell him he resembled the beauty of the demonlords in their human form. He'd heard it from others, men who thought him too frail to put up a fight to them, who didn't know half-bloods were far stronger and faster than any human. And women...

Je'Rol shook away the painful memories conjured by the suggestion. With his arms crossed, he closed his eyes and shut out the room and the sorceress.

Memories could remain buried.

"That is why you hide your face," she whispered. "Demonlords are more beautiful than any human, as are many of the half-bloods."

But demonlords used that to give their prey a false sense of security. Some still spoke of "culling their herds" of weak or old individuals, and they didn't always speak of four-legged livestock.

"What do you want from me?" The words ground in anger.

"You'll learn when we arrive in Dev Nadir, not before. That is for Lord Bannon."

Je'Rol grunted and slouched back, listening and waiting. If he wasn't getting anywhere, he might as well rest.

Scratching sounds from outside set his nerves on edge. Natters, the smallest, nocturnal predators, mindlessly attacked anything worth eating. He extended his claws in anticipation, but the lowest demons likely wouldn't attack with the sorceress able to control them. They couldn't enter anyway; the room was made of stone, and likely sealed, as in a fortress. Lord Bannon was probably one of the humans who afforded the expense of building a structure to keep all natters out, if he could afford the services of a sorceress.

Liandra tipped her head as if listening. "They won't bother us." The leather covering of her chair squeaked with her movements. "You'll go nowhere tonight. Why don't you rest…Go to sleep, Je'Rol."

Weighed down by the burden of a full stomach and the safety of the fortress after a long day of travel, his eyelids closed against his will.

"You're tired," her voice coaxed. "Close your eyes and rest, Je'Rol."

2

Je'Rol awoke to find himself stretched on the fur covering the floor of the room, his cloak off and the stench of his travels gone. Sometime while he'd slept, someone had bathed him and dressed him in a fresh tunic, and they had removed the blood stains from long ago and wiped the leather breeches with oil.

The sorceress, Liandra. A low growl rumbled from his throat. She had done this to him, not that he wasn't grateful to remove the stench of blood, but much of it had been the fresh blood of those sent by her to restrain him in the first place. It had all been her fault.

She was gone, having left him to wake on his own. The soft glow of morning through the clouded glass of the single narrow window illuminated the empty room. Besides the two chairs next to the cold hearth, only a small table bearing a pitcher and a small basin near the door for washing occupied it with him. The room was small, perhaps a sleeping room, but one without a bed. He had slept on the skins of animals.

This had been the sorceress's room for keeping him, where she had taunted him the night before, but she was gone now. Where had she gone and when would she return? What of the spell she had put in place to control him?

He still had his mind, his will, and she wasn't there to dull it with her control.

There was her error.

Je'Rol sat up and loose hair fell around his shoulders. The scent of herbs reached his nose. Why bother with all the trouble, and how had he slept through it all? He woke at the slightest sound whenever he rested in the wild.

Her spell had been more powerful than he expected, unless she had drugged him.

A low growl emanated from his throat. What had she done to him?

The burning in his chest; it had started with her.

He unlaced the tunic around his neck. In the light of day, he saw it—a green stone sunk into his chest, but he couldn't touch it. An invisible barrier stopped his fingers from any attempt to dig it out of his flesh.

Interesting, since she didn't need special marks or talismans to control him.

Unless the small stone had another purpose. Could she still control him? How could he remove it?

He could worry about that later. First to escape.

Je'Rol found his cloak hanging over one of the chairs. A little damp, but it was clean; the blood had been scrubbed out, although a faint hint of the odor lingered in the fabric. Someone wanted him presentable, but for what reason? Lord Bannon? He had wanted Je'Rol ready for something.

It wouldn't matter if he escaped; he had no interest in the humans' affairs.

After securing the cloak around his neck, he found the leather strap with which he had tied his hair and wrapped it in a tail once more. Satisfied with his hair out of his way and hidden by the hood, he tried the door, expecting it to be locked. At his tug, it whipped open and slammed into the wall beside him.

This was too easy.

Or maybe not.

He hesitated at the open door. Guards stood on either side in their light armor bearing the black and gold crest of their human lord master, which included a bear motif in the center. It didn't surprise him, considering the territory in which they lived. Honoring the bear clan with their likeness should appease them into allowing this Lord Bannon to rise in rank among the humans.

They crossed spears before him.

"You're to wait for *Serae* Liandra. Lord Bannon's orders." The one on his right spoke in a coarse voice, his face lined with age to match his confidence.

The other was young and nervous, by the flash of his throat when he swallowed and the rapid pounding of his heart in the silence of the empty corridor.

Beneath his cloak, Je'Rol extended claws in preparation. They were no threat to him.

Faster than they could blink, he grabbed the spears and splintered the shafts against the door frame. A second later, the old soldier pressed a sword to Je'Rol's throat, while the young man stood in place yet.

"Back into the room, half-blood," the man snarled.

The human was quicker than Je'Rol had anticipated but not near strong enough to subdue him. The scent of blood overpowered the stench of sweat. Wetness tickled down Je'Rol's throat, cooling his skin.

The beast growled in threat, but the man never flinched.

Je'Rol debated his chances against the swordsman. He was unusually swift in his reaction for a human guard, more like the elite Li'Ador, the warriors who trained the Adepts seeking to become demon hunters. That one was confident in his skills, too, a dangerous combination. Although not dressed in the black and silver armor, he had the skills of the demon fighters. How much had Lord Bannon paid him to give up his allegiance?

A wrong move and Je'Rol would be skewered. It wouldn't kill him, but it would disable him for most of the day, and Lord Bannon seemed to want him alive. The soldier was only one man. Je'Rol could take him, if he did this right.

Je'Rol backed into the room, the soldier following every step. Once inside, he waited for the soldier to retreat from the room. The point of the sword lowered from his throat, the tip shimmering with a red line of blood. The man backed away, his sword held in preparation to strike any second.

Another move—

Je'Rol whirled and slashed the space where the soldier should have been. A flash of silver swung at him, and he dodged left, swinging his arm to catch the young man and throw him against the wall. The boy was no threat, and killing would only fuel the desire for blood from the beast within him.

No. His conflict was with the old soldier. Hatred had flared in the old soldier's eyes while he had held the sword at Je'Rol's throat, seeking a reason to kill.

Je'Rol wouldn't kill, but he could disable.

Fire flared in Je'Rol's chest in that moment of hesitation, distracting him from the soldiers.

In a blink, metal glinted before him.

"Stop!" The woman's voice echoed through the corridor.

Je'Rol staggered away from the point pressing into his chest and blinked. Outlined in a dusty slant of sunlight from the window to his right, a lithe form broke from the shadow of the dark alcove.

Her shoes barely made a sound on the floor in her rush to join them.

She pressed the old soldier's hand down. "Do not hurt him."

"He attacked us." Menace snarled in the man's voice.

"He's needed *alive* by Lord Bannon. Would you reject your lord's orders?"

He glared at her for several seconds, and lifted the sword to her face. "I was defending my life."

Liandra whispered in a strange language and touched the bloody edge. It sizzled and bubbled, the blood caking and flaking off in seconds. "Put it away, Captain. He's not to be harmed."

"He tried to leave. Our orders were to keep him here until you returned."

Her glare lightened into a coy smile. "And where am I?"

The old soldier's sharp eyes darted to Je'Rol and back to Liandra, and he bowed his head in defeat. A moment later, he straightened and slammed the sword into the scabbard belted to his waist, a scowl darkening on Je'Rol.

"Good. Stand watch that we are *not* disturbed."

He said nothing but reclaimed his position next to the door, opposite the young man, who pulled himself to his feet and took his position.

The sorceress stopped before Je'Rol, her dark eyes staring into him. "Sit in the chair, Je'Rol."

Her knuckles tightened around something in her hand, but the fire didn't yet ignite.

Seeing little choice, he backed away to one of the two chairs.

The door thumped closed as she sat down opposite him. Liandra leaned back into a casual position and crossed her calves by sliding one slender leg over the other. She did nothing without a teasing, sexual appeal.

Her hand opened so only she saw what was inside. By the tint of green on her face, he could guess what held her gaze. The stone was important to her.

"Clearly I underestimated you," she murmured. In the silence of the room, her low voice rang clear. "You awoke sooner than I expected."

He didn't like the sound of that, but waited. Humans hated silence. It made them nervous.

Liandra stared at the stone. The hint of green on her smooth face vanished.

After a few minutes of silence gelling between them, her eyes lifted. "The journey to Dev Nadir will take several days and hundreds of servants and guards. You won't be so lucky if you try to escape, not with a dozen Li'Ador."

They could just as well have called the demon hunters. A dozen Li'Ador could easily keep him disabled, if not kill him. The warriors had earned the respect of normal humans by protecting them from demons and adhered to a rigid code meant to protect the public. They had no special powers, but their martial skills were unmatched. The Adepts of Te'Mea went to them to learn to become demon hunters.

Je'Rol had once fought and killed several Li'Ador who had dared to attack him when he'd wandered into the gardens of a local human leader. He'd fled to avoid the inevitable, but they'd chased him into an ambush with two others. The fight had been gruesome and difficult. On the brink of death by the unnatural speed and skill of the warriors who caught him, the beast had arisen. He remembered waking next to a dead horse and two bloody bodies shredded by claws, a horrible wound in his side.

He didn't want to think what a dozen Li'Ador might do to him. Death was a good possibility. Their speed nearly matched his, and their strength was extraordinary for mere humans. He'd heard rumors of the Li'Ador killing half-bloods, but not until his fight had he thought it possible. Several Li'Ador combined were as effective as the power of an individual demon hunter.

If Lord Bannon had employed a dozen of the warriors, he might have others protecting his fortress.

Liandra's smile taunted him from escape considerations. His thoughts might be his own, or they might not. Her power over him only led him to believe he was free to choose. How could he trust his own thoughts as long as she held that power?

"Do you like bleeding?" She closed her hand around the green stone with the gray ring around it, hiding it from his sight.

He had almost forgotten the guard's sword. Je'Rol swiped the coolness on his neck and studied the shine of blood on his fingertips. A small wound, it would heal before midday. He wiped his fingers on his cloak and crossed his arms, unconcerned by the small scrape. Here they were again, back to the game she played last night, but her body odor perfumed like a garden. "What do you want?"

She leaned forward, her free hand reaching for his knee while the one with the amulet balanced across her bent legs. That wasn't the hand he wanted. He'd let her have her fun, until the amulet came into reach.

"What do you think I want?" she asked.

"My cooperation in a scheme plotted by Lord Bannon," he grumbled.

She stroked his knee. "You know so little."

"Then tell me."

"You'll learn when the time comes." Her hand slid up his thigh. It brought her body with it and the hand he sought.

Je'Rol snatched her hand with the green stone and pulled it close. She made no attempt to fight.

"What is it, Je'Rol?" Her voice was silky smooth, a touch of the seductiveness haunting her tone. "What's in my hand?"

She was too calm. Or was this part of her game?

He pried open her fingers and dug out the gem, a deep emerald set into a narrow medallion of metal bearing symbols like those tattooed on her body. Was it the answer—the source of her control over him?

The smirk on her face said she wasn't worried about him having it. If it wasn't the source of her power, what was it?

He held it up between thumb and forefinger, his other hand still clamped around her wrist. "What is it?"

"If it were important, do you think I would risk you taking it?"

"What is it?" He tightened his fingers around her wrist, letting the claws extend to pinch her. No more games!

She winced but it didn't dull her smile or cause her to struggle. He caught a new smell, the subtle change of her scent hinting of something he knew well—fear.

Fire ignited in his chest. He tightened his grip, ready to crush her bones.

"You cannot hurt me, Je'Rol."

Heat flared through him from his chest so each breath choked as if inhaling the blaze. He gasped for air and scratched at the glow.

She backed away and the fire subsided.

He no longer held her or the green stone, but leaned on hands and knees, wheezing for clear air.

A soft touch ran down his head. "My poor boy. It seems you've learned nothing from our time together, but you will."

She knelt before him, a finger on his chin lifting his face to her. He growled but restrained himself from tearing her apart. Air filled his lungs, cool and a bit dank but welcome after the fire. He jerked his head away in defiance.

"You will obey." Liandra stood, the fingers of her left hand clenched once more around the stone held inches from him. "Come now, Je'Rol."

His body obeyed and rose from the floor, and his feet carried him to the door without question. She knocked and the young guard opened the door for her, a blotch of discoloration forming on his cheek.

"He's ready now," Liandra said.

The older guard gave Je'Rol a dark glare but said nothing.

Je'Rol pulled his hood over his head and followed the sorceress. The stone wasn't important. Hurting her did nothing but cause him more pain. Killing her was the last option, but he would if it meant his freedom.

No. That was her control on him. She didn't have to say anything. With her near, he couldn't trust his own thoughts; but she couldn't control him if she was unconscious. Or was that the reason for the stone?

She used him, and he wanted to know what Lord Bannon planned in Dev Nadir. Curiosity restrained him, not her.

The tromping of boots on stone echoed through the corridor. Liandra led him to the alcove, which made a sharp angle into another corridor lined by narrow windows.

As they passed, he looked out to his right on a rocky decline of land down to a village around which a protective wall rose up. Each glimpse through the glass gave him a piece of the picture he put together. Through the windows on his left lay a courtyard surrounded by the stone walls of the fortress, a pond in the middle with a tree hanging over it. A group of men in formal attire and ladies in fancy dresses mingled about, many sitting on stone benches lining the open area. Small etchings of bears climbed the corner columns.

Beyond the covered but open walkway on the other side of the courtyard rose the smooth stone wall of several floors of fortress topped by a tiled roof.

"This way, Je'Rol." Liandra motioned with her finger to follow her through a doorway.

He hesitated, until the old guard stepped close behind him. The scrape of his movements and the faint ring of metal hinted of his eagerness to skewer Je'Rol with that sword.

A low growl rose from Je'Rol's throat, but he followed the sorceress through a doorway and a short corridor on their right to another doorway. There, Liandra paused, giving him a moment to take in the dark columns throughout the hall almost blending in among the armed guards in their strict rows facing the center, where the rows of black and silver Li'Ador armor formed a clear aisle. Their eyes burned him in the fire of their hatred.

Je'Rol tensed, his claws extending in preparation to fight. The beast rose inside him but didn't try to escape. He would never win against that many Li'Ador.

Liandra whispered to him, "Follow me. Walk quietly and they won't move."

He glared down at her dark hair. Now was not the best time to attack her for his freedom. That time would come when they were away from the threat.

"Dev Nadir awaits." Liandra strode into the hall.

The beast waited on a breath for a reason to take over, while Je'Rol followed the sorceress's gliding steps and tried not to think about the danger around him.

Ahead, a double door with brass vines circling an inlaid brass and iron scene of bears in a forest stood open to a stone-lined yard filled by mounted soldiers around three carriages.

Once through the hall of soldiers, he stepped out into sunlight and pulled his hood low to shade his eyes. The soldiers sat quietly atop their horses, but their hatred penetrated the air around him with a menace that taunted the beast to rise.

Not yet. When the time came, he might not have a choice but to unleash the demon side. If he could avoid it, he would, and so far, the threat on his life was minimal. Patience would be his best ally.

On the cool breeze from the mountains towering over them, the scent of horses rose with the sweat of men. A path of road cut among the boulders and trees curved down among the natural barriers and the stone buildings of the village built on the same hillside.

Je'Rol took in the numbers of soldiers, particularly the black and silver armor with the black traveling cloaks. Lord Bannon must have had money to pay for all this. The bear clan was generous to allow him to rise to such power. A small part of him was curious why, but the matters of the humans were no more his than those of the demonlords. He wished to avoid them all.

Liandra motioned him to follow her to one of the carriages. In the open outdoors, he hesitated and twisted back to view the palace, for that was what it was, more than a fortress to keep out the natters, the lowest, stupidest of demons. A quick jump would launch him over the heads and spears of the soldiers to the roof. In a couple more, he could be down the rocky hillside or up the mountain.

He'd never make it.

Je'Rol blinked away the doubts tearing through his desire for freedom and turned with a growl to the woman at the carriage.

The dark eyes of the sorceress held him, a touch of knowing in her taunting smile. "Come," she said.

He stepped up to the dark carriage interior before her. She followed and took the seat across from him.

The guards that had followed them out shut the door. No one had attacked or stopped him. Either they had been given explicit orders or…"They don't know."

"They know *what* but not who." At the jingle of bits and fittings, she gazed out the window. "It was necessary to secure the Li'Ador."

He'd bet it was, and it would be a fair bet to win that Lord Bannon paid heavily for them to leave Je'Rol alive rather than kill him. Why was he wanted alive when they knew he was a threat?

How could he escape? For that he'd have to wait for the right opportunity.

With a call from somewhere in the waiting group, the clatter of hooves on stone surrounded them. The carriage lurched and rolled forward.

Je'Rol stretched his legs to the bottom of the seat on which the sorceress sat, bracing himself in a slouch with his arms across his chest. The carriage angled down the winding path, and the ring of hooves on stone muffled when they reached the hard-packed soil of the road.

"How long to Dev Nadir?" Rarely had he traveled the roads. Although he had arrived on the Karaligo continent a couple years ago in his search for the obelisk, he always traveled and avoided the demonlords where he could. Hiding who he was on a world that feared or despised him from either side meant never staying anywhere long enough to reveal himself.

"Three days." Her eyes fixed on the land passing outside the window to her left.

Three days by carriage would have been a little more than a day alone for him, or a rider on a fresh horse; but the carriage horses required rest and food and weren't built for fast travel. Three days meant plenty of opportunity to escape, if he could break the control she had on him.

3

Throughout the first day, Je'Rol held his tongue, watching the sorceress and observing her. The bouncing of the carriage made it impossible to rest while they traveled, but he tried. He would need to stay alert come nightfall.

His plans to escape at night proved futile, as a dozen Li'Ador surrounded him and the sorceress used her power of commanding him to sleep where they camped in the open. He couldn't resist her power and woke to her standing over him the next morning. A low growl rumbled in his throat with his irritation, but with the Li'Ador alert around him, he dared not retaliate and ate quickly.

Afterwards, they prodded him to enter the carriage. Je'Rol growled and extended his claws for the next man who dared crowd too close. Amid the soldiers half a head shorter, he caught a glimpse of the black-bearded Lord Cair Bannon in his finery among a group of armored soldiers.

A woman with long golden hair stood back from them, her amber gown fitting her tall, slim figure with an elegance not possessed of any human he had ever seen. She said nothing but glanced at Je'Rol, her face pinched in a dark scowl.

He froze at the steps of the carriage, struggling against the beast demanding release to defend itself, but not from the Li'Ador. The golden lady set off a warning within him by her presence. Instinct said she was more than a normal woman.

She watched him, a hint of menace on her face.

"Inside," one of the guards ordered.

Je'Rol snarled and all voices quieted. The woman approached, a motion to the guards all she needed for them to move aside in deference.

His heart raced with each step she took. The dignity and poise with which she carried herself multiplied the imminent threat of her presence, but he refused to back down. No human would hold him prisoner for long, not even one as terrible and beautiful as her.

"Do as you're told, half-blood." Her voice snapped the order as if trained in the art of command, something he fully expected from a lady of nobility.

He served no one and let her know in a growl.

Her eyes narrowed. Silence hung over the land as if no one dared breathe. From his position among the soldiers, Lord Bannon watched, the exposed areas of his face paling in sharp contrast to his black hair and beard.

"Be grateful for the mercy shown you," the golden lady said in a threatening voice.

Words betrayed him to argue with her. Or was it more? Something about her forbade him from arguing, but it wasn't for lack of words. The way she carried herself commanded respect, and fear. Only a fully trained sorceress might show such confidence, but the golden lady wore no tattoos like Liandra.

He didn't care who she was, or he tried to tell himself.

"Why should I care?" Je'Rol growled and held up one clawed hand in threat. Sunlight glinted off the nails extended into sharp claws ready to tear through flesh.

Her lip twitched, but she stayed her ground. Either very brave or very stupid, it didn't matter. When he made his move, anyone who stood between him and freedom would be slashed.

Lord Bannon came up behind her. "My lady, your carriage is ready." He made no move to touch her but stepped back out of her way.

For several seconds, she glared at Je'Rol. Then, without a word, she turned, her chin held high, and followed Lord Bannon to a second carriage. Lord Bannon bowed and offered her a hand to step up, before closing the door and leaving the carriage.

Interesting. Who was really in charge?

And who was this woman who could inspire a chill in *him*, Je'Rol, half-blood tiger demonlord? Her scent was carried away by the wind blowing from him, or he might have had a base to identify her.

"Inside, half-blood."

Je'Rol whirled on the guard with a snarl. Over a dozen Li'Ador closed around him, armed with spears and swords, some with bows taut with arrows and full quivers upon their backs.

"Come, Je'Rol," Liandra invited from within the dark carriage.

Unless he wanted to be slashed into a thousand pieces, he had only one choice. The damned sorceress had him, and she knew it. Next time.

Growling, he climbed in and sat down.

Liandra gazed at him, the corners of her mouth lifted slightly.

"What's going on?" he asked.

"You'll see in two more days."

"Tell me, sorceress." He lunged for her, claws ready.

Fire seared through his chest as he grasped her shoulders and pinched. It filled his body, consuming him in pain.

Not again. He refused to give in.

Through clenched teeth, he growled at her. "Tell…me."

Her face inches from his revealed a moment of fear beneath the calm façade, but it could have been a mistake. She smiled in spite of the rapid pulse within his grasp.

The burning increased in his chest with the glow from the stone. It both enraged and subdued the beast he wished to unleash upon her.

"You cannot hurt me."

The pain blotted out his surroundings, intensifying each second he held her. Claws retracted and he stumbled back, gasping for breath.

Sweat plastered his hair to his cheeks and neck, but the heat decreased each second he sat away from her. His clothes stuck to him. Although he'd lost to her power, Je'Rol had seen the truth. She feared him. But why rely on the stone and not her own power? Or was she weak?

"Sit, Je'Rol, and enjoy the ride." Amusement touched her quiet voice.

The beast vanished deep inside, but it could not escape in her presence. For a few seconds, she'd allowed him to think for himself.

"I hoped I could trust you, but I see that I'm mistaken." Her voice flowed in a silken serenity to match the lift of her full lips. She crossed her legs and, beneath her cloak, crossed her bare, tattooed arms, which poked out through the part of fabric.

He wanted to hurt her. He wanted to *kill* her for what she had done to him. The beast agreed, but now that he desired its cold compassion in bloodshed, it could not break the invisible cage of restraint she had built around it.

"What have you done to me?"

She leaned forward, her eyes dancing with cold malice. "You are mine, Je'Rol." Her voice bore a sinister edge that hadn't been there until now.

He'd heard rumors of the dark powers controlled by sorcerers, who seemed to thrive on the fear and mystery surrounding them. The demonlords would be right to massacre the Adepts of Te'Mea, but they had nothing to fear. Demonlords were immortal, untouchable by any magic, and they occasionally found both sects useful—sorcerers and demon hunters.

Je'Rol had never subscribed to any rumors, choosing instead to judge each individual on their actions.

Serae Liandra fit the dark descriptions of most rumors concerning the sorcerers, thriving on misleading him with wrong turns to freedom. Likely knowing none would survive, she had sent soldiers to plant something on him giving her control of all of him. Not only could she control the demon side, which she subdued with her will, but she also controlled his human side, and no Adept could do that. He needed to find a way to remove that stone, or the magic she used.

Until then, he could only sit and ponder the situation and the woman who had imprisoned him within his own body.

During the brief midday break, he was allowed outside only to eat and relieve himself with a full escort of Li'Ador watching his every move. He never saw anything of Lord Bannon or the lady with the golden hair.

By the end of the day, he yearned to stretch his legs and run the moment the guards opened the carriage door.

Over a dozen Li'Ador were ready for him.

Je'Rol clenched his fingers into tight fists. They held their weapons drawn and ready, a nasty blade at the end of each staff and arrows taut against bowstrings. At the memory of a previous battle with the Li'Ador and the pain he'd suffered after recovering control from the beast, he shuddered.

Over a dozen of those weapons aimed at him now. Despite connecting to the demonlord side, he could not release the beast. He could fight as he was, but he would be no match without the full ferocity of the tiger. Any other time he would be grateful for the restraint.

"Step down, half-blood." One of the officers said.

Je'Rol ignored him, his legs tightening in anticipation of a jump that would carry him over men and horses to the security of the boulders breaking the foliage beyond them. Once there, he could disappear into the crevices and trees of the mountains around them. Only the bear clan could stop him.

Fire flared in his chest, startling him off balance. The ground cracked against his shoulder and he rolled to his back as the sorceress stepped out, a satisfied look on her dark-complexioned face with her cowl off her head.

"You will follow orders." She spoke in that sensual, teasing voice. The soldiers backed away from her approach. "Come now."

The heat faded, leaving him cool in the crisp air. Je'Rol climbed to his feet next to the small, lithe figure. Those dark eyes gazed through him, demanding that he obey.

He let out a low growl, but it sounded like a whimper.

When she whispered in a strange tongue, a cloud of darkness blanketed everything, as if twilight had come, yet no one questioned it.

He blinked but could not clear his vision or the cold that settled inside of him. What had she done this time?

As if from far away, she whispered, "This way."

Now a shadow shimmering with strange symbols glowing on sections of her skin exposed outside her cloak, the sorceress stepped away from the carriage. The guards parted before her. Je'Rol followed through the shadows of the men. The myriad scents surrounding him muted with his vision and sounds muffled.

But through the shadowy darkness, a figure of normal lighting stood out behind the crowd of men. He hesitated, hoping for a better look. The golden hair bobbed over the shadows.

"Come, Je'Rol," Liandra's voice beckoned.

His feet moved against his will to obey the sorceress. He struggled to keep an eye on the figure through the shadows, but it disappeared.

A whisper touched the pain in his chest and the darkness lifted, revealing a cavern before him in the rocky side of the mountain.

"You will sleep here tonight," Liandra stated.

He growled his annoyance with the cave and the danger of dark places as nests to natters, despite the efforts of the Adepts and the Li'Ador to cleanse the world of the pests. It was no better than imprisonment in her room while she taunted him with her magic. Even worse were no windows or fire. But with the Li'Ador standing off, the threat of impalement eased from his mind.

"Any food with that?" His stomach rumbled as if to emphasize the ache in his gut.

A patronizing smile lifted her cheeks. "Soon."

Not soon enough. Je'Rol looked back at the two hundred or more men and a few women settling around the carriages and horses.

While the Li'Ador may not have followed them to the cave, they stood at rigid attention, their bows or staffs in their hands. Beneath a dozen helmets, their eyes watched him without wavering.

He snarled at them, but they never flinched.

"Wait inside, Je'Rol," the sorceress commanded softly.

Inside was out of their sight. He ducked the low overhang and entered a cavern larger than the room in the palace where she had held him. No natters and no scent of them having been there recently, but it would have negated Lord Bannon's purpose for him. He stood up under a tall ceiling, the sorceress behind him.

"Sit."

Her voice grated on his nerves, but he resisted the urge to bend his legs and collapse. The power of the request was lighter than other times. Had something weakened her, or didn't she care?

A weak sorceress might grant him a chance of escape. Claws extended beneath his cloak, ready to fight his way to freedom.

"Sit," she said more firmly.

The urge to sit rose strongly in him. Fighting her will over his made him tremble and stumble backwards.

"My will is yours. You will do as I command."

"No."

Her eyes narrowed and a faint light shone from beneath her cloak a moment before the fire flared in his chest. "You must give up, Je'Rol." Her voice whispered through his head with the seduction of relief from the pain.

He couldn't fight her, not when his chest burned, but he tried.

The fire seared through him, all consuming in its intensity. He gasped for air but it burned his lungs. The stone glowed from his chest and he clutched at it to scratch it off but could not touch it.

His knees weakened and he collapsed before the sorceress, struggling for air. Sweat stuck his hair and clothes to his skin.

She squatted down and lifted his chin with a finger. Part of him wanted to wipe the smile from her face with the swipe of a claw, but the other part of him restrained it, insisting he listen to her.

"My dear Je'Rol." Her other hand stroked his loose hair from his face, her touch gentle, almost loving.

It was wrong. She didn't care for him, except for how she could bend his will to obey and carry out whatever plans she had for him.

"I would comfort you and give you a place to lay your head, if you'd let me."

Yes, he wanted that.

No, he didn't. Damn her. She caressed him, touched him as if she loved him; but he felt nothing, only a shadow of a memory long buried.

This had to end, before he lost himself to the confusion of his thoughts.

Claws scratched on rock, but he could not raise them against her. Tears cooled his eyes of the burning still enveloping him.

"Why do you fight it? I can control the demon. You can be free, a half-blood accepted by others because you don't lose control. Isn't that what you've wanted all your life?"

Yes.

But not from her and not like this.

Through clenched teeth, he growled and blinked to clear his vision of her. "I would rather be a slave to the beast—" The burning raged through his chest and his arms ached— "Than a slave to you."

"My poor, misguided half-blood. I can give you freedom."

His ears deceived him, or she did. What game did she play now?

Quivering in agony but determined not to give in this time, he watched her for signs of truth. A faint hope lit inside him that she meant what she said in the way he wanted her to say it; but he doubted she played fair. Liandra had no reason to release him from her control, not when she could use him for her own means.

She leaned forward, her breath cool on his sweaty neck. "Trust me."

He wanted to laugh, but could barely breathe through the pain.

She backed off but, a few seconds later, set a plate of food on the ground before him. "Eat now and rest. I'll return after you've had time to consider."

Her feet padded softly away through the mouth of the cavern, taking the fire with them.

Weakened from fighting her magic, Je'Rol rested his head against the cool, dank ground and breathed to calm his racing heart. He was accustomed to traveling whole days on foot without exhaustion, but this was magic, and more powerful than he'd ever expected. What did they want with him?

He turned his head and stared out the low opening of the cavern. Several Li'Ador stood watch at the entrance, three with their backs to him and four standing alert facing him. Beyond them, he saw little, but the steady drone of voices and clinks and squeaks of armor merged. It was as if he didn't exist and the world went on without him.

To most of them, he probably didn't. This was the way he preferred it—that no one think about him. They did, though, or the Li'Ador wouldn't be standing watch.

Cold meat waited within arm's reach, along with a hard, dry roll. It wasn't much, but the meat would replenish his strength. He'd had the chance for water in the carriage.

Je'Rol's hand shook as he reached for the plate and pulled it near, the scrape of metal on stone echoing to the high ceiling of the cavern. Fresh, raw kill would have been preferable to the day old cooked meat, but he had no choice and chewed it down with the stale bread. Afterwards, he sat with his head back against the rock and closed his eyes.

Still weak from Liandra's magic, he rested. He'd need his strength if he had the chance to escape. Getting past the Li'Ador would be a challenge requiring everything he had, *if* he could disable the sorceress.

Small chance of that, but if the opportunity presented itself, he wouldn't be sitting around.

Except the more determined he was, the stronger the magic she used against him. How far would she go towards breaking him completely?

With his eyes closed, he listened to the buzz of conversations outside.

Soldiers speculated about the purpose of their journey to Dev Nadir and the territory under Lord Sidek Chandroya, the local governor. Apparently the man had a penchant for sports, particularly the more gruesome Dao'Larashi, where trained warriors fought to the death while a whole arena of spectators cheered them on.

And Lord Bannon was taking him to the city of this blood-thirsty ruler. Humans were no better than their demonlord masters when given enough freedom.

"I hear his best came from Ragren, a giant of a man. Undefeated in eight years, supposedly. Lord Chandroya bought him a few years ago for his weight in gold."

Bought him? As Je'Rol suspected from bits of conversation he'd caught in his travels, the Dao fighters were slaves.

"Right." By the tone, the other man was anything but agreeing. "No one has that kind of money sitting around."

"Ah, but rumors say the domain of the H'Shasa clan is rich with gold and gems and they freely trade with the humans through the ports of Dev Nadir."

The H'Shasa clan. Je'Rol had met one while traveling through their domain years ago, a large island named Hathaen. In their original forms, the demonlords who ruled it were strange, almost horse-like predators whose four long legs extended from a scaly, heavily-muscled body to claws. From that body, their spike-lined necks tapered to a head that resembled something between that of a horse and that of the dragon clan with sharp teeth for tearing flesh. Unlike a horse or dragon, they could snap their long, snakelike tails like whips. As fierce and swift as their beast forms, the H'Shasa demonlords were quite the opposite in nature, though no less discriminating, than any other demonlords towards half-bloods.

The demonlord had let Je'Rol go only after he promised never to return.

Je'Rol never looked back, but neither did he forget the gentle nature of the H'Shasa clan in contrast to their frightening appearance.

"Chandroya bought this fighter for his weight in gold?" The new man's voice was like rocks grinding. "Feh. Ain't no man worth that."

"Maybe not, but Lord Chandroya must think so," the third man said.

Another man chuckled. "Let 'im."

"Yeah. It's his gold to waste."

"No. I mean that," the calm, casual voice said.

"What?"

Their voices lowered, but Je'Rol focused on the source of the sound, his ears keener than any human's.

"What do you think is in *there*?" the calm man asked.

A pause, then a gasp.

"Yes."

"He wouldn't dare. In the blood rage—" the rocky-voiced man said.

"He knows. Lord Bannon hasn't said anything, but I suspect that's the purpose of this parade and the sorceress to keep him under control… until the right time. All the strength and agility of the demonlords but none of the control. Let a half-blood loose and—" He cut off.

So that was it.

Je'Rol let out a sigh. They wanted him to defeat the undefeated Dao fighter. What if he didn't want to fight?

Liandra would probably see to that. Maybe that's what she meant by his freedom—

turning him loose on an unsuspecting human who would be no match at any skill level alone with a half-blood of his experience. He was probably the oldest surviving half-blood; no wonder she had sought him specifically. Most died early at the hands of demon hunters or Li'Ador, or lost themselves when the blood rage grew too savage.

"So long, Lord Chandroya's Dao fighter." The man's voice muffled as if behind a mug.

"Hello, Lord Bannon as the top Dao fighter owner."

"Or all the gold Chandroya can throw at him for the half-blood."

A few mumbles of agreement followed that.

"Speculation and rumor," the rocky-voiced man scoffed.

"It makes sense."

Je'Rol growled, ready to strip Lord Bannon of his skin if he came near. Was that the reason for the sorceress and his captivity to her will? Perhaps she sought to subdue the beast to level his killing skills against the human fighter. He didn't need the demon side to kill. He was stronger, faster, and more tolerant of pain than any mere human. Coupled with a sense of smell and hearing that alerted him to the subtle reactions accompanying a human's thoughts, he often downed his opponents before they finished their attack posture.

"It's damned right speculation," another man said. "Messenger came a fortnight ago to deliver news of a Dao Larashi tournament. It opens seventh night after the rise of Karnoss."

"Five days from now."

"That's no coincidence."

The star of Karnoss only came into view for a limited time each year, though sometimes twice. It must have emerged from the western horizon during his night in Lord Bannon's palace. He was no astronomer and didn't care about the stars except for navigation across the domains, and this.

The men hushed, but Je'Rol had heard enough. Now he understood the reason Lord Bannon desired him.

He had one more day to plan his escape, if the sorceress let her guard down.

4

Liandra returned soon after the soldiers' conversation about the Dao Larashi moved on to other topics, but Je'Rol said nothing. Rather, he cooperated with her requests and didn't fight the commands forcing his body to yield to her will.

After the soldiers quieted, Je'Rol laid back on the dirt around the small fire he shared with the sorceress, one arm under his head and the other across his chest.

The dank, moldy scent of the cave mixed with the smoke of the fire to overwhelm the sorceress's human scent. Without that distraction, he could imagine that he was alone again in the wilderness.

Except that a dozen or more soldiers probably stood watch for natters. The lesser demons had never given up their taste for human flesh, but their numbers decreased every year through the efforts of the Li'Ador and the demon hunters. The chances of the average person being attacked by one of the lesser demons were less than being attacked by highwaymen, particularly along the main roads. Natters preferred dark places and only emerged to hunt at night.

"Not even a growl?" Liandra spoke in a quiet voice as if afraid to crack the silence. "This is unlike you. Not the least little bit of fight?"

How ironic. She wanted him to fight, now of all times. That was the last thing he would give her—what she wanted. It would seem that in not opposing her he was opposing her.

The faint scrape of fabric foretold her movements, but the soft footfalls told him more.

"I'm disappointed," she whispered, her voice close and irritating on his patience.

Through the open part of his hood partially obstructing his vision, he saw her legs. She knelt on the ground next to him, her knees pressing against his right side.

A second later, her hands rested on his chest. She lowered her face to peek under his hood and whispered in that strange language.

His hood slid back.

"Leave me alone," he growled.

One tattooed hand slid up his chest and pulled down the laced collar of his tunic. A sly smile spread across her face, pulling back the odd markings around her ears. The sorceress's finger traced what he guessed was the stone on his chest, but he felt nothing. Whatever it was, she had placed a spell on it to prevent touching that area.

How he would remove it, Je'Rol still hadn't figured out. He had tried to rip out his own flesh, but something prevented him from scratching it. The stone could only be removed by magic.

He tried to ignore her and closed his eyes to rest of his own free will, before she commanded him into a deep slumber.

The warmth of her cheek brushed against his. "Not yet, Je'Rol," she whispered.

Her words opposed his desire to rest, irritating him into snarling.

"That's my boy." She sounded far too pleased.

That's as far as he went. No more playing her games, not if she wanted him to fight her, or to fight anyone.

Her hands slid off, but only to support her body over him on four limbs with her legs straddling his hips. Black hair fell like a curtain around her face above his.

"We have one more night before reaching Dev Nadir." Her voice barely broke a whisper. "Tell me what you really want."

"I want to be left alone." He grabbed her shoulders and shoved her off.

A small grunted escaped her as she landed on her bottom next to the fire. Next time he'd aim for those flames, or what little remained.

Annoyance flashed across her face, and she stood and dusted herself. Whatever anger or shock she had felt passed, replaced by a satisfied smile; but he wouldn't soon forget that he had broken that calm demeanor.

Je'Rol tugged the hood back over his head and closed out the world, especially the sorceress.

Unfortunately, it didn't stop her from kneeling over his side again, this time by his head. "Sleep until I tell you to wake."

His eyelids fell heavily, and his mind blurred. A deep breath later, the world cut off.

* * *

Je'Rol walked through a world cloaked in black, chasing a light which shrank away the faster he ran to catch it. Through briars and lakes and deserts and valleys, he chased the light, almost certain what it was; but to no avail. The light diminished in the far distance.

The land beneath his feet gave way and he fell through nothing.

Until a faint voice called to him with the soothing tone of someone concerned: "Je'Rol!"

The sun rose on him standing on a thick branch high among the trees. Somewhere below, a golden shape strolled among the trunks, something on four legs, but he couldn't see it clearly. He crouched and watched, suspicious and extending his claws in preparation to defend himself.

The shape emerged from a place it logically should not have and much closer.

"Je'Rol," the gentle voice called to him. "I cannot undo this at once, but I will do what I can."

The sun grew brighter, and hotter. He fanned himself but it wasn't enough. He stripped off his cloak. Still, the fire burned. His body burned, stealing his breath to leave him gasping.

Awareness returned, and with it, a desire to disfigure the sorceress.

"Quiet," a voice firmly whispered.

The fire from his chest burned throughout his body. He clenched his teeth and released the claws to slash at the hooded shape over him with firm contact.

It jumped back and tucked an arm close, the face hidden behind a golden cowl.

The burning faded and his head cleared to make sense of what he saw. Beyond the figure next to him and the embers of what had been his fire, the bare feet of the sorceress were unmistakable in the faint light of the fires flickering outside. If the sorceress wasn't the figure, then who—

He sniffed. The smell wasn't human. The sorceress nearby gave off a pungent odor, and the whiff of wood smoke from the dead fire tangled with it, but he recognized nothing familiar about the stranger. This one bore a clean scent.

The stranger stood up in the dark of the cave, the faint scrape of cloth the only sound made. In the shadow of the hood, he could make out nothing of the face of the person who broke the enchantment.

"Stay, Je'Rol," the stranger whispered in a voice too soft for a man. "I'll do what I can to break the spell, but you must act as if nothing has changed."

"Who are you?"

"Another time. Return to sleep now or my efforts are wasted." She glanced aside at the sorceress and hurried from the cave.

He considered following, but not at the sight of the Li'Ador standing watch. They made no move to seize the cloaked figure passing their line, nor did anyone speak. They must have seen her, unless she was a ghost, but he could not have clawed a ghost.

Silence fell back upon his world. He scratched at the tingling in his chest but could not remove whatever was there. She had done something to the power but had not broken it completely, if he understood her.

He knew of only two groups of people who might break the magic of a sorcerer—another sorcerer or a demonlord. Neither group seemed likely to help him, but someone was; someone the Li'Ador trusted or who gave them no concern. He hoped she returned another night to finish what she started.

Until then, he would rest. Tomorrow would be an interesting day. Je'Rol closed his eyes and stretched out with a sigh. The questions slipped aside with his fatigue.

Sometime after he fell asleep, the soft scuffle of movement woke him. He listened.

"Come," a voice whispered, most likely not to him.

Je'Rol listened and remained still. The scrape of movement faded.

"What is it?" Liandra's voice cracked with sleepiness.

"What happened with him? I thought you had control." Lord Bannon's hushed voice carried a tone of anger.

"He is under my control. You'll reach Dev Nadir without problems."

A pause followed her words, then "I'm told he attacked you in the carriage."

"He tried, but the stone stopped him."

"I thought you didn't need talismans to subdue demons. You're an Adept."

"Yes, and I can subdue demons; but Je'Rol is half human. *Dispirit* only works on the demon side." She lowered her voice, her tone that of someone thinking out loud. "If the human side gains control, that may weaken my power over the demon side. That was unanticipated. I've never used *dispirit* on a half-blood more than two days. But I am testing the demon side to maintain control."

"You keep him subdued or I'll report this to the *Sect du Maistri Te'Mea*."

A long pause followed, and he imagined Liandra carefully concocting her reply. If he understood correctly, she'd committed an error that might have blasphemed the teachings of her precious founding teacher, Te'Mea. Amusement tugged at the corners of his mouth, despite the implications of giving in to the demon side.

"You would do no better for holding a fugitive half-blood, a crime against all clan laws." Smugness hung thick in her voice.

"The Ur'Asu allowed it." The stomp of his heavy steps faded quickly.

Liandra mumbled something under her breath and returned to the cave. After some movement, she quieted, her heartbeat rapid. Lord Bannon had upset her, despite her trying to hide it. She was good at acting.

But Je'Rol was better. He let out a small sigh and waited for morning. Falling asleep would be preferable, but unlikely with this new information playing in his head.

* * *

"Wake now, Je'Rol." Liandra's warm breath blew on his neck.

He'd been waiting for that command for a while, listening and pretending to sleep. He didn't know how much of the spell the woman last night had broken, but she'd indicated the time would come when he would be free. He'd rather act now, but he didn't have a chance of surviving. He had to wait, and to keep his demon side under tight control.

"Sit up and eat."

The sorceress could crawl back under whatever rock had hidden her. Unfortunately, that wasn't likely to happen.

He let out a low growl and sat up. She slid a plate to him covered in food, mostly meat and bread. If they intended him to be strong to fight, that explained the half-decent meals rather than starving him to weaken him, as he would have expected with being taken as a prisoner.

"Eat up, if you want to keep your strength." A wry smile curved up her face. Apparently satisfied that she had him, she stood and backed out the cavern.

He gazed past her at the Li'Ador still standing watch, the only reason she could leave him alone without worrying about him escaping. Beyond their line, the sun slanted through the trees, leaving shadows across the men eating and chatting about Dev Nadir. A light breeze rustled tree leaves and brought a hint of the scent of rain.

Liandra disappeared from sight, but the Li'Ador seemed more attentive in exchange.

Je'Rol snarled at the emotionless faces fixed on the cave entrance only a couple strides away, weapons poised to threaten him. Without them, he might have escaped, magic or not.

The desire to live overrode his need for freedom, for the time. He tore at the cold meat, trying not to taste it.

After he finished, he stepped out of the cavern. Half a dozen Li'Ador staffs and arrows trained on him. It shouldn't matter with the speed of a demonlord at his disposal. The urge to fight extended his claws and bent his legs into a position to spring above them. He couldn't take them all on, but he could escape.

From somewhere behind, the golden head of the lady emerged. Her liquid amber eyes bore into him, and she shook her head minutely, loose waves of golden hair shimmering in the morning sun.

Confused after yesterday's reprimand, he relaxed the tightening of his legs and frowned, but she turned away to Lord Bannon, who bowed to her with his arm extended to the open carriage door.

A second later, fire flared in Je'Rol's chest. It burned away any lingering intentions of escape, searing his lungs so each breath hurt and he could only gasp. Amid the blur of his vision, the sorceress appeared.

He fell to his hands and knees, trembling. Her face hovered close.

"Follow me," she said.

The fire lessened but did not cool. He stood and obeyed. Only when he entered the carriage did the fire vanish from his chest, leaving him to breathe deeply.

Liandra sat opposite him and let out a heavy sigh. "Why must you even consider it? You are mine, Je'Rol."

He pulled his hood down and crossed his arms. She could believe all she wanted about owning him or possessing his will; but someone had broken her spell, and he would bet good money it was the lady. The golden lady had to be demonlord for a human to show such deference and to be able to weaken a sorcerer's magic, but if she was, she was far from her clan's domain.

Who was she and why would she help *him*? The demonlords wanted him dead.

Next time she visited to break more of Liandra's spell, which she had promised, he would ask her.

5

Although Je'Rol did all he could to ignore the sorceress, by the time they reached the fields surrounding the harbor city of Dev Nadir, he sat with his claws grown long enough to mutilate her if she taunted him one more time. He'd sworn he wouldn't give in to her teasing, to leave his human side dominant, but *Serae* Liandra had ways of irritating him into losing his temper.

He would never get close to killing her, but he could cause some serious harm before she brought that magic to bear.

"You will obey my every word, Je'Rol," she said over the creak and clatter of the carriage and the horses and their tack. The soldiers rode without speaking, but they'd said enough last night for him to understand their purpose.

The land smelled different here, and soon he'd pick up the fishy scent from the ocean not far away. Lord Bannon must have lived on the edge of the Tundars Mountains. It should've taken longer to cross, particularly since a good part of that continent—shared by several demonlord clans—was mountains. He'd been further into the mountains when the sorceress caught him; they must have moved him a long ways before he'd awakened in her lair of Lord Bannon's palace.

Outside the windows, human adults worked in the fields alongside their children. While the men drove the horses pulling the cutting blades, several boys hurried to bundle the grain and run them to the nearest ring of women and girls, who separated the chafe from the grain.

The demonlords owned all the lands but were rarely seen. As long as the humans compensated the ruling clan with livestock fattened on their lands, the demonlords mostly left them alone. Humans were cheap labor for them. They used to be food, but that ended long ago, when the demonlords discovered their usefulness, in many ways.

His mother had been used to satisfy one demonlord's lust.

Je'Rol flexed his claws and stared at the results of that lust. He should never have been allowed to live. Somehow, his mother had hidden him from the demon hunters for fifteen years. The boys taunting him had been one thing, but he wasn't sorry that he lost control. Throwing rocks at him and kicking him were no worse than him attacking them in self-defense, even if he couldn't remember doing it.

It was the mutilation of his first true victim that brought the demon hunters after him. The boys had seen nothing compared to that.

Those same claws had slashed the body to bloody shreds, and the beast had fed. Now the humans wanted him to fight on their terms, to use that violence for their entertainment.

Je'Rol snarled and slashed at the side of the carriage, leaving deep gouges in the woodwork.

"Be still!" the sorceress snapped.

He turned to her, teeth bared and lengthening and a deep rumble emanating from his throat. She wanted him to fight for Lord Bannon, and the only way to fight effectively was to let loose the beast. Four days ago, he had been free. *Serae* Liandra had taken that from him, and now he had been cooped up for three days, unable to stretch his legs or seek the solace of being alone. More than any time in his life, he wanted to release the beast from inside.

"You will have your chance," she said in a silken voice.

Waiting wasn't an option. He jumped at her.

And seemed to have landed in a fire. Barely aware of his surroundings and the cloaked figure no longer where he expected it, he gasped for air and stumbled to the floor of the carriage.

"You cannot hurt me." Her voice soothed, although her words taunted. "Sit up, Je'Rol, and relax…"

The fire eased but only faded completely after he sat on the seat across from the sorceress. Covered in a layer of sweat that stuck his shirt to him, Je'Rol caught his breath.

"Conserve your strength. Soon, you won't be restrained, but you must never harm me, Je'Rol."

"Why? Because it would free me?"

The smile on her face hinted of dark satisfaction. "Far from it."

He raised his hand and extended the claws in threat; but, as he expected, she showed no fear. Rather, amusement danced in her eyes, which looked out the window a moment later.

He could take her unawares if she relaxed. He should have tried last night, except he wouldn't have gone far with the Li'Ador right outside the cave; if he could have. Maybe her power over him wasn't something she consciously exuded only while awake.

His fingers curled into a fist, the claws shrinking to normal nails again.

The demonlord lady better know what she was doing, if she'd done anything. He'd gained no advantage on the sorceress.

The carriage soon came to a stop with men on horses surrounding them. The scent of horse sweat and dirty humans blowing in through the windows overwhelmed him.

The door opened and an armored soldier gave him a long look before turning to her. "*Serae* Liandra. Lord Bannon wishes to know before we enter the city that you have the…" He hesitated, his eyes sizing up Je'Rol and the hood shadowing his face. "The half-blood under control."

"You can assure Lord Bannon that the half-blood will restrain himself. He won't hurt anyone."

The soldier gave a sharp nod of his head and shut the door.

Je'Rol crossed his arms and closed his eyes, cutting off the world and the harsh realities.

Except for a woman's voice he picked out among the squeaks and creaks of armor and leather and occasional clink of metal and horse's blowing or stomping. She spoke not in the common speech of the humans, but in the *Lexic* of the demonlords.

He understood nothing, except the tone. A man, likely one of the bear clan, was firm and sharp, allowing no argument; but the woman was also firm, and questioning in tone. They paused and the man yelled out, "Let them pass!"

Once again, the carriage creaked and bounced along the road.

Je'Rol peered out the window and caught the eyes of a man in meticulously detailed plated armor, his black hair pulled from the hard, angular lines of his face into a ponytail near the top of his head. His horse chomped its bit as they rolled past.

"He seems dissatisfied." Liandra sounded amused. "I suppose he should be to smell a half-blood in his presence. The Ur'Asu are less forgiving than the Su'Kora or the Je'Gri, of breaking sacred laws." She stroked something in the palm of her hand, her eyes dropping to reflect a green glow. "You should be glad I found you when I did."

He met her eyes with a glare and a low growl. He would have been just as well off without her "protection" from the demonlord laws, which was odd considering the demonlords ruled and answered to no human; or were they amused by his being forced to fight to his death in the Dao Larashi?

What had the golden lady told the guard of him? How had she convinced the bear clan to let him pass?

Next time she came to break the sorceress's spell, he'd ask.

In the meantime, he could do nothing but watch the city roll past.

Je'Rol noticed the smell first, a foulness blending with the sweat of horses and men. Every city bore the stench from too many humans living in cramped conditions, their waste and excrement flushed through streets or—as in some of the more prosperous cities—through underground tunnels. Dev Nadir was in the latter category, but that didn't mean people didn't throw waste into the streets.

City doors thundered a grinding welcome. He peaked out the corner of his eyes through the window of the carriage at the massive gateway and its immense wall. Like most cities, they were well defended against natters or invaders.

The carriages and their entourage entered the city outskirts, where the homes were larger and farther between with great swaths of open land sloping down to the heart of the city and the harbor. The tallest buildings of stone and masonry stood level with the modest homes on the higher elevation on the outskirts.

Not just any buildings stood level but three towers overlooking the harbor and the city. Similar towers stood sentinel at regular spacing along the miles of wall surrounding it all.

Dev Nadir was no ordinary city, but he'd seen more impressive cities.

Still, there was one sight he had heard about worth noting.

Je'Rol turned for a better look of an enormous structure below, an oval of descending tiers to a flat field on the inside. From a distance, it could have been small, but wide lanes radiated like spokes of a wheel from it with dots of movement around it in those spokes. It dwarfed the buildings, even the giant statues, around it.

The carriage turned on the sloping rode so he could see nothing but the few homes and the long stone wall on the outskirts.

The one time he'd been to Dev Nadir had been in landing in the harbor, and he had immediately made for the outskirts and jumped the height of the wall. Demonlord abilities gave him another advantage—he didn't have to pass through the normal checkpoints.

Je'Rol closed his eyes for a while and listened to the sounds around him, mostly the clap of hundreds of horses' hooves on hard-packed dirt. He tried to avoid noticing too much of the myriad scents, although he thought he caught a whiff of flowers. It passed before he could be sure.

On they traveled, down the sloping road. Where it leveled, the clop of hooves turned into loud claps on stone.

He opened his eyes and glanced out. The structures here were taller and more ornate, but the streets more crowded. The thick mass of mounted soldiers had vanished from each side of the carriage. He could only guess they had formed up ahead and behind. People in the streets stood and watched with curiosity painted across their faces. Some leaned against pillars supporting awnings or balconies, their arms crossed and faces pinched as if inconvenienced or unwilling to let any sense of curiosity show.

That would change when he was ordered to fight. The Dao Larashi was a popular sport, originally enjoyed by the demonlords, who watched their human animals fight, sometimes throwing them against particularly vicious natters. That had changed somewhere along the lines, as most demonlords retreated from the increasingly crowded cities. Je'Rol sympathized—humans stank.

The largest arena, the Kairashun, was a wonder among the feats of human engineering. Other arenas had been designed by the demonlords, who forced the humans to labor to build them, but the Kairashun was a monument of human ingenuity to imitate their masters and expand on what had come before. He'd heard of it before ever setting foot in Dev Nadir, but he'd avoided the city and its residents as much as possible, pausing only long enough to gather information for his search and be on his way.

They turned along a street parallel to the central city, giving him a clear view of the Kairashun and the banners waving in a stiff breeze around the edge of its bowl. He'd get a better look soon enough. The humans would force him to fight there; the humans who imitated their masters, seeking to become them.

Liandra watched him, a satisfied lift to the corners of her mouth.

Je'Rol looked away, studying the city layout while he could. He would need the information when the time came to escape.

They passed into one of the spokes of the wheel where the Kairashun was the hub. Mounted soldiers once more formed lines around them, blocking his view.

It didn't matter. He'd find his way out, one way or another, after the sorceress's spell was broken and the Li'Ador were gone, or when most of them were.

With the windows blocked of the breeze carrying the city smells—good and bad— the sweet musky scent of the sorceress closed around him with the stench of dirty humans.

He glared at the sorceress from under his cowl, but she simply gave a sickening smile, her dark eyes hinting of reproach.

After some time, they rode under the archway of the Kairashun entrance, the interior of the carriage darkening as they passed into a livery, based on the overwhelming odor of livestock and their waste.

There the carriage stopped and most of the soldiers dismounted in a clamor of armor and tack. The door of the carriage opened to a semi-circle of Li'Ador spears. Once again, he stepped out, but this time a ceiling stopped any thoughts of jumping clear. In the tight space of what appeared to be an entrance tunnel, he had no room to maneuver. If he dared to fight his way out, he'd likely be skewered.

Je'Rol stepped down with the sorceress following.

"Bring him," a deep voice commanded.

The Li'Ador opened a path to an archway under which Lord Bannon and the golden lady stood, her simple amber gown like a second skin on her slim figure. Only the frightening beauty of the demonlords could turn ordinary into extraordinary. No matter how much they tried, the humans would never achieve the same effect with their hands as the demonlords did with their magic.

"Follow Lord Bannon," Liandra whispered.

The closing of the Li'Ador behind him gave Je'Rol no choice but to obey. They moved with him through a dingy corridor slanting beneath the main arena. In those torchlit stone passages, they passed sections housing dozens of horses and other animals. Caretakers backed into their nooks as the entourage passed. After local guards unlocked several gateways, they entered an area of men chained and behind bars, most of them in their own cells and all of them well-fed and sturdy. The clink of chains accompanied the shift of their movements.

They stank, like the rest of the closed-in underground corridor. But it was nothing compared to what stopped Je'Rol from continuing.

The reek of blood and death drifted from ahead, the stench of demons, more specifically, natters.

"Keep moving."

A sharp prod in the back triggered an explosion of defense and a growl that filled the narrow corridor. He whirled and knocked the staff away, but in reaching for the man who poked him, several points stabbed into him. Je'Rol roared and whirled to knock them away, but the soldiers backed off.

Tense silence surrounded him. They feared the blood rage, but how many knew the sorceress had silenced the demon side?

He glared at the men wearing the silver-accented black uniforms, daring them to force him to fight. They pointed their spears and kept their distance. After a dark look to each, he turned and continued with the others nearer to the natters, blood oozing from the fresh wounds cool on his sides. They would heal in a day.

Whispers trailed around him from the men behind bars, questioning his status as an opponent. They'd witnessed the speed at which he moved—unnatural for a human—and heard the beastly roar.

The clamor of natters behind sealed doors rose up in earnest, the clinking of chains muffled by what must have been inches of solid metal and stone. The entourage stopped before a metal door blocking the rest of the corridor, an open cell to their right. The last cell before the natters section would be his.

Je'Rol stepped past the golden lady and Lord Bannon into a room of stone. Shackles secured to chains above a wooden bench along the back wall. The Li'Ador stepped forward to secure his wrists in the heavy bindings. He almost laughed in their faces that they expected it to hold him; but the moment they slapped the bands around his wrists, his strength waned.

He lifted his arms, which weighed ten times heavier than a second ago, as the Li'Ador stepped back. He could barely reach up, much less fight his way free. Such cuffs weakened him to be less than a human. Curse them all!

"He won't escape." A man in the dark blue tunic of the local soldiers stopped at the cross bars of the cell door.

"You have no idea what I have here," Lord Bannon said.

Liandra's fingers traced the symbols around the cuffs, a smile sliding up her face. "Powerful magic." Apparently satisfied with his incapacity to escape, she stepped back outside with the others.

"Well?" Lord Bannon questioned.

"We can leave him. He'll go nowhere, my lord."

"You're certain?"

Her lips curved up into a sly smile. "Yes."

Lord Bannon turned to the golden lady, who gave a bow of her head. That seemed to satisfy him. "I want no less than two Li'Ador here at all times, rotated throughout the day and night."

"Understood." The nearest soldier gave a crisp nod and motioned to two of his men to take up positions.

The local soldier grunted. "As you wish. Unnecessary, but you're payin 'em."

"I'll protect my investment."

Je'Rol caught a glance from the golden lady before they left and he staggered back to the bench to sit, his body feeling like a ton of bricks. Two Li'Ador stayed behind, both in the middle of the corridor facing the direction they had come. If not for the magic restraining him, he might take them on. Any ordinary shackles he could have broken with little effort.

He hadn't anticipated magic. But the magic only weakened him. It didn't dull his senses.

The natters reeked nearby, despite the heavy door closing them off from escape. The humans were no better. The filth of the underground prison overwhelmed him, and likely did the same to the golden lady, except she didn't have to stay in the intolerable stench.

After the long carriage ride with no chance to stretch his legs, the need to move had coiled inside him, latched by the sorceress's commands and now by the magic of the shackles.

He stood and gathered that strength and pulled on the chains. The Li'Ador soldiers watched him, their weapons ready. His muscles strained against the weight of the chains with each pull forward, his legs adding their force to free him of the chains.

The cuffs cut into his forearms, but he didn't care. Je'Rol grunted with the exertion, sweat beading on his brow and sticking his clothes to him.

The Li'Ador stood ready.

Je'Rol continued for some time, until the warden came with a scrawny boy in a plain tunic. The tousle-haired boy carried a plate loaded with food.

A key clinked in the lock of the cell door. "Ain't no use tryin to break magic-bound shackles. Not even them natters escape." He opened the door and prodded the boy to take the plate in.

Je'Rol waited for the boy to leave, which he hurried to do after setting the plate on the floor close to Je'Rol.

"Eat up."

"Maybe I'm not hungry."

The warden shrugged and locked the door. "Not my concern." He prodded the boy away ahead of him and disappeared.

Je'Rol's stomach growled. Hunger stretched his foot to hook the plate and slide it into reach of his hands. What he told the warden had been a lie of defiance; in truth he wouldn't give up a solid meal when he needed his strength more than ever. Soon he would fight for more than their entertainment.

6

—————

The burning on his chest alerted him to the dark shape next to where he slept on the floor. In the green glow caught beneath her hood, he made out the hard lines of the golden lady's face.

"Hold still," she whispered, her hand pressed against his chest.

He did as she commanded, in spite of the fire burning through his body.

After some time, she sat back, and the fire faded with the green glow.

"This is strong magic," she said in a low voice. "Arcane. The sorcerers have grown too powerful."

He didn't care what kind of magic it was, only that she could break it.

The demonlord turned to him, the light of the torch in the quiet corridor catching part of her face and adding an orange glow to the pallor of her fair skin. "I'll need more time to weaken it. The spell grew strong again…" Her eyes dropped, unfocused.

"How?"

"Exposure to the sorceress, I expect."

But Liandra had left him, apparently satisfied that he couldn't escape. If the demonlord was right, Liandra was also sure that she had strengthened the spell binding him.

"The cuffs are another matter."

He lifted his hand, and strained to do so, aware of the clink of the chain. They still weakened him. "You can't break their magic?"

"Not now. I haven't the time." She glanced towards the open door of his cell. The Li'Ador soldiers lay crumpled on the ground. "The change of guards will wake them. I'll return tomorrow night, but you must obey the sorceress. Give her no reason to stay by you."

She rose to her feet, again glancing furtively towards the cell door.

"Wait." Too loud. She cringed. Je'Rol listened for any signs of movement and heard only the patter of rodent feet nearby. He lowered his voice to a whisper. "Why are you helping me?"

After a few seconds, she said, "I could not live with myself if I didn't try."

"Why?"

"I haven't time to explain, but can say that the Su'Kora believe as Je'Dron does, that all demonlords can work together with humans. You represent not only the rightful ruler of the Je'Gri, but the ideals he and his allies value."

The ideals Je'Dron and his allies valued? What ideals—raping human women and forcing them to watch their children slaughtered because of what they could become?

She strode for the gate and closed it, turning the key in the lock where she had left it hanging.

He let out a low growl of frustration. "That's it?"

She pulled the key with the clink of metal. "A terrible war is coming. These humans have grown too powerful and the demonlords won't tolerate it."

"What can I do?"

She glanced down the corridor. "Hope," she said and hurried away.

Hope. For what—freedom? That the humans lost? That the demonlords gave up?

The humans had grown too powerful. He agreed with that assessment but could not argue against the reasons for the humans' revolt. Demonlords had once used humans for sport and as their main courses. It was only fair for the humans to turn that around on the ones who once hunted them.

He was nothing to either of them.

Je'Rol shivered and rolled over, the clinking of his chains shattering the silence.

If the Adepts of Te'Mea found the power to confront the demonlords as equals, the war would be bloody for both sides. Both sides would be matched in power, but not in numbers. The demonlords still far outnumbered the demon hunters, but not the total population of humans. If the humans could hold a half-blood against his will, they might have the power to hold demonlords also. Get enough sorcerers together and they could secure the demonlords for the demon hunters to kill at their leisure.

Maybe the demonlords deserved what they had coming, but they had guided humans into civilizations and a cohesive society that could work together and create wonders equal to them.

Let them do as they would, destroy each other for all he cared. Neither side cared for him.

Forget it. He'd fight his way to freedom and be gone, out of sight and once more alone to wander a world that considered him an abomination—too weak for the demonlords yet too strong and unstable for the humans.

Sleep came from the fatigue of the cuff magic.

* * *

Je'Rol awoke to the slam of the cell door and a plate of food within his reach.

"Eat up," the warden barked, his keys rattling in the lock. "You'll need your strength."

Je'Rol let out a growl and the man stepped back from the crossed bars. The warden's mumbles about dangerous half-bloods deserving to be killed and looking forward to the champion defeating him reached Je'Rol. He's heard it all before, but this time anticipated the fight and taking down, if not killing, whatever "champion" challenged him.

Only one concern weighed on his mind—that they intended him to fight wearing the cursed cuffs, thereby weakening him and allowing Lord Chandroya's precious champion to handily defeat him.

If he could unleash the beast, not even the cuffs could stop him, or so he hoped. If they could restrain natters, the cuffs might have the power to restrain his demon side.

He'd find out soon enough.

Je'Rol choked down the plateful of food, wiping up the last of the meat juices with the last of the loaf. Afterwards, he shoved the plate aside. Satisfied with the fullness in his belly, he sat back on the bench and closed his eyes, listening to the chatter of guards and the scratching and snarling of the natters in the section next to him.

Among the tangle of scents floating through the stuffed air of his prison, an odd one reached him. Je'Rol pulled to the end of his chains and sniffed, seeking the faint hint of something different than the reek of men and horses and natters and filth.

He sniffed again, wondering if he had been mistaken.

He hadn't. There it was, a scent he rarely caught, but he knew it—half-blood.

Another one.

He should have noticed sooner, but the commotion when they brought him in had distracted him, and he hadn't cared in his struggle with the cuffs. Unless the other half-blood had been brought in while he slept.

Whatever the case, he might find himself fighting another man or woman as strong as himself—not exactly inspiring for escape—unless he could convince the other to join him in escape instead of fighting him. That could work. Liandra couldn't possibly control them both at once.

But she could still control *him*. The demonlord had been unsuccessful breaking the spell.

Surely she would return again.

Je'Rol hoped she would return.

* * *

The golden lady didn't return that night, but she did return the night before the scheduled grand entrance of the Dao Larashi.

He awoke to the burning on his chest again.

"Shh!" The green glow highlighted harsh lines of concentration on her human face.

Je'Rol breathed deeply and, by concentrating on the odors, forced his mind from the pain flaring through him. Her clean scent came to him with a clarity that cut through the stench of the holding area. Light and soft, a spring breeze whispering of meadow flowers and open lands, it might have been only a dream. He remembered that dream of freedom.

The fire cooled with the fading of the green glow.

"It's all I can do. The sorceress is stronger than I expected." Wincing, she put a hand to her forehead and sat back.

He sat up with the intent of helping her, but the fatigue of the cuffs slowed him.

She put a hand up to stop him. "I'll be all right."

He waited with respect to her, his ears open for the alert of the guards; but once again, the Li'Ador lay crumpled in the aisle outside his cell.

"Are they all asleep?"

"Yes."

"What of the other half-blood?"

A wan smile touched lips outlined in the torchlight shining through the bars. "So, you're aware of him. Yes, he sleeps."

"Will they make us fight each other?"

Her smile faded into the shadows. "I don't know their plans. Lord Chandroya has advertised a half-blood fight, but nothing about you against each other. It would be an unfair fight—you against a boy. I believe he has other plans for each of you."

"A boy?" Rage fired through him at the thought. They would send a boy to fight?

"Not yet a man but close—twelve I believe he advertised."

"He's a child!" Je'Rol caught himself, but the anger roared through him, stirring the beast. Who would put a child to fight men? In the right circumstances, even Je'Rol could be killed by men, but a child had less advantage.

"Hush!" The demonlord rose to her feet. "You would wake them all."

He clamped his jaw and glanced aside, avoiding her reprimand but accepting that she was right. As a full demonlord, she should have had greater power; perhaps they weren't as skilled in magic as he had assumed.

"I'll do what I can to finish the task, but I'm already too weak." She stepped to the open door.

Another concern rose to the forefront, something he'd considered asking her since her last visit, after he confirmed she was demonlord. "One more question."

She stood at the door and turned to him.

"What do you know of the obelisk of Mai'Kari?"

Her head lowered and her hand twisted around the bar of the cell door. "Ancient magic must remain hidden, Je'Rol. The obelisk would ruin our world. Why would you seek such an object?"

Her condemning tone gave him hesitation, but he had to know. "I was told it would give me absolute control over the demon side."

"It would give you control…over all demons." In the silence of the section, her breath blew like the roar of a wind. "In the days of the clan wars, it was created by the Mai'Ekam using deciphered magic of the Master Race to dominate the other clans. It was taken by the humans, until a half-blood killed the one bearing it. *That* is why the clans hid it and erased all clues to its location. You must not seek this, Je'Rol. I won't return to you if that is your goal, no matter my loyalty to Je'Dron."

Her words stabbed his spirit like a knife in his back. She knew but she would deny him his right to live free of the monster within him, the monster Je'Dron himself cursed him to bear. "Then there is no hope to contain it."

"None I know. Je'Dron spared your life; do not betray him." She slipped from the cell and locked the door. "Swear to me you'll forget the obelisk."

He couldn't. What she asked was to give up and die. He might as well if he gave up his search, because he would never find peace.

"Swear it, or you won't see me again."

He sat down, unable to obey her but not wanting to have to obey the sorceress any longer. The lie on his tongue stung and refused to voice itself. Instead, he bit it, letting the silence speak for him.

She flipped up the hood of her golden cloak and whirled away. The soft patter of her feet faded.

He should not have asked her, but he had to know. Long ago, he had met an old man at a tavern who had recognized the demonlord in his youthful features; the man had told him it could help. In his quest, Je'Rol had found no evidence or history of the obelisk but his desire for control had driven him onward. Now he understood why— the demonlords had hidden it and erased all traces of its existence—but it was real. One of the clans must have known where it was.

The Mai'Ekam clan had disappeared long ago, passed into legends. In his search, he'd heard rumors of their grand creations, but he'd found nothing. Now, he knew they had existed, but something must have destroyed them.

If they could render something as powerful as the obelisk, what else might be hiding? Where was their domain?

More than ever, he wanted to find them. He had to escape that prison and seek the burial place of the Mai'Ekam, if not also the obelisk. All their secrets seemed to have been buried with them, but he would find them, or die trying.

First, he had to escape, but he wouldn't be going anywhere until they removed the cuffs, *if* they removed the cuffs to let him fight.

Je'Rol let out a soft growl and laid flat on his back on the hard ground. He needed his rest; tomorrow would be interesting.

7

The noise of the crowds faintly reached him through the stone, the occasional trumpet blaring a deep salvo of irritation to his keen ears. The fighting hadn't even started, but he could guess there was entertainment throughout the day.

The fighting didn't start until after midday or at least after the second meal of the day, which should have been around midday, perhaps beyond that. Then periods of commotion in which soldiers escorted fighters in and out disturbed Je'Rol's occasions of peace, what little he found with the natters disturbed by the ruckus above and adding their own discordant chorus.

Several days passed, and he welcomed the periods of quiet.

The golden lady never returned.

But the sorceress did. He didn't see her face through the shadows of her hood where she stopped outside his cell, but he recognized the lithe movements and the smell.

From the bench where he sat, Je'Rol growled the moment he recognized who she was, but it was a low growl masked by the commotion of the natters.

The guard unlocked the door and stepped aside for her.

"I'll be all right. You may return to your post." Although she directed her seductive voice to the guard, it reached deep into Je'Rol's spirit and sparked defiance.

The guard gave her a doubting look.

"He's no challenge to me. Go now."

After a few seconds, he disappeared, and Liandra stepped inside, her full lips pouting. "How neglectful I've been, leaving you alone all these days." She spoke as if regretful of wronging a lover, but the only regret Je'Rol expected from her was not being able to taunt him.

He scowled at her, refusing to play her game; and the demonlord had warned him that something in her presence strengthened the spell. If he didn't have the golden lady's help, he couldn't afford to risk Liandra's power over him deepening once more. He had to stay calm, no matter how she grated his patience.

In her slippers peeking out from beneath her cloak, Liandra stopped just out of his reach, if he pulled to the ends of his chains. "How are you?" She spoke as if she sympathized with him.

He wouldn't fall for that. "What do you care?"

She clicked her tongue. "My poor boy. I care very much. I'm here; am I not? I came to see you after all this time."

And he should believe she came out of the goodness of her heart? The woman didn't have a heart, he'd bet. "What do you want, sorceress?" he growled.

"Only to know that you're treated well. Lord Bannon has bet good money on you, so you must win...at all costs. He would not let anyone sabotage his investment...*my* investment." The last two words purred off her tongue.

He should have expected that, but no grown men dared enter his cell. They had to force a helpless boy to bring his food, a young man he had no intention of hurting. Attacking anyone would only hinder his efforts, and likely mean no food, not that what they provided was enough. On his own, he would gladly eat twice the amount. What they fed likely satisfied the human men, but he wasn't purely human.

"You're not weak or injured?"

"No."

She paused and stepped closer, and leaned over so her warm breath blew against his cheek. "We heard someone has been in here."

"Lots of people have been in here."

Her eyebrow arched up. "Several guards were found asleep some nights ago and one other night since we arrived. Have you seen anything, Je'Rol?"

"No one."

She straightened, a hint of suspicion playing across the shadowed features beneath her cowl.

"I was sleeping!" He clenched his claws around the bench to restrain himself from sinking them into her soft flesh.

"But you feel well?"

"As well as I can with magic enslaving me and locked in a cage with so little to eat and none of my freedom." Claws extended, piercing the wood on which he sat.

She backed off, a rueful smile playing on her lips. "Very well. Good night, Je'Rol," she whispered and slipped out the cell door. A few seconds later, the jangle of keys announced the arrival of the guard, who locked the door.

Good riddance. He hoped the sorceress's presence had not renewed the magic binding him through the stone implanted on his chest. If it was weak enough from the help of the golden lady, he might be able to break it himself.

He wouldn't know until he tried to escape, if he could resist Liandra and escape from whatever challenge they put before him to fight; and he imagined the worst.

Surviving was his first priority, escape his second.

A low growl rumbled from his throat as he glared at the Li'Ador in the corridor outside his cell. He'd have to work fast at the precisely right moment to escape, but he'd need the cuffs removed if he would have any hope of that happening.

Breaking the sorceress's spell would mean nothing if he didn't get out of those cuffs. He'd need his full power.

That meant relaxing and doing nothing to resist the magic of the cuffs or to arouse the guards outside. He'd learned that much in his wanderings—keep your head down and your mouth shut to avoid trouble.

He did that for three more days, the boy who brought his food showing more bravery at each feeding. The Li'Ador never wavered in their attention, but they rotated frequently.

Two nights later, he awoke to soft hands on his face and the faint scent of clear air among the filth of the prison.

"Wake, Je'Rol," someone whispered.

He blinked his eyes open and stared in surprise at the figure with golden hair beneath the tailored cloak. "Who are you?"

A smile played on those fair features in the flickering torchlight. "Someone who would rather see you out of Lord Bannon's hands."

"You didn't answer my question."

She dropped her eyes and took a deep breath. "I would not have you forced to give that name to the sorceress. If they knew I was here, my work would be at risk."

"She suspects already, my lady. No one else could leave all the men sleeping."

The demonlord met his eyes, a flash of horror across her face measured a moment later. "Of course, but there are many other demonlords in the city in recent days. They haven't given up their thrill of humans killing one another...and the bodies have been carted from the city for their feasts."

Disgusting. Je'Rol snorted at the prospects. "The demonlords haven't given up their taste for humans."

"No."

"What of you?"

Her eyes caught the firelight with a hungry glint, or it might have been something else. He couldn't be sure.

"The Ur'Asu invited nobles from all the clans to the Dao Larashi tournament. I believe they're using it as a means to revive the old ways. They pushed Lord Chandroya to this tournament. Lord Ur'Makus put up the purse for the winning owner."

"But you didn't answer my question." And he suspected why.

She stood and took a step away. After a few seconds she turned, her back to the light from the corridor and her face shadowed from the cowl. "I am an ambassador of the Su'Kora. I was invited to the Dao Larashi by the Ur'Asu, and whatever social occasions they offer."

"You're no better than the other demons." The words ground out in a deep snarl, his fists clenched to restrain the beast and his disgust.

"It was our way long ago that humans were among many creatures we hunted. Their bodies are wasted with burning."

"Excuses," he grumbled. That's all he heard. She was no better than the clans who never denied their tastes for humans.

"I've made no excuses. You should not ask questions for which you don't want to know answers." Her tone might have struck him like a whip.

Je'Rol winced but she'd confirmed what he suspected—she'd also retained her taste for human meat. "Why are you here this time? I thought you disagreed with my search."

"I do." She paused, taking a moment to glance out at the sleeping Li'Ador. Silence closed in on them; not even the natters dared rise, but their voices had decreased over the last two days, likely many of them having been killed by the human warriors fighting for their lives.

In a lowered voice, she said, "But I've heard troubling rumors from other domains." She hesitated and knelt at his side. "The stakes are higher than you and me, but I must stay here. You must escape, Je'Rol."

He'd gladly escape any time, if someone would remove the cuffs.

She started to reach for them and hesitated with her hand inches away. "I can't touch them any more than you. That's part of the problem. It seems the sorcerers are finding new ways to bind demon powers. Some of us suspect they may have deciphered the secrets of the Master Race. Others think the power may already lie dormant in the humans, and that power is activated by something, which has given rise to the Adepts of Te'Mea."

He sat up, the clink of the chains ringing in his cell.

"You must find the obelisk…and destroy it."

Destroy it, his only chance of gaining control over the demon side of himself? "Why should I destroy it?"

"Because if you don't, the blood of humans and demons will be on your hands. The demonlords have spoken of slaughtering the humans to stop them before they can rise against the clans. But if the obelisk is out there, the clans will turn on each other for control of it; the humans would fare no better. Its destruction could save this world."

If the humans gained power over their former masters, the demonlords would be justly punished for their crimes. He took a perverse pleasure in that idea. But he didn't like the thought of the Adepts playing with the power of the extinct beings known as the Master Race.

Aside from that, the humans aspired to become like the demonlords and sacrificed their own kind for sport, as the Dao Larashi tournament proved.

Either the demonlords gained the obelisk's power and controlled one another and killed the humans, or the humans used the power to purge the world of demons, but the Adepts of Te'Mea would be no better than their former demonlord masters. Humans had already proven they would make war on one another for power many times, showing that their hearts were no better than the demonlords they wished to conquer.

Je'Rol didn't want to care about anyone except himself. He wanted the obelisk's power to control his own demon side. Only then would he find peace.

"Destroy the obelisk," she said.

"If I find it, I'll consider it." Consider and reject the notion.

"Consider it carefully." She rose again and strode to the cell door. "I've weakened the spell as much as I dare without arousing the sorceress's suspicions."

He reached down and felt something where his hands could not before touch—the rough scabbing around the stone on his chest.

The squeak of the cell door and the clank of the keys jerked his eyes up to the demonlord. After a pause at the locked door, she hurried from sight.

While he couldn't agree with her partaking of the demonlord feasts, she demonstrated a deeper concern for more than herself. The Su'Kora ambassador was a noble woman who couldn't help what she was. The demonlords were, after all, predators who took the form of humans to camouflage themselves among what had for much of their history been their main prey. He had assumed most of them had given up the taste of human flesh.

The Dao Larashi was an excuse for their fine dining.

Je'Rol shuddered and lay down on the hard ground. Soon he would fight, and he would break the final thin strand of the sorceress's spell.

He didn't want to consider the numbers of demonlords who might be ready to attack when he made his escape.

* * *

The next day, the same noise disturbed the air of the prison. Somewhere in the midst of it, a cluster of Li'Ador appeared outside his cell with the sorceress. The warden jangled the keys and unlocked the door.

"It's time." Liandra glided through the door past the husky man, a Dev Nadir soldier right behind her.

Je'Rol glared at them, glad to see the hesitation in the man's movements as he approached with keys. It appeared they would remove the cuffs. With those off, he could make his move.

Liandra murmured in the strange language, and his surroundings darkened. She'd done it once before, along the journey there.

"Stand still, Je'Rol, and listen to me," she said.

Someone fiddled with his hands and a heaviness lifted from his body, as if he'd been carrying a burden so long he'd forgotten what it was like to be free of it. He stood upright, feeling as if he could sprint from the shadows around him before they thought to move.

"You will obey me," the sultry voice of the sorceress whispered from the shadow nearest to him.

He stood without his cloak and searched the dark face with the light marks of her tattoos. It was time to fight, and he was more than ready after being locked up without room to move. They had taken his freedom, but the energy and the need to move had built up, restrained only by the cuffs they had used to bind him.

The dull clank of metal resounded from behind him as shadows backed away.

Except the sorceress.

"Come, Je'Rol."

He followed her from the cell into the dim corridor. Behind bars, in dark alcoves, a few shadows stirred.

Behind him, the muffled tromp of boots followed. The Li'Ador closed in, blocking any retreat.

Ahead, Liandra led him through the arched corridor to a side tunnel sloping down. Down? Shouldn't they be going up to the arena?

Although the spell muted his senses, the scent of blood overwhelmed him. They were close.

They reached level ground before a set of tall double doors. Three shadows stood to either side.

"Open it," a deep voice ordered from somewhere behind him.

Je'Rol shook his head, but he knew he couldn't clear the darkness induced by the spell. Instincts had arisen to react without rational thought. His heart pounded in his chest and claws extended, as if he could fight his way out of the spell; it wasn't the spell but opponents bent on killing him that challenged him.

The darkness dissipated in a line between the doors, the muted sunlight washing through an ever increasing chasm of space that stopped at twice his width.

"Go, Je'Rol," the sorceress whispered from his right.

His feet moved forward, carrying him into the dim light of a large round enclosure surrounded by walls at least four times his height. Across the circle, the bloodied remains of a few natters lay strewn across the arena, along with what looked like the body of a goblin in fine garb torn and bloodied—likely tossed in by a demonlord unhappy with its service.

The roar of the crowd crescendoed with the brightening of the sun.

The doors boomed closed behind him and all senses awakened as if emerging from a heavy fog.

The Kairashun was enormous, and apparently dug out of the ground. He might be able to jump those walls to gain freedom, but it would be questionable. Whoever had designed the structure had done so with a sense of the abilities of demons.

Tiers of faces looked down from above, and if the golden lady had been right, demonlords blended in among them. *If* he jumped clear, he would have to contend with them.

Let them. He let out a low growl in threat, not caring that they would never hear over the thunder of voices.

Two other sets of doors stood closed at approximately the exact third spacing around the circle. He'd bet one of those led to the natters section. Maybe both did, depending on how much space it took beneath the spectators.

And the arena was full of spectators, whose voices hushed to a minimum.

From around the arc before him, five men in armor and helmets and bearing various weapons of brutal designs approached. These men had seen vicious battle already, judging by the dents in their armor and the blood splattered over them, but they'd faced nothing like him. He would show them what a true demon could do.

Claws extended fully with the rage of the beast hammering for release against the spell restraining it. With that in effect, he could maintain his control for this fight, possibly to escape. That was all he needed to let loose the true power of his demon side.

Too many days penned up charged through him like lightning. Je'Rol waited, watching every step the men took. One of them swung an axe every few steps, another brandished a spiked club in one hand with a couple of swords and knives strapped across his back and chest. Two of them dragged metal nets that clinked behind them. Another twirled a chain weapon not quite a mace but with spikes along the length of the end.

He'd bet those metal nets had barbs on them also.

Five men with human-made weapons and armor, and him with his claws and superhuman abilities; not an unfair fight. It was a challenge, but not one he couldn't overcome.

Je'Rol waited, the murmur of the crowd low now. An occasional cough or comment reached him, but even those decreased as his adversaries approached.

The men closed in, a few of them casting sideways glances to the others. The black-bearded man to his right held his axe steady in his hands. At the far left, a man with a net unsheathed a broadsword. The middle man motioned to the others. They stopped several strides from him, and the crowds hushed to nothing.

Je'Rol growled, the anticipation of the bloody fight coursing through his muscles and tightening them in preparation. Someone had to make the first move. He squatted in preparation to leap.

He'd have to move fast to avoid their weapons. If he let them surround him, he'd be trapped. And his claws wouldn't do more than scratch their armor. He'd have to strike for the weak points—under their arms and along their necks and legs. Yes, the legs, low but vulnerable. They only protected their heads and bodies, the vital organs, but the extremities were left unprotected, or most of them were. The men wore shin guards and bracers and shoulder plates, allowing them the flexibility and lightness to move while protecting the most vulnerable areas.

He knew his targets of soft flesh, but getting in and getting out before they brought their weapons on him would pose the greatest challenge. The sponsors of the Dao Larashi armed their fighters well, but none were perfect.

If he had to fight, he would survive.

Clearing the wall would be another matter. With the two men next to the wall, he realized it was closer to five times the height of these men, likely too high for even him to jump clear.

He'd have to fight his way out of this and wait for a better opportunity for escape, but when the moment came, he'd be ready. Survival was the first challenge.

The arc of opponents slowed their approach.

He could reach them quickly, but not before they reacted; a risk, but he'd only get one chance at the first move and it had to take them by surprise to gain the greatest advantage.

A little longer and a little closer. Je'Rol waited, his blood burning through him with the transformation of his demon half. Teeth sharpened and claws extended their full, curved length. Muscles tightened.

Close now.

He bared his teeth with a loud growl, his tongue sliding over the sharpening points. One of the men hesitated but continued in the next second.

Sensing the threat and the thrill, the beast struggled for escape, but the magic worked for him this time. This was his fight, and he needed his reasoning. Blind instinct for killing wouldn't save him in this battle.

They paused as if expecting him to make that first move into their midst.

The axe would be slowest to move.

Je'Rol sprang forward, ducked towards the wall and dodged back as the axe came down where he had been. A split second later, two inch claws sank deep into the man's neck. One down.

But the others had already moved.

A flash of movement.

Je'Rol rolled away and sprang up before the metal net rang its song of links. Not exactly a swift weapon, but the broadsword swung a heartbeat later, too late.

Too slow. These humans couldn't match his speed.

Je'Rol landed several lengths away. The sport raced through his veins and the beast raged but stayed within its cage. The scent of fresh blood invigorated him with the desire for more, especially knowing the beast was under control.

Four men fanned out, abandoning their dead companion.

The man with the chain would be next, on the far left now. Je'Rol had only to wait for them to close the distance.

He crouched in preparation to make the leap, feeling the distance and the effort he needed to close it.

One of the men dropped his net and charged with the spiked club ready to strike.

Bad timing, but he'd make the most of it. Je'Rol leapt for the man with the chain, which swung towards him. Upon coming down with claws poised to strike away the links, pain stung his leg. He caught the movement of a spear swinging through the air trailing droplets of blood.

On landing, Je'Rol collapsed but rolled before the chain smashed him. Barely did he roll to his feet that the chain swung to catch his wrist and wrapped itself around. Stinging points of blood oozed over his sleeve, shredding fabric and sinking into his flesh.

Without thinking, he grabbed the barbed chain end and yanked it from the fighter. He immediately swung it at the other three rushing him, ignoring the pain in his wrist. It drove them back, but only for a moment.

Je'Rol leapt clear as the man whose chain he'd taken stabbed with a sword. Two knives sunk into the soil barely a breath after he left it, thrown from behind.

Blood ran down the sleeve of his shirt, the wounds stinging but not intolerable.

At the pinnacle of his jump, he twisted his arm to free it of the chain with his other hand grasping the smooth end. Upon landing, he swung the spiked end and caught one of the fighters in the jaw.

The man staggered back, but Je'Rol found himself fending off three others amid boos and cheers from above.

The beast growled for escape as he swung his claws blindly and whirled and ducked a metal net and a spear. A second later, he slashed and caught soft flesh. A knife fell to the dirt.

He twirled the chain above his head, driving them back and giving him a moment to catch his breath.

It didn't last. The moment he took his eyes off the men on one side, the clink of metal warned him a fraction of a second before they struck.

Je'Rol tipped the chain and twisted his body to follow. It made contact with metal, knocking one of the fighters to his back and sending the two parts of a shattered spear rolling into the remains of the goblin and the strewn guts of an arachnoid natter.

A heartbeat later, Je'Rol leapt clear of the net ringing through the air. When the chain gave a tug, it pulled him down faster than he expected.

He twisted, catching sight of the man with the broken jaw sitting in the dirt, severely wounded but not dead.

Two down. Three to kill.

Je'Rol landed with the three before him, where he could see them all at once. The pain in his leg and wrist rose to his awareness, but he refused to let it distract him from survival. He could give it attention after defeating these Dao warriors.

The end of the chain had caught the net, but the man who'd thrown the net now held the end of the chain beyond the barbed end. Foolish humans.

Je'Rol yanked, intending to rip it through the man's hands, shredding them in the process, but the man let go. The chain flew back at Je'Rol, who stepped away for it to thump into the dirt.

Pain struck his side, knocking the breath from his lungs.

Je'Rol slashed back with a roar and whirled on the man with the club. Every movement now consisted of pain ripping through his right side and every breath caused agony.

But the demon in him fought back and gave him strength. He pounced on his attacker.

A swift duck of the barbed club spared his shoulders and head, and a low slash in the same movement left the man staggering. Je'Rol swiped up into the man's jaw as a new pain landed upon him and blocked part of his vision.

His victim stumbled and fell back while he whirled, or tried to, beneath the metal net. His movement to face his newest attacker dug hundreds of tiny needles into his head and shoulders. He threw off the net, ignoring the puncturing of his flesh, more concerned by the sword he narrowly avoided.

One clawed hand shot out and grabbed the man's wrist, digging in to draw blood. Still the man clung to his sword, a defiant gleam in his eyes.

It died with a slash of claws across his throat in a movement that landed Je'Rol facing his last opponent.

Breathing hard, he swiped his sleeve across his face, smearing his own blood from his eyes in time to avoid the thrust of a sword in his side. The man's only calculated mistake.

The human didn't have the chance for another. Je'Rol jabbed his claws under the man's arm, a merciful blow but only because he'd lost his speed from the distraction of the pain in his side. The man swung his sword in a futile attempt to recover, but Je'Rol was quicker, despite slowing down, and gave a half-hearted slash across the man's throat that left the man gasping and gagging on his own blood like the others and finally falling to his knees.

Silence surrounded him, except for the scrape of movement to his left.

Blood dripping into his eyes nearly blinded Je'Rol to the man with the broken jaw attempting to stand. Je'Rol straightened from his hunched fatigue and walked to the man.

"Gi' 'e. 'ea'!" The man begged in a whisper without using his bottom jaw, which was knocked out of place and bleeding.

The Dao Larashi was a fight to the death. This was the last man, and one begging for death. He had no use living with a broken jaw, but the pitiful sight stayed Je'Rol's hand. Sharp teeth and claws shrank with the quieting of the beast, his chest heaving for breath.

Je'Rol looked up at the faces staring down. They had their show. He'd proven his skills against five men at once. Why did he need to kill the last?

From a section at the farthest end of the crowds covered in a deep purple and gold canopy, a few dozen men and women in the finest raiment gazed at him.

The doors through which Je'Rol had come opened to his right, releasing a river of Li'Ador in their black and silver armor, weapons poised. They formed a circle around Je'Rol and the last fighter, but moved no closer.

"Oo i'," the man said. Without the use of his tongue, he was hard to understand. He'd never survive, even if Je'Rol spared his life.

Claws grew out at his bidding. The man stood his ground but made no move to fight.

In one slash, it was done.

The Li'Ador closed in and the sorceress stepping forward, her tawny skin and long black hair standing out from the circle of uniforms and weapons. She stopped two strides away, her eyes on the covered area at the farthest end.

His escape would have to wait for another time. He had no energy left to attempt it there. The loss of blood and his internal injuries weakened him, but he would recover in a couple days, thanks to his demon side; while he wasn't immortal like a demonlord, he healed much quicker than a human. And he'd endured worse.

The crowds sat in silence, waiting as a figure under the awning rose in his dark robes.

Je'Rol ignored the sorceress, who stood close enough to cool his skin when her breath blew across his neck. "You did well," she whispered.

"You will live to fight again, half-blood," a deep voice rang from the far end of the arena.

A collective sigh rose from the stands, releasing him as if he'd been held by strings. The buzz of conversations rose into a din.

"Come." Liandra directed him out with the Li'Ador. He didn't object, desiring instead to rest and clean the stench of blood from himself.

8

After two days of rest, Je'Rol stood in the arena again, this time topless. Most of his wounds had healed already, although his ribs still ached. None of the external wounds had gone deeper than a couple inches into non-vital tissues, and his muscles healed more quickly than humans'.

The moment he stepped into the light, the audience's roar echoed through the arena, making his ears ache. He pressed his palms over them, his eyes fixed on the two open doors ahead to his left and his right.

Through one, a young man ran out in rags, his pants torn from his shins, exposing bare feet. He appeared to wear a helmet of scales over his head and neck and armor over parts of his shoulders and back

Je'Rol inhaled sharply. It wasn't a helmet but actual silvery scales, which reflected the sunlight in mini-spectrums at certain angles when he moved. A half-blood of the sea demonlords? The boy's eyes caught Je'Rol's and dark claws extended from the boy's fingers longer than Je'Rol thought possible.

The boy couldn't be a half-blood from any of the demonlords of the sea, not with claws like those. Those weren't fish scales, but something worse. He hoped he didn't have to fight the kid; it would be no match for him, claws or not.

Behind them both, the doors closed.

But the third door remained open. A high-pitched shriek followed by a thump rang from inside.

The crowds above quieted.

Voices shouted and something shrieked and groaned in a deep, threatening tone.

Je'Rol tensed and backed away with the boy, his claws extending for whatever demon appeared. Something dark slithered through the doorway and hesitated. Not slithered, but wound on countless tiny legs.

"Stay close. If we work together, we might both survive."

The boy's eyes shot to him in a look of panic. "Who are you?"

"You're only ally. Watch yourself!"

Something in red and black stripes scurried out on two legs, with two odd arms—

the best comparison he could make—that ended in long, hooked claws opening and snapping shut. Tusks curled up from its jaw.

The first natter twisted its segments to bring its head around and rose up, revealing five holes along its bottom puckering and opening to expose snapping beaks. Its tiny legs rippled with movement in the air.

Although no bigger than young children, both demons were nasty creatures that could disembowel a man in seconds.

Still more natters came, evading the voices of men shouting from within. Some had four legs, some eight, some slithered on none. None was like another, but natters came in any combination, as if in the creation of the world, the universe couldn't make up its mind, until it finally settled on the lowly insects and animals that now dominated Derandria.

But natters were still demons, the lowest, but still of some nasty abilities.

They went for the boy first. He slashed and growled and ripped at them with the ferocity of the blood rage.

When they came for him, Je'Rol was ready.

A couple managed to inflict some injuries, but nothing serious. The Dao fighters had been harsher and far more cunning.

The fighting wasn't done, though.

More natters were driven in to face them, surrounding him and the boy, who roared in the blind fury of the blood rage, claws extended and teeth sharp, his face extending slightly in the partial transformation. The kid wasn't ready, and a sinking feeling dropped into Je'Rol's gut that the boy wouldn't survive.

No time to worry about him. The natters swarmed around them.

One of the many-legged insectoid natters wrapped itself around his leg while he fought off several others. Five small beaks speared into his flesh.

Je'Rol roared and slashed at the hard, shell-like segments covering its body, but only when he caught the body tight around him and pulled it in half did it release itself.

One of the furry creatures caught his claw in its mouth and shrieked. Je'Rol twisted his hand to slice claws along the softer flesh. The creature opened its mouth to howl in pain, releasing his arm.

While he finished that one, another leapt at him. Je'Rol sprang free of the natters around him and caught the jumper in the air with a swipe of his claw.

A cry yanked out his heart and made him look. Natters swarmed over the boy, overwhelming him. Anger rose up, taunting the beast within Je'Rol. They should never have expected a boy, even a half-blood, to be capable of fighting off so many demons. He wasn't ready. Faced with the dozen that had attacked him, Je'Rol had barely survived. How could they expect a boy to fight?

Damn them—natters and the men and demonlords who supported the Dao Larashi, especially the demonlords and their lust for human flesh. If he ever found the obelisk of Mai'Kari, he'd control them and command them to give up their ways.

Je'Rol landed amid the swarming natters, slashing left and right to free the boy somewhere beneath while the demons turned to attack him.

Sweat and blood poured over him amid the growling, snarling, shrieking, snapping, biting mass of bodies.

After enduring countless wounds, Je'Rol finished off the last of the natters. He reached the boy too late. Only a bloody pulp of flesh and bone remained. The natters had worked fast, but Je'Rol bore the wounds to prove that not even he was quick enough to avoid their hungry mouths. The boy could have been him at one time, a lifetime ago when he didn't want to fight, before he'd left home.

Before he'd lost his innocence to the beast within him.

They had no right to force this on the boy!

The scrape of doors alerted him to the opening from which he had come in.

Rather than the Li'Ador as he expected, a lone figure stepped in wearing armor like that worn by the warriors he'd fought a few days ago gleaming in the height of the midday sun.

Je'Rol stepped past the bloody body of the youth, his emotions boiling into a rage. The lone figure would be no match for him, even in his weakened state. Claws and teeth extended and a growl rumbled from his throat. He'd had enough of this fighting and bloodshed. What was one more death?

He raced to the warrior, claws ready to end it quickly.

As the doors slammed closed, he ducked a swift stroke from a curved blade that flashed into existence, not like any weapon he'd seen before and definitely not a sword, not with a point at both ends and a handle in the middle, but more like a double sword.

Je'Rol rolled in the dust and sprang to his feet.

Three strides away, the warrior stood facing him, a lust for blood glinting in dark eyes beneath the helm with its extended bottom fanned out to protect the neck. They'd learned his swiftest killing method and prepared this one. Then Je'Rol would have to find another way.

Still breathing hard from his fight with the natters, Je'Rol stood his ground, the rumble of his growl drowned by the voices above, which hushed over his continued stillness.

The warrior twirled the wickedly curved blade in a threatening demonstration of skill.

A small laugh ground from Je'Rol's throat. The man was good with his weapons, but take those away and he'd have nothing.

Blood continued to cool his body where it flowed from fresh wounds, and its heavy scent overpowered any others that might have provided clues about the man. The warrior before him was fresh and unharmed, but that would give him no advantage over Je'Rol's anger and the beast within him.

That beast hungered for death, but the blood rage wasn't from the beast. Rather, it came from Je'Rol. Vengeance surged through him, as if this man represented those he hated for what they had done.

The warrior stepped aside, and Je'Rol followed, keeping his distance so he moved around a circle with the man.

After a few steps, the man frowned. "Attack, half-blood."

"Make me." No one commanded him. Here he was free of the sorceress to make his own decisions, and he was injured. The brief reprieve had cooled his emotions, but anger still raged in his heart over the senseless waste of the boy's life for their entertainment. Reason had taken over once more, the reason to judge how best to survive this fight.

The man settled his blade into a position and launched himself at Je'Rol.

Finally.

Je'Rol dodged the blade once, but the man was fast. Pain shot through Je'Rol's side.

But the blade was nowhere near him.

Not that blade. From somewhere hidden, the man had pulled a dagger.

Je'Rol glanced down at the red slit across his ribs. No time to contemplate. The warrior moved swiftly at him again with the intent of finishing him.

Je'Rol dodged both blades and whirled to catch both arms in his claws and squeezed, but the leather bracers were thick. He squeezed with all his strength to penetrate the thick leather, and his claws sank deep into soft flesh. Blood dripped to the dry ground, blending with the stains of countless others, including himself.

The warrior's arms slackened and a hard helm slammed Je'Rol in the head. The ring of metal against his skull startled him into releasing his grip and threw him off balance away from his attacker.

What had he been doing?

No time to think. The armored man stabbed with his blade and Je'Rol rolled away.

As the blades whirled and stabbed down, Je'Rol kicked up and caught the middle handle.

The double-ended sword-staff flew from the man's grasp.

Encouraged by his success, Je'Rol rolled to his feet. A second later, his claws slashed down the man's ribs under his left arm. Two leather straps caught but gave under the sharp edge of his claws, loosening the man's armor.

Pain stabbed through Je'Rol's shoulder, crunching through bone and muscle. He'd forgotten about the dagger, now sunk deep into his shoulder. The beast snarled for retribution, guiding his claws across the man's arm to knock it away.

The warrior staggered back, his nearest side and the underside of his opposite forearm bleeding, while Je'Rol yanked the small weapon from his flesh. Pain surged through his arm, making it all but useless.

The warrior recovered his double bladed sword and wielded it in both hands. The pulpy right arm moved little, the man wincing with each movement now.

The end was near, and the gasp from the crowd said they knew. One of the combatants would die soon.

It wouldn't be him.

Je'Rol snarled through clenched teeth to hide the whimper from the pain of his movements. He held his injured arm close to his body to keep it steady. His other hand flexed with five daggers of his own ready for striking and, by his own will, the teeth of a tiger extended.

The warrior faltered, his weapon tipping in a hint of weakness.

Je'Rol rushed forward, knocked the weapon aside and sank his teeth into the warm muscle of the man's good arm.

The warrior dropped his weapon as Je'Rol stabbed four long claws into the soft area beneath his ribs.

Two seconds later, those same claws sunk into the exposed narrow gap of the man's neck between the helm and the armor.

Lord Chandroya's champion crumpled to the ground in a bloody mess, the metal of his armor clanging through the silence hanging over the arena.

Je'Rol breathed hard, standing over the man as the life faded from his eyes. He'd seen it more than he ever wanted, but in other battles, he'd fled before he caught the end.

Claws shrank and teeth returned to normal with the numbness of pain threatening to steal him into unconsciousness.

He staggered backwards and dared to lift his head. The group of well-adorned lords and ladies under the canopy to his left whispered amongst themselves. Opposite them sat another group of men and women, the goblins among them staring with their large, bulbous eyes. A familiar face among a halo of golden hair met his eyes with a hint of a smile, the only sign of approval among the severe scowls or neutral gazes of the representatives of the other clans.

The thunder of footsteps accompanied the clatter of weapons as the black and silver of the Li'Ador surrounded him. He had no strength left to fight.

"Well done." The sensuous voice sparked the beast into a growl.

He wanted to wipe the smile off the sorceress's smug face but the will to fight seeped away with the blood of many wounds. Too weak to argue, Je'Rol followed her from the arena.

"It is done," she said in the dark corridors of the holding area. "You performed better than we hoped. After you rest, your greatest performance is to come."

9
_____

In his dreams, Je'Rol found it hard to escape the surge of natters rising like a tidal wave to overcome him. His feet refused to move as panic swept over him ahead of the growing mountain of snapping, biting, drooling fangs, teeth, pincers, and mandibles.

The beast roared in challenge, extending claws and teeth and deepening into a rage he could not nor would not subdue.

At the first of the wave, he slashed wildly, and still they came at him. He snarled and fought, unable to move his feet, while determined not to let them eat him alive.

From their midst rose a form, the boy. A second later, the boy's skin melted away, exposing bone and shredded flesh. The corpse lunged for him.

Je'Rol growled and tried to fight him off, but the figure grew and squeezed him between giant, bloody palms, strangling and crushing him.

He gasped and bolted upright from a soft pad, loose hair brushing one bare and one bandaged shoulder with the sudden movement. He lifted a claw before him and noted the trembling in the sunlight from the three small windows along the wall beside him. The claws retracted to normal hands.

"Bad dreams?" A familiar voice shook away the horror of the dream.

Je'Rol held a hand up to block the sun. In the corner of the room, a lithe figure stretched her legs as she sat up from a red chaise, the exposed areas of skin covered in tattoos. Liandra. Now what did she want from him?

"Where am I?" This obviously wasn't his cell in the holding area, the prison of the Kairashun. His wounds had healed, although a few wraps still covered him, and his shoulder still ached where the fighter had stabbed the dagger in deep.

"Lord Chandroya's palace in the upper gardens. You put on a very good show and earned your reward." Liandra brushed aside a loose strand of black hair, exposing the tattoos along her face. "A long rest, compliments of Lord Bannon."

Compliments? His being there was anything but complimentary. They wanted something from him yet. "You promised my freedom."

Her lips twisted into a sly smile. "So I did, but you haven't put on your best performance yet." With all the seductiveness he expected, she slid from the lounger and crawled to him on hands and knees.

He should kill her and escape, but the spark of fire in his chest warned him from such thoughts. Her scent surrounded him, the bloody reek that had overwhelmed all other odors in the arena only a memory.

She leaned her mouth close to his ear and whispered, "You will be presented to Lord Chandroya as a gift. When that happens…you must kill him, Je'Rol. If you wish your freedom, that will be the only way. The Li'Ador will not be present. Lord Chandroya believes I have full control, but I won't stop you."

"Why?" Why should he kill a man for their purposes? But now he understood the reason for the Dao Larashi; he had demonstrated that he could fight while keeping the beast in check, gaining the trust of the local human lord so he would be allowed alone with him to carry out the assassination planned by another who sought his power. Afterwards, they would probably present him to the demonlords for execution.

She sat back on her legs and smoothed away the hair from his face, brushing it behind his shoulders and watching her hands rather than meeting his eyes.

"He is a traitor," she said, her fingers tracing the muscles of his bare chest, pausing at crusted sores nearly healed.

Je'Rol tried to ignore the soft caress, but when her hands went to the light blanket still covering his legs, he caught her wrist.

Amusement lit in her dark eyes. "So modest."

Reason caught up in that moment and he released her wrist. He'd been lying there naked while she'd likely treated his wounds and assisted with whatever process had cleaned the blood off. She'd had plenty of opportunity to poke and prod to her pleasure. Her pleasure was the least he cared about, but she seemed to like what she saw.

It was the last time she would see it.

"Where are my clothes?"

Liandra turned to a low table a ways behind her. A fresh shirt and leather breeches lay across it.

Conscious of her watching him but not caring what she thought, he stood and walked past her.

"You really should reconsider."

He'd reconsider nothing, except escaping to continue his search for the obelisk.

Je'Rol lifted the shirt up and over his head mostly with one arm. The bandaged shoulder stung when he lifted that arm too high, but he clenched his jaw on the pain of pushing his arm through.

The shirt hung loose, a light blouse that tied at his chest, much like his old one. He pulled on the breeches, glad he stood with his back to the sorceress when he winced in pain as he shoved his leg through; each of the five wounds from where the natter had taken chunks of flesh with its beaks stung on contact from the scabs still healing. He pulled the breeches up and finished dressing, inhaling sharply at a jolt of pain when he lifted his shoulder the wrong way.

"You haven't healed fully."

"It's enough." He slipped the vest on and fastened it over the blouse, his long hair loose over his shoulders falling in the way. "Where's the strap?"

She rose and glided to him, her hand rising to dangle a leather strip between her thumb and forefinger.

He grabbed for it, but she snatched it away, her other hand reaching for his hair. "You should reconsider staying longer."

A low growl rumbled from his throat. "I won't be a part of your games." He grabbed her wrist and pulled her close to reach her other hand. The smirk on her face grated on his patience, along with her tight fingers around the leather piece, which required both his hands to pry open.

"Your demonlord mistress won't help you."

He hesitated only a moment, but she caught it; the smirk on her face climbed higher.

"Was she good to you, Je'Rol?" Her sultry voice slowed his fingers around hers. "Tell me what she promised you."

He met her dark eyes with defiance, which ignited the burning in his chest. He could fight it. He *must* fight it. Liandra was a sorceress, the last person who should learn of the obelisk and the mission the demonlord had asked of him. What the golden lady had promised had been nothing. She'd never promised to help him. That thought cooled the burning.

"Nothing."

She gave a soft snort. "I find that hard to believe. What does a demonlord want with a mere half-blood?"

He yanked the strap from her loosened fingers and stepped back. "Nothing that concerns you."

"Everything about demons concerns me," she said.

To escape her, he turned his back. For all he cared, she could watch him use his claws to comb through his hair and tie it back.

"Tell me what she did, Je'Rol."

No, he wanted to argue. Instead he bit his tongue and focused on the tranquility of the sunlight on his face. The pressure to open his mouth and explain the lady's work to break Liandra's spell on him waned.

He'd been right—she had no power over the human side. Only when the beast rose with the faltering of his control could she control him.

A smirk of triumph touched his lips.

"Did she please you?" The hands on his side could have been reaching for his heart with a knife.

He inhaled and let it out slowly. Let her do as she wanted; he wouldn't let his irritation take root and call up the demon side. That was her goal. She needed that to control him. Staying calm was his best defense and the one she hated most.

"Tell me what she did, Je'Rol," the sorceress whispered. "You are mine. You obey me."

Not any more.

He finished tying his hair after wrapping the leather strap down a length of tail and his ears caught the faint snick of a door.

"Excuse me, *Serae*." The young girl at the door blushed, her hands full with the silver tray. "I was told to bring food for you and your guest."

Liandra's fingers dug into his sides, while the clatter of laden trays told him the young servant set them on the table. The faint scent of cooked meat, seasoned vegetables, and fresh bread teased his tongue.

Any reason to move away from the sorceress was good for him. Je'Rol turned as the young woman backed out and closed the door. Hungry, he lifted the shiny silver cover from a steaming plate heaped with a variety of foods and another with lighter portions. Delectable scents poured from the food, begging him to fill his empty stomach.

The food disappeared from the full plate faster than Liandra finished one portion of her meal. Afterwards, Je'Rol wiped his face and stood, having no intention of waiting. He'd waited long enough to escape the sorceress's control. With his health restored and his stomach filled, he was ready to return to the wilds and continue his search for true freedom from the demon side.

"You can't leave yet," she said.

Yes, he could. He grabbed the door handle. Fire burned through his chest. Not this time. He refused to let it stop him.

Grunting in exertion, he pulled the door open.

Two Li'Ador stood on either side of the door, with others spaced throughout the airy corridor.

His heart beat faster, but the fire didn't increase. It didn't have to—the soldiers turned to face him.

"Come back inside with me," Liandra's voice coaxed.

No. He refused to listen.

The Li'Ador approached with swords and staffs drawn. He'd faced a swarm of natters and five armed men at once in the Dao Larashi, but he wouldn't be a match for all the Li'Ador.

"You'll be more comfortable. I can assure you."

Growling, Je'Rol backed in and slammed the door closed. When the time came, he'd escape. She said the Li'Ador would not be there when she and Lord Bannon presented him to Lord Chandroya.

The recent nightmare flashed its gory images from the depths of his memories. He closed his eyes, but the mutilated body of the boy grew clearer. He couldn't forget. That boy could have been him. They had no right to make the child fight. None!

The beast rose up with his anger, clawing his emotions for release to satisfy the need for vengeance. He refused to soothe it.

Liandra's touch snapped the leash on his emotions. The fire burst from his chest and he clawed to tear it out, snarling.

"Stop it!" Worry shrieked in Liandra's voice, the pitch ripe with fear.

His fingers touched the scab on his chest around a small, smooth object. She hadn't revived her magic; then she must not have known.

Je'Rol dug claws into his own flesh, determined to dig out whatever her soldiers had planted on him before he'd killed them all.

Pain coursed through him but nothing worse than what he had endured from the natters or fighters. Liandra's fingers dug into his arm, but he wouldn't give in. He couldn't.

If he would listen to her, everything would be all right.

No. That was her *dispirit* power over the demon side.

No! Je'Rol ripped the skin off his chest to remove whatever she'd planted on him. "No!"

The fire stopped and Liandra stepped back, nearly stumbling over the lounger. "No! That's impossible!"

Je'Rol opened his bloody hand and turned over the crimson flesh. On the other side, a pea-sized stone peeked its green face from the smear of blood with blackened skin around it. He held it towards her, aware of the cooling lines of blood gluing the blouse to his chest. "What is it?"

"Impossible." Her eyes rose from the pulp in his hands to his face. "How did you—"

He threw the small chunk of flesh and blood at the wall, spattering the white linens on which he had slept with specks of red. "You will not control me!"

She stared at him, a glint of fear in her eyes, but didn't back away. As much as he wanted to slash her to death, he couldn't. Instead, he opened the door, ready for the

Li'Ador.

* * *

Coming out of the blood rage was never easy. Je'Rol remembered only bits and pieces, glimpses of fighting a dozen different Li'Ador throughout the palace and later sinking his teeth into an innocent women of tawny skin like the sorceress. He could only guess that some part of his mind had imagined the woman was Liandra and punished her as he had only hoped to do to the real sorceress.

He had let Liandra live, being more intent on his escape than another death at his hands. Besides, if he had attacked her, she would have gained control over him once more. He'd fled to avoid that confrontation. Unfortunately, an innocent young woman had died at the hands of the beast in retribution for her torment.

The stench of blood filled his nostrils and covered him head to foot. The beast had been sated. But it wasn't blood that soaked him; or, rather, it was, but it was diluted.

A wave of dizziness tried to send him falling into the cold around his legs, but something caught him.

"Careful," a man's voice said.

Je'Rol blinked away the hazy images, the face staring at him vaguely familiar. Dark eyes matched a dark tail of hair at the top of a man's head, but the armor with its ornate details now smeared with blood gave away his status as bear clan. His mouth formed a hard line that could have been a verbal reprimand.

"Deep breath."

Je'Rol barely had time before being shoved down into the cold depths of water. He struggled against the arms securing him, his lungs ready to burst, but not even his strength could free him of the hold on each arm and the pressure on his shoulders.

Demonlords; more than one.

His brain barely had time to register through the panic of drowning when the pressure holding him down vanished and he sprang above the surface of the water, gasping for breath and coughing.

"Better," a different voice grumbled. "He'll need more than a dunk to remove the stench, but it's tolerable now."

Je'Rol twisted, his arms still held firmly by two of the bear clan in their armor. Other demonlords surrounded him, but not all of them were bear clan; actually, only the two holding him were Ur'Asu. The others stood among bushes and trees on the banks of the river, in whose cool waters he stood with the two Ur'Asu. By the fancy robes on some and the breeches on others and the colors of skin and hair on others similar to their natural states, he recognized a few of them in their human form. Still others didn't bother to hide their true forms.

The golden lady was not among them.

"What do you want?" Suspicion gnawed in his gut, especially since he was still alive.

They sloshed through the water with him to one side of the river, still holding his arms as if he was a threat to them if turned loose.

A woman in brown breeches and tunic stepped forward, her hair knotted around her head in a crown of myriad shades of brown. She reached for his chest and yanked the shirt open, and her face tightened in a clear show of irritation. "Where is it?"

"What?"

"The *am'taerad*, the stone. It was sealed in your flesh when you fought. Where is it?"

If they meant the stone Liandra had fixed on him to control him when she wasn't awake, he had left it with her. "The sorceress."

Rage erupted across the woman's face, but she quickly regained control and motioned to a group across the river. From the rustle of leaves behind him, he knew they had departed.

"You should have brought it to us."

"Why?" Why did they desire that damned rock? What would they do with it? What was special about it? Why would they even think he would help them?

The two Ur'Asu shoved him to the ground at the woman's feet as a man in silvery white and black robes stepped forward, his white hair shimmering over his shoulders in the slant of sunlight with the black mixed in it. His face was among the fairest of the demonlords in human form, his movements smooth and purposeful with nothing wasted. "All should fear the *am'taerad* in the hands of the Adepts of Te'Mea." His voice matched his movements, steady and confident but without the arrogance of most demonlords he had encountered.

Pale blue eyes fixed on Je'Rol, a slight lift of one white brow sparking curiosity. A voice whispered in his head, *"I have been searching for you."*

"It must be destroyed," the demonlord said. "Only a few remain in existence, and we are fortunate to have discovered this one linking you to the sorceress. She will give up her precious control, if she wishes to live."

"Why didn't you take it from her?"

"We could not. The magic of such talismans is old, from a time before our kind."

"The sorcerers possess a power you can't control?"

"Enough!" The woman cast a severe look to Je'Rol.

"You must join me, or your life is forfeit."

Je'Rol blinked, unsure if he had heard what he thought he heard as a voice in his head. If he had, he wasn't going down without a fight, whether he had to risk another blood rage or not. The sorceress had said the same thing as that voice, although in her own dominating way.

"You've said too much, Lord Je'Kaoron." She scanned the faces around her. "We'll soon have the *am'taerad*. Getting them out of human hands is our only concern."

How could the mortal sorcerers control a power the demonlords didn't understand? He had a feeling the man before him would explain, but if he understood correctly, the situation for him was grim. The demonlords wouldn't let him live.

"Dispose of him," the woman said.

The beast rose in defiance within, its growl rumbling in Je'Rol's throat as claws extended. They might have caught him while in the blood rage, but as himself, he could think through his actions with reason rather than react with the instincts of the beast. He could figure out how to escape, if he survived a battle with demonlords.

"Wait." The calm command of the tiger demonlord stopped the others from moving in. "He is mine by the *caer sekiya numa*. His judgment is the right of the Je'Gri."

"Judgment?" A man in green robes snorted, his shoulder-length dark hair twisted around a crown piece that passed over his brow. "What judgment but death is there? He is half-blood, an abomination and unsuitable for this world."

"But he is of my clan. By rights of the *caer sekiya numa*, he is ours to judge with the traitor who soiled our clan's purity. You cannot deny that."

Death here or death later—what did it matter? Je'Rol prepared to flee. While they argued in their own language, he waited for a chance to escape.

The Je'Gri representative glanced down at him. *"Calm yourself. You have one chance to live, if you join me."*

The demonlord *had* spoken to him. He was the voice in Je'Rol's head. It had to be, but none of them had ever bothered to speak in his mind before. Obviously, the demonlord didn't want the others to know of their conversation. Why? What did he plan?

His curiosity piqued, Je'Rol shrank the claws and calmed himself. The beast reluctantly retreated to the deep recesses of his heart. One less blood rage was one more chance to live.

The others fell silent, lending an eerie quiet to the wilderness which no animal dared break. They turned to Lord Je'Kaoron.

The woman in brown curled her lip in a snarl. "He is yours, Lord Je'Kaoron, but the dishonor is yours if he escapes."

The tiger demonlord bowed his head to her. "That is well understood. We will go now." He motioned to Je'Rol to stand. "Walk with me."

Je'Rol obeyed, if only to satisfy his curiosity. He had not left the humans to become a victim of the demonlords' laws concerning half-bloods.

"Do not look back. You must show subservience, or I will have to kill you."

That would never happen as long as he stayed alert, but he was no match for the demonlord. As ordered, he didn't look back, but heard the assembly of demonlords moving and wondered how many prepared to follow to ensure that he didn't escape from Lord Je'Kaoron.

Away to the right, across the river and through the trees, loomed the outer wall of Dev Nadir. They should have sent soldiers after him, unless the demonlords had made arrangements.

"What happened?"

The demonlord lifted his chin higher. "I assume you mean before you returned from the blood rage?" His voice contained a calm that contrasted the spite of every other demonlord Je'Rol had crossed.

"Yes." The blood rage, aptly named for the desire of the demon side for the flesh of other creatures leading to the heavy blood spillage. He reeked of it, most of it not his own, despite the dunking in the river, which had left him soaked and chilled.

"You escaped Chandroya's palace…with some help from Lady Su'Tari. But you were unreasonable in the blood rage and attacked everyone. How fortunate that you should escape then, as we met to discuss…details."

The way he said that irked Je'Rol, but he restrained his desire for "details" of his own. Instead, he clenched his fists and said nothing, waiting for the demonlord to explain further.

"The Ur'Asu warriors restrained you and carried you from the city to where the rest of us had agreed to meet. Your timing was no less than perfect, Je'Rol."

Perfect for them, but it had done nothing for him. "What do you want of me?"

The demonlord's lip curved up slightly at the corner in the barest show of amusement. "You know the answer."

"My death?" Je'Rol growled, his muscles tight in preparation to fight. He should have jumped clear at that moment, but something held him back, a curiosity piqued by the whispers in his head. Those words hinted of something more than death awaiting him.

The demonlord tipped his head as if listening to something for a few seconds. "We must leave this land. There's nothing here for you."

"But you would take me away only to kill me anyway."

"Hush! We're being watched. I'll tell you after we're away." The harsh lines of reprimand replaced the soft lines on the demonlord's face.

Je'Rol turned his head at the rustle of leaves to his right but caught only a glimpse of colorful plumage before it disappeared.

Why should he go with this demonlord? He owed them nothing. Worse, Je'Kaoron was tiger clan, like his father, the man Je'Rol had sworn he would kill after the first time facing the realities of what he was and again since realizing the life he could never have.

They traveled through the wilderness along the river and crested a rugged hill to gaze down on a small harbor far from the city walls, which shrank away as they traveled. Je'Rol hadn't expected to find another harbor up the coast.

It wasn't as much of a harbor, though, as it was a natural occlusion of land hooked around an inlet of water at the mouth of the river, where fresh water and salt water mingled in a dance of blues and greens. In the darker blue near the hook of land, a ship berthed.

How strange to consider traveling to the Je'Gri domain. He'd never visited it for fear of his life and being unable to force himself to set foot in his mother's homeland. Her dire warnings had stuck in his mind with the other hard feelings, building a resistance to the idea of ever searching the land of Tikeros for the obelisk.

That resistance slowed each step he took, the mental effort of fighting it equal to walking through hardening mud.

He could escape. Only one demonlord would pursue him, but it was upon Je'Kaoron's honor to do so and he probably wouldn't give up. Je'Rol stood no chance against a demonlord in battle, and he had spent the last year searching the continent of Karaligo and found nothing. No matter where he went, his life was at risk, but the tiger demonlord seemed more generous than most in allowing him to live. Going would also provide safe passage to Tikeros, where Je'Rol could escape to continue his search.

They continued in silence to the harbor, where Je'Rol noticed a crew preparing the rigging upon their approach. The scent of sea air broke through the reek of blood, which had transformed into something putrid as it dried. Changing, or at least cleaning, what he wore would be his first priority, then rest. Whatever he had done in the blood rage had left him fatigued.

Upon setting foot on the plank ramp to the main deck, Je'Rol noticed a familiar odor—dirty, sweaty humans. Men labored on the ship, not a crew of demonlords. It only made sense, as humans were also slave labor for their demonlord masters, like any animal.

Je'Kaoron watched him, those pale blue eyes cool. "Go on." His voice was too calm, as if he expected no argument.

Seeing no other choice except death, Je'Rol climbed the ramp to the top deck with his host behind him.

A man in a stiff blue tunic and gold-edged shoulder guards with a curled hook design on the front stepped forward and offered a bow to Je'Kaoron, his dark hair tied back into a short tail at the nape of his neck. "My lord."

When he straightened, his eyes slid over Je'Rol with a curl of disapproval in his lip.

"Captain Mankin, make ready to depart."

"We are stocked and ready, my lord."

"Then set course for Tikeros."

"Yes, my lord." The captain paused and gave his tunic a tug at the bottom.

"Do not test the patience of a half-blood any more than you would your lord." Je'Kaoron's stern tone left no room for doubt. The captain's throat flashed with a swallow, his eyes wide on Je'Rol.

They would fear him more than their lord for the instability well-known of half-bloods. Je'Rol appreciated them knowing—they'd likely leave him alone, as he preferred.

"He will be judged by the Je'Gri, as is our right...Go now. Cast off, Captain."

"Yes, sir." Mankin bowed again and hurried away.

"Follow me," Je'Kaoron said, leading Je'Rol to a square opening and the steps leading to the lower decks.

Behind them, orders shot from the captain to the men, the clatter of rushing feet on the deck echoing below.

10

Je'Rol followed his host into the darker holds of the vessel. There, the demonlord led him to a room, where a mat laid on the floor next to a low table, and closed the door, sealing them in darkness. The muffled tromp of footsteps and the calls of voices sounded above them.

The demonlord lit a globe on the table and the flutter of wings drew Je'Rol's eyes to the cage in the corner, where a pair of birds folded their wings and blinked.

"No doubt you're curious why I spared your life." Je'Kaoron adjusted the glowing orb on the low table next to a stack of papers and a small brush and sat down with his legs crossed beneath it. "I'm sure you expect me to fulfill my obligation once we arrive in port."

Not a difficult assumption.

Je'Rol stood near the door, ready to run but curious why the demonlord would so willingly turn his back as if inviting him to flee.

"Lady Su'Tari said you were the quiet type." Je'Kaoron uncorked a bottle of ink. "You should know I'm as surprised by this as you."

He paused to dip the fine tip of the delicate brush into the ink and marked something on the paper. "It was not my plan to bring Je'Rol the fugitive half-blood to Tikeros. Nor is it my plan that you be judged with Je'Dron in the only punishment fitting of his 'crime'."

"Then what do you want from me?"

Je'Kaoron paused, his back straightening. "I want only what is best for our world. No clan should rule another. We were made to rule this world equally." He dipped the brush again and wrote something. "This world was made to serve our needs. To force any clan to servitude is to upset the balance of our world."

"*Your* world?"

"Yes." The demonlord's calm voice scoured Je'Rol's patience. "Unfortunately, our mistakes have done much of that already…as you, of all individuals, are well aware."

"Half-bloods." The word growled from his lips.

The demonlord paused in his writing and stared at the soft light of the orb. "Many blame the humans for the degeneration of the demonlords' power over this world, but the problems started long before the demonlords began experimenting with the humans, before they even considered only taking out the weak and infirmed to allow a stronger species to survive each generation.

"Our problems started with one of the oldest clans, the Mai'Ekam." Je'Kaoron paused for several seconds before dipping his brush and scribbling a note. "One of the dead clans."

Je'Rol waited, his breath caught on what the demonlord had to say. The golden lady's words returned.

"Su'Tari warned you of their power and their downfall."

Something clicked in his mind, the pieces snapping together—the Su'Kora representative he thought of as the golden lady and the confirmation that a demonlord named Su'Tari had told him about the Mai'Ekam. "She was the golden lady?"

The huff of air from the demonlord almost sounded like a hint of a laugh. "I imagine her smiling to hear you refer to her that way. The Su'Kora have a gold color, yes, as you and I bear the color of our true natures."

Je'Kaoron spoke to him as if he was a part of the clan, but in Je'Rol's experience, the demonlords despised the half-bloods and didn't acknowledge them as belonging. But Je'Kaoron hadn't *included* him as part of the clan, only as much as they bore the marks of his demon side. That was more than he expected.

"She refused to give me her name," Je'Rol said.

"Understandable. Her life would be taken for her treachery, as would mine." At that, Je'Kaoron peered over his shoulder. "If you ever spoke of this."

The gaze of the demonlord caught him in a question of his intentions. Je'Rol shook his head. "No. I have no reason to tell anyone of your help or hers."

"Good." Je'Kaoron returned to his writing. "But intentions do nothing where coercion is used. If you are taken by another Adept of Te'Mea, I'll deny everything; you will be on your own."

"I won't say anything," Je'Rol growled. "I resisted Lord Bannon's sorceress."

The demonlord set down his brush and turned to face him, the paleness of his eyes standing out among the shadows cast by the light behind him. "Can you resist their *dispirit* control?"

Je'Rol thought back to the times he had resisted and the conversation he overheard between *Serae* Liandra and Lord Bannon. Only the spell—or rather, the *am'taerad*—had given her power over him when he controlled the beast. "I believe so. They have weaknesses."

Je'Kaoron sat up straighter. "What weaknesses do you know?"

"The human side and time. Controlling the beast, the demon side—" He hesitated at referring to the demon side as a beast in the demonlord's presence, but Je'Kaoron didn't react. "As long as I'm human, her power over me is weak."

"That is something we didn't know. No half-blood has lived to tell, nor would any Adept admit this, although it *is* known their powers only work on demons. That explains her reason for using the *am'taerad*." His eyes shifted, as if he watched something only he could see, but a second later, Je'Kaoron turned back to the table and continued his scribbling without further explanation.

Je'Rol stared at the birds in the cage, sympathizing with the creatures as he had never before with any animal. The sorceress had caged him within her power with the intention of using him to facilitate Lord Bannon's rise to glory, by eliminating a rival lord, one who controlled a prosperous city. Je'Rol would never forget the horror on her face when he tore the stone from his chest and tossed it away.

Je'Rol dropped his eyes to his hands. Human hands, but bearing the strength of a demon and the knifelike claws of a beast at his bidding.

He clenched his fingers tight. No more killing. He had sworn long ago to never hurt another person; but he couldn't uphold that personal vow. The world was a dangerous place, and some humans deserved to die; others were less fortunate, the innocent lives he regretted. He would control the beast…eventually.

"What do you know of the *am'taerad* that I've not already told you?"

Je'Rol blinked and released his fists, recalling too clearly the pain the sorceress had caused him through that stone. "Only misery. What magic is it?"

"One of the stones of an arcane power no clan has understood, except one…It's believed the Mai'Ekam deciphered the writings of the Master Race to create the obelisk you seek. The sorceress must have known what she had. Wouldn't you agree?"

"Yes." Liandra had known exactly how to use the stone to subordinate him, but she had a larger, matching stone that seemed connected, although she denied it. "Maybe." Something wasn't right.

"Is there something more?"

"She had a stone on me but I don't believe it was the source. She carried a green stone set in an amulet etched with strange symbols." While he couldn't care less about a stone, Je'Rol didn't want the sorcerers gaining more power than they already possessed any more than the demonlords wanted them to gain an advantage.

Je'Kaoron scribbled on the paper, dipping the brush in ink and making furious strokes for a few minutes before pausing. "A larger stone…as the source of control to the one on you? Then the one on you wasn't the *am'taerad*, or at least not the control stone. Two stones connected by magic. You said one was larger, set in an amulet the sorceress bore?"

"Yes, about this big." Je'Rol hooked his fingers around in an oval shape to demonstrate. He'd had a good look while holding it in his hands briefly that first night after his capture, although he wasn't sure if it was significant or a trick.

Je'Kaoron mimicked him and returned to his paper. "Did you recognize any symbols? Do you remember anything?"

"No. Only that they closely matched those she wears." The demonlord seemed confused rather than satisfied, with more questions than Je'Rol expected.

"Like those she wears?"

"Her tattoos."

"I see…" Je'Kaoron dipped his brush and wrote something on the paper. What did he see about this?

Despite a rising tide of questions, Je'Rol kept them to himself. He didn't care what the demonlords wanted. He was done with the stones of the sorceress and the control they had exerted over him. Once he had the obelisk, he would be free.

After a minute, the demonlord paused. "You may leave. You'll share the main quarters with the crew, I'm afraid; but it should chain their tongues until we dock."

A clear dismissal without answers, except that this news bothered Je'Kaoron more than the idea of some ancient control stone in the hands of the humans.

The door let out a soft creak when Je'Rol pulled it open.

"Do change clothes while you're out?"

Je'Rol looked down at his torn and blood-caked clothes.

"Ask Captain Mankin." The demonlord dipped his brush again.

Je'Rol shut the door, leaving himself alone in the narrow alley between the captain's quarters and the demonlord's. The captain would be on the top deck, directing his crew, if the voices and clomp of feet over his head were any indication.

He would do well to clean the breeches; soft leather lasted longer than wool or plant fibers for hard travel but required special care. For his purposes, he preferred it to other fabrics. Lord Bannon had paid well for the breeches and vest to make him presentable to Lord Chandroya.

But they were no longer his concern. Je'Rol, the fugitive half-blood, would soon arrive in the homeland of his ancestors.

A low growl rumbled in his throat at the rising anger and the beast gnashing its teeth to escape. Without the stone or the sorceress's power to restrain it, the struggle was his again. Facing the Li'Ador in his escape had released it from his weakened grasp. He'd learned to rely on the stone too much.

Now, he curled his fingers, aware of the claws extending to shred the next person who dared threaten him, one of the many triggers he'd learned to control; except he was stuck on a ship afloat at sea with no way to avoid trouble from the sailors. With luck, the crew wouldn't dare to challenge him; he could run nowhere to escape trouble but would have to suffer the same pent-up need to move as he had in the hands of the sorceress.

The voyage would try his greatest patience, but he would suffer it for the chance to search Tikeros for the obelisk and the chance to control the beast within.

Je'Rol emerged from the hold into the light of day. The sails billowed in the wind as the crew finished tying the ropes. The captain stood by the wheel at the aft part of the ship, talking with one of the crewmen.

Their eyes caught his, a frown on the captain's face and a grimace under the mustache of the other man. They could think what they wanted; it wasn't Je'Rol's concern, although he wished for human ears that he wouldn't hear their whispers about him. No one had warned them of the abilities of half-bloods apparently. Je'Rol wasn't about to start.

He would have preferred keeping away, but he needed a fresh shirt. The breeches would clean up well with some work. Removing the stench of dried blood would ease his mind, although the nightmares would linger, as they had in another lifetime, the first time the beast had actually fed.

He'd seen enough bloodshed and killing in the last few days to haunt him for many lifetimes. Removing the gory reminder would be the first step to forgetting.

For that, he needed the captain. Je'Rol took a breath and crossed the deck, the splash of water against the hull catching his ears. The foul sea air overpowered the dried blood covering him, small comfort on the confines of the ship.

"Captain." He spoke in a deep voice to hide the growl. "I was ordered to see you for clothes."

Captain Mankin's lip twitched, and the man standing behind his shoulder tensed. "Clothes, eh? Lord Je'Kaoron, I assume?" He tapped his fingers on the wheel. "Hm...Not much spare on a voyage; room for food only—" For a man of dark skin, the color change was remarkable. He must have heard about the appetites of half-bloods somewhere, or assumed it, based on the preferences of his master. In their natural forms, demonlords were all predators, a fact as well-known as their hunger for humans in the long ago past, among the many animals they hunted. For all he knew, his crew was considered food by the demonlord, and possibly by his new half-blood guest.

"I only need a shirt." A cloak would be preferable for a sense of separating himself from the crew, but they likely would have nothing like a traveling cloak on board.

"That I will have." Mankin strode past him. "This way...Take the wheel, Carrik...Follow me."

Je'Rol followed the man toward the hold, but before they descended, Je'Kaoron's head emerged from the hole and the captain halted and bowed. "My lord."

Je'Kaoron stepped from the hole, his hands wrapped around a bird, and gave

Mankin and Je'Rol no more than a passing glance on his way to the deck rail.

"Come…Je'Rol."

He waited for the captain to descend into the dark interior. Curious about the demonlord, he paused to watch the release of the bird, which fluttered madly to gain altitude.

Lord Je'Kaoron stared after the bird headed east, the direction of their travel. It quickly disappeared into the sky, but the demonlord continued to watch.

The message had been sent, but what had it said, and to whom had he sent it?

"Are you coming?"

Je'Rol looked into the darkness and climbed in. He'd likely find out soon whoever the demonlord contacted, when they arrived on Tikeros.

* * *

Her boots clapped loudly on the smooth tiled floor of the Je'Gri palace, each step adding to the thunder of others accompanying her. Nadia adjusted the black leather bracers bearing the crest of the *Sect du Cantir Te'Mea*, a silver engraved beast with bronze horns and its jaws open to bite with fangs. An arrow pierced through it, the tip inlaid with a green *imera* stone blessed by the priest of her sect for protection. The bracers were a gift to all who completed their training as demon hunters.

High Lord Je'Rekun had called for her specifically, Nadia TuFalan, the closest demon hunter in the western coastal province and also a recent guest in expectance of the suspected birth of another half-blood. The child was due within the next month, and would be taken from its misery before it could breathe. The mother was already in custody, the poor wretch.

Nadia had given her comfort in understanding the hardships her child would bear, should it be allowed to live. A handful of female Je'Gri had demonstrated a surprising amount of solace to the girl, whose situation proved yet again the reason the Adepts of Te'Mea secretly preached the downfall of all demonlords. One day they would have that power.

That day may not come in her lifetime, but she would do what she could to follow the code of all Adepts, building their power to eventually overthrow the demonlords and rid the world of all demons to make room for the rise of mankind.

Until that day came, she answered to the summons of the demonlord masters and purged the world of the dangers of demonlord lusts.

Nadia arrived at the immense ebony and jade doors of the throne room of the High Lord of the Je'Gri, an orange tiger sitting guard at either side. Without hesitating, she marched past them. Four columns connected arches sectioning the ceiling and marking the center of the room, where a crystal skylight etched to concentrate the sun on images along the outer walls shimmered in the sunlight. Beneath it in full light was a marble seat of elegant craftsmanship padded in the deepest blue.

Behind the throne stood half a dozen men and women in black and orange armor reminiscent of their true forms, while on the chair sat a man of regal bearing, his white and black robes opened upon the arms of the seat to expose the matching tunic with its shimmering pattern beneath, all of it the effort of converting his tiger hide through magic. Hard blue eyes sent a shudder down her spine; Lord Je'Rekun's gaze never wavered from her.

Two small goblins stood in simple hand-made robes on either side of the throne, half the height of their masters with oversized ears on either side of bald, green heads from which dark, beady eyes looked out.

She would have preferred the goblins to Lord Je'Rekun; they weren't too bright. She hated the High Lord but respected his authority and the beauty of his human form, the perfect camouflage for a hunter of humans but perhaps too perfect. He inspired fear in his domain, a fear that the old ways would return after the prosperity that had come in the years of his brother's rule before him. Only once did she make the error of mentioning Lord Je'Dron; one didn't ask twice in the presence of High Lord Je'Rekun.

Nadia reached the edge of the arches and fell to one knee, her head bowed so her tight brown braid fell over her shoulder. "My lord. Summoned, I come."

The faint scrape of the fabric covering the seat and the soft ruffle of his 'clothes' marked his movements. "I have a task for you, Huntress." His voice growled with the menace of a foul mood. One wrong word or show of disrespect and even her life would be forfeit.

Nadia held her pose, despite the cramp tightening in her thigh.

His steps padded close and only stopped when he stood next to her. "A ship will arrive in Durmin in a few days bearing my emissary, Lord Je'Kaoron. He brings a gift." At that, a soft purr escaped him, and he stepped away, granting her a moment to breathe. "After all this time, I'll have the chance to end this pointless rebellion led by my brother."

Rebellion, nothing. From what she had heard, Je'Rekun had been the one to steal the throne from Je'Dron almost thirty years ago, but it was probably no time in the ageless immortality of the demonlords.

Nadia bit her tongue, hoping to keep it with her life rather than rile the High Lord. Her place wasn't to openly judge the politics of the demonlord clans but to eliminate the half-bloods and lead the Li'Ador to protect her kind—humans—from demon attacks. Her opinion was reserved for those she trusted.

How could a gift from his emissary end the feud with his exiled brother? While she wished for an explanation, she doubted he would offer it. Je'Rekun was no fool to give away his plans.

"He'll need your services to secure my prize."

Her services? Suspicion gnawed in her mind. Only one purpose would require a demon hunter, the task for which she had been born with the power. "You will have your prize."

"You are authorized to use any means to secure him, but if he tries to escape, you may kill. I prefer this prize alive, but too long he has eluded capture."

"Him, my lord?"

"The half-blood my brother 'honored' with a name only fitting the rightful pureness of the clan—Je'Rol, the fugitive."

Her blood ran cold and hot all at once, the hardening of her heart failing with the memories of her youth and of the deep feelings unrequited in a time of innocence and hope, left cold as the night was lonely. Je'Rol, the bastard.

The ringing like metal on stone sent shivers through her body, snapping her attention to a furious High Lord.

"Mockery!" Lord Je'Rekun roared, his true nature merging with the word.

Nadia tightened her fists, her jaw clenched to contain the roiling emotions ignited by the memories; those she had left to cool with the experience and wisdom of the years since.

"Rise, Huntress." His voice was hard with a snap of impatience.

After a breath to cool the embers of her forgotten anguish, she obeyed.

"Accompany Lord Je'Kaoron on his return with the half-blood."

She gave a slight bow to the composed High Lord, forcing back a smirk at the irony. "Yes, my lord."

"You're excused." He flicked his wrist in a clear indication for her to leave.

Nadia spun on her heel and marched out. Finally, she would confront Je'Rol, after all these years of healing from the heart break he'd left her before the *Sect du Cantir Te'Mea* found her. They had taken her in and taught her how wrong it was to feel mercy for any demon, much less a murderous half-blood.

11

Only eight days at sea and Je'Rol had taken to pacing the deck to expend the pent-up energy, his wounds healed and his muscles were strong and ready to act. The crew had avoided him from the first day, a much-needed distance to maintain his patience for the voyage, which proved to be as effective a cage as the sorceress's control.

He stopped at the prow and gazed out over the waves and the line of land at the horizon. The whistling of the wind through the rigging behind him and the roar of the sea—perhaps at the command of the demonlords who called it home—drowned out the whispers of the crew.

"Durmin."

Je'Rol whirled on the voice behind him.

Je'Kaoron stepped up beside him, his gaze on the land ahead; the hint of smile on his face that of someone glad to be home. Those pale blue eyes casually fixed on Je'Rol. "Are you prepared for what's to come?"

"No." Je'Rol had never had the inclination to talk with the demonlord, nor had Je'Kaoron, who spent most of his time in his natural form, offered to inform him of any plans when they arrived. How could he be prepared?

"You'll be greeted by the Li'Ador and perhaps a demon hunter, if I know High Lord Je'Rekun. He would not send his own with the resistance causing trouble." The demonlord spoke in that nauseatingly cool voice of confidence.

"How would he know?" The words ground out in a growl. Je'Rol had assumed from their conversation that Je'Kaoron intended to help him escape. If that wasn't the plan, he had no intention of cooperating.

The demonlord turned and strode back along the deck.

Betrayal! He should have known better than to trust a demonlord with his life. That bird must have carried the message to the High Lord he spoke of. If Je'Kaoron was anything less than a demonlord, Je'Rol would finish him for this. Already the beast raged inside him for release, the claws extending in anticipation; but he couldn't do it. Rather, he would be prepared and no amount of taunting by the demonlord would hold him back when his chance for freedom came. He would escape, whether the demonlord pursued him or not.

That time was soon. Je'Rol watched the land fill the horizon, the details of a harbor town growing every minute with smoke rising from a dozen places among the tiled roofs of the tight rows of homes and the movement of people along the shore and the boats rocking next to the dock with the waves. Soon they would arrive in port, but he wouldn't let anyone take him. He had too little time to prepare, but ideas washed through his mind.

The captain rang out orders to his crew, whose adjustments of the sails slowed the ship as it approached the pier.

Je'Rol scanned the faces while trying to ignore the waft of sewage and mold reaching him from the muddy town. Most of the citizens went about their business without more than a glance. The men at the end of the nearest dock yelled orders to the crew, guiding the ship safely to the wooden pier among the sloshing waves.

Men tossed heavy ropes to those on the dock, and the crew extended the plank and secured it.

The voyage had ended. Je'Kaoron waited at the top of the plank, watching him with a look of calm expectation.

A low growl vibrated from Je'Rol's throat, but so far the town was clear of anything to worry him. The expected welcoming party was nowhere to be seen. Perhaps Je'Kaoron was wrong, but why?

Questioning his fortune would only bring misery. Je'Rol had no intention of letting the demonlord take him to his High Lord, and rushed across the deck and down the plank, each step clattering on the wood until he reached the muddy ground.

"You must go now."

The voice froze him and pulled him around to face the demonlord.

"Go! They'll be here soon. You will find the obelisk."

He knew? Of course, he must have known. Je'Kaoron had mentioned knowing about the lady's visit with Je'Rol in the prison beneath the Kairashun. Lord Je'Kaoron must have been one of those she had trusted, except he had sent a message to the ruler of the Je'Gri, a man who would order the—

The thunder of hoofbeats scattered the citizens as a couple dozen mounted warriors rode through the streets to the pier.

"Jump! Now!"

Je'Rol sprang to the nearest rooftop peak, confused by the demonlord's actions but determined to escape. Arrows sang through the air, but it only took one sinking into his thigh to knock him off balance. He slid down the roof tiles, but regained his footing at the edge.

"Bring him down!" The cold, feminine voice sent chills through his spine with its vague familiarity, but the face remained hidden beneath a dark cowl.

The grunts of horses and clatter of metal accompanied the splashing of mud as he limped along the edge of the roof overhanging the nearest side.

A dozen Li'Ador sat with their arrows nocked on taut bowstrings.

Clenching his teeth on the pain in his leg, he sprang to the opposite side of the house.

"Get him! Go! Go! Go!" the woman shouted.

The thunder of hooves followed him with a couple of arrows.

Je'Rol leapt to the next rooftop, but the riders were ready. He couldn't avoid them. Given those options, he ran along the peak, intending to leap over their heads to the next row. The stinging in his thigh was nothing compared to his determination to escape.

The end came, and went. He sailed through the air, the next rooftop closing fast.

Pain stabbed through his left shoulder, and he twisted, dropping his posture so he barely landed on the rooftop and rolled off. The ground knocked his breath out and cracked through his head.

He choked for a breath amid the spots in his vision.

A hooded figure dismounted and approached on foot from the nearest group of riders, a slender figure, the woman who had given the orders.

"Calm yourself, Je'Rol." The quiet tone of that voice chased away the tension from his muscles. He had no reason to fear her. "That's it. Now come to me."

His breathing returned, giving him the strength to obey her and satisfy the curiosity nagging his mind about the face hidden in the shadows of that hood. He stood as several soldiers dismounted.

The woman held up a gloved hand to stop them, her eyes unmoved from Je'Rol. "You will join me, Je'Rol. Come now. We'll take care of you."

He knew that voice. It whispered of fond memories and peace amid the turmoil. She would take care of him; she had once before.

Unsteady on his feet, he took a tentative step towards her, the desire to obey strong in his mind and his heart.

"Come." She backed out of his reach towards the other riders.

He shouldn't follow her. He should run. But he wanted to know why she seemed so familiar that the beast quieted instead of rising in defiance. The answer was clear by the dark cloak with its demon head clasp, and the fitted clothes and weapon belt across her chest and the second around her waist—demon hunter, a warrior with the power to control his will, an Adept trained by the Li'Ador. But there was something more about this particular huntress.

Pain stung through his thigh. The arrow wasn't deep, but the head would hurt worse coming out. He limped on it for now, following her to see the full features beneath the hood.

"Who are you?"

Something cold passed through those eyes in the shadows. "I suppose I shouldn't expect you to remember, if you ever cared." Her tongue lashed the last words as she reached up and pulled the hood off.

His blood ran cold on a wind of distant memories, freezing his feet. "Nadia?"

"Sleep, Je'Rol."

No! Not again. His mind closed in around itself, cutting off the outside world.

* * *

Je'Rol collapsed at her feet into the oozing mud.

Finally, after all this time, she'd found him and caught him. Je'Rol was no human. That stunt on the rooftops proved it, but she had known half a lifetime ago he wasn't human. Back then she thought he had been a full demonlord, back when she was young and naïve, before she'd traveled across a dozen domains.

No more.

Je'Rol was a half-blood and dangerous. He deserved whatever High Lord Je'Rekun had waiting for him.

"Pick him up."

Four Li'Ador rushed past as she returned to her horse and reached up for the saddle horn, intending to mount; but she hesitated. A graceful white figure stood out from behind them in the dreary mess, alerting her to the presence of the demonlord, High Lord Je'Rekun's emissary. She owed him a sign of respect.

"Tie him in the saddle," she ordered the four carrying the half-blood. It wouldn't hold him if he broke her control, but it would keep him from falling.

Confident her orders would be carried out, she squeezed between horses. On her approach of the demonlord she bowed her head. She would have knelt in proper respect but for the muck, or that's the excuse she would use. The demonlords deserved no respect—they ruled by fear—but she would continue her feigned subjugation. "My lord."

"Well done, Huntress."

The compliment passed through her like a gentle wave, carried on the unusually calm voice of the one she assumed was Lord Je'Kaoron. He took no offense of her lack of formality. This one was different, but it changed nothing. "It is my honor to accompany you to the palace of High Lord Je'Rekun with the half-blood."

"You serve well. Go and carry out your duty."

"Yes, my lord." She offered a deeper bow and whirled away, intent on keeping Je'Rol unconscious until she was ready to deal with him.

From the corner of her eye, she caught a faint light. A second later, a white tiger splashed through the mud well behind their horses.

By proper tribute, she should have offered him a mount; but the demonlord hadn't seemed interested in riding back for the seven days it would likely take to return to the palace, and they had no horses to spare.

The men sat Je'Rol in the saddle of a horse with one on each side holding him while two others wrapped a rope around him and the horn of the saddle. They had pulled the arrows from his leg and shoulder already, something she would have liked to have done herself while he was conscious, if only to hurt him as he had hurt her.

* * *

He stood in a clearing, the clicking, growling, skittering of natters surrounding him from the darkness of the trees. Claws extended, the beast inside snarling to escape for the fight and bloodshed.

They came. Not a few, nor even a dozen, but hundreds of creatures drooling with hunger. A wave of them rose up and arched over. They surrounded him, blotted out the trees and the moon, until a sea of them rose up, and they tightened into a writhing figure. Arms formed and legs, and a head. The mass of natters merged into a bloody, half-eaten figure—the half-blood boy from the Dao Larashi.

It reached down for him, but he couldn't run. The demon side tore away so he faced a bloody, snarling partially transformed image of himself, but the bloody giant grabbed it.

Seconds later, the beast was the giant.

"Je'Rol!" A woman screamed as the beast slashed him.

* * *

"Wake up, Je'Rol!"

The scream echoed through his head, fading with the materialization of a face. Or was he still dreaming? He reached up, but she backed away.

"Keep your hands to yourself."

He blinked, the frightening dream fading with the focus on that familiar but different face. She had changed as he had with time, but the remnants of the gentle face he recognized were still there, identifiable. "Nadia?"

How could she be on Tikeros? He had left her long ago at a village on Meko.

She crossed her arms, a haughty air about her. This wasn't the young girl from his youth but a woman in a black uniform similar to the Li'Ador, though much less restrictive with a layered chest plate shifting with their movements and shoulder guards. Demon hunters didn't have much need for armor but did need to be able to move quickly.

Je'Rol sat up, and winced with the sting of pain in his shoulder. The escape attempt flashed through his mind, along with his fall after the arrow pierced his shoulder.

"What do you have to say for yourself?"

"I should have fled sooner." Je'Kaoron had urged him to flee, yet he had been the one to send the message to the High Lord of the Je'Gri of his coming. How was he, Je'Rol, supposed to know if that order to jump had been a help or a hindrance? Maybe the demonlord had set him up for injury. He should never have trusted a demonlord, but the golden lady—Su'Tari—had helped him; the proof scarred his chest.

His head hurt thinking about it.

A slap across his cheek didn't help. Nadia's face turned red, her pretty lips pressed tightly together. Of all people, she should have been the one to help him.

"Huntress." One of the soldiers handed her a plate of food, which she set on the ground and shoved towards him.

"Eat, Je'Rol. High Lord Je'Rekun wants you alive."

He took the plate of food and brushed off the dirt that had scooped onto it when she shoved it at him. Unlike the owners of Dao fighters who wanted to strengthen their chances—literally—of winning the tournament, the Li'Ador and demon hunters would do all they could to weaken him. Stale bread and some greens would never sustain him. He'd eaten better on the ship that brought him to Tikeros.

While he ate, Nadia never took her eyes off him but sat against a boulder with a scowl. Like someone poking him lightly but incessantly in the side, her eyes irritated him, until he had to gulp the bite of dry bread.

"What did I do wrong?" he growled.

"Figure it out yourself." She stood and glanced at the men checking the tack on the horses.

Through a break in the clouds to the west, a spear of sunlight touched a mountainside across the valley between peaks.

Then he noticed it—the white tiger languidly draped over a large protrusion of rock along the road. The demonlord had taken his natural form for the journey.

"Hurry up and eat. You'll need the strength to walk." Her eyes returned with all their scornful hatred.

A low growl rumbled in his throat, but the beast made no attempt to escape; and why should it in the restraining power of one of the Adepts of Te'Mea? She had the same power as Liandra the sorceress, but Nadia was trained to kill demons rather than manipulate the complexities of magic. That *dispirit* power explained much of what he had felt around her when he was young, and she had been young and apparently an untrained Adept at the time.

"You cannot defy me, Je'Rol."

He didn't want to defy her, only to understand why she hated him. He'd left to protect her from the beast, so she wouldn't end up dead. How could she appreciate that? She was a demon hunter now.

Je'Rol growled and ripped at the food with his teeth, refusing the memories refuge in the present and concentrating on eating. He'd allowed himself to forget, as the only way he could go on living. In her training, Nadia must have learned about the risks of his loss of control and accepted why he had left in such a rush, but she trained to be a demon hunter, indoctrinated to loathe all demons, including half-bloods.

What was the point of making her understand? She had every intention of killing him when she had her chance.

He finished the food as the Li'Ador readied the horses to travel and threw the metal plate at her. "Satisfied?"

She caught the plate at her chest, her eyes never leaving him. "Lieutenant!"

A man in a Li'Ador uniform rushed to her. "Yes, Huntress!"

"Bring my horse."

He gave a slight bow to her and a dirty look to Je'Rol, and whirled away.

"You will walk quietly, Je'Rol. Banish all thoughts of escape."

His thoughts scrambled at the tone of her voice, a sultry but commanding tone that threaded its way through his head and suffocated his better instincts. He had to hang on to the last whisper of defiance, the last voice of reason, the fading shriek of the beast imprisoned. It shrank into a tiny corner of his mind.

Before he realized, the group moved around him, Nadia directly behind and the demonlord at his side. Every other step sent pricks of agony through his thigh where the arrow had sunk deep. When had that happened?

Her *dispirit* power was strong, but she didn't rely on magic stones to control him as the sorceress had. She didn't have to; the tiger next to him would win if he tried to escape, but that didn't mean he wouldn't be watching for the right opportunity.

The long walk and the constant supervision with no further contact from the demonlord gnawed on his patience like a natter on a fat calf by the time they stopped to rest for the night. While they slept, he might have a chance to escape, if he could stay awake. After eight days at sea and the long walk all after midday, he was tired.

He fell asleep soon after eating, her command irresistible.

12

Upon several cut ledges of the steep, rocky bluffs of the mountain stood the palace of the Je'Gri High Lord in all the splendor one expected of the ancient rulers of the world. Old but well-kept by the blood and sweat of the humans who served the demonlords, *Acropa Je'Gri* stretched over an area the size of a city, but most of it at different levels connected by stairs cut out of the rock and bridges across sheer drops. A vast garden of flowers and trees descended from the lower levels and the valley floor through the hills towards the simple human dwellings. Tigers and humans went about their business throughout the tiers.

It was a city unto itself, though nothing like Dev Nadir, or, rather, Dev Nadir was nothing like this, with its stylized arches and levels of tiled rooftops alternating with decorative stone peaks. Throughout it all, as if placed by an artist, spindly trees covered in blossoms provided their touch of color and shade.

The gateway to the city was a bridge over a chasm into which a ribbon of water fell. On either side of the bridge rose two massive statues of sitting tigers, their eyes staring down in judgment upon those who sought entrance with ears tipped back and lips curled to bare their teeth in warning.

Je'Rol glanced up at each of them as he passed between, feeling small and helpless trapped between the gazes of the giant tigers. The dozen orange tigers accompanying them didn't help matters. Je'Kaoron had ordered them to the perimeter, but their presence had dimmed any hopes of escape the last few days; a half-blood was no match for one full demonlord, much less thirteen.

The clop of the horse's hooves on wooden planks drowned out any sound of the tigers, if they made any noise besides the occasional growl to one another the last six days.

Ahead of Je'Rol, three pairs of riders rode two abreast without hesitation about the steep drop a couple feet on either side of the rails. Beside him walked Je'Kaoron in his natural form. The demonlord had said nothing to him since his capture by Nadia, who rode directly behind with the leader of the Li'Ador and the rest of the soldiers and tigers behind them.

They crossed the bridge to solid ground and circled him. Behind him, the clink of metal and squeak of leather warned of the dismounting warriors. Nadia stepped next to him as the Li'Ador ahead moved aside, her slim figure beneath the black suit and armor poised with confidence.

A moment later, Je'Kaoron stood in his white and black robes on Je'Rol's other side, the calm visage a welcome change from Nadia's cold, harsh glare. The demonlord stretched an arm towards the entrance before them, which arched from the sides but never to meet above. "This way."

He led them across a courtyard, where orange tigers lounged among a smaller variety of men and women of the same unnatural beauty as Je'Kaoron but of different styles of dress and colors indicating they were not Je'Gri. The demonlords parted for the group, their eyes burning through Je'Rol and aggravating the beast with the threat they posed.

Je'Kaoron led them past the stares through an open door and across a small chamber to a high-ceilinged corridor lined by life-sized tiger statues spaced in the center of tall columns.

While the opulence of the demonlords impressed him—Je'Rol had never set foot inside their dwellings—the thought of walking into a prison darkened his mood. In the silence of the corridor, the low rumble in his throat drew a critical glance from Je'Kaoron.

"You'd best stay silent in the presence of High Lord Je'Rekun."

Why should he? The High Lord wanted him dead. No demonlord would tolerate a half-blood living, or not for long. If he was as good as dead, he had nothing to lose by expressing himself.

Behind Je'Rol, Nadia said nothing. She didn't have to. Her powers worked on him without speaking, or he would have at least attempted to escape many times on the road there; something always dampened his thoughts of escape with hopelessness. The demon hunter fulfilled her purpose, and would soon receive her reward from her master like a good little human servant.

At the end of the corridor, they stepped through a doorway to a room divided by four columns around a throne in the center. Through the etched window above, sunlight washed it in a brilliant glow. Upon it sat a man in silvery white robes bearing lines of black, his human legs crossed and his head held aloft. White and black hair draped over his shoulders and chest. Je'Rol might have considered him regal, if he had shown anything but a sneer.

At the boundary of where the columns divided the entrance from the brilliantly lit throne and its occupant, Je'Kaoron fell to one knee.

"Kneel." The whispered command from Nadia pressed through Je'Rol's mind, challenging the beast, which rose in defiance until he blinked and found himself on hands and knees behind the demonlord.

"My Lord," Je'Kaoron's calm voice said. "I bring Je'Rol, the half-blood fugitive." He stood and stepped aside, his head bowed as the High Lord rose from his throne and approached.

Je'Rol watched as if through a fog, aware of his body and surroundings but unable to command his limbs to anything but Nadia's will overpowering him.

High Lord Je'Rekun stopped before him, close enough to notice a faint scar along his left cheek to his neck, like claw marks; someone had disfigured him in a fight, possibly with one of his own. "No half-blood deserves the honor of a clan name. My brother was wrong to secure you away as a babe with your mother. He was weak, but I am not!" The last part turned into a raging snarl and ended with a blow to Je'Rol's cheek that snapped his head aside.

Amid the stars dancing in his vision, Je'Rol noticed the bitter, metallic taste he'd grown familiar with during the Dao Larashi fighting. He spat out crimson on the red velvet carpet at the High Lord's feet. As the stars and black spots shrank, he focused on the droplets staining the High Lord's robes, a distraction from the ache in his jaw.

Je'Rekun whirled and motioned to someone. From next to the throne, where Je'Rol hadn't noticed it, a goblin rushed out and knelt before the High Lord. Rather, not knelt, but his movements indicated activity low to the floor with a rapid lapping sound.

"That insolence won't last. *You* won't last…not long, but long enough for my needs." He whirled around, the goblin following and apparently obsessed about the bottom of the High Lord's robes.

"Guards!"

In seconds, orange tigers stood on each side of Je'Rol. Where he thought his eyes blurred, the tigers transformed into armored men.

"Secure him."

The men each grabbed one arm and forced Je'Rol to his feet. His head pounded from the movement, making walking difficult. The demonlord had hit him harder than he first thought.

"Lock him up."

* * *

From her kneeling position, Nadia watched them drag Je'Rol away until they disappeared through the side passage.

"Huntress." The High Lord's tone softened, the anger no longer present, replaced by an almost purring satisfaction. Or perhaps that really was a faint purr she heard in him speaking her title. "Your reward is waiting in your chambers. But first, the woman is close to term. You would do well to check in."

She rose to her feet and bowed her head. Despite her exhaustion from the travel and the focus on Je'Rol, she had no choice but to obey. "Thank you, High Lord Je'Rekun."

A smile touched his lips at the full address. Yes, she understood how to flatter the demonlords, and she knew how to use their favor to her advantage.

Nadia strode out, glad to escape the High Lord's scrutiny and potential lethal temper towards lesser demons and humans. While staying to observe the woman held in a lower room of the palace, she'd observed his disregard for anyone less than a demonlord, as if their lives were no more valuable than the herds they raised for hunting. And why should he and the other demonlords not consider them any better? The clans had hunted humans and were known to still enjoy their flesh.

Past the other demonlords she hurried, anxious to check on the woman. Such a child would be a threat to their world, as Je'Rol was. He should never have been allowed to live, but as she understood, Je'Dron himself had cared for the half-blood son. Never had any demonlord taken such an interest in the results of their affairs.

It didn't excuse the fact that Je'Rol was alive and a threat. If he lost control, no one was safe. She was lucky he had never gone into the blood rage with her, but with all she had learned in her training, she concluded that her untrained power had influenced him.

Enough Je'Rol! Nadia swiped a hand over her face as if to brush aside the thoughts. When she saw him leap onto the roof, as beautiful and graceful as that day long ago when he'd jumped down from the trees to protect her from a swarm of natters, the confusion of her emotions had tangled inside her. She hated him for what he'd done, yet without him she would be dead.

Without her he might be too—the demons had taken their toll on him in the end. She'd nursed him back to health in secret, lying to her family and the village about where she went a couple times a day and stealing food from her mother's pantry for him.

Now, she might have the chance to do what she should have done then—end his life. The miserable, bloodthirsty half-blood who'd preyed on her emotions until she couldn't imagine her life without him then left without even a farewell would suffer in kind for using her.

Je'Rol was secure with the demonlords now. She didn't have to keep a constant vigil or rely on others who might have failed while she slept. Je'Kaoron's vigilance had helped, but Je'Rol was her responsibility. She had succeeded in carrying out the High Lord's wishes, a bonus in her reputation.

Executing an infant before it could turn into another Je'Rol would be child's play by comparison.

She descended outdoor stairways, ignoring the view of the mountains around them and the thunder of the nearby waterfall, and passed through corridors. All the while, the demonlords who crossed her path paid her no attention, going about their business with the same grace and calm as usual. They had nothing to fear.

They should. One day, her kind would rebel against the overlords of the world.

That day was generations away, however. For now, she hoped the woman would be soothed knowing her child wouldn't suffer with losing the human half in time. Eventually all half-bloods lost it, transforming into a beast neither full demonlord nor human. Je'Rol was one of the oldest she'd ever heard of, but that would soon end.

A tiny part of her heart gave a whimper and retreated back into a dark corner of her soul as she determined to rid the world of another potential danger.

She reached an area of sleeping rooms dotting the corridor with their single doors. Outside two of the dozen doors alternating along each side of the corridor were the orange tigers Je'Rekun preferred for guards. Both turned to her but did nothing more than blink unconcernedly.

At her approach, the farthest tiger blurred and transformed into an armored guard, and opened the door. "Here, Huntress."

She marched past him through the door. Inside the room, a woman turned from gazing out the window, her swollen belly swinging around with the rest of her body.

The beauty of the young woman—barely sixteen—was marred by the worry upon her face. "Huntress!" With a hand on her belly, she made an attempt to kneel—the general human population regarded all Adepts with nearly the same reverence as their demonlord masters.

A sickening feeling burned in Nadia's stomach, but she cooled it with the rationalization that this had to be done. The girl would go on with her life and eventually find a human man worthy of her, if any would take her as a wife after this. Morana was exceptionally beautiful, though, which is what had probably attracted the attention of the demonlord father in the first place. She might stand a better chance for a future than most girls of finding a human man to care for her.

"Don't." Nadia grabbed her arm and helped her stand. Morana kept her head bowed, her loose black hair hanging around her delicate face, but the tear running down her cheek and the sudden sniffle revealed the truth she tried to hide. "It's for the best."

Morana rubbed her belly and nodded. "They keep saying that, but he came while you were gone. He apologized for this. He said…He said he loves me."

Acid coursed through Nadia's heart, and she brushed the girl's hair behind her shoulders in a gesture meant as much to calm herself as it was to soothe the girl. "What do they know of love?"

"But he cares." Morana's eyes pleaded with her to believe.

"He only cares about himself, Morana. He should never have ruined your life by putting you through this. Don't listen to his lies. Listen to me, to the women attending you. Tell me his name and you'll feel better." How she wished her powers worked on humans! But some reasoning and appealing to the girl's emotions would do the same, and a lie wouldn't hurt, although for all Nadia knew, it was the truth. "He's using you for his pleasure and now he doesn't want to pay the price for ruining your chances at a normal life. This demonlord is already moved on to the next girl. I can bet my life on it. They all do, Morana. It's not about you, but about what they can get from you. It's not right for him to use you. Tell me his name so we can stop him from hurting anyone else."

The girl sniffed, and Nadia pulled her close, stroking her hair to soothe away the trembling of her tears. "I know it hurts, but you know it's the right thing to do. I'm here for you. We all are. You'll come out of this stronger and more resilient, go on to live a long life with a man who really loves you and won't abandon you. Didn't you say a young man in your village had brought you cakes, even though he'd seen you with the demonlord?"

"Kallen. Yes." She wiped her eyes, a hint of a smile emerging. "But I didn't listen. I should have listened."

The girl erupted in choking sobs.

"Ssh. I'd bet a fortune Kallen will be waiting for you after this."

Morana wrapped her arms around Nadia and cried into her shoulder. This was the hardest part—convincing the girls to move on with their lives after being seduced by the sweet talk of a demonlord determined to satisfy his carnal needs. The female demonlords were often aloof and cold, turning the males away to find easier targets for their lusts—young, innocent human girls too naïve to see through the flattery of demonlord beauty.

"Tell me who the father is, Morana."

The girl shook her head, rubbing her eyes in Nadia's shoulder. "I can't. They'll kill him."

Damn! She'd hoped the girl had changed, but the visit by the demonlord lover while Nadia was gone had set back her progress. Morana had been closer then to convincing than now. He must have been a royal to get past the guards.

"I'm sorry. I didn't mean to upset you." The belly pressed into her as the girl continued her sobbing, and a well-aimed poke of the child nudged Nadia.

After a few minutes, the sniffling lessened, and Nadia pulled away from the girl "I'm here for you, to help you through this."

With her eyes downcast, Morana nodded and wiped them dry. "Thank you, Huntress."

Nadia brushed hair aside from the girl's face. "Let me know if you need anything."

"I will." The girl forced a smile, her eyes red from crying.

"Good. I came here as soon as I returned, but I have to finish a few things and can't stay. I'll see you later?"

"Yes."

A redundant question, since Morana was no better than a prisoner in the room until the child was born, but it was more a permission for Nadia to return, a means of giving the girl a choice and the power that came with it.

Nadia leaned forward and kissed the girl's forehead. "You're in good hands, Morana. Soon, it'll all be over and you can go on with your life."

The girl's lip quivered but she nodded and stroked the bulge of her belly.

Nadia turned away and hurried out the door, escaping the stranglehold of emotions in that room. The worst was soon to come, but she couldn't tell the girl. She'd done that a couple times fresh out of training and discovered the girls trying to flee, even as the contractions gripped them. With practice she had learned the fine art of winning their trust, and most did move on to better lives. A few died in child birth, most often those bearing half-bloods by a few particular demonlord clans.

This child would come soon. Once that was finished, Nadia would move on to the next hunt.

In the meantime, she wanted to know what payment Je'Rekun had left in her chambers.

Through the grand halls and up a stairway winding around the side of a cliff corner, she returned to the chamber she had left twelve days ago. The double doors opened silently to a room bearing a long bed—a full-sized soft bed she couldn't wait to sleep on that night—and a tall dressing closet with a stand next to the bed. A fresh, gentle breeze blew in through the open doors to the balcony.

Nothing looked out of the ordinary, except the fresh linens on the bed.

Wait. A box. Small, but it was new.

Nadia hurried to the bed, where the box sat on the blue and black covering. Was it the reward High Lord Je'Rekun had left? It barely covered her hand.

She opened the lid and folded back a black cloth. A gold medallion radiated the power of the Je'Gri Clan in a trio of tigers chasing each other's tails with obsidian stripes on different shades of jade; not only did it demonstrate the prowess of the clan's natural form but also emitted an aura of magic. This had been made by the hands of the demonlords themselves.

Upon her touch, power sizzled through her hands to her arms, numbing her into releasing the medallion. Feeling returned within seconds, but the damage had been done—she couldn't bear such a gift. This had belonged to a demonlord, and only one of their kind could bear it. Their power was too strong for her.

Or was that the statement Je'Rekun hoped to make—that the demonlords would always overpower humans? Had he known the effect it would have on even an Adept of Te'Mea? Did he suspect *her* duplicity, or was he aware of the work of all Adepts to find a way to overpower the demonlords one day?

Or did he expect she would simply accept it in awe of his generosity of such a lovely piece?

Maybe her power would work. She hadn't exerted her will on the demon magic.

"You are powerless," she whispered but hesitated to touch it. *Confidence. Overpower it, as any demon.*

But it was demon*lord* magic. They were the most powerful beings on Derandria.

But that hadn't always been the case, if the teachings of the secret books of Kirian were true. Hidden in an underground cavern beneath the Temple *Katuna Te'Mea*, where she had first trained as an Adept to subdue demons, the books were sealed in a vault accessible only by a sorcerer. The demonlords would destroy all Adepts if they knew of such writings, instead of using them to clean up their messes, like Morana's child.

Confidence. It will yield. Just as Je'Rol had yielded. She was one of the strongest, if her teachers were right.

"You are mine." Focused on the amulet as if it was a demon with a will of its own, she reached for the prize.

Her palm tingled, but the power didn't hurt her.

Nadia held it up in the light with a triumphant smile. The Adepts were gaining ground on the demonlords.

A knock on the door startled her. Pain ripped through her arm, making her drop the amulet and grab the numb arm.

"Who is it?" She called the words through clenched teeth as the numbness faded. Demonlord magic. She'd have to stay focused without the slightest distraction to handle the amulet. No one could safely hold it but one of their own kind. She'd have to return it. Damn him! High Lord Je'Rekun must have known she couldn't keep it. What was he trying to prove with this?

"Lord Je'Kaoron, my lady."

Her heart stopped. The demonlord who had brought Je'Rol to them, and he had called her by a formal title of nobility, not her given title. He had spoken little to her over the return journey. What did he want to say now?

The numbness faded enough for her to move her fingers again. She couldn't keep the demonlord waiting, nor could she let him see the amulet.

"A moment please!" She had to get it back in the box as if nothing had happened, or carry it as if it didn't affect her. Neither option promised much hope of convincing the demonlord of her abilities to control their magic.

She couldn't keep him waiting long either.

Nadia adjusted the black cloth in the box and took a deep breath. Focusing on shaping the power of the amulet to her will, she reached for it. Her hand tingled, but she dropped the amulet into the box before losing control of its power and covered it again. There. The High Lord wouldn't know she had even tried to touch it.

Now for the demonlord at her door. She hurried to the double doors and pulled the left open. "My lord." She bowed her head to the tall man in the white and black robes. "To what do I owe this honor?"

Bemusement touched the lips on that beautiful face. "Your ear and your time." He spoke in a voice of quiet strength, nothing like the energetic moments he'd taken off hunting in his true form along the journey. She could picture him seducing young women with that gentle expression.

"May I come in?"

Nadia blinked. Lord Je'Kaoron assumed nothing but granted her courtesy? That was unusual for his kind. "Yes. Of course." She stepped aside for him to enter and closed the door behind him.

"You've done well for yourself, Huntress." He studied the room, continuing towards the bed.

"Thank you." He must have seen the box. Did he know? Had the High Lord sent him to test her? What did they want from her? What was the right choice? She forced the quiver of doubts from her voice. "What can I do for you, my lord?"

He sat down on the bed and picked up the box. "Je'Rol recognized you."

So that was it, or was this part of an elaborate game?

She wouldn't play. "How is he in his last home?"

Je'Kaoron opened the box and parted the black cloth. "I haven't seen him since High Lord Je'Rekun sent him away."

The calm tone carried a note of admonishment, along with the warning glance from those blue eyes. She had overstepped her boundaries questioning the demonlord in such a critical tone, and was lucky he let her live.

He held up the amulet in one hand and traced the design with his fingers. "Quite the prize. High Lord Je'Rekun must be very pleased with your success of Je'Rol's capture." With it still in his hands, he approached her. "You're a very skilled demon hunter, my lady."

"Thank you." She swallowed, aware of the demonlord standing inches from her with the amulet in his hands. If he handed it to her, she'd have to be ready. "But it was you who captured him and sent the message of your arrival so I could be there on time to catch him before he fled."

"Your flattery is appreciated, but it was not I who brought him down and subdued him the entire journey. You must be exhausted."

"I couldn't have done it without your help. Knowing you were on guard allowed me to sleep."

The bemusement lifted into a genuine smile. "I'm glad to be of service to my clan and this world." His eyes returned to the amulet for a few seconds.

Uneasy seconds in which she feared he would hand it to her. "Was there something you wanted?" Besides flattering her and possibly testing her powers.

"How is it a demon hunter and a half-blood have met before but the two both live?"

Her blood ran cold at the implications loaded within the question. He made it sound like she had failed and turned this into a personal vendetta. "I was young when he saved me from a swarm of natters, and I nursed him back to health in return. I didn't know he was a half-blood."

"Ah!" Je'Kaoron returned to the bed with the amulet and picked up the box. "Without Je'Rol, you would not be here to serve us. An ironic turn of events." After placing the amulet inside the box and closing it, he stopped before her and offered it.

"A rich reward from the High Lord. He thinks highly of your work."

She took the box, but he held firmly for a second, the soft visage hardening slightly.

"It would be a shame if his expectations were not met after such a gift." He released the box with a coy smile. "What a waste for the most lovely demon hunter to be marred for the rest of her life, however short that may be."

A shiver raced down her spine, but the demonlord couldn't scare her away with his threats. Nadia stood unmoved before him. She had faced far worse than a single soft-spoken demonlord.

"Good day, my lady." Je'Kaoron bowed his head and walked to the door.

That was it? Not even a test?

He didn't have to test her, though. He must have known she would have trouble handling the amulet. Why had he visited?

At the door, he stopped and looked back over his shoulder. "Consider where your loyalties lie. The wrong choice could cost you what you most desire." He stepped out, closing the door behind him.

What she most desired? She desired to see all demonlords gone from the world, along with the rest of the demons.

Lord Je'Kaoron wasn't what she expected. What had he hoped to gain from her?

She looked down at the box, and his words—a warning?—sharpened in her mind. She'd show them what she could do. Not even High Lord Je'Rekun would scare her.

13

_____

Je'Rol's arms ached so he could barely sit up on hands and knees. A lone tiger at the entrance of the circular chamber watched him, but the guards had chained his wrists and ankles in the center. Although not marked like the shackles in the Kairashun prison, the demonlord-made shackles pained him into weakness made worse by his stomach aching without adequate food.

Only a day had passed in that dreadful place, the sun setting and rising once since his arrival. He planned his escape but at the same time was too weak to stand, much less to fight. In the silent prison, thoughts of Nadia distracted him from those plans. He couldn't figure out why she hated him, and she refused to tell him.

As much as he tried to ignore her betrayal, it stung all the same. Those who trained her must have cleansed any of the innocent child she had been and hardened her into the demon hunter she had become. Training with the Li'Ador wouldn't have helped. From his understanding, they discouraged women from martial training, pushing them towards sorcery or teaching instead, where they could still raise children. He could only imagine how rough they had been on the girl he had known.

Women were to be protected and honored. The men fought to defend their homes, while women tended the children and the fields. Not even the demonlords dared to kill the women; but why should they? The men were the real threat, and women bore the children to continue the human species, the most tantalizing food source for demons. Women were only targeted if they were weak or too old to waste resources feeding.

Yet that didn't stop the demonlords from having their fun.

A soft growl reverberated in his throat in the quiet chamber, and the guard's yellow eyes met his with a lift to his lips in a hint of a snarl.

The clap of boots on stone tiles echoed from beyond the door. A figure stepped into the sunlight illuminating the room from the three small windows high above. The sharp lines of her face accented in shadows of harshness with her dark hair pulled back into a tight braid gave her a hard look. A familiar scent carried on the air stirred by her movements, touching gentler moments from the past.

The cold line of Nadia's lips lifted into a smile as she stepped aside to make room for one of the royal Je'Gri.

"As I assured you, Huntress, he cannot escape."

She bowed her head to the demonlord. "Thank you, but High Lord Je'Rekun has left his care in my hands; and I will ensure the half-blood's captivity for whatever purposes he wishes."

The demonlord's blue eyes caught Je'Rol for a moment before he departed.

Nadia's eyes burned through Je'Rol as she walked along the perimeter outside the attachment of the chains, where he couldn't reach with all four limbs secure.

Without his cloak, he could only curl up with his head tucked within his arms to pretend she didn't exist. The clap of each step irritated him, though, her pace slow and methodical, as if she knew it drove him mad; but he wouldn't give her the satisfaction of seeing his irritation.

"Je'Rol the fugitive, the half-blood son of Je'Dron." She paused behind him. "You lied to me. You let me believe you were a full demonlord."

"And you were more than anxious to take me to your bed."

"You used me and left me for the demon hunters!"

Was this the argument she had sought all this time, the one she had wanted him to figure out himself?

"I left to protect you."

"Protect me." Her voice wavered slightly but she scoffed in derision as if to hide the emotions. "Is that what you call leaving a young girl in love without any explanation?"

"Yes."

"Do you know what the demon hunters do when they suspect a young girl of an affair with a demonlord?"

No, but he could take a fair guess.

"I was watched for several cycles for signs of child bearing and not even my bleeding would satisfy them. I had no freedom; they feared I would run away. No matter how many times I told them we never got that far, that you ran off before you undressed, they refused to believe me. I was trapped and alone. My family disowned me."

Despite not wanting to care, her words pricked the heart of the young man he used to be. "I'm sorry."

"It's too late for that, Je'Rol." Her words stung like the lash of a whip.

Anger touched the beast inside him, as the impending loss of control of his emotions had that night so long ago, this time touched by anger at her refusal to understand. A growl rose from his throat. "I left to protect you."

"Yes, you say that now."

Claws extended for defense but retreated at the tingle of power from the cuffs on his wrists. "You don't understand." No one did. He'd buried the memories deep inside, and with the peace he'd found in her presence, he thought he had escaped the grief of that first time, the first love haunting his nightmares recently with the rest of his fears and regrets.

"Oh, I don't understand that you were using me, or tried to? That you fled so you could escape the demon hunters?"

"No!" His growl echoed through the chamber, forcing out the lump of the painful memories of sexual desire and mutilation. "I left so you wouldn't end up dead!"

Nadia said nothing, leaving the silence to stifle him in the choking hold of the past.

"I would have lost control…I would have killed you. I couldn't let that happen, so I ran when I felt the beast rising to escape. I can't control the demon side…in any passionate emotion."

Memories glared at him in accusation. Temari had died because of him. They were young but the emotions had run deep. He remembered losing himself in her kiss and sinking deep into her body with the intention of satisfying the urgency of their attraction; but there it ended. The next memory he woke up next to her naked body mutilated to the bones and almost unrecognizable. His stomach wretched, heaving out masses of red. The implications sickened him until he had nothing more and stumbled weakly away to the river. He couldn't wash the stench of her blood from his naked body. It stayed with him for days, months, even years, haunting him as he stayed a step ahead of the demon hunters.

It was within that time that he'd met Nadia. He'd never seen the natters swarm on anyone like they did on her, but he couldn't let them kill her. Knowing now that she was an Adept, he'd guess they knew something about her, as he had felt a peace in her presence. He almost never had to think about the beast rising up when he was with her, except when the other boys flirted with her. He had watched from a distance after healing from the wounds of the attack, inexplicably drawn to her as more than someone who had nursed him back to health. He'd known there was something special, just as the natters must have known, and he had wanted to be near her; but he couldn't see her in the open and watched from afar, where the other villagers didn't notice him. She always returned to him, but he was cautious with thoughts of Temari's fate and recognizing the beast inside him. Feeling Nadia close to him eased the troubles of the beast, and her body within his arms chased away the loneliness. He had loved her.

But when the time came that he thought he could consummate their feelings, the beast returned.

He could never let himself love another like that again.

"I've heard half-bloods lose control in times of intense emotions, but how was I to know then? You left me in tears, Je'Rol."

"I'm sorry." He'd never wanted to hurt her, but leaving was the only way to protect her.

"Sorry isn't good enough." The voice wavered again with her struggle to restrain the emotions. She wanted this argument. She wanted the truth to be simple, so she could hate him; that's why she was there. He saw it clearly now.

"Then do your job. Kill me. It'll make your life easier." And his.

"You're not mine to kill…yet. High Lord Je'Rekun has plans for you."

He'd ask what plans, but the demonlord probably hadn't explained that much to her. Her job was to keep him alive, but tamed for whatever purpose the High Lord of the Je'Gri clan wanted with him. The demonlords didn't have to explain their ways to anyone, and certainly not to a human.

"Why are you here?" he grumbled.

"I had to know. After all this time, all these years when you never came back to me, I realized the truth." She swallowed, normally unheard but loud in the echoing silence of the chamber. "You never cared. You ruined my life, Je'Rol. I will never have peace until I see you dead!"

The beast growled in defiance, but he said nothing. She wouldn't listen. She never had. She had begged him to stay, even when he insisted and knew he should leave; but he had stayed by her. He had loved her enough to spare her, though, when it mattered most, and she betrayed him to the tiger clan.

Maybe death would be his only escape from the beast inside him and the painful memories of its conquests.

"Leave me."

Nadia huffed out a breath and stomped around him to the doorway. "It will be my pleasure to watch you die in the end."

He bit his tongue on a remark and listened to the clap of her boots fade away beyond the chamber. Now he knew why she hated him, but she didn't want to hear the truth from him. He had no allies there.

He was alone. Life was better that way, what life remained to him.

* * *

Damn him! Nadia stormed through the corridors, aware of the tigers occasionally passing, and made a concerted effort to show respect to the demonlords with at least quick bows.

Her throat burned with the tangle of emotions threatening to lump together. She'd barely restrained the tears and felt foolish for letting her emotions reach that deep, especially in front of the tiger guard. The whole journey from Durmin to *Acropa Je'Gri*, she'd restrained her need to hear it from Je'Rol, not wishing for two dozen ears to overhear her personal troubles. She was a demon hunter, expected to remain unemotional while carrying out the necessary tasks of her position. She had fought hard for the respect of the Li'Ador, and they would not forgive her showing pain, much less personal involvement with a half-blood.

Once in her room, she slammed the door. The echoing thunder could have been the destruction of the dam on her tears. They flowed down her cheeks in spite of her efforts to stop them.

Je'Rol, the bastard! How dare he make excuses for leaving her and never returning! He could have come back after he regained control, at least to tell her that much, instead of leaving her to the demon hunters and the agony of wondering what she had done to make him run. For years she had blamed herself, until she realized after a few half-blood kills how much she had resembled those innocent girls. Only then did the healing begin and she found her real strength.

So why did it all crumble while questioning him?

Nadia sat on the bed and wiped her eyes. It would do no good for the demonlords to see her weak.

Through clearer vision, she caught sight of the box on the table by the bed, the amulet. After the puzzling visit by Je'Kaoron yesterday, she had almost forgotten. The amulet was dangerous, not only for her to touch, but also for her to carry. Traveling with it could bring trouble if another demonlord assumed she had stolen it. Some took a perverse pleasure in killing Adepts, if rumors were true, but never without a valid reason; although she had heard stories of a few Adepts abusing their powers for personal gain and attracting the punishment of the demonlords.

The sooner she returned it with her gratitude for the gesture to the High Lord, the better she would feel. The weight of expectation that came with the reward had burdened her mind since Je'Kaoron's visit. He was right that she should be concerned, but why warn her, if that was what he intended? What had he meant?

Ploys and politics. She didn't need that. She worked alone, for no one but herself and her species.

Through a doorway on the wall opposite the balcony, Nadia stepped into the bathing room. She washed her face at the basin on the stand, hoping to cleanse away the red around her eyes from crying. After checking herself in the mirror, she took a deep breath, resolved to forget Je'Rol, and grabbed the box bearing the amulet.

Through corridors and up outdoor staircases winding along the cliffside to the next level of the palace with its own courtyard, she passed tigers and other demonlords in human form served by their silent goblin attendants and the occasional human. By the time she reached the great hall with the throne room, any hint of her tears had vanished, leaving a steady resolve to complete her tasks with honor to her sect.

The throne room was empty. Not even a goblin lurked in the shadows.

Where would she find the High Lord after midday? In the large gardens? Unlikely. Je'Rekun didn't seem the type. Then again, one never knew. At least it would be a pleasant sight.

Nadia wandered through the corridors of the main hall, passing through arches and the grand hall with its neat rows of dark-oiled beams carved with intricate details of life on Tikeros. A few royals lingered in the grand hall, mingling and conspiring in the demonlord *Lexic* with their goblin servants under foot, but no sign of the High Lord.

She passed through a side door out to one of the lesser gardens, where she caught sight of Je'Rekun on a covered walk way. He strolled along the level to an open room which extended over the edge of the cliff as the peak of a tower. Another demonlord dressed in white and black robes joined him, one she recognized...Je'Kaoron.

What did he want? What would he report about her to the High Lord?

Under the cover of the trees and brush in the garden, she slipped closer. They spoke in the demonlord *Lexic*, a language she had studied in depth in her training as an Adept.

["They'll listen?"] Je'Rekun asked.

["He suspects nothing, my Lord. Je'Dron believes I report on your movements to benefit him."]

["Good. Take the message and do all you can to bring him alone to the Nik"Terek Gate, if he wants his precious half-blood son alive. He'll trust your word to confirm Je'Rol lives. With your help, this feud will finally end."]

They stopped on the jut of the wooden walk way hanging out over the cliff side and looked down.

["And what of those who follow him? Someone else will simply step up where he left off."] Je'Kaoron lifted his nose in the air.

Je'Rekun leaned on the rail overlooking the valley, his head tilted as if to look aside. ["Some still believe he may return to power and reinstate the changes he began before we seized control. If he dies, their ideas of change will wither and die; he is the idea. Granting life to the half-blood son was too much tolerance for most of our clan. The humans are food and labor, not equals, and certainly not mates. Some hold out for his belief that we can share this world with the humans, but that is not, nor will it ever be, the rightful order. This course will only lead to our ruin."]

Nadia caught her breath. She knew the demonlords thought that way, but to hear it from the mouth of the High Lord of the Je'Gri stopped her heart. What would happen if Je'Rekun had his way? Would they return to the old ways, when the demonlords took the weak and the old to spare resources for the healthy, or pursued the occasional strong man as sport? What about the Adepts?

["He is the leader. Without him, this rebellion will fall apart. Then our plans can be set into motion without interference."]

["Yes, my Lord."] Je'Kaoron bowed his head, and both looked out over the valley surrounded by mountains.

After some minutes of silence, Je'Kaoron laid a chain holding a decorated cylinder around his neck. ["In twenty-two days we will meet at the Nik'Terek Gate."] In a blur of magic, where the man had stood, a tiger appeared in silvery white with black stripes. Je'Kaoron jogged off into the tower and disappeared.

The High Lord waited at the rail, gazing out upon the valley below. "And how is the demon hunter this afternoon?" Blue eyes turned to her, sending chills down her spine.

They knew she was there.

"Your scent is strong, Huntress."

Nadia cursed herself for forgetting their keen senses, and stepped out from behind the tree and dropped to one knee. If the High Lord was in an unfavorable mood, that view would be her last. "Forgive me, High Lord Je'Rekun. I wished not to interrupt but needed to see you." She swallowed, each soft pat of his steps on the wood playing an ominous death knell in her heart.

"My servants are to be reprimanded for their lack of attentiveness." He continued towards her, a goblin rushing from the shadows to his side. The short, big-eared demon withered under the High Lord's glare, his ears drooping with his posture. In her travels across five continents and three seas, she'd never heard a goblin speak once, yet they never objected to nor fled from the harshest of demonlord masters.

At a motion of his hand, she rose to her feet. "What brings you, Huntress?"

The corners of the box pressed into her tight fingers as she lifted it. "I'm afraid your reward is far too much for my humble service, my Lord."

He took the box and opened it. "But you served me well and brought the fugitive to justice. That is worth far more than this." He lifted it out, the three tigers chasing each other's tails in the sunlight.

Here it came, the test he sought. While Je'Kaoron had not pushed the matter, the High Lord would; it had to be his purpose. Nadia took a deep breath and focused her will on taming the magic of the amulet as she had tamed Je'Rol.

A hint of a smile touched the demonlord's lips. To her relief, he set the amulet back into the box and closed it. "This is insufficient. What then do you seek as payment for your services?"

"Payment is as you deem, my Lord. But nothing would satisfy me more than to be the one to end the half-blood's life when you decide his use is done." And she would finally move on with her life without wondering about Je'Rol.

Moving on meant revisiting the temple and contacting the leaders of the Adepts about what other demonlords might be organizing. If for no other reason, she had to warn them that something was amiss.

"You've served me well, but are you not forgetting your primary purpose for which I called you?" One white eyebrow arched up.

She clenched her teeth to fight the grimace. Morana, but she could birth the child any day, long before he decided Je'Rol had served his purposes. And one of their own could dispense with the child, although that would soil their claws. "I have not, High Lord. But if fate should choose favorably, I would take the opportunity."

"Well said." A smile spread up his lips. "A true hunter, a path rightly chosen. I will grant your wish, *if* fate decides. We leave in twelve days for the Nik'Terek Gate. Satisfy your duty of one half-blood for the opportunity for another."

"Thank you, High Lord Je'Rekun." She bowed her head and waited for him to pass. The goblin hurried along beside the long strides of his master.

Did he suspect that she had overheard, or didn't it matter? The *Lexic* was taught in secret with every Adept swearing upon their death not to reveal their knowledge.

She would have the vengeance she had sought all these years for the pain Je'Rol had caused, the pain she had put behind her while it had driven her through the hardships of training with the Li'Ador.

The wars of the demonlords didn't concern her; she had a job to do. They would all be gone one day, when the Adepts gained control and destroyed all demons…one day.

14

While Je'Rol waited for death in his prison, weak from little food and refusing to talk when she checked on him from the shadows outside the cell, Nadia awaited the birth of the half-blood child and watched the preparations under way for the journey to the Nik'Terek Gate.

A few days before the expected departure, she stood in the lower gardens, admiring the white blossoms so thickly covering the scattered *telipa* brush that the bushes looked like pillows of snow. The garden was large, with water diverted from the falls near the high gate of *Acropa Je'Gri* forming a small waterfall into a stream meandering through the lower garden. A person could wander the garden for days without seeing it all.

Not far was a human town, the nearest to the palace. The human homes were modest, most only made of a single room, and the nearest was close to a thick wall of tree-like plants twice as tall as any man and without branches; the long, narrow leaves grew directly from the single stems. The demonlords had nothing to fear, except their privacy.

This was the garden where Je'Dron had seduced a young maiden, or perhaps more than one over the hundreds of years he had lived. Perhaps one of the reasons the demonlords found entertainment with each other so boring was their immortality, except for the frequent killing of each other in their territorial scuffles.

Like the intrigue between brothers, Je'Rekun and Je'Dron. Neither was good for the humans; one wanted to return to the old ways of eating them and the other wanted to treat them as equals, which caused more problems than it solved, if half-bloods were allowed to run loose.

There was a better answer. Eliminating all demons was the only way to allow her species to expand and rise to their real potential. One day…

Until then, humans would continue to suffer, and she would serve her purpose.

Nadia bent down to sniff the white blossoms, inhaling the sweet aroma and letting out a heavy sigh.

The Adepts of Te'Mea would find a way. She had heard hints in her training of arcane magic discovered by the sorcerers but not fully understood, something dark mentioned in the book of Kirian. While she was wary of sorcerers, Nadia could not deny the connection to them as fellow Adepts and the benefits of their spells. Some of their knowledge was said to come from the ruins of an ancient temple or palace, a dead race believed to be more powerful than demonlords, one more commonly referred to as the Master Race. If they had been eliminated, then there had to be a way to fight the demonlords too. One day the Adepts of Te'Mea would unlock those secrets. Until then, she served the call of demonlords as well as humans.

The crunch of steps on the gravel path through the garden grated on her nerves, interrupting the peace she had found to escape the frustrations around Je'Rol and the impending birth of Morana's child. It would be a race to achieve her goals.

"Huntress." No growl in the voice in the slightest.

Nadia turned to face a pair of men in traveling cloaks over their close-fitting pants and belted tunics; the tattoos around their faces marked them as sorcerers. Although a different sect, they were fellow Adepts. She acknowledged them with the greeting— curling her fingertips of one hand around those of the other at her chest, representing an intertwining of the two sects. They returned the gesture.

"It is an honor, *Serion*," she said in formality, aware of the oddity of two sorcerers traveling together. Like the demon hunters, they worked alone, their "services" spread thin on a world where their skills were needed by humans but held in suspicion by demonlords.

"The honor is ours," the man on her left said. He wore his light brown hair pulled from his face into a knot while the rest hung to his shoulders. "Marcos," the man said, pointing to himself. "And Kennan."

The right man, Kennan, was taller with tawny skin, short black hair, and a mustache. {"We come with a warning,"} he said in an ancient tongue taught only to Adepts from the book of Kirian.

She knew two sorcerers was a bad omen, but for them to use that language confirmed it. They didn't want anyone outside the sects to understand.

{"We've been sent, like others of our sect, to warn any Adepts we find."} Marcos stepped closer and swept his eyes over the garden.

She had wandered from the company of others to think, so no one was near enough to overhear now.

{"One of our kind was found dead with her client in Dev Nadir. She was a keeper of one of the five control stones. We believe the demonlords are after two more known to be in the hands of sect members."}

{"Control stones?"} She hadn't heard of any such magic talismans, but she was a demon hunter and untrained in the intricacies of magic, except for the one spell she had been taught to aid her task.

{"The stones are set in amulets bearing the sacred writings of *sect du Cantir Te'Mea*. We believe the demonlords seek the stones because they fear them, as they fear us."}

Her recent lesson with the amulet brought to mind heavy doubts. {"They don't fear us—their magic is too powerful."} Or did they? {"But I think they suspect something. I...overheard High Lord Je'Rekun talking about not accepting the changes Je'Dron wanted to instate, something about never sharing the world, that the demonlords would always rule."}

{"Interesting. We've heard such statements from others. The Counsel of Dev Nadir recently points to a new cooperation among the clans. If they're working together..."}

He didn't have to finish. Her heart sank at the prospects. If the demonlords organized against the Adepts of Te'Mea, humanity's main hope for seizing control over the demons who hunted them would fail. They had to protect that. The demonlords needed them to protect the humans at the least; the Adepts were useful, else the demonlord Te'Mea would never have trained the first of the Adepts for that purpose.

{"I understand."} She couldn't let High Lord Je'Rekun succeed in killing his brother. Perhaps Je'Dron was their best hope, or at least a temporary ally, to surviving long enough for Adepts to destroy all demons.

That meant cooperating with the demonlords, for a while; but it also meant she needed Je'Rol alive.

That thought burned like acid through her heart. Je'Rol didn't deserve to live; how ironic that she needed him to reach Je'Dron alive to prevent Je'Rekun from murdering their one chance to delay the demonlords from whatever plans they had discussed in Dev Nadir; where Je'Kaoron had been present.

Je'Kaoron knew! Is that what he hinted at in his warning? Was it a warning to help her? Why? It didn't make sense if he was a traitor to Je'Dron and loyal to Je'Rekun and his beliefs.

{"Then you know what must be done,"} Marcos said. {"Finish your duties here and travel south to the Temple *Nasal Te'Mea*. We're headed east across the land to find other Adepts to warn. We must gather and plan our defense. Warn any Adepts you encounter on the way."}

{"When my work here is done."} First the baby, then Je'Rol. How was she going to prevent Je'Rekun from killing Je'Dron? Or should she avoid the entanglement altogether? If Je'Rekun discovered any subversion, he might kill all Adepts in his territory, prematurely beginning a feud they could not win.

They needed time, and if their histories were right, Je'Dron's policies of fairness for humans would give them more time to plan a defense, or to decipher the magic of the Master Race. At the least, Je'Dron might form an alliance that would save the Adepts of

Te'Mea from ruin.

"Travel safely." Kennan clasped his fingertips at his chest.

She returned the gesture. "Stay well."

The sorcerers pulled up their hoods and followed the path to a break in the foliage fence.

Nadia shuddered in consideration of their warning about the demonlords and their recent gathering in Dev Nadir. Je'Kaoron had brought Je'Rol from there and must have been sent by Je'Rekun to attend the gathering of demonlords as his representative. Now he was gone to deliver the message to Je'Dron.

She wouldn't care, except that Je'Dron now seemed their greatest ally to preventing an early end to all Adepts. Killing Je'Rol was no longer an option, or at least not allowing Je'Rekun to kill his brother was no longer an option. She had to stay with the High Lord to stop his murderous intents; that meant Morana had to give birth in the next few days.

Or Je'Rol had to escape.

By Te'Mea, that was the last thing she wanted. It left a foul taste in her mouth. She wanted to be there to end his life, to bury the ghosts of the past still haunting her in quiet moments.

No. Je'Rol had to die, but he couldn't be used to lure Je'Dron out. If only she could stop Je'Kaoron from delivering that message.

He was long gone, wherever he went to find Je'Dron. By the sounds of the overheard conversation, the demonlords knew where the former High Lord hid. Why hadn't Je'Rekun taken his army and gone to kill his brother sooner?

Or maybe the better question was what did he fear that he hadn't gone sooner?

Nadia's pulse quickened in realization, her fingers pinching off a flower bud she had caressed. "Leverage." The word whispered on a breath.

Je'Rol was leverage against the forces commanded by Je'Dron. Je'Rekun feared his own brother and the support he must have. It had to be!

If Je'Dron was that powerful, why hadn't he returned to claim his rightful throne?

Her head throbbed with the questions and possibilities circling her thoughts. The demonlords didn't deserve such attention.

Except their tactics had repercussions on the future of the Adepts of Te'Mea.

What was the right choice? What should she do?

First things first—Morana's baby. Once the girl gave birth and the child was dead, Nadia could focus all her attention on the High Lord and his captive.

She rubbed away the tangled web of demonlord intrigue splitting her head and followed the path through the garden to return to the palace.

Through the quiet halls, past statues and real tigers, she strode with confidence to

Morana's room. The girl showed no signs of labor, although she complained about her discomfort and being anxious for the child to be out of her.

Luckily, one of the tigresses knew a few things about humans from her experiences as a midwife and cooperated with Nadia in feeding Morana a meal that always seemed to bring on labor within a day.

The next morning, Nadia got the call. None too soon—the High Lord planned to leave within two days. The human servant who brought the news to Nadia in her chambers retreated as she raced out the door past him.

She reached the room to the screams of Morana in agony. Still no child, but the labor had begun in earnest.

Three human women attended Morana, while two tigress women of the exquisite beauty common among their kind stood watching in long white robes with black markings matching the hair flowing down their backs.

"Nadia!" Morana gasped her name and Nadia rushed to her side as one of the attendants stepped away. The girl clasped her hand tightly. "Stay with me."

"I'm here. You'll be all right." She stroked sweaty hair from the girl's face and kissed her forehead. "I won't leave you. I promise."

She knew of no women demon hunters, but in situations like that wished more would join *Sect du Cantir Te'Mea*. They were uniquely suited to these situations, rather than the men, who would wait outside until presented with the child, giving no concern to the poor girls who suffered through the births.

Perhaps that was why she had seen an increase in the demand for her services as a birth attendant rather than a true demon hunter. She would prefer the latter, though. The defense of the innocent against the demons still plaguing their world was easier on her emotions. A head-on confrontation with danger was preferable to the killing of a helpless infant half-blood. *A half-blood who would become a threat to helpless humans*, she reminded herself.

Morana clutched her hand through the morning, squeezing her fingers in a white-knuckled grip through the contractions. Despite her hunger around midday, Nadia stayed with the girl, as she promised.

By then, the contractions were close, Morana's suffering apparent in her tears of pain and her pleas to make it stop. Nadia pitied the girl, but could do nothing until the child was out, or could do nothing short of killing Morana.

"Ssh! Take a breath. Good, Morana," Nadia soothed. One of the other women wiped the girl's forehead with a wet cloth. "It'll be over soon. Remember, this is his fault. He left you to suffer like this. This isn't love, Morana. This is selfishness."

Morana groaned and stiffened. "No...No..." She gasped, her face contorted in pain.

Tiger Born

"Breathe. Remember Kallen, the boy from your village. You can go back to him when this is over. You'll have your life back."

As the girl relaxed, tears flowed and she sniffed. "Make it stop," she cried into Nadia's arm. "Make it stop. Get this out of me, but make it stop."

"It'll be over soon. Giving me the name of the father would make you feel better."

Morana said nothing, but clenched her fingers on Nadia's arm and sucked in a breath.

She said nothing more before pushing down with a tigress at each leg and the human attendants taking places at each hand. Nadia stepped back as the woman at Morana's feet encouraged her with the others.

Watching the birthing always gave Nadia shivers as the baby emerged slimy and wrinkled, nothing like what she saw of older human infants.

Once the child was out, the midwife wrapped it in a blanket and cut the cord attaching it to the exhausted mother. While the baby screamed through a gurgle and found its voice, the woman handed it off to Nadia.

With her dagger already in her hands, she rushed the child from the room. Morana would never see her child, or its death, despite her protestations. She would never form a bond to a future terror of humanity.

The child's will was easy to dominate and it settled into quietude with little effort from Nadia. She lifted the dagger to the child's throat, the ancient symbols of magic on it a reminder of the spell to call forth the child's life, so it would die before feeling the slice of the blade.

That was why the demonlords called the demon hunters to clean their mistakes. She could finish the task with little mess and not a sound from the infant. It would be over quickly.

The tigresses joined her in the corridor, silent but waiting.

Nadia put the dagger to the child's throat, the spell on her tongue, the little magic she knew to simplify her purpose. The blade glowed faintly against the tender, blotched and slimy skin of the infant.

It looked up at her, its lips twitching into an almost-smile.

Je'Rol had been a child once, but spared by the will of his demonlord father. That infant should never have lived to enter her life.

She would be dead without him, though.

He wasn't a terrible person, but he was dangerous if he lost control of the demon side. The human side could never contain the power of the demon.

The child in her arms with the jagged black lines across the top of his scalp could be another Je'Rol.

A lump of emotions knotted in her throat, but she swallowed it down. This was not

Je'Rol, nor would it ever be. He should not have lived.

The tigresses waited. Now was not the time to hesitate.

Nadia whispered the words of the spell and the dagger glowed brighter against the baby's skin. It opened its dark blue eyes, unaware of the threat she posed, and, mouth open in search to suckle its first milk, it turned its head into the blade point. She had done nothing, but the trail of red across its throat had completed the spell. Blood poured from the large vein of the throat and the child ceased its movements as if fallen asleep. The glow of the dagger faded.

She covered the infant in a dry corner of the reddening blanket and handed it to one of the tigresses, her stomach twisting with the harsh reality of her job. With a quick swipe, she wiped her dagger clean on the blanket and walked away. She couldn't return to Morana.

After dozens of mercy killings, this should have meant nothing. But it didn't; this was a Je'Gri half-blood, like Je'Rol. She could have been killing him, but it sickened her to look at the dead child.

She didn't know what to believe, especially after the demonlords' conversation she had overheard and the visit by the sorcerers. She needed time alone to clear her head, but her duties called her.

One thing that would put her mind at ease was to travel with Je'Rekun to end Je'Rol's life herself. All of this would be over and she could move on once and for all knowing she would never see him again.

15

The guard never moved but, like a statue, sat frozen until the replacement took his spot. The orange tigers all looked the same to Je'Rol, but their scents changed a minute amount. He caught it on the air stirred by their movements. One took the right side of the door while the replacement took the left. They alternated each time, but only one guard sat watch. They were demonlords; they didn't need more than one to watch him.

He had lost track of the days, the power of the shackles keeping him bound to the floor in weakness. Every two or three days by his best guess, they brought him meat, enough to replenish him but keep him hungry. Water came regularly in a bowl pushed within his reach.

Until last night. The meat portion had been double, giving him the satisfaction of his strength that morning as the sun rose. They must have planned something for him, but he couldn't imagine what.

Je'Rol looked up as another orange tiger stepped in and took his place on the opposite side of the doorway as the other, who tilted his head and blinked. Whiskers twitched with a low growl. The new guard made a simple "urf" noise that seemed to satisfy the first, who walked out on four paws.

The squares of light crept up the high walls of the chamber from the sinking of the sun in the sky. Je'Rol only noticed because the guard woke him with a growl.

Through the haze of exhaustion, he caught the blur of the guard's transformation to a man in armor, his hair in a chestnut and black tail near the top of his head. He strode around behind Je'Rol and grabbed his ankle.

Instinct screamed to pull away and turn and thrash his attacker, but Je'Rol kicked out once and fell. The magic stole his strength, leaving him aching and numb.

A few seconds later, the weight lifted from his leg. He turned and noticed the guard working on the other ankle, which he quickly released, leaving only Je'Rol's wrists bound.

If he intended to release him, Je'Rol was ready to run. Already strength returned to his legs. He waited as the man came around before him.

"You'll follow me if you hope to survive." The whisper barely reached him in the silence of the chamber. Amber eyes met Je'Rol's.

"Why should I trust you?" Je'Rol growled. He thought he could trust Je'Kaoron, but the demonlord had left him to rot in that prison.

"I know the old tunnels, unless you'd rather alert every Je'Gri soldier to your escape."

Escape? Caught on the prospects, Je'Rol barely noticed the clatter of the shackles from his wrists.

"Follow me." The guard helped him to his feet, but with the shackles off, Je'Rol's strength flooded back, though not as greatly as he had expected.

Standing left him dizzy for a few seconds. How long had he been chained to the floor?

With an arm around him, the guard supported his weight. Movement brought back steadiness. Before they left the anteroom, Je'Rol found his feet and let go of the guard, who stopped him at the doorway and peered out.

From the shadows behind the guard, Je'Rol watched and listened. Why was the guard helping him? Was this another set up or was someone on his side?

"Who are you?" He whispered the question inches from the man's ear.

"Je'Sikar. Hurry." He waved Je'Rol forward and they jogged through the corridor past several doors, until they reached a dark doorway. By the shadows cast, Je'Rol made out stairs winding down into some fathomless hole. Je'Sikar started down a few steps and paused.

The dank scent wafting up from below carried a vaguely familiar blend, including the sour odor of decay and rot.

"It's the only way without being seen," Je'Sikar whispered.

The demonlord was probably right—he would know the palace better than Je'Rol—but every instinct in Je'Rol's body screamed to flee that hole. The odors might bear the dusky tinge of time, but the threat had been there.

Hesitant, but eager to escape without a fight that might end in a final blood rage, he followed behind the demonlord. What light he caught was swallowed within a spiral of the stairs, leaving only a heavy blackness and stale air and the tap of their steps disturbing the tomblike silence.

After another spiral, a flash of light erupted from the demonlord's hand—a rock of some kind glowed from a scepter. Given that Je'Sikar hadn't held anything when they descended, Je'Rol assumed he had found it along the wall.

In a short time, they reached a landing where Je'Sikar stepped off.

Glad to not continue to wherever the bottom was, Je'Rol followed his guide through an archway into a room of stone slabs decorated with pictures and symbols etched upon them partially obscured by ages of dust, and the webs of something that must have lived there at one time. Loose threads of webbing scattered sprinkles of dust into the air disturbed by their passing and hung in the glow from the scepter light.

A dozen sarcophagi spaced throughout the room bore signs of age. Passing through a wide arch into the next room was no different. They walked through a tomb.

That didn't bother Je'Rol. The dead couldn't stop him from escaping.

The husks he saw laying around could. Natters had once made the tombs of the Je'Gri their home. That explained the smell.

It also aroused the beast inside him in defense, although from the looks of the shells and bones, no natters had lived there for probably hundreds of years. He caught a low growl rumbling in his throat.

"The dead deserve our respects."

A snarl rose in defiance. The tiger clan of the past deserved no more respect than any demonlord, alive or dead; none of them deserved respect. The guard could leave him if he didn't like that.

Je'Sikar said nothing more and Je'Rol quieted.

Their steps tapped an echo through each chamber, half a dozen, each the same as the other and branching to the sides also. Hundreds of Je'Gri were buried there, and who knew how many more further down.

They continued to a rough-cut doorway blocked by a large stone.

Je'Sikar handed the scepter to him. "The catacombs are free of natters now, but the mountains still harbor many of the beasts. We may encounter them, but it will be nothing compared to facing the forces of High Lord Je'Rekun."

The possibility angered the beast, but Je'Rol restrained it. The demonlord was right that he'd fare better against natters than demonlords, and he had faced swarms of them before and survived.

"Why are you helping me?" The growl in his voice was strong with suspicion.

The demonlord said nothing but grunted and strained to move the stone. It scraped and ground as he slid it aside. "Bring the light."

Je'Rol stepped forward with the scepter. They squeezed through the opening, and Je'Sikar closed the path behind them.

After taking the scepter again, the demonlord caught his breath and pointed with the light down a pocketed tunnel, where countless feet had worn any jagged edges smooth. The air stank of excrement and death. Natters lived there recently.

With claws extended and senses alert in anticipation of an attack, Je'Rol followed the demonlord. He had no choice if he hoped to find his way out of what proved to be a winding, branching labyrinth of darkness. The occasional hiss or skittering of dozens of feet echoed to them.

"You know where you're going?" Je'Rol asked.

"I helped clean these tunnels recently."

How convenient. Je'Rol followed through the dark maze, aware of the nearby gnashing of pincers and mandibles, the crunch of teeth on bone, the scrape of a body on stone. If the demonlord meant cleaning away the various natters who called the tunnels home, he hadn't done a very good job.

"They move in quickly to breed and feed, on each other most often."

Except when they had the delicacy of warm flesh.

A skitter of feet close behind made Je'Rol whirl as a giant many-legged natter attempted to drop on him from the ceiling. He slashed out before the five puckered mouths opened their beaks and shredded it into a sticky carcass.

As they moved away, other denizens of the tunnels emerged to devour the remains.

"Hurry," Je'Sikar said.

Je'Rol didn't need to be told twice. The death occupied the natters, distracting the small demons from his escape. But something didn't sit right as they passed other natters stepping back from the light—the demonlord hadn't answered his question.

"Where are we going?"

"These tunnels lead to the passage around the mountain. From there you'll have a clear route to reach Mount Serako."

Suspicion swelled in Je'Rol's chest, extending the claws to fight. "Why would I want to go there?" he growled.

Je'Sikar stopped at the mouth to a pitted area of tunnel almost opened completely with natural columns wider at the top and bottom around the holes forming a chamber. The light cast shadows upon his calm face. "You must stop Je'Dron."

At the mention of that name, the beast snarled for release. Je'Rol restrained it with the satisfaction of lifting the demonlord by his armor and pinning him to the wall.

Je'Sikar made no attempt to fight him, which would have satisfied the beast growling for escape.

Rather, the demonlord remained calm. "Je'Rekun plans to kill Je'Dron at the Nik'Terek Gate. He sent a message demanding a meeting, with you as the incentive for Je'Dron to show himself."

The sounds of natters surrounded them. Although he wanted to demand answers from the demonlord, Je'Rol couldn't ignore the threat closing in, and he was no match, something Je'Sikar knew.

Je'Rol whirled as a spike shot past his shoulder. After too much time spent chained in the palace and the frustrations of being used for other's purposes, he attacked the swarm in a release of pent-up rage while barely restraining the demon side. Je'Sikar fought beside him until only oozing piles of body parts littered the chamber.

As other natters converged on the remains, Je'Rol hurried away with the demonlord, breathing hard and feeling sore where one of the pests had sliced his shoulder that the Li'Ador arrow had recently cut. The fight had rejuvenated him, erasing any concerns about Nadia. If it did nothing else, killing the bastards in those tunnels made him feel better.

The politics of the demonlords were another matter. They wanted to use him for something, but he had no intention of helping them. He would not go to Mount Serako, wherever it was.

Je'Sikar hesitated at a simple intersection of tunnels curving around. "You must stop Je'Dron from meeting Je'Rekun at the gate."

"Why should I help you?"

"Because Je'Rekun plans to kill Je'Dron by forcing him into the gate. Those who pass through disappear from existence. It is death, even for a demonlord. Once he eliminates the rebels, he'll lead the clans in a purge of humanity. First the Adepts, then back to the old ways of hunting humans as the primary meat source."

"Maybe that's the way things should be." Rather than the demonlords raping human women in their camouflage forms and impregnating them with half-bloods they only sought to kill.

"Je'Dron doesn't think so."

The low rumble in Je'Rol's throat echoed in the tunnel. "Maybe he should."

"Maybe." Je'Sikar met his gaze with steady resolve. "If you wish our world destroyed."

"Why?" How could going back to the old ways destroy their world?

"Je'Rekun suspects the Adepts use of the power of the Master Race, something the demonlords have been reluctant to acknowledge until recently. He'll go after them first. If he learns to use their power, he'll use it to control all life on this world."

Je'Rol curled his lip back in a snarl. He didn't like the idea of demonlords possessing such power anymore than if the Adepts had it.

After a long pause, Je'Sikar continued through the tunnels without another word.

A hint of fresh air stirred Je'Rol's heart to follow from that awful place and the echo of movement behind them.

"The Nik'Terek Gate stands among the ruins of an ancient city in a wide valley to the north east, south of Mount Serako. If you hurry, you can intercept Je'Dron before he meets Je'Rekun at the appointed time."

Je'Sikar stopped at a stretch of tunnel dotted with what looked like giant, oozing pustules ready to pop. From the random holes, it looked like a few had. The putrid stench nauseated Je'Rol, and from the disgust on the demonlord's face, Je'Sikar didn't like it either.

"I'm not here for the demonlord's entertainment." Je'Rol nearly gagged when he saw one of the head-sized bubbles explode outward in a spray of slime triggered by a sharp point from within. The point tipped the leg of a multi-eyed natter with a bulbous body tapering to a long tail with what looked like a nasty stinger at the tip. The newly hatched demon arched its tail up, pincers clattering at the beak of its mouth as it hunched back on slimy legs.

They'd have to fight and run, before more of the stingers hatched.

Je'Sikar put a hand to his chest to stop him. "Don't get stung. That venom is lethal, even to you."

"Do we have a choice?"

The demonlord shook his head, his eyes never leaving the approaching hatchling. "Watch behind us."

Je'Rol turned away, curious what the demonlord planned, but all too aware of the clicking, sucking, and hissing growing louder from the darkness. Dozens of natters closed in on them. Apparently the bodies of their own dead didn't satisfy their appetites.

From the shadows, crawling, clattering bodies emerged, dark eyes reflecting the light held by the demonlord.

The first attack came from the right, a slimy tentacle that slithered towards his foot. Je'Rol lifted his foot and stamped it down to squish the appendage into a pulpy mess under his boots, eliciting a squeal from the shadows. The tentacle receded, trailing a dark liquid. Something scurried past Je'Rol's leg, following the injured appendage.

A shift of air behind him and a growl followed by a high-pitched squeal that cut off caught his attention for a moment.

"Let's go. Quickly." Je'Sikar and the light he carried raced away.

Je'Rol followed, careful to avoid the tunnel walls and ceiling until they cleared the worst.

Fresh, cool air blew away the putrification behind them, which erupted as natters fought the hatchlings emerging from their cocoons or egg sacks or whatever those were. Let them feed off each other.

"It was worse before, but they'll go after anything injured." The demonlord turned from the battle behind them. "We're almost out."

Je'Rol followed the guard, glad to be away from the natters but having a difficult time imagining it worse than that. He'd seen worse, but only because the keepers at the Kairashun had kept the natters starved while sorcerers must have kept them under control. The lesser demons had no real intelligence and were mortal, but could be controlled by Adepts.

The air freshened the further they traveled, and the natters they encountered from that point were the few common demons sometimes seen in light. Despite the weariness of the travel and the fighting past the natters, Je'Rol picked up speed.

Around a corner, a glimmer of light emerged ahead. They were almost out of those natter-infested tunnels.

Relief sprang up inside him, spurring the urge to run for freedom.

"Wait." Je'Sikar's arm snapped out to stop Je'Rol. "I'm not the only one who knows about these tunnels."

The demonlord didn't have to explain further. The realization that freedom taunted him with its nearness while threatening captivity once more tainted the sweetness Je'Rol had tasted for that fleeting moment.

"What if they're waiting?"

"I don't know." Je'Sikar dropped his hand, a thoughtful expression on his face. "It wasn't important if we made it through quickly. The others may not know yet that you're missing, but I'm not sure how much time has passed."

Je'Rol growled. Claws extended with the snarling rage of the beast to escape and fight anyone who tried to take him captive again. He wasn't going back. They'd have to kill him before he would submit.

After some time, Je'Sikar started towards the light without a word.

Je'Rol followed closely, his senses alert to the natters following in the shadows behind them.

"If someone is waiting, I'll do what I can do distract them. Don't hesitate but run, escape. Find Je'Dron and warn him."

Je'Rol said nothing. Once he was free, he'd continue his search for the obelisk, not for his father, but he didn't dare to say it to the demonlord who'd risked his life to help him escape.

As they approached daylight, they slowed their progress, pausing frequently to listen and smell. Je'Rol caught nothing to indicate anyone waited outside the low opening nearly closed around by grasses.

They stepped out in time to catch the sun dipping among the mountains. A slant of hill stretched down to a valley curving around the mountain from which they emerged.

"Head north, around the mountain. The odor of natters hides your scent, but the guards will be out soon to search. Stay hidden and you should be safe from tigers."

As Je'Rol stepped past, the demonlord caught his shoulder, those amber eyes chill with caution. "Even if you don't take my word, going south will mean your death. Je'Seni is unmerciful as her father's right hand, and she has no reason to let you live."

"I'll keep it in mind." Je'Rol pulled away, determined more than ever to escape the threats surrounding him. The obelisk would be his, and then *he* could control the demonlords and stop them from harming any humans in any way. And he could control himself and save his life from the slow inching towards the oblivion of the final blood rage.

He set off on the narrow path along the cliffside and found a way down into the green valley, where he followed the river's course.

Night fell quickly, leaving him in the open with steep peaks surrounding him. Je'Sikar's warning stuck in his mind, but it was a given that the Je'Gri would be out searching for him once they discovered him missing. Je'Rol hid in a crevice where no natters called home and laid his head back to sleep.

The night brought a coolness that woke him to the moonlight illuminating movement across the river.

From his hiding place, Je'Rol made out the black stripes of a tiger on the dark shape, one of the guards. The tiger walked with his head to the ground in the pale light, stopping at the river to drink before lifting its head, ears pricked forward.

The tiger's tail twitched and it moved off along the river.

Je'Rol watched until it disappeared from his vision. After it was gone, he closed his eyes and tried to sleep again. He'd need his rest. Tomorrow would be his greatest challenge.

He should never have come to Tikeros.

16

Nadia opened her eyes to the shadows of her bedroom in the palace. Dawn approached, but not for some time. It was too early to wake. Yesterday had been a long day of counseling Morana about her baby. The tears had flowed nonstop from the girl, and nothing Nadia did seemed to help. Nadia wanted to forget it happened—the birth, killing the half-blood, and her hesitation.

She adjusted her pillow under her head and closed her eyes.

The pounding on her door made her wince. That explained the early wake-up.

She groaned and threw off the covers. Whoever woke her up before dawn was going to receive the short end of her temper without mercy.

Across the cold floor in bare feet she hurried to the door, her gown swishing around her legs. Whoever disturbed her better have a good reason for it.

She pulled open the door as a yawn fought its way out. "Yes?"

A white and black armored tigress in human form stood at the door.

Nadia's heart thumped against her chest as her thoughts caught up to drop her to one knee in deference. "My lady."

"Dress quickly, Huntress. High Lord Je'Rekun demands your presence."

The High Lord? At that time? It couldn't be good. A shudder passed through her at the possibilities, but it would mean definite death if she failed to obey the summons.

"Right away, my lady." Nadia rose and closed the door. Damn! This could not be good at all. High Lord Je'Rekun had never interrupted her sleep for any reason. Had she upset him? What could she have done? Did he know about her and Je'Rol?

A brick dropped into her stomach. The guard could have told the High Lord of her conversation with Je'Rol. She'd given away that part of her past. No sense avoiding him; that would be like admitting she was wrong. No, she had to play along and pretend everything was as it should be; after all, he might not know.

Nadia rushed to change clothes and ran a quick brush through her hair. Only after tying it back in a tail did she open the door to the tigress waiting, a second tie strap in her hands and her bracers hooked on her belt.

The tigress led her through the dark corridors while Nadia braided her hair. They climbed stairs while she strapped on her bracers with the demon heads. She finished securing the second one as they entered the holding area.

Je'Rol! She hurried into the chamber, where it wasn't Je'Rol chained to the floor but an orange tiger.

High Lord Je'Rekun looked up from the panting tiger, his face shadowed by the light of the scepter held by the guard. "Huntress. You finally arrived."

She winced from the sting of his voice, but the proper response flowed from her tongue as she dropped to one knee. "It would be disrespectful to stand in your presence without proper attire, High Lord Je'Rekun."

The demonlord was quiet for a couple seconds. "Rise, Huntress. I have a task for you…two actually."

She did as commanded, her eyes on the chained tiger and relief washing through her that the High Lord had seemed to accept her explanation.

Je'Rekun stepped around the perimeter of the tiger's reach, which wouldn't be far with each leg chained separately.

Now she knew why they had chained Je'Rol as they had—the shackles were positioned to hold tigers, not humans. Interesting, but not surprising, that he would imprison his own kind.

"This was the last guard to see Je'Rol alive."

"The last guard…to see him alive?" He might as well have kicked her in the gut.

"Yes, before he escaped." Je'Rekun kicked the tiger in the ribs, knocking him over. The clink of chains echoed in the chamber.

Then Je'Rol wasn't dead; but he was gone. He lived to spoil Je'Rekun's plans to kill his brother and end the rebellion. She might have been glad to have the decision taken out of her hands, if not for the fact that the message had already been sent to arrange the meeting. And she didn't get to personally end the years of misery Je'Rol had caused her.

"Escaped?"

Je'Rekun motioned with his finger for her to join him. "Last evening we discovered this one and Je'Rol gone. After some searching, Je'Sikar was found and brought back for questioning. Although he claims to have pursued Je'Rol, that is clearly a lie. Escape is impossible without help."

"You wish me to search for Je'Rol?"

"Yes, but not yet." A sly smile spread up the High Lord's cheeks. "First, I have use for you. Our methods might kill one of our own before gaining information, but yours may be more effective. I would like you to make him wish we would kill him."

Her? Nadia stared at the tiger, who attempted to stand, his head low. The demonlord was right—she couldn't kill one of them with her methods. She could inflict pain and suffering on one of their kind, though.

Je'Rekun straightened, looking down his nose at the tiger. "I want to know where Je'Rol is."

"As do I." One way or the other, she was going to settle the score with Je'Rol.

But she had to wonder about Je'Rekun's true motives in asking her to torture one of his own kind. This was too convenient for him to observe what she knew about demonlords. She'd have to be careful what she revealed.

"In his form, I won't understand him," she said.

"Not to worry. One of my *trusted* guards will stand by when I must be gone." He glanced aside at the man holding the scepter of light."But I expect that won't be necessary."

In other words, he intended to observe.

Nadia swallowed her hesitation. Refusal would show insubordination, giving Je'Rekun good cause for her termination.

"And, I want to know who his accomplices are. The timing on this escape was too perfect for Je'Sikar to arrange it alone." A slight growl rumbled in this voice.

"Yes, my lord." She walked around the tiger lying on its side and breathing heavily as if exhausted. Je'Rol had fared no better in the shackles, but if she was right, they inhibited demon strength. It made her task almost too easy.

A good thing, since the sooner she obtained the information sought by the High Lord, the sooner she could leave to pursue Je'Rol and close the book on that chapter of her life.

"When do you wish me to start?"

"Immediately. Food and drink will be brought for your convenience."

"Then if you'll permit me…" Nadia pulled her dagger and approached the tiger.

Je'Sikar lifted his head, still panting but strong enough to pin his ears back and bare sharp teeth. Another guard stepped forward in human form and took a firm hold of the prisoner's neck. Nadia focused on the power within her. Although normally immune, a demonlord weakened like this might submit; she had to try.

"Tell me your name." Something in his eyes touched her, and the power of her will dispersed like dust in the wind.

Je'Rekun watched in silence. She had to try again.

"To dispirit a demon, you must want him to obey without question. It must come from your deepest desire," her teacher, Master Adept Tomashin, had instructed. Unlike other demons, though, demonlords could redirect their thoughts and focus them upon others, even using it for secret communications with their own kind, according to rumors. They were more than mere demons, something far more powerful, which was why they were the rulers of all lands.

This one was still strong enough to repel her. That would have to change.

Her stomach growled in protest to the stress before a meal. She wouldn't maintain her strength to *dispirit* any demons if she didn't eat. Rest would be helpful too, but she couldn't afford to rest, or to let Je'Sikar rest.

Je'Rekun ordered food before she could ask.

She had one other tool more powerful than her innate ability. Nadia pressed the tip of the dagger to the tiger's forehead. He struggled to escape it, but the guard held him. With all her will focused on dominating the demonlord, she whispered the spell she had used on the infant. The blade glowed, but she didn't draw blood with it yet.

"Tell me where Je'Rol went."

This time his will weakened and didn't dispel her power, but he still struggled.

That struggle bumped his head into the dagger to draw blood.

Not yet! She had never used it on a full demonlord and didn't know what would happen.

The tiger howled in pain, a pitiable sound that reached inside her and tore her heart. She jumped away to avoid his thrashing amid the efforts of the guard to subdue him.

She had one chance to use this to her advantage if he died. "Where is Je'Rol?"

The tiger snarled and blurred for a moment as if caught during transformation; but he solidified as a tiger and collapsed, his sides expanding and contracting with each deep breath. He had lived, if barely, through the spell, one of her most powerful demon killing techniques.

He growled something.

"Interesting," Je'Rekun knelt to meet the gaze of the tiger. "Now tell me the truth."

The tiger breathed heavily, but made no further sound.

Nadia focused her power on Je'Sikar. "Tell him."

The tiger shuddered and didn't deflect her power, but he made no sound.

"She'll do it again," Je'Rekun said. "Tell me the truth and the pain will end."

The tiger grunted.

Je'Rekun stood and motioned to her to proceed. "Huntress."

Nadia approached the tiger. This would be harder than she expected, but at least the spell hadn't killed him as it had dozens of half-bloods. She gripped her knife, aware of the power she held over the demonlord and those watching.

The tiger growled, his teeth bared and ears back. The guard knelt over him, hands pinning the tiger's head to the floor. Blood stained the orange and black coat.

Nadia took a breath and focused on her deepest desire—to learn where Je'Rol had gone. That focus gathered her power. The closer the demon, the stronger the *dispirit*. She put her hand on the tiger and gazed into those amber eyes. "Tell me, Je'Sikar, where

Je'Rol went."

The demonlord jerked, but the guard held him. The power didn't disperse, but the tiger made no sound.

"Tell me."

He only grunted.

The growling of her stomach broke her focus. He was close to breaking; she felt it. The killing spell had weakened him.

"Use your magic again, Huntress," the High Lord said.

"If I do it again, it may kill him. I think the first time weakened him. His resistance to *dispirit* has been affected, but he refuses to talk."

High Lord Je'Rekun's frown sent a shiver through her, but she stood her ground. His temper was lethal, but her killing of his—and her—one chance to track Je'Rol would bring a swifter death than her argument. She'd bet her life on it.

Je'Rekun stepped towards her, his height over her imposing. He knew it, by the nearness of where he stopped. "You dare question me?"

Nadia lowered her head, afraid to gaze into the fire of his glare and hoping he might show conciliation with her demonstration of respect. "No, my lord…but the magic is lethal to half-bloods. I know not how a full demonlord will react. I share your desire for Je'Rol's life, and I would not jeopardize our best chance to learn where he might have gone. I have only your best interests in my heart, High Lord Je'Rekun."

In the silence of the chamber, she quietly swallowed the lump in her throat and prayed to her ancestors that the High Lord showed leniency.

"Very well said, Huntress, but I will decide what my best interests are." He moved off, and she let out a breath she hadn't realized she was holding.

Je'Rekun approached the chained tiger and stared in silence. Nadia could only guess he used the mysterious power of theirs which deflected the *dispirit* control. "Tell me, Je'Sikar. Where is Je'Rol?"

The tiger whimpered, still breathing hard from his near death.

Je'Rekun motioned to someone—a servant had stepped into the doorway with a tray. "Your food is here, Huntress."

The human servant left the tray at her feet and backed out. While she ate, one of the guards beat the prisoner, breaking to offer him a bowl of water while promising more, like the food she ate, if he cooperated; but Je'Sikar refused. Afterwards, in their own language, Je'Rekun promised comfort to the prisoner, even stroking the orange coat with a gentle touch. He coaxed the tiger to sit up and drink.

With her stomach satisfied, Nadia stood by and watched the manipulative game played by the High Lord throughout the morning.

After some time, he stepped back to her and straightened his robes with a brush of his hand. "Use your death mark again, Huntress."

Like the High Lord, she had reached the end of her patience. Nadia pulled her dagger and approached the tiger. He struggled, the chains ringing in his futile efforts to scramble away. Je'Sikar growled, but the guard pinned him down once more. She squatted near his head and pressed the point of the dagger to his skull.

"Tell me where Je'Rol is," she commanded with the force of her will behind it.

The tiger whimpered in a soft mew.

"He doesn't have to tell me."

She looked up. What game did Je'Rekun play now?

"You sent him to warn Je'Dron of my plans. He's heading north to Mount Serako."

How did Je'Rekun know? What if he was wrong? She bit her tongue, the High Lord's warning fresh in her mind.

Mount Serako was the center of rumors of the Master Race's secret domain. The Book of Kirian mentioned it, but referenced a different name on the map. It spoke of incredible power hidden there, but no one had ever found a hint of the Master Race or any knowledge left by them.

The mountain was a powerful symbol of authority, and Je'Dron did well to use it to his advantage.

Cool blue eyes met hers with a sly smile. "It's obvious he knows. You'll have your kill, Huntress. Do it now."

She pressed the knife to the tiger's skull, the spell whispering from her lips making the blade glow with the power to take away life.

Je'Sikar whimpered and mewed softly, his eyes pleading for mercy. If High Lord Je'Rekun was right, then she would only need to follow Je'Rol and let him present himself to counter Je'Kaoron's message before she recaptured him. If Je'Dron was ready for Je'Rekun, perhaps this situation could turn around and Je'Dron could regain the throne of High Lord of the Je'Gri. Without Je'Rekun, the other demonlords might hold off on their plans to return to the old ways.

But she wanted her revenge on Je'Rol. If Je'Dron really did care about his half-blood son, he probably wouldn't allow her to kill him. Damn them all!

The tiger let out a mournful "urmf" that stayed her hand, but he dared not move. She had to finish the task. Je'Rekun observed closely. But if she killed Je'Sikar, the demonlords would learn as she would that she could kill their kind under the right circumstances. It would confirm the potential danger of the Adepts to their power.

Nadia gazed into the amber eyes of the tiger and licked her lips.

"It is in my interests. I assure you." Je'Rekun's soft voice vibrated with a purr of satisfaction.

His interests in punishing Je'Sikar's betrayal, or his interests in testing her abilities?

Although Nadia wanted to know for herself how far she could push the demonlords to death, Je'Rekun was the last of them for whom she wanted to demonstrate the abilities of the Adepts.

A whispered word changed the spell the moment before she drew blood. The tiger thrashed and howled in mournful agony. This time his body didn't blur. Instead, he flopped against the chains for a few seconds and fell still, his sides again rising and falling rapidly.

Nadia sheathed the dagger at her hip and waited.

Je'Rekun strode around the panting tiger and stopped opposite her. "Prepare to depart, Huntress. You have a half-blood to kill."

She bowed, letting out a small sigh of relief. "Yes, my lord."

Leaving the chamber lifted the weight of Je'Rekun's judgment from her mind. Now for the job for which she had been trained. Je'Rol wouldn't escape again.

17

The next few days brought several close calls for Je'Rol. Although a swim in the river to wash away the crusted guts of the natters called to him, that odor seemed to be his best chance of throwing off the searching tigers. When he hid, they passed him with hardly a sniff.

But he needed a cloak and food, or better food than what he found in the mountains. He also needed to find supplies for his journey and information about any artifacts known on Tikeros. If he hoped to find something in the tiger clan domain, he needed to know what its citizens knew. That meant listening to people, the only time he didn't mind others around him.

From a ledge high above, Je'Rol gazed over the wide valley stretched beyond a bend of the mountain across the river. Not far from there, trails of smoke climbed into the sky. Smoke meant fire, but these smoky trails came from chimneys. Those chimneys were attached to a few dozen houses and, very likely, shops and public gathering places. A boisterous tavern or the common room of an inn meant plenty of stories from locals.

It also meant food and shelter. His stomach gurgled its opinion of that. He'd been lucky to catch a swift rodent, one a hair too slow for a half-blood's agility. The little meat it provided was insufficient, and it had been tough. The roots and berries he found weren't any better.

The thought of seasoned meat along with some filling vegetables and bread made his mouth water and his insides churn. He wanted to reach that town. He had to reach that town.

But they wouldn't appreciate a stranger covered in the filth of natters. His condition would draw immediate suspicions.

He'd have to bathe in the river before setting foot in the town. Besides, the crusted guts didn't hide his hair color. The townspeople would expect demonlords to show more polish, but they would know he wasn't full demonlord by his clothes. He'd need that cloak to cover up no matter how he presented himself, especially in tiger clan territory.

And he was disgusted with wearing the natter filth already. He'd escaped other demonlords tracking him in other domains. This would be no different.

Except the other demonlords didn't need him for their political gains. High Lord Je'Rekun wanted him for his plans. That incentive made it imperative to find him rather than ignore him as those in other domains had done.

He hadn't seen the tigers since last night, and they had turned north, perhaps expecting he would seek out Je'Dron. Instead, he traveled east, deeper into Tikeros and hopefully out of the control of the Je'Gri.

A swim in the river would refresh him, and at the opening to the valley, the river slowed. Up through the highlands, it had rushed and crashed over boulders beneath the white waters, too lively to safely bathe.

Je'Rol scanned the land from his perch again before finding the steep grade he'd climbed to reach that grassy ledge. After a tricky slide down in which he nearly sent himself tumbling head over heels, he hurried to the water and pulled off his clothes.

Clothes first, then the rest of him; the clothes could dry while he rinsed off in the cold water.

The leather cleaned easily, but the shirt was another matter. The grime of his captivity and tunnel escape refused to wash out, leaving what had been a white blouse grungy with faint blotches of gray and brown. It would have to suffice. As he would have to steal a cloak for warmth on his travels, he might as well swap shirts somewhere.

Satisfied with the results, he hung the clothes over a few bushes along the river and waded into the chilling water.

The cold bath refreshed him, but also turned his body to ice. Je'Rol submersed himself only as long as necessary to scrub his hair free of the caked on remains that had hidden his scent. He'd be easier to track by the tigers, but he'd feel better running and he could enter the town without bringing too much attention to himself.

His hair flowed freely when he finished and dressed. Although the clothes were still wet, they were better than the mountain river. He shivered in the damp shirt and tacky wet leather while sitting on one of the boulders and tying his hair. The warm sun dried him and warmed him, in contrast to the chill of the breeze.

While he sat still and studied the land, something snuffled in the shadows next to the cliff.

His heart jumped from his chest, and he froze on the boulder, sniffing for the scent of whatever was there.

Through the brush and grasses, something moved. Not something, but a fat brown boar. Although small, it would more than satisfy his needs.

His stomach rumbled at the anticipation of fresh meat.

The boar grunted and rubbed its back under the brush as it passed. Insects buzzed around the groove following its spin down the middle of its back, despite the temporary disturbance.

Je'Rol waited, forcing the beast inside him to keep quiet, although the demon side of him relished the anticipated kill and feeding nearly as much as his stomach. He shifted slowly on the boulder to tuck his feet under him.

The boar grunted and paused, its snout twitching in the air.

If he wasn't careful, his next meal would escape. Je'Rol froze on the boulder and waited for the boar to step closer.

It continued its winding course towards the river, likely to drink.

Je'Rol struggled against the burning hunger of his physical need and the desire of the beast. Just a little closer…

The board hesitated about ten feet away and turned.

Je'Rol leapt from the boulder and the boar squealed and fled on its short legs. Although he could outrun the young boar, he couldn't predict its quick reverses.

After a few abrupt changes of direction, Je'Rol bent low, inches from its hindquarters. The boar ducked.

Je'Rol's claws dug deep into its side.

The boar squealed and dropped away, but Je'Rol caught a leg. The jerking of the boar to escape wasn't enough to stop him from securing the second leg on the same side and flipping the runt onto its side. He dropped a knee onto the struggling boar and with one quick stab of claws to its throat, left the boar gurgling for air amid the rush of blood from its neck.

The struggles slowed, the legs kicking with less force, until only a couple twitches finished it and the animal ceased. Finally, a satisfying meal.

Someone gasped.

With his knee on the boar, Je'Rol twisted to find the source of the voice.

A boy stood some thirty feet away, a quiver of arrows on his back and a strung bow in his hand. His tunic and trousers matched the colors of the rocky cliff and brush, unlike the shag of auburn on his head. The boy's complexion paled. "I— I'm sorry, my lord. I—I—" He dropped the weapon and fell to his knees in the grass. "I've never seen your kind hunt this way. I've never seen your kind hunt. Forgive me for interfering. I was following the boar when I saw you."

Je'Rol let out a sigh of relief. Only a boy, and one who didn't know a real demonlord from a half-blood. He posed no threat. On the contrary, he might prove useful.

A bloody pool formed around the boar, one that would attract natters come night fall. Looking at the animal now, he saw far more meat than he could eat in two sittings. The rest could be worth trading, and if the boy needed it, so did a family somewhere. That family would likely have what he needed for his journey. This situation could work to his advantage.

"What's your name?" Je'Rol spoke low, hoping to hide the growl in his voice.

The boy trembled but lifted his head. "A—Arak, my lord. I'm Arak."

"You were hunting the boar, Arak?"

"Yes," he whispered. "I'm sorry. I didn't intend to offend you, my lord. I didn't know—"

The scent of fear blew strongly from the boy.

"Where do you live?"

A tentative hand lifted with the boy's face, a lone finger stretching out to point north. "There. My father's farm outside of Labbers. He told me to hunt natters, but I saw the boar and…and we don't raise pigs."

So the boy thought he'd have better luck and a better meal if he brought down the boar; not untrue, but at least much safer than natters.

Je'Rol stood up, a smile on his lips with his face away for a few seconds. He grabbed the hind legs of the boar and turned to face the boy. "Natters could kill you."

"I know." Arak looked behind him as if afraid one of the small demons was sneaking up to attack.

"But I won't."

The boy lifted himself on hands and knees, the color returning to his cheeks. "You're not mad?"

"No. I need your help."

Arak blinked and stood with his bow. "My help? But you're a demonlord. Why do you need me?"

Je'Rol swung the boar over his shoulder so the head hung behind him to drain away rather than down his damp clothes. "I need someone to cook this thing, and I need information." Mostly, he needed information and trade; he could have eaten the meat raw without hesitation.

"Ah…All right." Arak ducked through the bow so it hung across his body, strung and ready if he needed it in a hurry, a wise move if natters attacked, although in the light of day that was unlikely. "What do you want to know?"

"While we walk." Je'Rol stretched a hand in the direction the boy had indicated his home to be.

"Right. This way." Arak led him parallel to the river, towards the town in the valley. "So…what do you want to know?"

Je'Rol plucked the end of a blade from one of the brush and chewed it. Bitter, but it would settle the desire to tear into the raw flesh of the boar immediately. "Legends, Arak. I'm young. Tell me about the Legends of Tikeros."

The boy looked him up and down, an expression of awe on that face of youthful roundness. "You're young?"

"For a demonlord," Je'Rol grumbled. He didn't have to admit being a half-blood. "Have you ever heard of the ancient races and their magic objects left behind?"

"Not much, only what Tessa tells us."

"Tessa?"

"My sister. Since mom died, she took over the house. She hears things from the ladies in town. They gossip about everything, she says. Sometimes old man Kiron visits the shops, and he likes to tell the best stories. Hey! I bet he would know of any magic objects."

Aha! An old man who told stories would have been around long enough to have heard some things, and, depending on his occupation, maybe he'd traveled a bit in his lifetime to learn those stories.

Je'Rol patted the boy's shoulder. "Thanks. What kind of stories does he tell?"

"The best!"

Je'Rol chuckled at the boy's enthusiasm and the answer. Throughout his travels and the struggle to survive on a world that didn't want him, he couldn't remember the last time he'd laughed. "Like what?"

"Like the time he said he killed a hundred natters all by himself, or…or how about the time he was young and swimming, and a big fish saved him from drowning."

"Big fish? Demonlord, I'd guess."

Arak shrugged. "That's what he said, but he isn't from Tikeros. I want to travel the world like him when I get older." He dropped his head and slapped aside the tall leaves of a tuft of grass. "Soren's older and Pa says he'll get the farm one day. I'm on my own then."

"Older brother?" That could be trouble.

"Mm."

"And a sister?"

"Yup."

"Any others?"

"No."

Good. That many was too much already.

Over the crest of the hill, Je'Rol spotted a few farms outside the town, and the valley was an open plain surrounded by mountains. Along with the clusters of two or three stone buildings surrounded by pens of animals, a few scattered orchards where the trees grew in neat rows dotted the landscape with a patchwork of fields. Livestock grazed contentedly in pastures surrounded by stone fences.

"You're the youngest?"

"Yup. It's not fair either. Soren gets everything, and Tessa acts like mom, but she's not, and I don't get anything. It's always 'Arak do this. Arak do that.'" He quieted, his face flush. "But I...ah...I'm sorry. I shouldn't say things like that to you."

"That's all right." Je'Rol couldn't help but smile. The boy had an innocent way about him that cleared out the concerns of the last cycle. He felt almost human in his presence.

The beast seemed to have found some peace too. Or maybe that's what he liked—not struggling with the beast to keep it restrained. After all the darkness in his life, the boy shone a light of what the world could be, of what *his* world could be once free of the struggle.

"I suppose you want to know about ancient magic and stuff."

"Something like that. I'm looking for an artifact."

"What's that?"

Je'Rol adjusted the boar over to his other shoulder to relieve his shoulder, and by the looks of it, most of the blood had been spilled immediately after the kill.

"It's a very old object of a civilization that's gone from this world."

"Oh." Arak walked in quietude down the slope of the hill into the immense valley. Near the bottom, he asked, "What is this artifact thing?"

"An obelisk."

"What's that?"

"It's kind of a tall pyramid, but this one isn't very big...I don't think. Near as I know, it's about your height."

Arak plucked the string of his bow. "I don't know of anything like that...but old man Kiron might know. He talks about all sorts of stuff that I don't know."

"I'd like to talk to this Kiron."

Arak's eyes lit up with the smile he turned up to Je'Rol. "I'll take you to him! It's not far from the farm..." His enthusiasm reigned in with a grimace. "But I have to ask Pa."

"I'd like that, and maybe if I asked your Pa, he'd give you the time." Although he could probably find the place by asking around town, the boy's presence had a calming effect, or maybe that enthusiasm infected him with something he needed.

"You'd do that?"

"You're a good kid, Arak."

The boy's cheeks flushed and he looked down for a few seconds. "Thanks....What's your name?"

"Je'Rol."

"Thanks, Je'Rol." Arak seemed content with that, until something caught his eye down the road along the river. "Uh, oh."

"What is it?"

"Soren. He looks mad." A young man cleared a wooden fence enclosing a pen of long-necked birds and marched towards them along the worn wagon tracks of the road. That must have been the older brother, and he did look mad.

"Arak!"

The boy flinched under the scorn of his brother's voice.

Soren intercepted them on the road, his eyes meeting Je'Rol's with a hint of fear for a second before fixing a glare on Arak. The older brother looked to be in his mid teens, about the age when Je'Rol had left home, but this young man carried himself with a maturity of someone much older. "Arak! Where were you?"

"Out hunting the natters."

"While you were playing, we had an attack on the kimas. Next time, hunt a little closer to home." Soren looked up this time and swallowed. The voice changed with the expression and a bow of respect. "My apologies, my lord. I appreciate you bringing my wayward brother home."

A second later, that expression hardened once more on the younger brother. "Go on home. Pa'll have your hide after what happened."

Defiance rose up with memories of the boys harassing Je'Rol. The beast growled low in his throat.

Soren's face paled but he didn't look up. "Go on, Arak," he said in a milder voice. "Quit being a bother to the demonlord."

"He's not a bother." Je'Rol made no attempt to hide the rumble in his voice.

"Yeah. I'm not a bother!"

Arak's outburst startled the beast into quietude. Je'Rol caught the boy's eyes and the silent plea and smiled. Yes, he'd meant what he said.

Soren's cheek twitched but he bit his tongue on whatever retort brewed there. "You're still in trouble for leaving."

"Maybe this will help." Je'Rol lowered the carcass. "Have your sister cook it and I'll forget this happened."

Soren studied the dead boar. "That's up to Pa." His eyes narrowed on his brother. "What were you doing?"

"It's a long story." Je'Rol tired of the older brother's accusations and of the lack of food in his stomach. "For later. Food comes first."

"All right…this way." Soren turned and marched ahead, putting distance between them.

"You're not like I've heard about demonlords," Arak whispered.

"Good." He wasn't demonlord, but if they knew the truth, Je'Rol wouldn't be welcomed.

18

"Tessa!" Soren's voice called through the house as they stepped into an open sitting room that blended into the dining room and kitchen as one large area with the panels pushed away. Je'Rol set the boar on the brick steps outside and followed the boys. "Tessa, where are you?"

"I'm coming!" The frustrated voice came from around a corner to a hallway, along with the fast thump of steps. A girl in a yellow dress, her light brown hair pulled back out of her round face, stepped around the corner and hesitated, her face going pale.

"We have company," Soren said.

"I see that." The girl must have been in her early teens but already a woman in figure.

"The demonlord brought dinner. Get the oven going. I'll get the boar gutted and cut."

Tessa's eyes fixed on Je'Rol and her throat flashed with a nervous swallow. "And who is our guest?"

"Je'Rol," Arak said.

"Lord Je'Rol, it's an honor to have you." She gave a slight bow, a wavering smile on her fair lips.

Soren scowled at her. "I'll be in the smokehouse." That scowl darkened on Arak. "You can run and tell Pa."

"But—"

"No 'but's, Arak. It was because of you that the natters attacked. Go and tell him what happened. He might need your help anyway. Go on."

Je'Rol caught a glance from the older brother as of someone hiding a secret.

"So-ren," Arak whined.

"Go! The sooner you go, the sooner you get back."

Arak turned, his head down. "I never get to do anything interesting," he muttered a second before the door slammed behind him.

"I'll be back soon, my lord." Soren followed Arak out the door.

"Lord Je'Rol." Tessa started towards the kitchen area. "How can we serve you?"

"I need clothes and information."

She stopped and turned to him, a curious expression on her face. "Clothes, for a demonlord?"

"Something warm."

"I'll…see what I can find." She walked to a stone hearth and opened a small bottom door to a ready stack of wood. "What else can I do to serve you?" Her hands trembled on the flint as she prepared to light the fire, the scent of fear rising from her over the house odor of smoky wood and spices.

He backed away to a low table and pulled out a cushion to sit down, as much to make himself comfortable as to ease the discomfort he saw in her. The girl must have had some unpleasant encounters with the local demonlords to show such fear of what he might ask. He could imagine what they had proposed. "I need information."

She struck the flint a couple times before the sparks caught on the kindling. "What information could you possibly need?" With steadier hands than a few seconds earlier, she closed the lower door of the oven and stood up.

"I'm looking for artifacts of the extinct races. Arak said you might have heard something."

"Did he?" She let out a huff of air and shook her head. "What else did Arak say?"

"He mentioned an old man named Kiron who might know something."

Her shoulders dropped and she smoothed a wrinkle in her dress. "Kiron might know something, yes. I'm sorry I can't help you more."

"Then food and a traveling cloak is all I ask."

She forced a smile, her expression more relaxed. "And you want that boar cooked?"

"I don't need it cooked, but *you* might prefer it."

"You're sharing your meat?" Tessa stared at him, her mouth agape in a look of disbelief.

"In exchange for your help."

She blinked and busied herself with a door off the kitchen, the color returning to her cheeks. "I didn't know demonlords could be so generous. I'm sorry I misjudged you."

Je'Rol said nothing as she disappeared into a dark hole with only a candle to guide her. The less he said, the less his chances of being turned away, or turned in to any local Li'Ador. Once he had what he needed, he'd be on his way and the family would know nothing better. He'd leave them in peace.

She climbed the steps back up, a pail in one hand and the candle—which she blew out—in the other. Her demeanor was more pleasant while she prepared the vegetables she had brought up from the cool cellar.

Soren later returned with what was left of the boar, its hooves and head gone with its skin, leaving the best of the carcass, which he brought in a metal tub already cut into pieces for Tessa. He gave his sister a questioning look, and she answered with a glance at Je'Rol and a slight shake of her head. The hard lines of Soren's mouth relaxed, and he retreated to the open floor with a knife and a block of wood.

Tessa shoved the smaller pieces through the top door of the hearth onto a metal rack over the fire.

While he waited, Je'Rol took the bread she offered and satisfied the rumbling in his gut. The scent of roasted pork made his mouth water for more food, but he'd have to wait if he expected cooked meat. The girl busied herself with cooking, letting the clatter of pots and the sizzle of the meat fill in the silence while her brother whittled on his block of wood. Neither seemed inclined to speak much and Je'Rol had nothing to say.

The father arrived after some time with Arak, who bore the marks of sweat under his arms with the dirt and grime on his clothes and face. The odor barely broke through the scent of roasted boar. At a basin near the front door, both washed their hands and faces.

The old man wiped his hands on a cloth laid on the same table. "Lord Je'Rol." The man's graying dark hair stuck out at odd angles from beneath a hat, his pants tattered at the bottom. Unlike his children, the father offered no show of respect, and the wrinkles around his squinting eyes deepened. "This is an honor. Arak says you offered to share the boar you caught. My son is inclined to exaggerate."

"I offered the boar as compensation for trade."

The old man's eyes flicked in suspicion to Tessa, who shrugged. "Trade?"

"A cloak for warmth and information for my search. No more." The father suspected his motives by the suspicious tone in his voice, and Je'Rol understood. Tessa was a lovely girl, but he had no intentions of bedding her.

The old man took a seat at the table opposite him and stroked the beard on his chin, the boys taking places on either side of him in silence. "No more?"

"No. I'll be on my way."

"That's it? Just a cloak and information…You're not like the tigers we see around here."

"No. I'm not," Je'Rol growled in irritation. The man had a suspicious mind and wasn't afraid to make that clear.

"Pa…" Tessa's voice trailed off in warning.

"Get back to work." The line of his mouth hardened with his stare at Je'Rol. "The sooner this man eats, the sooner he leaves this house."

No one said anything, but the atmosphere of the room transformed with the old man's sudden aggression.

"You say you only want a cloak and information, but there's more to it. Ain't there?" The old man stepped closer, the lines of his face deepening. "No demonlord ever gives fair trade, and I'm tired of your kind coming in here and demanding all you want. If that makes me a traitor, so be it. Kill me if you want; I've lived my life. You can tell your High Lord that I'll give no more animals for his dinner, and no man is taking my Tessa unless I give my permission. Do you understand? No one!" His eyes widened and his fists tightened.

"Yes." Je'Rol wished he had a cloak now to hide his face. The old man had a right to his misery, but Je'Rol wanted nothing to do with it. That glare burned through him, hitting a nerve that made him restless to leave. Maybe he should go, forget the boar and return to his journey alone.

He hurried from the house and pulled the door behind him to close it, but it caught.

"Lord Je'Rol?" Arak's eyes pleaded with him from around the door. "Are you leaving?"

He should. He really should, being unwelcome in that cold house, but he would be giving up a meal he desperately needed.

"Your Pa has a right to be angry."

Arak followed him out and closed the door. "I'm sorry about that. Pa hasn't been the same since Ma died."

Caught by a pang of guilt, Je'Rol sat down on the step, leaving room for the boy beside him, and watched the sun dip into the peaks to the west.

"It's been two years since they found her remains."

Remains. Then she hadn't died peacefully.

"Someone said they saw the natters swarm over her." His voice wavered and he sniffed. That the boy could talk about the horror of losing his mother amazed Je'Rol. "I could have protected her, but she told me to stay home. She was…She was just going to the store to trade for some sewing stuff to make a new dress." Arak sniffed.

Although he barely knew the boy, Je'Rol wished he could take away the pain and the guilt. The nightmares of the damage he'd seen from natters still haunted him. Hopefully the boy hadn't seen the horrid sight of his mother's remains.

"I'm good with killing them. You know? They just freeze and give me a clear shot. She should have let me go with her." Arak wiped his eyes and sniffed.

The boy's words rang through his head, along with the way the beast stayed in control near him. Nadia had the same effect on him, and she had turned out to be an Adept. The boy had the gift; he was sure of it. Arak was an Adept.

Je'Rol studied Arak, a demon hunter in the making, and his emotions tangled. On one hand, he could give the boy hope to escape the misery of his family's shadow, but that meant starting him down the path to being a killer. Nadia had been a sweet girl when he'd met her, but her training had killed that part of her. He shouldn't say anything to Arak, but the boy needed something, since he wasn't going to find any love in that house.

"You have a gift, Arak. Not everyone can *dispirit* a demon."

"I do? What's *dispirit?*"

"You take control, impose your will over theirs." And that was probably what affected Je'Rol to like the boy. Arak wanted someone to like him so much that he probably used that power on Je'Rol without being conscious of it, like Nadia had.

"You mean like a real demon hunter?"

Je'Rol nodded, his insides knotting around the fact that he'd given the boy power over him, but Arak needed something to believe in. "If you get the right training, you could be a great demon hunter."

Arak's eyes widened in excitement, erasing the sorrow that had reddened them minutes ago. He gazed out at the mountains, his jaw hanging slack. "Me, a demon hunter. Wait until Pa and Soren hear that!"

"I wouldn't tell them. I don't think they'd take it well."

"No," Arak muttered. "I suppose not. But they'll see when I'm older. I'll travel the world killing demons, saving people."

"Killing people."

The excited gleam vanished from the boy's eyes. "What?"

"Half-bloods, innocent babies and children. Can you do that, Arak?"

The boy dropped his eyes and his shoulders drooped; an air of disappointment hung over him. "I don't know. Do they hurt anyone?"

"Sometimes, when they lose control, but not until they're older. But they don't want to."

"They don't?"

"No. They didn't ask to be born cursed in a world that doesn't want them."

"Are there grown up half-bloods?"

"Yes." Je'Rol wiped his face with his hands. Maybe the boy would listen, or at least take something to heart or plant a seed of doubt before the Adepts found him and twisted his mind.

"Are they dangerous? Are they mean? Pa says Tessa needs to be careful or some demonlord will impregnate her with a half-blood."

Je'Rol peaked out of his hands at the boy. "You understand more than I expected."

Arak shrugged and wiped at a crust of dirt on the knee of his pants. "I hear things…sometimes when I'm not supposed to."

He wouldn't doubt that.

The click of the door opening pulled his attention around to Soren with a plate of food. "I guess we owe you this much for bringing the meat." He stepped out and handed the metal plate to Je'Rol. Blackened meat piled high. "Tessa didn't know how much you would eat."

"This is enough."

"Oh, and…ah…Here." He turned around for a moment and turned back with a cloak in his hands. "Fair trade."

"Thanks." Je'Rol set the cloak beside him. Now he could hide the white and black hair betraying his heredity. First for the food. His stomach ached for the meat with its delectable scent. Fresh, cooked meat at that.

"Arak, come inside and leave the man alone."

With the plate on his thighs, Je'Rol met the boy's eyes. Despite his favorable influence, the boy was likeable without the power. "He can stay."

"And I suppose he expects me to bring a plate for him too." Bitterness lashed from Soren's words.

"That would be appreciated," Je'Rol said.

Soren clamped his jaw and stomped away into the house and ordered Tessa to make a plate for Arak.

Je'Rol sank his teeth into the roasted meat and savored the hot grease flowing down his chin, despite the steaming heat rising from it. Soon, Arak ate next to him on the steps, tentatively picking pieces from the portions on his plate. Neither said a word until the food was gone.

For the first time since his imprisonment for the Dao Larashi, Je'Rol sat back, satisfied with a full stomach, and watched the stars light up in the sky. The tigers hadn't found him or had given up for reasons he couldn't imagine, he had a full stomach, and he'd discovered a fragile peace he hadn't known in a long time. For a few minutes, he closed his eyes. Too soon, that moment would be gone.

"It's getting too late to go out," Arak said.

"Why?"

"The natters will be out."

"I can't stay here." The words left a sinking feeling in Je'Rol's heart, but it was the truth he couldn't deny. He was unwelcome. "I need to see Kiron, to learn what he knows."

"And then you'll just leave."

"I have to go on."

"Why?"

The whiny voice grated on his nerves, but Je'Rol set the plate aside and grabbed the cloak. "It's complicated." He stood and secured the tie around his neck.

"You promised I could go with you."

Je'Rol winced, his face away from the boy. He had said he would like Arak to show him the way, but the boy had already said it best—the natters would be out. They were mostly nocturnal hunters, and Je'Rol wouldn't be responsible for them getting the boy while walking home alone, and he wasn't about to take the boy with him.

"It's too dangerous, Arak."

"But you said I had the gift of a demon hunter."

"You're not trained…And the demonlords are after me."

Arak fell silent, staring as if seeing him for the first time.

"I can't take you with me. I don't want you to get hurt. Stay here with your family. Please, Arak."

The boy's shoulders dropped. "You didn't really care. Did you?" He stomped up the steps to the door.

Je'Rol opened his mouth to object—he did care, which was why he didn't want the boy with him. He wouldn't put Arak in that kind of danger.

"Good bye, Je'Rol." Arak stepped in and slammed the door.

A low growl rumbled from the beast inside. As he suspected—the boy's will was strong and would have held him there. The last statement had freed him. Now he could go on with his search, and hope that someday a demon hunter named Arak didn't cross his path.

Bad enough to have Nadia determined to kill him.

Nadia…All this reminded him of meeting her long ago.

Pushing her from his mind, Je'Rol flipped the hood over his head and strode past the pens of feathered kimas. The odors of animals and their wastes faded as he followed the road away from there for the lights of the town a couple miles away.

Someone there would likely tell him where to find Kiron. In such a small community, nothing could be hidden, at least not for long, which was why he had to leave as soon as possible.

In the quiet peace of the early night, the fresh air of the mountains carried on it the occasional animal scent, but nothing of the natters. The small demons could stay away. He'd never miss them if the demon hunters killed them all. After the Dao Larashi, he had hoped never to see another swarm in his life. The tunnels he used to escape his prison in *Acropa Je'Gri* made him leery of any dark places. They haunted his dreams with the occasional visit by mutilated bodies he recognized and abhorred.

Ahead, lights glowed from the windows of houses, which clustered closer as he neared the town with its many buildings along narrow, hard-packed streets. A man crossing a street at the edge of the town glanced at him and continued on his way.

Je'Rol hated to speak, but he had to say something, growl or not. "Excuse me!"

The man turned, his face shadowed with the dusty light from a window at his back. "I'm looking for a man named Kiron."

After a pause, the man said, "He likes an evening drink. Try the Tiger's Claw." He turned, clearly intending to hurry away.

"Where's that?"

"Two streets down, then left. Can't miss it." The man rushed away into the shadows between houses.

The growl had given him away. Je'Rol couldn't hide it, but he'd do what he could at the tavern. The Tiger's Claw—an obvious name either in spite or in honor of the demonlord masters of that territory.

Couldn't miss it, he'd said.

Je'Rol strode down the dark street, staying out of the light from windows. He counted two streets down, assuming by streets the man had meant areas between houses wide enough for a horse and carriage to pass. At the second street, he spied a few placards hanging outside their respective shops among the houses. Cast in the light of a window, one of them bore a rough outline of a paw with claws extended. As he approached, he made out the words confirming it.

Je'Rol pushed the door open to the tavern lit by lamps on the beams throughout a single room, which was only half full of patrons. They looked up at his entrance, except for an old man with a pipe sending up curls of smoke in the corner who seemed to be deep in thought, the gray-sprinkled hair on his head poking out in odd directions. That's where he'd start. If it wasn't Kiron, the old man probably knew where to find him.

"Thirsty?"

Startled, Je'Rol whirled on the voice, reflexes ready. The sight of a friendly-faced man in a red-plaid vest halted him and his thoughts. After a couple seconds, everything caught up. "Not now."

The server shrugged and wandered away to a table of men around a game, their cheeks flush with too much drink.

The old man at the table by himself looked up, a spark of intrigue in the lift of his brow. Je'Rol wove through the tables and chairs and stopped across the table where the old man sat. "Kiron?"

"Who's asking?" The man took a couple quick puffs and blew the smoke out over the table. The scent of burned leaves with a hint of spice overwhelmed Je'Rol.

He clutched the back of a chair opposite the old man to avoid collapsing from the nauseating odor. "Someone who heard he knows his history."

The old man set down the pipe on the table and leaned forward, his eyes narrowed. "You're not human," he said in a low voice. The smoke trailing from his mouth choked Je'Rol on the odor of burned leaves.

"No." The growl in Je'Rol's voice was unmistakable and undeniable.

"What do you want with Kiron?"

"Information."

The old man sat back in his chair and crossed his arms. "What information?"

A low rumble rose in his throat; Je'Rol refused to play these games. "I only speak to those who can help me." He turned—

"You seem so sure that only Kiron can help you. Maybe I know something he doesn't."

Je'Rol hesitated. The old man had a point, but he wasn't about to tell anyone his secrets. Maybe someone else there knew where he could find the right man.

The scrape of the chair and hurried clapping of boots on the wood floor warned him before the hand grabbed his shoulder to halt him.

"Wait."

Je'Rol shrugged away from the hand and scowled under his hood. The old man abruptly pulled away.

"I can take you to him."

Was this some sort of trick or was the man sincere? It came too easy, but he didn't have much of a choice, and with no sight of the Li'Ador or the Je'Gri anywhere in the valley so far, he felt some security trusting the old man. "All right."

"Good. Good…One moment." He hurried back to his chair and grabbed a jacket hanging over the back, and his still smoking pipe propped on the table. On his way to returning, he slipped on the jacket. "Let's go."

Je'Rol followed him out into the street and past several homes. In the silence, the muffled voices of families and friends filtered from the houses, where they were safe from most natters.

Although the Li'Ador should have been on patrol to keep the small demons out of the town, he saw no sign of them. Every town paid to keep at least a small contingent of Li'Ador to protect their residents. The Je'Gri High Lord didn't impress him as a generous man to pay the upkeep of such skilled warriors to protect his livestock. Je'Rol would have to be careful.

With his senses piqued for the slightest hint of trouble, Je'Rol followed the old man. If the Li'Ador expected him, they could be lying in wait.

They stopped at a quiet house with two narrow windows dimly lit from the inside, and the old man knocked.

Steps rose from inside a moment before the door opened to reveal the shadowed visage of a man with a spark in his eyes. "Gram! I'm sorry. Got a bit busy here." His eyes lifted to Je'Rol. "Who's your friend?"

"Not sure, but he sounds demonlord, and he insists on talking to you."

Je'Rol knew that wary look, but the real Kiron wasn't getting anything until he invited them inside. Someone could overhear. He couldn't risk exposing himself.

After a few seconds of hesitation, Kiron opened the door. "Don't know what you want with me, but I'd be interested in your story."

"Missed ya for our usual drink," Gram said as he stepped in. "Kept me waiting. Good thing this lad came looking. Didn't fool him, though." He chuckled and waited for Je'Rol, who took the cue to step inside. "What was your name there?"

Je'Rol hesitated, waiting for Kiron to shut the door. Once it clicked into place, he pulled off the hood hiding his face and hair.

Gram's smile twisted into something sly, and he nodded. "Thought so, since you weren't arrogant like most demonlords."

"I'm not most demonlords."

Kiron's gray eyes narrowed. "Half-blood."

A growl rumbled in Je'Rol's throat at the man's quick deduction and the implied threat that accompanied anyone knowing. He glanced about the home for a quick escape if he should need it, but it was a simple home with three areas, including the hall in which they stood, which branched off to a room to the side and another area to the rear closed off by a sliding panel. Dark oiled beams only a couple feet above supported a peaked roof with the usual stone and masonry forming the walls to keep natters out.

"That explains it. You're wise to hide that head, although the face is a sure giveaway under the beard…Put away the claws, boy."

Je'Rol took a breath to calm himself and the beast ever present for release. The claws shrank the little they had extended in his defensiveness. Being called a "boy" would normally have irritated him even if he qualified in age as a "boy", just for the fact that he'd endured a man's life earlier than most boys before they became men.

"Not many make it to your age. Royal Je'Gri by the looks." Kiron's scrutiny fell over every part of him, but settled on his face.

Enough speculation. Je'Rol wanted information and the man obviously knew something. "You're familiar with the demonlords."

A slight lift of the old man's lips confirmed it. "I've been around."

"Where?"

"Every domain... Je'Rol, is it?"

He knew without being told.

The beast snarled. His heart pounded and reflexes sharpened, ready to fight his way out of an attack. Kiron had indeed been around.

Gram jumped back, thumping against the wall behind him. "Dammit, Kiron! Don't get him mad!"

Kiron made no move, but the gleam in those old eyes now hinted of something else, the same confidence as the soldier in Lord Bannon's palace, the old soldier whose reflexes nearly matched his own; the old soldier who couldn't be mistaken for anything but a member of the warriors trained to fight demons. Je'Rol growled, "Li'Ador."

Kiron's jaw shifted and he limped away into the front room. Even if he had been one of the elite soldiers, an old man in his condition was no match for a half-blood. He was no threat.

"I spent my life protecting humans from demons." Kiron grunted as he sank onto a padded chair near a stone hearth. "I was fresh out of training when we received the news to watch out for a woman with a half-blood tiger child…She hid you well. I was a commander of my own company hired by a southern city when I heard you'd been discovered as a young man and to keep a watch for you. After all those years, I was surprised to hear your name, then nothing…until now."

He chuckled. "The irony doesn't escape me. You come to me, now, when I'm old and weak. Je'Rol, the fugitive half-blood son of Je'Dron. And you expect me to help you?"

"No." This was a mistake; that was obvious.

"Come now. Sit. Tell me what you could possibly want that you would risk the Li'Ador." Kiron motioned to his friend, giving a tick of his head sideways. "Would you mind bringing some tea, my old friend?"

"I thought you'd never ask." Gram stepped around Je'Rol out of the front room.

The man's footsteps faded through the entry hall, but Je'Rol never took his eyes off the old Li'Ador in his chair. As a soldier, he would have traveled where needed, eliminating demons of all varieties and playing favor to the Adepts of Te'Mea and the demonlords, possibly even Je'Rekun. If he was loyal, Je'Rol had no time to waste. Word would reach the palace, and Nadia, and they would find his trail.

But the damage had been done and it would take some time for any message to reach them. He might as well ask what he came to ask before leaving that town. "Did you ever hear of the obelisk of Mai'Kari?"

Kiron leaned back, his gaze distant for some time in the silence of the house. "I suppose it's an object of power."

"In a manner of speaking." Je'Rol already had his answer—the man hadn't even heard of it.

"So, you want to do what—destroy the Adepts, sorcerers and demon hunters all? Kill everyone who's ever wronged you?"

"No. I want to be free."

"Free? Free to kill? Free to destroy?"

"Free of the beast!"

Kiron blinked, those gray eyes focusing on Je'Rol as if seeing him for the first time.

"The beast?"

"The demon side."

"And this obelisk is supposed to help you with that?"

"If old legends can be trusted. I've been searching for years."

"This obelisk of Mai'Kari?" Kiron rubbed his hand around his neck as if to relieve some discomfort. "Obelisk…I don't know about an obelisk of Mai'Kari, but I know the mountains to the north were home to some ancient civilization. The abandoned ruins are infested with natters, unless the tigers cleaned them out. Last I heard, Je'Dron settled in that area when his brother led a coup against him some thirty years ago." He shrugged, his eyes on Je'Rol. "But you'd know that better than me, I guess."

Je'Dron had made some old ruins his base? If the obelisk was there, he must have found it; but why was he still the one exiled? If he had the obelisk, he should have used it to retake his throne from Je'Rekun. The obelisk couldn't be there.

"Is there anywhere else something like that might be?"

Kiron shrugged. "There are ruins all over this land. Some of the clans disappeared in their wars with the others and their abandoned cities were taken over by the surviving clans and humans. If this obelisk exists, it would have to be buried deep, or hidden by magic."

Magic. The thought had occurred to him. It was likely he had passed the infamous talisman and didn't realize it. But he didn't want to consider his search to be in vain.

"You have no ideas?" Je'Rol asked.

"None."

"You wouldn't help me if you could."

A bemused smile touched those thin lips, lifting the sagging cheeks. "Maybe, if I thought my life was in danger."

Je'Rol growled and turned to leave. He didn't need this. It was a waste of his time; time he needed to put distance between him and Je'Rekun's forces.

"You'd walk away?"

"Yes." He didn't look back but reached for the door handle.

"You'd rather give up? Not even give in to the rage simmering inside you?" Kiron paused. "You're not like other half-bloods."

Je'Rol gripped the handle but hesitated, curious what the old Li'Ador had to say.

"I thought you gave in to the blood rage, just let it all go, not caring who you killed."

"I don't kill," he said with his face to the door. The need to make his point overrode his urge to leave.

"Tell that to the dead you left in your wake."

"Only those who were innocent." Like Temari, and the woman in Dev Nadir who resembled Liandra, or the handful of others unfortunate to be near when the beast escaped. "Others preyed upon the weak."

"Then you admit to killing."

His grip on the door handle tightened, the beast growling for escape to end the argument in bloodshed. More than ever, he had to restrain it, to control the anger rising, or not only prove the man right—even if it meant his death—but also send up an alarm of his whereabouts. "I don't like it!"

"That doesn't justify what you've done. You're a half-blood, prone to losing control of the demon side when your emotions are out of control. You're a threat to people everywhere. You should be dead; Je'Dron shouldn't have spared your life."

"I know, but the blood rage will kill me soon." Je'Rol's eyes stung with the harsh reality the old man turned on him. Maybe the world would be better off without him. Maybe he should kill himself, or turn himself over to Je'Rekun's forces to be killed or to Nadia to give her satisfaction. Ending his life might be easier than continuing his search.

The Su'Kora ambassador had confirmed that the obelisk did exist, at one time if not currently, and that its power was a threat. Maybe the world would be better if it remained hidden.

"Then give yourself to the Li'Ador."

"No." Something within him refused to quit, no matter how vividly the memories of death and gore spilled through his mind. He wanted the life denied him. "I want to live. I deserve to know peace."

"Deserve? What do you deserve for your crimes?" Kiron huffed a heavy breath.

Damn him! "I never asked to be born. I never asked for this burden. I've suffered all my life because of what I am. If the obelisk will give me peace to live like a normal man, I'll find it." Je'Rol gripped the door handle, intending to pull it open.

A voice outside the door stayed his hand. The streets had been empty when he arrived, except for Gram.

Gram! The old man hadn't returned, nor had he made a sound from the kitchen. Since he hadn't left by the front door, he must have gone out another door.

Kiron had stalled him to give Gram time to retrieve someone, and it was probably to capture him. He'd worked fast, which meant someone had been ready or nearby, and Gram moved like a younger man. They had been waiting for him—the Je'Gri guards must have reached the town first and warned them to set a trap.

Je'Rol backed away from the door, the beast growling from his throat. The ceiling was low in the brick and wood house, not having an upper floor. The ceiling supports were open to him, and it wouldn't take much with his strength to punch through the rooftop.

"No one asked to die at your hands," Kiron said.

"No one asks to die at anyone's hands. Humans kill humans with purpose, for power and control. Are you any better than a half-blood who does all he can to control his demon side but is hunted and condemned for existing when all he wants is to live a life like any human?"

Kiron frowned, opened his mouth to speak, and closed it again. He knew the truth. Humans were no better than their demonlord masters.

Satisfied that he made his point, Je'Rol looked up again. Perfect. That cross beam above would give him the leverage he needed to punch through the roof in one attempt.

He sprang up to the beam, bumping his head on the ceiling. The moment he landed on the creaking horizontal beam, he gathered his legs and, fists covering his head like ramrods, he sprang through the boards. Wood splinters flew everywhere as he landed with his legs splayed over the hole he'd left, the clatter of roof tiles scraping down around him. There were some advantages to behind half-blood—demonlord strength surpassing them all.

Multiple voices shouted from the street. Je'Rol sprinted away, ready for the spring to another rooftop. This time, no arrows sang after him. His escape was almost too easy. That made him wary.

19

Je'Rol fled the voices shouting through the dark of the night, keeping to the rooftops where they wouldn't reach him. Each spring over a wide street brought back memories of the Li'Ador arrows that had brought him down for Nadia, but no arrows came this time.

Too soon, he reached the edge of the town and landed on hard ground. Shouts chased him from somewhere among the homes.

After a moment to catch his breath, Je'Rol sprinted past fields and pastures. He launched himself easily over several stone fences and continued his course towards the mountains of the north side of the valley. He was closer to the mountains on that side. Reaching them meant putting distance between him and the humans, who would be hard-pressed to keep up with him.

He would search for the ruins Je'Dron called home. From his understanding, Je'Dron himself had spared his life, but Je'Rol had no intention of returning the favor. Meanwhile, he, Je'Rol, would find the obelisk and gain its power. Once he gained control of his own demon side, he'd turn that control on the demonlords and end the conflict.

No more half-bloods.

No more hunting humans.

No. More.

At the steepening incline at the edge of the valley, he leapt up rather than ran. He stopped after a few jumps, which landed him on a rocky ledge, and looked back. Among the shadows of the valley, nothing moved. The distant shouts of men barely reached him over the wind flapping the corner of his cloak. The lowing of a cow nearby drowned out the calls from the town. The only scents to reach him were those of dank places and the perfume of flowers with the occasional hint of an animal.

He turned and continued into the mountains alone and headed north. He'd never wanted to set foot on Tikeros, but fate had brought him back to his homeland; and it seemed he would have to confront his own father, something he'd never wanted, even while he wanted to kill Je'Dron.

Sometime during the night, he found a nook beneath two sheared stones and curled up to sleep, secure on all but one side, but one side was easier to defend against from the cold or attackers.

Nothing disturbed him that night, and he woke with the sun already well up in the sky to warm the morning chill away. Although hunger gnawed in his gut, the meat from the boar would sustain him for a couple days. Unlike humans, he could survive without problems on little food for a few days, as long as he ate well between fasts. Water was easy to come by, like the stream a short trek from where he'd slept during the night.

And where there was water, there would be game.

After a short wait, he caught a large bird in the nearby brush, its colorful head and tail plumage contrasting the green of the foliage. Feathers were easy to pluck and, even raw, the bird's meat satisfied his hunger. He threw the bones and feathers into a thick brush with the hopes the natters would find what remained of the carcass before anyone realized he had been there.

Eating raw gave him more time to travel too. The sun reached its zenith before he set out again, making sure before he did that he'd sated his thirst. It might be a while before he drank, and he didn't have anything for carrying water. That was one thing he wished he had for his journey. He'd lost his water bag before Liandra had found him, but Karaligo had been blessed with an abundance of fresh water from mountain runoffs. Tikeros seemed to be much the same; if he was right, he would cross streams or rivers every day or two—not ideal but sufficient. He didn't have much choice but to continue without a flask or storage bag for water.

Survival was harsh for a half-blood like him already, without basic necessities lacking, but he had learned how to rely on himself.

Je'Rol encountered steep cliffs and passed rotted caverns where the filth of natters reeked of fresh kills. A few times, the crawling demons tried to close in on him, but a swift attack left their guts spewed.

This was the life he'd known for years. No sorcerers or demon hunters; they were too few and preferred hospitable areas where they could be among other humans, the reason for learning their skills—to protect their own kind.

A few times in the years of his travels, he had crossed paths with young half-bloods wearing tattered clothes, their bodies lean of flesh. They rarely said anything, afraid of strangers with good reason. Only one had ever tried to stay with him, but Je'Rol had lost him when the boy ran out of the cave they used for shelter during a thunderstorm, because natters attacked.

He'd learned to keep to himself, but the kids escaping the demon hunters, the children whose mothers had hidden their identities as long as they could, were often unprepared for the wilderness or had bad experiences with strangers luring them to the demon hunters for a bounty. Like him, most trusted no one.

He shouldn't have trusted Kiron, but he'd needed information and the old man had been recommended as the best source. Now he understood why. While the Li'Ador often stayed in one place for long periods of time, their fees paid from town coffers, some traveled the world following assignments from their commanders. Kiron had traveled the world, likely meeting demonlords of most of the domains. While that made him a rich source of knowledge of the lands of Derandria, it also made him a threat.

But the accusations bit at his core. Je'Rol couldn't let it continue. He wanted someone to listen to him, to understand. He wanted to change their minds about what it was like to suffer as a half-blood, to always live as an outcast, feared and persecuted for being born.

It would never happen. As long as half-bloods lost control in the blood rage, they would be hunted and killed.

What would happen if he obtained the obelisk? Su'Tari had said it was a threat.

The Adepts would likely never leave him alone, and they would want that power for themselves, as would the demonlords. He would never know peace, unless he hid away.

No. He would obtain the obelisk and its power. If he had it, he could command the demonlords. If he hid it, no one would find it.

The arguments ran through his head as they had other times.

Je'Rol pushed them aside in the afternoon to focus on the narrowing ledge along the steep mountainside covered in grasses and mosses, which made the footing slick. He would have preferred dry rocks.

Instead, he had to pay close attention to the end of that ledge and climbing along the steep face, until he reached the grassy shelf across the drop. There he could rest for a short time to warm in the sun. A nap would refresh him for the latter part of the day.

Je'Rol set out along the steep face, his heart pounding with the desire to keep his toes on the short jags of rock protruding from the cliffside. His fingertips strained to keep their grip on the sharp points against the threat of a good hundred foot drop nearly straight down if they failed. Not even his demon strength could save him from splattering on the fingers of rock below.

He lifted one foot and slid it along the cliff to find another hold.

This was not what he'd had in mind when he started. It had seemed like the better option when the ledge he'd been following tapered to nothing. Turning around meant losing a good portion of a day of travel and risking the natters that probably lived in the crevices of the rocks below. That meant lost time and a chance for Je'Rekun's forces to catch up to him. He couldn't afford to back track.

Je'Rol's foot caught on something solid. He tested it, his fingers gripping for his life. At his moments of panic, the beast fought him for escape from his tenuous hold, breaking his concentration.

Slowly, he crossed along the wall, until his feet reached the wider ledge. Sweat poured from his body and his fingers ached from the strain. He sat on the ledge, curling and uncurling his fingers into tight fists to loosen them, but he couldn't rest yet. The wider, gentler slope was a quick climb above him. Once there, he could rest.

Je'Rol unrolled his fingers amid the aches. Forget it. One good jump and he'd be there. Had the gap he had crossed been less, he could have leapt that too.

He gathered himself, but the moment he launched, the ledge cracked beneath him. His first jump was his last.

While the shelf thundered away beneath him, he threw his arms out to catch the upper ledge at the pinnacle of his jump, where he could see over the edge.

Ruins!

The realization startled him into barely catching the grassy edge of the rocky face. Claws sunk deep into the soil until they hit the rock not far under it. Beneath him, the ledge crumbled and crashed down into the valley.

Determined not to join the shattered remains of the ledge, he reached up with his other hand and sunk his claw in as deep as it would go. Despite the ledge angling out at the top, the demon side refused to give in to death and urged him on with more strength than he expected for the ache of his fingers.

After reaching the top, he backed away from the edge and rested against a stone to catch his breath.

He hated mountains.

But he'd found ruins. Where there were ruins, there might be clues about the obelisk. He might not need to face Je'Dron after all.

After regaining his strength and settling the beast, Je'Rol climbed to his feet and stared at the vast city around a tall building. From the mostly intact structures, he discerned a city of stone, simple in its beauty but ornate in the central structure towering above the rest, the only one still having a roof. Arches surrounded it, the columns decorated with weatherworn figures tangled by tree branches that had grown around them. The lost city of an ancient race, perhaps the vanished Mai'Ekam whose magic he sought.

Je'Rol stepped beyond the first walls and a chill swept down his spine. The open doorways whispered of ghosts of the past haunting the ruins.

He peeked in a couple simple dwellings, feeling as if he'd stepped into another world. No natters attacked him; but the place seemed devoid of the lesser demons to the extent that he saw no signs that they had ever set their little claws there. Nor did he catch any hint of their rancid odors. The remote city was safe.

He breathed easier and wandered through the homes, noting the remains of metal containers and the stone counters with columns down to support them over collections of carved stone, clay, and shaped metal containers. Dust and debris filled many of the rooms, often stones and rock that must have collapsed from the walls or roofs. In a couple, he noticed stone stairs cut off after a few steps up, tufts of grass long having overtaken them, while one had steps descending into a dark hole.

The houses varied, but most contained the same three rooms in different layouts and proportions. He assumed they used sleeping rooms, bathing rooms, and kitchens like those he had seen intact.

After a few houses, he continued along what seemed to be a main street from the entrance to the central structure, since it was wider than any of the spaces between houses. If he would find anything important, he'd bet it waited inside that building.

The figures on the columns supporting the arches looked familiar, despite the cracking and chipping. They appeared human, not some odd race he had imagined of something so ancient. Nor did there seem to be any sign of tigers or other demonlord forms; only humans. Writing scrawled in frames carved to look like banners across the arches in a language he couldn't read, but that meant nothing. He only knew the human language. This could have been the demonlord *Lexic*, but something in his mind said it was something else. He'd seen the writings before. They almost reminded him of Liandra's tattoos, but that couldn't be right.

Could it be the Master Race? Why would they glorify the human form? It didn't make sense. Even the demonlords decorated their palaces with their natural forms, despite being able to mimic humans.

Curious, he climbed the few stone steps surrounding the structure and stopped in the center of the five arches on that side, between columns that appeared to be women in long robes with their hands bearing different objects before them—one supporting a book and another with a globe. The other figures all appeared to hold different objects, one with a sword pointed down between their feet. Some of the clearer faces appeared to be more masculine. Perhaps they were men, very beautiful and elegant, like the demonlords in their human forms and this was simply another ancient city of a demonlord clan long gone.

What lay inside pushed aside the questions. Ahead stood a double door with one half on the ground while the other slanted on one remaining hinge, both tarnished with age to a dull amber. Upon the door still standing were more of the markings like those across the tops of the arches but here around images of men and animals.

Je'Rol traced the stiff lines and left a streak of brass shining where his finger had swept away the dust of ages. Brass doors on the largest, most decorated building in that ancient city sparked his interest to what lay inside, besides dust. Or had someone broken down the door and stolen the contents from within? What secrets about the obelisk might they have hidden?

The thought lured him into a small chamber—too small to be the whole building—where plain round columns supported the tall ceiling. Light trickled in through a few holes in the roof. Shelves of books and scrolls lined the walls with cluttered tables taking up much of the floor space. A single ladder bent at odd angles to make it unsafe for use lay among the mess, while another stood perfectly useable, if time hadn't warped it. Fixtures spaced throughout the chamber must have held lamps or something else for light.

The air was still, but for his passing, which stirred motes of dust to dance in the beams of light. The staleness of the air was disturbed by an odd scent.

Another door waited on the opposite end of the chamber. Je'Rol took a few steps and stopped when a ray of light hit the dust at the right angle to show it been disturbed. Footprints, and fresh ones at that. They were small, though, and had the shape of shoes. In the quiet of the room, he sniffed—dust and mold dominated, but the odd scent broke through, faint but different, something he hadn't encountered for a long while.

No, there was once recently. The memories coalesced with the strengthening of the scent into the next room. He'd been forced to kneel in Je'Rekun's presence and had spewed blood on the High Lord, who had motioned to…a goblin! This scent reminded him of the goblin. The short, greenish-skinned creature with the big ears and beady eyes had made no sound but obeyed without question. They all did.

He'd never met goblins anywhere but in the presence of the demonlords, didn't even know where they lived. Were these free goblins or servants of the demonlords? What did the demonlords learn from this place?

He sniffed again—no hint of the oddly refreshing odor of the masters of the world.

Were any goblins still in the ancient city? The scent was still strong enough for him to pick up, which meant they had been there recently, if they weren't still.

A low growl rumbled in his throat, barely audible but vibrating with the beast's arousal to defend itself with the claws extending.

He stepped through the doorway into the inner sanctum, where a strange statue filled the center of the room—three bronze women in sleeveless gowns, their hair flowing over their shoulders and backs. The lithe figures stood around a ring raising them off the floor while they held between them a group of rings interconnected but open through the center. Around the bottom was the same language he had seen on the outside arches. The light from the cracked roof shone down on the ancient statue, accentuating the slender curves of the feminine figures.

The scent of goblin was stronger in there. They'd spent a great deal of time in the old ruins. Why?

A scuff of movement echoed through the chamber, and the beast inside struggled for the chance to defend itself. Je'Rol extended claws fully, his senses alert for danger.

Another scuff came, the direction clear this time—the far left corner from where he stood. Darkness shrouded it behind a shaft of light from a crack in the roof above.

"Who's there?" He caught no scent of natters or demonlords, only goblin.

A squeak echoed through the chamber, followed by the quick patter of feet. He was right in one respect—a goblin was still there—but it was alone.

Something slammed and a shrill yelp magnified in the chamber made Je'Rol cover his ears.

Damned if the little demon didn't have a piercing shriek! He'd never heard them speak, but apparently they had voices. "Who are you?"

After a slur of words from the shadow at the back of the chamber, silence returned.

"I'm...hmm...Who are you? Or what are you, if you don't mind me asking? Human? Demonlord?" A moment later, the high-pitched voice lowered to muttering again. "No, no, no. Stupid. Do not speak to demonlords." A gasp and slap followed.

"Neither." Je'Rol relaxed. The nervous goblin was alone and certainly not a threat. But where had he come from? Why was he there? "Who are you, goblin?"

"You know? Of course, you know. Not that I could hide it." The high-pitched voice squeaked with anxiety. "I'm...Skar."

"Skar?" Je'Rol stepped into the room, squinting to make out the shadow on the other side of the statue.

"They call me because I study texts."

Skar...What did that have to do with texts? "Texts?"

"Books and scrolls of Old Ones. I read all."

"You can read?" Wait. Goblins spoke? The revelations made his head reel.

"Oh, yes." Confidence steadied the voice and the goblin stepped forward. "I am Skar of masters before demonlords."

A Skar? He studied ancient texts? That confirmed the suspicions rising in Je'Rol's mind. The goblin was a *scholar*. If he was so intelligent, why couldn't he speak clearly?

A bigger question was who were the masters before the demonlords? He couldn't mean— "The Master Race?"

"Hmm...Yes, you say; you being outsider, like others, call them. Good logic—Master Race—they ruled Derandria before disappeared. A sad fate. Not all believed but all suffered." The goblin spoke quickly in that irritating voice.

"Suffered?"

"Not suffered...Suffered? I am not sure of word. It does not matter. Old Ones left knowledge for goblins to use."

If the goblin studied the Master Race, then he might know their secrets, like the rumors that the Mai'Ekam had deciphered the magic of the Master Race to create the obelisk he sought.

"You are not demonlord?"

"No."

The goblin grunted as if lifting something heavy and shuffled towards him. "Yes. Not demonlord. I could not speak to demonlord. Old Ones cursed goblins. You show yourself?"

Je'Rol hesitated. If the little scholar—he didn't even realize goblins were that smart, but the broken language didn't impress him—*if* the goblin couldn't speak to demonlords, how would he feel about a half-blood?

The goblin stopped near the central statue. In the diffused light, the pallor of his skin contrasted the darker shades of green Je'Rol had seen on other goblins. This one had the usual big ears and a long nose on which rested a strange contraption of round glasses with other round parts jutting out above at odd angles, as if he should have eyes elsewhere than the two dark orbs that stared out through the central glasses.

"You have name?" Skar asked, clutching a book half as big as him, but he was less than half Je'Rol's height, average for the few goblins Je'Rol had seen.

He didn't exactly want to give it, but the little demon couldn't give it to a demonlord anyway if he'd been cursed not to speak to them. "Je'Rol."

Skar hissed and backed away.

"I'm not a demonlord...I'm a half-blood." Je'Rol threw off the hood, hoping to prove that he meant no harm while hating the situation.

"No, no, no, no. No half-bloods." Skar shuffled aside with his book, which was clearly growing heavy as his feet slowed.

No one wanted to help half-bloods, only to kill them, even a weak little goblin.

The book slammed to the floor, sending up a cloud of ancient dust, and the goblin grunted and groaned to lift it. "Go. Leave Skar...No more I..." He grunted under the strain to lift the book again. "...talk to you."

Je'Rol watched, his teeth clamped in frustration. The goblin must have found the tome important to risk reclaiming it in the presence of a half-blood he didn't want to speak to. What was in it? What did Skar know about the Master Race? Would he know about the obelisk, or perhaps the *am'taerad* stones? The sorceress had subdued the beast for him to fight in the Dao Larashi. If he could find more, he wouldn't need the obelisk, or maybe the Master Race knew something else that would help him. The goblin might know something if he could read the books of the "Old Ones".

In a few quick steps, Je'Rol reached the tome and lifted it.

"Ah! Thank you. I—"

The goblin reached his knobby fingers for the book. "No. No. Must not touch books! Delicate. Old. Be very careful and put it down."

"You dropped it without consequences." The books might be old, but they could withstand some abuse, if the resounding thud had been any measure.

Skar's ears drooped, and a second later he perked up and reached for the book again. "Not for you!"

Keeping it out of the goblins hands was a simple matter and not without its comedy. "I'll give it back if you answer a question." In curiosity, Je'Rol flipped open the tome to pages of the odd text like that over the figure columns outside.

"No! No! Not for you!" the goblin shrieked.

Je'Rol flipped a few yellowed pages dense with text to some with detailed pictures of human and animal figures in what appeared to be scenes of worship, or performing magic.

"Give back to me!"

"Will you help me?" He closed the tome and frowned at the wiry goblin jumping futilly for the book.

Skar paused and blinked. "One question."

"Or more," Je'Rol growled.

Where there should have been eyebrows, the ridges pressed down over Skar's eyes, his mouth set in a stubborn frown. "You will give me book?"

"Yes." If the goblin didn't know, harassing him wouldn't produce any better results. Besides, the world was a large place to search for the obelisk. Je'Rol didn't need to waste his time harassing a goblin.

With his arms crossed, the goblin said, "Ask."

Je'Rol met that hard, determined gaze through the odd glasses, configuring the phrasing of his question. After some seconds of staring at the short demon, he closed the book. "What do you know about the obelisk of Mai'Kari?"

The thin line of the goblin's mouth twitched. A blink later, the goblin transformed as if hit with a decompressing magic. His ears wilted and his shoulders sank. "Mai'Kari was Mai'Ekam clan, now gone from Derandria. Mai'Kari was Skar of her clan, took knowledge of Master Race and burned books so no one else learns."

Interesting facts but— "What do you know of the obelisk?"

Skar blinked and stepped forward. "Yes, you ask about obelisk. Why? What will you use for, Je'Rol? Obelisk is powerful control…" Dark eyes widened. "You seek control. Yes, half-blood. Human half is not strong to contain demon. Or is there more?"

The goblin's implications stabbed to his heart and the growing desires building with thoughts of wielding the obelisk's power.

"Tell me what you know about the obelisk," he growled.

"This not I can do."

"You promised to answer my question."

"I did. I know nothing about obelisk."

The beast growled to satisfy its frustrations with the shredding of the goblin. "You know about Mai'Kari. Why not the obelisk she created?"

"It is not written."

"Not written." Of course. This goblin was nothing more than a scholar. He would only know what his precious books said.

"History is recorded in Gung Horsh archives but obelisk only exists as warning. It is dangerous to control all demons and destroyed…"

"By a half-blood. I heard this story."

Skar blinked dark eyes magnified behind his glasses. "A half-blood? That is not known. But if it is destroyed, why search?"

Wrong question. Je'Rol handed the tome back to the goblin, who grunted with the weight. Su'Tari had warned him to tell no one, and this goblin didn't know it still existed. Skar would be no use in his search.

Je'Rol strode from the chamber and the squeak of the goblin yelling for him to stop.

After an echoing thud, the tap of feet hurried after him.

"Stop, Je'Rol. How do you know obelisk exists?"

Je'Rol didn't stop, but neither did the goblin leave his side. "Leave me, alone!" he growled, fighting the insistence of the beast for release to eliminate the annoyance of the goblin.

"But how can you search?"

Je'Rol whirled, his teeth sharpening. "I must find it…alone." Without waiting for a response, he strode from the ruins. Once he found a way down, he could continue his search.

He'd head north, to the ruins inhabited by Je'Dron.

20

Nadia gazed over the quiet mountains surrounding her and the group of Li'Ador, while the horses drank from the cool river. The tigers had sworn Je'Rol wouldn't have come this way. High Lord Je'Rekun was certain he had gone north to warn Je'Dron, but that could be a touch of paranoia about his plans. She had been careful to argue that if he had eluded capture for so long, Je'Rol was too clever to have gone straight north.

Instead, she had insisted on leading her hunting party east. Despite the cold threat of the High Lord's impatience, Je'Rekun had conceded to sending a pair of his most trusted guards with her. She doubted he did it for help but, rather, to monitor her and report back to him if she should betray him. Losing Je'Rol had put him on a blade's edge of losing his temper; even after she spared Je'Sikar's life, Je'Rekun had ordered his immediate death.

Shadows of the mountains filled the low areas where they rode. Dusk came and, with it, the threat of natters. They'd have to set up camp soon, but she'd hoped to find a secure place to settle the horses for the night. They'd been skittish in the narrow valley, likely from the scent of natters.

The tiger guards had one redeeming quality—they kept the lesser demons away, those that dared attack. But with the cleansing of their world of the nasty predators, which would rather eat their own than mate, their numbers grew scarce. Only in dark places did one find them in any measurable quantities.

Unless one was an Adept and the natters sensed it. They had an uncanny knack for swarming those like her with the gift to *dispirit* demons. That's why the hunters had tested her while they watched her for signs of pregnancy after Je'Rol left. It was a telltale sign. The power must have triggered a response in the little demons to defend themselves against that kind of control.

Lucky for her that Je'Rol had been there to protect her.

*Je'Rol...*Her life was his fault. In some twisted way, gratitude might be due, but he'd cut out her heart in the process.

Nadia scowled as her horse lifted its muzzle from the knee-deep water. Je'Rol deserved no mercy. Not only had he hurt her, but he'd left dead bodies along his trail throughout the world, every time he lost control of the demon side. As long as he lived, the world was unsafe. Killing half-bloods would save them all the trouble.

"Let's move!" she called to the group. They splashed from the river to the dry bank and continued a ways through the mountain.

Around a bend, a valley opened wide.

One of the orange tigers sniffed along the water's edge and tracked whatever they found to a place on the ground. A few seconds later, the tiger blurred and stood as an enchanting woman in bronze and black armor defining a slender but obviously feminine figure with a helmet shaped like a tiger's head over her human features. "Huntress."

Nadia rode to the tigress.

"He was here."

A chill raced through her at the prospects. Je'Rol had been through there! They were on the right track. They hadn't picked up any trace of his scent until then, tracking only natters, which had kept them on alert. She was beginning to worry that Je'Rekun had been right, until now.

"How long ago?" In other words, how close were they to catching up to him?

The tigress knelt down and sniffed. "It's too faint to say, but there is the scent of half-blood, and look—" She pointed to spots of brown on the foliage and leading back to a large browned area that appeared to have been mostly cleaned up, likely by natters. Something had been killed and carried away—she saw no signs of broken foliage that would have indicated an animal having been dragged away.

Je'Rol, most likely. His scent plus a killing. He must have come this way.

"Boar's blood," the tigress said.

From atop her horse, Nadia picked out a faint trail of blood from what had been a pool of it, but it faded to nothing among the grasses and brush. "Can you follow the scent?" If Je'Rol carried the boar away while it dripped, he would have left a clear path for them, at least for some distance. But why wouldn't he have eaten his kill there?

She would have expected him to eat what he could and leave the carcass, but the distant town and the farms spotting the valley might explain that, if he wasn't avoiding civilization.

"Yes." The tigress didn't wait for orders but blurred in her transformation and trotted off along the trail of blood, her tail lashing.

Nadia rode after her with the Li'Ador close behind. As the stars lit in the sky above, they arrived at a farmstead, where the cattle along the fence line snorted and kicked up their heels. She followed the road to the front door of a simple house as a young woman stepped out from the door. A boy squeezed past her, his eyes wide.

"Demon hunter!" The boy stepped down from the door but stopped before the two demonlords, who transformed into their human forms, both female.

"Demonlords!" His eyes widened and his jaw fell slack.

Belatedly, the boy knelt down in respect, and the young woman bowed her head. "We're honored by your presence," she said and looked up again. "How can we serve you?"

Nadia scanned the pasture—fenced solid all around with stone, except the wooden gate. The horses would be safe for the night and likely appreciate the chance to truly rest. "A safe sleep for the night...and we've tracked a half-blood to your door. What do you know of a man, perhaps bearing a boar?"

The boy's face hardened and the girl paled.

"Je'Rol was a half-blood?" she asked.

He had been there! The thrill swept through Nadia, threatening to overwhelm her with a false sense of success. She hadn't found him *yet*, and fought to temper the excitement in her voice. "Yes. When did you see him?"

"Two days ago," the boy said.

Two days. Then they were close. One night of good rest would give their horses and the tigresses a well-deserved break to continue at a faster pace, at least for a little while, hopefully long enough to catch up to him.

"He was supposed to take me with him to visit Kiron."

"Kiron?"

"The old storyteller in town." The girl frowned at the boy. "Quiet, Arak! Let me speak. Besides, it was late. You know it's too risky to be out alone at night."

Nadia dismounted and stepped towards the boy, who seemed to have been most affected by Je'Rol. "Did he say what he wanted?"

Arak shrugged. "Information...something...something about an artifact thing."

"Artifact?" She looked up, but the girl wore a blank expression. What would Je'Rol want with an artifact?

"He only told me he wanted food and clothing, a cloak to keep him warm."

"What was your name?"

"Tessa."

"He didn't tell you anything else?"

Tessa shrugged. "No. He didn't really say much to me. Arak brought him home, though."

The squeak of leather rose from the shifting of several soldiers, and the land darkened with the coming of night. This conversation would best be left until after they took care of the horses, when they sat around a campfire—the house was clearly too small for their group and she wasn't about to leave her entourage speculating into the night without her ears present.

"I'd like to hear more about your visit with Je'Rol, but if you don't mind, our horses could use a rest in your pasture."

Tessa grimaced but nodded her head. "I'm sure Pa would allow it for the night."

"Thank you." Allow it, nothing. It was expected of the people to do what they could to support the Li'Ador and the Adepts in any way necessary. Still, there were always those who gave the rest of them a bad reputation by association with their greed. Not everyone liked the Adepts or Li'Ador.

Nadia returned to take the reins of her horse and ordered the rest to untack there. Afterwards, Arak led them to the gate of the pasture, where they turned the horses loose. They watched the horses take turns in a couple dusty places grazed down to the roots by the cattle. After each had a chance to roll, they lowered their heads to enjoy the green grass.

"How did you get to be a demon hunter?"

Nadia blinked and looked down at the kid shadowed by the encroaching twilight. She should have expected something like that from the boy. It wasn't often anyone saw a woman hunting demons, if they did chance to meet a trained Adept.

She didn't mind telling him, but no one needed to know her connection to Je'Rol. "There was a half-blood when I was young who made me mad, so I decided I had to get rid of them. I trained with the Li'Ador after I finished my studies at the temple with the other Adepts. I can kill a nest of natters or a full-grown half-blood." Only the High Lord's plans had restrained her.

His jaw dropped open. "I want to be a demon hunter. Je'Rol said I had the *dispirit* power."

Several Li'Ador moved around Arak, no doubt ready to ask the question that sprang to her mind, but it was her task, not theirs.

Nadia put a hand up, her interest piqued by this news. Had Je'Rol noticed something about the boy? Had the boy influenced Je'Rol in some way? How could he have known if the boy had the gift?

"He did? What else did he tell you?"

Arak looked around at the faces staring at him and sagged under the weight of the attention. "Ah…I…Not much. He didn't stay long."

Perhaps the boy needed less pressure. With a hand on his shoulder, Nadia guided him through the others, but found Captain Karik and leaned close to give him orders. "Set up camp away from the house. We don't need extra ears."

"Yes, Huntress." He gave a quick bow and turned to his men.

"Now, Arak," she said with an arm over the boy's shoulders. "I'd like to hear all about your visit with Je'Rol."

They walked back to the house, the boy starting off slowly but gaining momentum as he talked. He seemed a bit smitten with Je'Rol, who'd apparently not bothered to tell them the truth—that he was a half-blood—although she could understand his reasons. He'd said little but left the boy and the house after some unkind words from the father, who apparently had no liking of the demonlord masters of that land. She'd discovered a lot of animosity towards the demonlords in her travel, always deserved, but no one still alive after expressing such views. The father didn't seem to care about the consequences of upsetting a demonlord. She'd have to keep the tigresses away.

And from what the boy said, he might indeed have the gift of *dispirit*. How odd that Je'Rol would explain it to the boy. She would have expected someone in his position to keep his mouth shut about it, unless he had a death wish.

No. If he wanted to die, he wouldn't have fled.

Why would he say anything, though? The boy showed a lot of enthusiasm for demon hunting. For that matter, why didn't Je'Rol kill him outright and end a potential threat?

"But he said you kill babies?"

The way he said that made Nadia wince. In the light from a window of the house, she avoided his eyes by picking at the tie strings securing her shoulder plates. "Only half-bloods."

"Why?"

"Because they grow into killers." Je'Rol was proof of that, as were the couple of late-teen half-bloods she'd hunted and killed. "They lose control in the blood rage, Arak. You were lucky Je'Rol didn't hurt you. In the blood rage, he'd kill anyone."

"I don't believe you."

Nadia halted, her mind tangled with facts and emotions. Even Je'Rol would kill anyone in the blood rage. She'd seen it happen to half-bloods. All humanity disappeared and only a beast determined to kill every living thing in its path remained. An Adept could subdue them, but even her powers were put to the test against the blood rage. It took total focus until the human side regained control.

"You should. When they lose control of their emotions, the demon side takes over and they don't recognize anyone…" She stared across the landscape into the past and the resurrection of that night when she'd questioned Je'Rol in the chamber of *Acropa Je'Gri*. He said he'd left to protect her. He'd left the boy home to protect him from the natters that would have swarmed him as they did her that fateful day. It was inevitable, and he must have realized that.

No. Even if he had cared, he was still dangerous. He deserved to die.

Then why did it bother her so much? Because she had cared about him, been so infatuated with her savior that she had nursed him back to health? That was long ago. She had learned the truth since then. He could have killed her.

But he didn't. He'd protected her, from himself as much as the natters. He'd stayed with her for several cycles of the moon, caressed her gently, held her in his arms as if needing her as much as she had needed him. He'd been so sad that she had wanted to help him.

Damn him!

Nadia fought the tears burning in her eyes and stepped into the shadows.

"Did the half-blood you met hurt you?"

She swallowed the lump of emotions forming in her throat. "Yes." She had to get away from the boy and his poisonous words. His denial made her question all she believed. Je'Rol was no exception of the danger half-bloods posed to their world, to humanity.

"What did he do? It musta been something bad."

She cleared her throat. "It's complicated."

"Oh…ah…All right." He scratched his neck and adjusted his belt and looked over the group of men and the two large cats gathering in the small square between the barn and the house. Two shadows approached from a field nearby. "I better go explain to Soren and Pa." He dashed off before she could speak.

Just as well. She didn't want to hear anything more about Je'Rol's visit with the boy. She wanted to believe he was a murdering fugitive who didn't care about anyone he met. That made her job of finding and killing him easier. Then she could put the past behind her for good.

21

The bleeding corpse rushed after him and a woman screamed his name. "Je'Rol!"

He blinked and the dream faded, leaving the face of a goblin hovering over him, the odd glasses in a different configuration of lenses on his large nose than the last time Je'Rol had seen him.

He had to be dreaming yet.

The scent of dusty pages accompanied the image before him. That confirmed it—not a dream.

Skar blinked but said nothing.

Je'Rol shivered in the cool air and rolled over, glad for the scent of grass to mask the goblin's scent. "Go home, Skar." Wherever that was. What *was* a goblin doing out there by himself? Were the books that important? If so, wouldn't there be guards standing watch? The books must not have been too valuable, except to Skar alone.

As the sun had set yesterday, Je'Rol had hurried from the grassy plateau and found a steep cliff that challenged him like the climb, but he had made it without hurting himself too much. The landing after losing his grip those last twenty feet had jarred him, but he could jump that height and tolerate the impact without injury. His fingers ached, though, with the strain of all that climbing.

He never would have expected a goblin to make it down, least of all one he'd tried to frighten from following. Now he understood how they could tolerate serving the demonlords.

The shuffle of fabric accompanied the feet hurrying around to stand before him.

"I cannot yet. I must know more about obelisk."

"You didn't answer my question. Why should I answer yours?" Je'Rol grumbled and pulled his hood over his face to ignore the goblin. He'd have to get up soon, though. Already the sun rose, and he hoped to cross the gorge he had spied to the north within two days. He really wished he didn't meet the demonlords at the ruins.

"I could not. That is your answer."

"Not the right one. Go home."

Skar stood in silence for some time, during which Je'Rol let out a heavy sigh and closed his eyes. Maybe if he went back to sleep, the little pest would be gone when he woke up again; or maybe he was having another bad dream.

"I keep natters away, lead you to more information?"

Je'Rol cracked his eyes open and looked up at the robed figure. "You know where I might find something?" He was curious how the goblin fought off natters but pushed the question aside to focus on the issue piquing his interest.

The goblin shrugged. "Not certain but I know ruins of Old Ones. I found old maps of world and continents and cities. Details. Lots of maps."

Je'Rol sat up, the temptation of the goblin's offer hanging before him with the appeal of fresh meat to the beast within. "Where?"

"In books. Protected by clan now in sacred place."

Je'Rol grimaced at the thought of the local ruling clan possessing these maps. "Demonlords."

Skar snorted. "Goblin clans. No demonlords have knowledge." After a moment, he wrung his hands together, his ears drooping. "You do not tell them."

"No. Not if you get me these maps." He'd be set in his search if the little demon could produce maps of each land and the ruins to search, if not for the obelisk, then something of the Master Race that might control demons.

"I cannot, but I know some cities after studied maps."

How convenient. The little goblin couldn't or wouldn't take him to these maps that he just happened to have seen? That left Je'Rol no choice but to take the scholar with him, which would slow him down.

The aggravation tempted the beast, and Je'Rol might just let it free if not for needing the demonlords to revive him from the blood rage the last time he gave in. He didn't have much time, and couldn't risk the demon side taking control again. Already he was older than any half-blood he'd met or heard about, but the struggle to restrain the demon side was a losing game. Without the obelisk, he would eventually fall into a blood rage from which he would never recover.

But he needed those maps. Desperation took hold, sinking into his soul like the claws of the beast, which extended now.

In a flash, he held the goblin by the collar of his robes, small feet kicking in the air high above the ground. Skar's fingers grasped futily at Je'Rol's wrists.

"Tell me where the maps are!" The words growled with the ferocity of the beast desiring fresh kill, even a goblin.

Skar gasped, his glasses no longer on the thin nose, leaving his eyes as beady as any goblin's. "I—I—I cannot! Not for demonlord…Not for half-blood."

With a snarl, Je'Rol threw him aside. Skar grunted as he hit the rocky face of a cliff and rolled, coughing, to the ground. The goblin was no use.

Now that Je'Rol was awake and standing, he might as well get moving. His stomach gurgled for food, but he'd have to hunt later. First, he wished to put distance between him and the goblin. He almost felt sorry for the servant who had been forced to Je'Rekun's feet or those thrown into the Dao arena, but now he saw why the demonlords treated them like fodder.

Still, something in him regretted the harsh treatment of the scholar, and he'd expected such an answer. But his temper grew short, especially when waking up to a pest like that.

"Don't follow me!" Before the goblin could respond, Je'Rol raced away. Those short legs wouldn't catch him anytime soon.

He ran roughly northeast, following the narrow valley curving between the slopes of mountains and hills. After a good distance between him and where he'd left the goblin, he slowed to a walk, satisfied that if Skar followed, he'd be too far behind to catch up any time soon.

As an opportunity to rest, Je'Rol stopped to let his senses take in the landscape. The sounds of animals scraping through underbrush, the flap of wings, the faint roar of a waterfall somewhere nearby, the dusky scent of feathers, and a hint of blood. These and more reached him. But the scent of blood fueled his hunger.

The faint sweetness of berries lured him to a nearby bush bearing its mostly red fruit. The small berries satisfied him temporarily, giving him some strength for hunting. The rodent he caught soon after provided some meat, but not near enough.

The waterfall would lure larger prey. He followed the sound and the scent of game grew stronger.

Trees thickened as he neared the water's edge. Where the mountains he had crossed had been steep and barren of much but grass and low brush, the gentler inclines gave way to denser foliage among rocky bluffs.

He leapt into the trees and landed on a branch almost twice his height from the ground. Another thick branch jutted out ahead, closer to the canopy top. From there, he might have a view of the landscape that had eluded him in the narrow valley of the mountains.

He sprang to the other branch, his claws catching the bark of the tree as he landed and securing his balance. The top of the canopy was close, requiring only a short climb, since no branches strong enough to hold him stretched any higher. With claws out, he pulled himself up the swaying, tapering end of the branch. Once he reached the height that would tolerate his weight, he moved aside small, leafy twigs.

The gorge he had spotted from the plateau of the ruins stretched out around him. He'd reached the nearest edge. Among the trees, tables of rock rose like step stones across a green valley.

The call of an animal echoed from somewhere. Birds roosted in tree tops, their chatter returning after his disruption. But he wasn't as much of a disruption as what flew overhead—a winged demonlord, its long tail snaking behind it.

Je'Rol let the branches cover most of his view again, not wishing to alert any demonlords to his location. After meeting High Lord Je'Rekun, he wouldn't have expected the tigers would share any of their domain.

Being watched from the sky would make it hard for him to hide from those hunting him, but he'd done it before, on most of the continents he'd visited. The only difference was that he rarely saw the flying demonlords in their natural state.

The raptor soared lazily, arching towards him. The colorful plumage of the body and wings gave way to a saw-toothed beak and a scaly head with few feathers. The long, scaly tail ended in a tuft of red and black feathers. Claws graced the wings and long talons on the legs tucked close to its brown and gold body.

He'd seen others of that clan from a distance but had never heard the name. Rather, he'd always avoided the deadly creatures.

As it circled closer, he slowly let the leafy branches cover him and froze in the tree top while it passed overhead, its shadow dwarfing him by double.

Silence accompanied its presence, as if the local fauna granted a show of respect for the demonlord, or hid from those hungry jaws. His own breath froze in his lungs until the demonlord veered off to the north, its wings unmoved from their massive stretch to continue the lazy glide.

Je'Rol watched through a gap between leaves until he was sure it continued away, before pushing aside the branches once more to scout the landscape. From the looks of it, he'd spend most of the day crossing the gorge before reaching a fissure on the other side. The jagged teeth of mountains broke the skyline to the north, beyond the hills rising to increasing heights to blend into those mountains.

He didn't want to go north, to encounter Je'Dron. It wasn't a matter of life or death; from the implications of Je'Rekun, Je'Dron would likely be glad to see him alive. Je'Rol wanted nothing to do with the man who had sired him. If there were any other ruins to search for the power to control his demon side, he would seek them.

Or he could go back for the goblin who claimed to have seen some maps showing where different ancient cities of the "Old Ones" were located. That idea irritated him into extending his claw deeper into the tree where he held on for balance.

No goblins. He had to keep moving. Unfortunately, that meant either meeting the man he wanted to kill or walking the land as he had in other domains to seek out any artifacts like the obelisk.

Su'Tari, the golden woman, had urged him to find the obelisk and destroy it. Je'Kaoron also knew of his quest, but he had been loyal to Je'Rekun. Maybe Je'Rekun already had the obelisk and Je'Kaoron had only toyed with him.

Je'Rekun couldn't have had it, though, or he wouldn't have needed Je'Rol to lure Je'Dron out. He would have had control over all the demons.

No one possessed it yet. Maybe it had been destroyed. Maybe he searched for nothing but the slow death of himself through each blood rage as the beast transformed him. Maybe it was all a futile effort and he should give up.

Giving up meant admitting that all these years had been a waste.

No giving up; he'd continue east. Maybe by the time he circled around to the south, Je'Rekun and the tigress who ruled the south would be out of power.

Then again, if Je'Dron would let him live, maybe helping him return to power would serve Je'Rol's purpose. With Je'Dron in power, he might have the freedom to search the entire tiger clan domain without being hunted, *if* the demonlord truly cared to let him live.

His fingers tightened around the tapered end of the branch, compressing the wood with the indentations of his claws. He gazed out at the hazy mountains to the north, his mind searching for another reason to avoid Je'Dron.

He found nothing, which agitated the beast. If Je'Rekun felt he could be used as leverage to lure out Je'Dron, the former High Lord wanted him alive. If not, then Je'Rol would lose his life.

Take his chances with Je'Dron or avoid the forces of Je'Rekun?

Je'Rol withdrew the claws and let out a deep breath. He would find Je'Dron, and maybe he'd have the chance to release the frustrations of a lifetime of fighting the monster bred into him by the demonlord.

He sprang to a lower branch but stayed in the trees. A few jumps along the lower branches brought him to the water's edge and a gap in the trees. Not a wide river, it flowed along the length of the gorge. On a low, thick branch tapering out over the river, he squatted next to the tree, gauging the distance and estimating the strength of the limb.

A familiar scent made his hair stand on end. Senses piqued and he sniffed, but the scent vanished as it had come. Had it been real? They couldn't have found him already! Yet, he was surprised they hadn't found him sooner.

No sound broke the soft melody of the wind gently rustling the leaves, insects buzzing in the still pockets of air, or the fast patter of a tiny heartbeat above him in the tree. Still, he twisted to scan his surroundings, searching for a hint of the scent again.

Nothing.

That didn't mean they weren't close. He didn't have the luxury of estimating his best chance of leaping across the river. He had to cross quickly.

Je'Rol braced one heel against the tree and stood, his eyes on the goal—a branch on the opposite side. He could grab it and swing or land on it; one way or the other, he'd get it.

Confident in his balance, he sprinted for the end of the branch. When he pressed down and gathered his legs, it dipped under his weight.

As he pushed off, a loud crack sounded, stealing his momentum and the arc of his jump. The river bank came up fast. He splashed down in mud and rocks and cold water up to his chest, spluttering and gasping. Using the roots of a tree to pull himself, he scrambled up the eroded bank to the grassy ledge over the water.

The damned branch! No one could have missed that crack, least of all the keen ears of demonlords. Hopefully his dunk in the river would erase his scent, although a true hunter would figure out that where a scent ended at water, the prey had crossed.

He didn't have time to hunt his own meal. He needed distance between him and the tigers he expected to be following. If he found something on the way, he'd eat, but until he returned to the mountains, he needed to cover ground.

Reaching Je'Dron before Je'Rekun's forces or Nadia found him might be his best chance of finding the peace he sought.

* * *

The wind rushed past her cheeks, the horse stretching out beneath her with legs pounding the earth. Nadia caught up to the tigresses running full out through the valley.

After spending the night at the farm, they'd discovered an impossible climb— except for the demonlords—and had to find a way out of the valley. While one tigress followed Je'Rol's scent up the cliff, the other stayed with her and the Li'Ador.

After a long day of travel, the tigresses had spied each other from rocky bluffs. Late in the night, they'd met and finally rested.

Since then, a few days had passed before the tigresses picked up a strong scent again.

Through the valley between mountains, Nadia led the Li'Ador after the orange tigers. Her horse kept up to them as they approached a shape ahead. Like a pile of dirt, it seemed innocuous, until something shifted and a green face caught the glare of the sun.

The tigresses slowed, and Nadia sat back on her horse and slowed it from the mad dash.

The robed figure's eyes looked oddly larger than usual behind a strange adornment of glasses balanced on his nose. A goblin.

The tigresses blurred and transformed. One of them revealed a head of copper and black hair tied out of her face. Je'Mika had transformed fully human a couple times since meeting the boy, Arak. She had given the boy long looks, making Nadia wonder if the demonlords sensed the controlling aura of the Adepts the way natters seemed to;

but demonlords never talked about their true powers.

The tigress's lip curled back in a snarl. "Goblin," she spat.

It looked ready to object but cowered at the glare from the two armored tigresses.

"I thought you found Je'Rol's scent." Nadia rode her horse near, wishing she had the demonlords' senses.

Je'Raoni sniffed, her face mostly concealed in the tiger-styled helmet. "I did, or do."

"I get it too."

The goblin blinked its dark eyes and opened its mouth. A moment later, it grabbed its throat, the line where a brow should have been pressing down over his eyes in a confused look.

"You can't speak?" Nadia asked. Couldn't any goblins speak?

He shook his head.

"Cursed." Je'Mika crossed her arms. "With good reason. I hear their voices could curdle milk."

In all her travels, Nadia had never seen a goblin wandering alone, but she seemed to remember a brief mention in her training about goblins being cursed.

"Legends say the oldest demonlords cast a spell on them never to speak in their presence. I tend to agree that goblins should neither be seen nor heard, that they perform their duties as if invisible." Je'Mika's eyes narrowed in warning at the goblin, who took a step back.

"But he smells like Je'Rol?" Je'Mika's story wasn't the one her teachers had recited from the Book of Kirian, but the sacred text was unknown to demonlords, and she wasn't about to argue and reveal her knowledge.

Both tigresses wrinkled their human noses. "He bears the scent of the half-blood."

Nadia gazed at the goblin. He seemed to want to speak, but the curse of not speaking in the presence of demonlords forbade him from saying anything. How far away from the demonlords would a goblin have to be to regain his voice? Sending the tigresses away while she used her power to make him tell her about his encounter with Je'Rol could wait for nightfall. With the sun up, they needed to regain their trail of the real Je'Rol.

Nadia's horse chewed its bit, clinking the metal and distracting her for a moment. "Bring him along." She'd question him later.

Je'Raoni snatched the goblin, which kicked and clawed at her to no effect. He landed on the saddle of one of the Li'Ador, where a growl from the tigress warned him to cease his struggles.

The demonlords transformed once more and circled the area for a few minutes. Oddly, they picked up the trail in the direction the goblin had been traveling. Had he been following Je'Rol? For how long? Why?

Questions filled Nadia's head, drawing her eyes to the odd little demon squeezed between one of the black and silver uniformed soldiers and the high pommel of the saddle. Wiry green fingers turned white clutching the rise of the pommel rolled over and stitched. The odd glasses tilted on his nose. He was not like any goblins she had seen before, but she'd only seen them in the presence of their demonlord masters, never alone. None of her teachers knew anything about goblins, except their relationships with the demonlords. It inspired more questions to ask, if she had time.

They followed the trail until nightfall, when they arrived at a gorge where trees grew thick and the rush of a waterfall blended with the calls of animals. A more perfect place to camp she couldn't imagine.

The tigresses followed the scent to the water's edge, where it vanished. One of them climbed into a tree, gripping with long claws and sniffing out onto a limb broken off over the water. Her tail whipped side to side and black-tipped ears perked up as she stared across the dark water into the shadows of the opposite bank.

After some time, the tigress rushed down head first and transformed, spooking the horses at the abrupt change of shadows in the night. "He jumped across, but didn't make it. It's too dark to see where he might have climbed out. With the sun, I'll know more."

In other words, this was the place they would camp among the trees. In the morning, they'd have better luck finding a place for the horses to cross too. From the darkness, Nadia could only make out the outlines of an eroded bank too steep for the horses to climb out. One of the tigresses could jump it and keep to the trail, as they'd done before, while the other led her and the Li'Ador to catch up.

This was how he'd done it all those years—making it nearly impossible for a human alone to track him, and the demonlords really only cared when they encountered a half-blood by chance. It wasn't their job to hunt for anything more than actual food, and they didn't eat other demons, especially not half demonlords.

Nadia ordered the men to set up camp there and heard more than a few relieved mumblings. Amid the clinking and squeaking of tack and equipment, she caught the eyes of the tigresses in the wan light of the rising moon. The lithe shapes detached from the land to join her. "My ladies, might I be so bold to ask for some protection from natters?"

She didn't have to say any more; they understood. One of them gave a low grunt and both shadows trotted off to merge into the night.

Now for the little demon.

Nadia found him with his hands tied and his shoulders held by one of the men. The flicker of two fires outlined his features with an orange glow and deep shadows.

Although she'd never had a reason to control a goblin, she discovered his will easy to master. Nothing blocked her. Her teachers were right—only demonlords stood out with the power to resist the Adepts of Te'Mea. "Tell me where you met Je'Rol."

He opened his mouth but only a gurgle came from his throat. The tigresses must have been too close yet. She'd have to wait.

So be it. Nadia had patience. They had all night. The soldiers set up camp while she watched, several of them caring for the horses and others started meals. Two of them remained with her, one holding the goblin and the other for reinforcement.

As the men settled, she returned her attention to the goblin. "Can you speak now?"

"Yes."

Nadia winced. Je'Mika wasn't too far off when she said goblin voices could curdle milk.

Nadia refocused on his will. "Tell me where you met Je'Rol."

"At ruins of Old Ones."

"Ruins? We didn't pass any ruins."

"High above valley."

A mountaintop? "What was he doing there? What were *you* doing there?"

The goblin blinked. "He found me in learning place. I am Skar of my clan. I read. I learn. I teach others."

"Skar? Is that your name or a title?" Or was she hearing wrong and he meant scholar?

"I am Skar, not other."

"All right...Skar." Whatever it was, he seemed to prefer it. Not even her *dispirit* could determine how he interpreted what she asked or force him to give a clear answer she would understand, but she didn't usually use her power to interrogate demons. Rather, she used it to stall them for the killing blow. "What was Je'Rol doing?"

"Searching."

The boy had said Je'Rol mentioned searching for an artifact but didn't know or didn't remember what. Did the goblin? "What was he searching for?"

"Ancient artifact—obelisk of Mai'Kari. We believed it destroyed, but he believed it exists."

Obelisk of Mai'Kari? She hadn't heard of such a device. "Why? What does he plan to do with this artifact?"

"Control demon side. He is half-blood."

Control the demon side? Did the goblin mean that Je'Rol wanted to prevent the blood rage or was there something else to it? Was it possible for a half-blood to stop the demon side from taking over? "How?"

"Old Ones controlled all demons, ruled demonlords. Knowledge recorded was discovered by Mai'Ekam. Mai'Kari was creator of many objects with magic. Obelisk was one to control demons."

Her blood ran cold at the prospects. The Mai'Ekam had used the power of the Master Race to create talismans for controlling other clans? The two sorcerers who had visited to warn her about the demonlords' gathering in Dev Nadir said something about control stones feared by the demonlords. Could those have been creations by this Mai'Kari demonlord or something of the Master Race? She should have questioned them further when they visited, but they'd only said the stones…

"*Sect du Cantir Te'Mea*," she breathed. What were the sorcerers up to? What dark magic had they discovered? A shudder passed through her from the possibilities springing up in her mind about the real reason for the demonlords wanting to eliminate the Adepts of Te'Mea. She hadn't wanted to believe they would, but if they suspected Adepts of already possessing the ability to control demonlords, they had a reason to act to protect their dominance.

When she finished with Je'Rol, she'd return to Temple *Katuna Te'Mea*. If something big was going on within the inner politics of the heart of their sects, while she risked her life for them to pretend status quo, she wanted to know what she risked her life for. She wasn't a pawn in their game for dominance of Derandria.

"Huntress?" one of the men asked.

Nadia shook her head. "Nothing." They didn't need to know.

She refocused on the goblin. "Where is this obelisk?"

"We thought it destroyed. Je'Rol searches ruins for answers. Closest known are north."

North, then maybe Je'Rekun was right after all, *if* Je'Rol did indeed head that way, and only in a roundabout way. By the movement of the sun, she estimated they currently headed northeast following his trail.

The tigresses would track him. They were close. Nadia was sure of it.

"What else did Je'Rol tell you?"

"To go home."

Like his encounter with the boy, Je'Rol wished the goblin to leave him alone. He probably traveled faster, but he had only himself to depend on for his needs, which probably slowed him down. Hunting, hiding, natters…they all cut out time from his running. She'd catch him soon.

"Tie him up," she told the soldiers. "He may still be useful."

"Yes, Huntress."

Although she didn't know what use a goblin might be, she didn't want to let him go to warn Je'Rol, if he was close. And if Skar knew something about the Master Race, she could question him alone when she had the chance.

22

The scent was stronger. Je'Rol froze in the branches of a tree, all senses alert to his surroundings.

After a filling meal by a chance encounter with a grundling, a meaty, flightless bird, he'd slept well, or as well as he could amid the horrible dreams. The images of mutilated corpses had chased him into a chasm and trapped him, then transformed into swarms of natters that bit and clawed him. Upon waking, he'd discovered a particularly hungry young one gnawing on his thigh and squashed it with one blow of his fist.

The pain in his leg interrupted his sleep the rest of the night, along with his fear that he'd slept too soundly and needed to stay alert, especially since his wound would attract other natters. He'd been overly exhausted after covering more distance that day than he had the previous two days together.

If Je'Sikar had told him right, he'd need to reach Je'Dron before Je'Rekun sprang his trap. He'd lost track of the days that had passed since his escape from the High Lord's chains, but avoiding the demonlords serving Je'Rekun kept him alert. Not knowing which demonlords he could trust made the journey difficult.

They would find him with their acute senses, but he wouldn't give up without a fight.

His thigh ached from the crouch on the fork of two thick branches. Where the natter had chewed, he had a small dip in his muscle. He'd torn off part of his tunic to tie around the wound and stop the bleeding. It would be safe to remove it in a few days, but in the meantime, the scent of an open wound would attract demons of all kinds. They'd hunt him like the wounded prey he was.

But this prey had claws of its own.

The wind shifted slightly and the faint scent vanished again. Had they picked up his trail or not? Or did the demonlords not care what he was? He might have a chance of slipping past them if they were the typical clan members in their own territory. Many didn't care to bother him in his travels when they could have easily stopped him. He wasn't a problem to them and they didn't want to create one.

He couldn't risk being caught there, one way or the other, and had to keep moving.

Finding Je'Dron before Je'Rekun's forces found him was his goal now.

He dropped to the ground, and nearly collapsed at the ache in his thigh, and took some comfort in knowing the small natter had eaten its last meal.

On the ground, he ran as fast as the pain allowed, passing along the narrow trail worn smooth by animals. He made out the impressions of split hooves, but there were other prints there too, larger than his hands—tigers most likely. They knew the game trails.

It meant he'd find food as easily as they might find him, but it didn't matter. He had to continue, and this was the best way to avoid the trouble of the low areas, which would make a chance encounter with a tiger more likely.

Winding up and down the mountains, the trail continued roughly north. Je'Rol stayed on it through the day, finding sufficient water a couple times as it crossed large and small streams from springs in the low areas.

But it was while drinking the cold, clear water of a larger stream that the thunder reached him. From his kneeling position next to the water, he sat back and pulled the hood away from an ear, his head tilted until he found the strongest sound—from behind him, not above.

Something with hooves raced towards him, and he'd bet it wasn't a stampeding herd of goats.

Horses, most likely with riders.

The wind didn't bring their scents. It blew from him. Damn! He'd been too distracted by the wound and keeping to the trail to realize the wind had switched.

The realizations shocked his heart into skipping on that moment. In the next, he was on his feet and in the air across the stream.

The roar of tigers echoed from behind. He'd never outrun the demonlords, but he might outsmart them.

There was nowhere to go. Steep cliffs on one side and rough terrain on the other blocked his escape.

And the scent of tigers came from ahead.

Je'Rol froze, scanning his surroundings for something to help him escape. Two tigers bore down on him from behind, their orange and black flashing with each swift stride, bodies elongating and condensing with the grace and prowess of demonlords.

He leapt up the steep angle of the grassy incline next to him, but the demonlords were faster.

Before he could gather his feet to launch himself farther, one of the tigers beat him to it. Snarling fangs threatened him from above with the body pressed close to the grass and rocks. He couldn't fight on the incline.

The other tiger crept up from below.

The thunder of hooves slowed and splashed in water. The riders spread out along the low area little more than a wide trench through which the stream flowed.

He was surrounded, and by the black and silver armor, he didn't have much of a chance.

The black-cloaked figure threw back its hood and he almost fell from his precarious position. Nadia stared up at him, the severe lines of her face cut the light into areas of shadow, carving out a woman's face rather than the smooth roundness of the young girl from his past. The Nadia he had known was gone.

"Come to me, Je'Rol." She called, and his heart sought to obey.

The tiger above him slid closer, kicking loose gravel onto him.

Je'Rol snarled at them in a futile effort to frighten them off, but the tiger's claws flexed, its ears pinned flat to its head and lips pulled back to bare sharp teeth.

The beast took the challenge, growling in defiance.

No. Nadia called him.

"Je'Rol."

He turned to face her. She sat astride her horse below, dressed in the black of a demon hunter.

No. He couldn't obey, the beast insisted on fighting, yet each second also tempered its defiance.

A clatter of rocks rained upon him, drawing his attention to the tiger sliding towards him.

Voices whispered below, but his eyes focused on the threat above.

The pull of Nadia's presence quelled the beast's determination in the face of the tiger—

Until an arrow sank its biting pain deep into his sore thigh. He whirled and lost his security on the grassy tufts. In a blink, he rolled down the steep incline and knocked against the other tiger.

Teeth clamped around his upper arm.

"Give up, Je'Rol, and she won't hurt you." Nadia spoke in a soothing but commanding voice.

He would not give up. He would not return to Je'Rekun. And he would not face Nadia the demon hunter.

The beast growled for escape, clawing at the tiger holding him. She bit harder but not to make him bleed, and the beast struggled against his control and Nadia's *dispirit*. His claws extended, and with his free hand, he swiped at the tiger's face. She howled, releasing her grip, and he kicked away to roll past her to the feet of the horses shying back. As he reached the bottom, he untangled from the cloak wrapped around him.

The other tiger jumped mid-slide, but he was too late to avoid being knocked back into the water. He opened his mouth to gasp but choked on the frigid water. Panic swept over him to breathe. In that moment, the beast ripped free of his control.

* * *

"Give him air! Let him up!" Drowning Je'Rol would do no good.

Nadia was too late. Je'Rol's head lifted from the water, the sharp teeth of a predator exposed from lips pulled back in a visceral snarl.

Her heart pounded in her chest, her eyes meeting the pale blue of his, but it wasn't the eyes that stole her breath. His whole face transformed into something neither human nor tiger, with his nose wider and lifted into his forehead to a jaw that had extended to accommodate the teeth.

"Blood rage!" one of the men shouted. "Get back!"

The tigress held her ground, and the second joined her.

But Je'Rol was quick and jumped clear. Instead of fighting the tigresses near him, he leapt and ripped the throat from one man before he could scream.

Nadia focused on her power, but the clatter of arrows knocking on bows stopped her heart. "Don't! We need him alive." Dead only if absolutely necessary, and Rissan was already dead.

They hesitated while the horse spooked and the soldier thumped to the ground. Je'Rol jumped for the horse's neck and brought it down amid the snorting and whirling of the others. Several Li'Ador jumped down to regain control and handed off their reins to others to better handle their weapons and defend against him rather than run.

Four soldiers stood ready to loose their arrows, while four others held the horses, the rest gone.

His face and clothes bloody, Je'Rol looked up from the still horse and met her eyes with a snarl, but he made no move to attack. His attention shifted to the tigresses circling him warily.

The soldiers on the ground were ready to take him on foot and more than capable as a team. They left the others, who had calmed the horses, and circled wide around him, intending to cut off his escape route and aid the tigresses closing in.

Two orange and black blurs knocked the tigresses away.

Bowstrings twanged.

And a white and black blur interrupted their flight, solidifying as a man in leggings and a tunic of a tiger-striped pattern, his silvery-white hair with the black in it pulled back from the sides out of that angular face. He whirled to face her, holding three arrows in his hands.

Je'Rol roared, then sank his teeth in deep and ripped out a chunk of bloody flesh from the horse he'd brought down. With it still in his mouth, he looked up and snarled in warning.

Now was their chance. "Take him!"

"Stop!" The demonlord royal stepped between them and Je'Rol, his eyes unwavering from Nadia. She recognized him, but he shouldn't have been there. In what seemed no effort, Je'Kaoron snapped the arrows with his fingers.

Nadia looked past him to Je'Rol and the Li'Ador awaiting her command and noticed the tigresses pinned beneath two other orange tigers. "Je'Rol…"

Blood smeared his face and hands, but that face wasn't human. She hardly recognized him.

"Remember who you are, Je'Rol." The command was more than an attempt at control. It came as a plea from the girl she used to be.

He growled and, with a chunk of bloody muscle and hide in his mouth, ran off.

"After him."

"No! Leave him." Je'Kaoron growled and the horses of the nearest soldiers snorted and backed away.

"I can't let that murderer escape." Why would Je'Kaoron let him leave like that? Lord Je'Rekun wanted the half-blood captured, or killed if necessary. Je'Kaoron served Je'Rekun.

Je'Kaoron marched up to her horse as if it wasn't there, his gaze fixed on her with a hardness she wouldn't have expected from him. "You will if you wish to live."

"High Lord Je'Rekun—"

"Je'Rol is wanted alive, Huntress." He threw down the broken arrows. "Chasing him in the blood rage will only make it worse. It should never have happened. If you wish to see him human again, you will end this pursuit now."

She met his hard gaze with the strength of her will, but he deflected her power as if it was nothing but a pesky insect.

"Do not forfeit your life, woman!" He growled and her horse stiffened and snorted, distracting her from him to settle the frightened animal. After a few seconds, the rumble from his throat subsided and he exhaled a deep breath that seemed to steal his anger. "Je'Rekun needs him human for his plans. If you wish to finish your task, I suggest you meet the High Lord at the Nik'Terek Gate in six days."

A shudder passed through her, and the horse let out another snort. "Easy boy." She spoke to calm the horse but watched the demonlord.

A second later, he turned away, his figure blurring and dropping. A white tiger growled and ran off. The two orange guards which had accompanied him ran off after him, leaving the tigresses with no more than hurt pride.

Already the two growled after the trio, their ears pinned and tails lashing. The tigresses were right to be upset. Je'Rol was their responsibility. Je'Kaoron's was to deliver the message to Je'Dron. From the lack of the cylinder around his neck, she guessed that task had been completed. So why had he been there? Why would he pursue Je'Rol only to let him go?

The desire for answers drove her heels into the horse. "Camin. Markos. Bring the others. Sarkin took the goblin. I want him. Lady Je'Mika—" She calmed her voice from the commanding tone, begrudging the tigress the respect they'd chastised her about last night. The Li'Ador deferred to demon hunters as their superiors and all were required to grant demonlords of either gender the highest respect. How easily she forgot when addressing the demonlords during their pursuit. After the harsh words from the two in the early hours, she wouldn't soon forget again. "They'll need you to track us, if you would join them. The rest of you, after Je'Rol." She didn't care what Je'Kaoron said about following. Nadia TuFalan didn't lose a hunt.

23

It all happened as he remembered—bits and pieces—but the pieces he could remember were less. He was losing to the beast.

Je'Rol recognized only one moment of light in the darkness of the beast's savagery. The beast had wanted to kill Nadia, but from the corner where he resided in that part of him, humanity screamed to leave her unharmed. Her *dispirit* of the demon had soothed it. Her voice had coaxed him from the farthest corner of his mind, the humanity returning for that moment and struggling to regain control. But the beast had won and resorted to eating the horse to satisfy its hunger for the warm flesh of a fresh kill. Rather than let it attack anyone else, he'd taken some control to flee. Nadia's power had given him that much.

He remembered nothing else except for waking covered in blood with a full stomach and his left leg aching. The arrow was gone, though.

"You reek."

Je'Rol lifted his head and stared into the face of the demonlord who'd brought him to that domain, the once immaculate white and black clothes now smeared with blood. Anger seethed within him at the betrayal, tempting the beast to return. It growled in anger, and he leapt at the demonlord.

Like Je'Sikar had in the tunnels, Je'Kaoron did nothing when Je'Rol attacked and pinned him to the hard ground with its scattered tufts of grass. The demonlord could easily have thrown him aside like a child's doll. Instead, Je'Kaoron lay beneath him, calmly accepting whatever punishment came.

Je'Rol pressed on the demonlord's shoulders, aware of the two guards standing over him.

When Je'Kaoron lifted a hand, the two backed off. "You're entitled to your opinion," he said with that irritating calm.

"Leave me alone!" Je'Rol growled. Claws extended, sinking into the demonlord's shoulders, but Je'Kaoron gave no reaction if he felt any pain. The demonlord's blood blended with the overwhelming stench of human and horse blood. "You brought me here for your High Lord Je'Rekun's amusement. I won't be used like that!"

"I never wished any harm, or you would not be here. I warned you to escape."

"You gave me to the Li'Ador and Nadia."

A hint of a smile turned up the corners of the demonlord's human face. "I could not jeopardize my position of High Lord Je'Rekun's trust. The humans would speak if I gave any indications of my duplicity and I would have been executed. I had to play my part in every way. My true loyalties belong to Je'Dron."

"Liar!" Je'Rol roared, digging his claws deeper into the soft flesh of the demonlord's shoulders.

Je'Kaoron lay still, his face showing no signs of pain. "You're entitled to your opinions, but Lord Je'Dron awaits your arrival."

The crunch of feet on grass and gravel indicated movement behind Je'Rol. If not for the blood covering him, he might have caught the approach of others by their scents. In the silence, the heartbeats of at least four individuals reached his ears.

Je'Rol peered over his shoulder at half a dozen different demonlords standing on the hillside grass and rock. Even if he wanted to kill Je'Kaoron, he'd never escape, but he didn't want to kill anyone. He just wanted an honest answer. Whose side was Je'Kaoron on?

He'd probably never know until he was betrayed, but he didn't have much of a choice at the moment. He had to trust Je'Kaoron.

He shrank the claws and backed off.

Je'Kaoron stood with the grace and calm as of nothing happening and extended his arm to point through the five non-tiger demonlords to the peak towering in the distance. "Your presence is expected at Mount Serako."

The others made no move to close in but stood in their human forms in silence, waiting. Je'Rol recognized a couple other than the tigers. Their presence on Tikeros meant something big was happening. The demonlords rarely accepted other clans into their territory for fear of diminishing their hunting; thus the many wars in any given year. The golden lady had said she supported Je'Dron. Apparently more than the Su'Kora were on his side, and this was more than a little intra-clan dispute, like the meeting in Dev Nadir organized by the bear clan. Was this why Je'Rekun needed him alive—as leverage?

Je'Rol snarled but went ahead, while the others closed in on him and Je'Kaoron and his tiger guards.

They walked as a group, he and Je'Kaoron in the center of a rough circle of other demonlords, who remained quiet. Ahead wound a road along the mountain ledges, hewn to form a wide, flat ribbon along the mountainsides. It went on into the distance, where one mountain rose above the others. Although he'd never set foot on Tikeros since his mother fled with him overseas as a young child, he would guess that hazy-peaked prominence was Mount Serako.

Next to him, Je'Kaoron glanced aside as if something caught his attention, but he said nothing. Only a faint twitch of the corner of his mouth hinted of any reaction, but the demonlord gave nothing more away.

If he wasn't covered in blood, Je'Rol might have detected whatever his host caught on the wind, but a bath would have to wait.

Je'Rol ignored him the rest of the walk along the road. He'd decided Je'Dron was his best chance of freedom to search Tikeros for the obelisk, but two questions now plagued him—who could he really trust and what happened if Je'Dron lost this dispute?

* * *

"They're taking the road north."

Nadia glanced aside at the soldier next to her. The intricate curls and the fanlike shape of ears formed into the black helmet with the silver trim worn by what had become her primary lieutenant for the Li'Ador accompanying her—Captain Karik. After Je'Rol's kill, she was down to ten, and that shouldn't have happened.

"Mount Serako," she said as a cool breeze billowed under her hood. Upon the summit of a small hill, they sat astride their horses. The goblin sat in the saddle with one of the other men, his knuckles no longer white. He seemed to have grown accustomed to balancing on the horse, squished between the man and the pommel of the saddle.

She couldn't hope to win against one demonlord, much less eight. Even worse, she couldn't return to High Lord Je'Rekun empty handed. He might have sent the tigresses to aid her, but he'd also sent them to observe.

"Lead the way," she said.

Dark eyes in the shadow of the helmet met hers. He gave a nod and turned his horse. She gave the demonlords and Je'Rol one more glance and followed the Li'Ador—Captain Karik knew this land better than she did.

* * *

As on the voyage of the ship, Je'Kaoron said nothing to Je'Rol, except to order him away some distance due to his stench. The others also kept their distance.

At the end of the first day of walking, they found a place to rest on a plateau above the land stretching far around and below them, corralled only by mountains towering as an impassable fence. A few trees and boulders called the plateau home, large enough to provide shelter from the winds and from sight.

Most of the demonlords took on their natural forms to rest. One of them matched the raptor he'd seen from the tree, confirming his suspicions that Je'Kaoron had been searching for him.

Je'Rol watched the colorful plumage on the giant lizard-bird blend into the night sky, the flap of its wings fading quickly as it gained altitude.

"Val'Tiro. They used to share the Je'Gri domain." Je'Kaoron sat down with his back to a boulder and stretched his legs. "Until High Lord Je'Rekun ordered their nests destroyed if they didn't leave."

Je'Rol grunted and scanned the shadows of the ground for a grassy patch; the demonlord had taken the best boulder. "So, I'm supposed to believe Je'Dron was a benevolent dictator, one who spared half-bloods?"

"No." Je'Kaoron leaned back with his hands behind his head and let out a heavy sigh. "Je'Dron led his share of battles against clans to the north and east. He protected the Je'Gri domain, but he would never betray his allies."

Je'Rol stared away to the north, to the edges of their plateau high ground. Beyond the nearest tree, the shadows of predators haunted them. All but Je'Kaoron had settled into their natural forms and arranged themselves along the perimeter of the plateau, ranging from a lion and the two orange tiger guards to a large canine with spines down its back to a black bipedal dragonlike creature he recognized as a Ra'Lof. Why didn't the royal tiger change? It would save Je'Rol from talking to him. Or did he prefer the human form?

Or was this a way of making him feel more comfortable while surrounded by demonlords?

Whatever the reason, Je'Rol felt no gratitude, only a begrudging reluctance to cooperate. The demonlords could do as they wished. He only wanted the consent of Je'Dron to continue his search, and for that, he had to reach him, which meant letting Je'Kaoron lead him to the mountain.

After some time, Je'Rol found a patch of cool grass to stretch out. He closed his eyes and drifted into strange dreams where he roamed the land as a tiger.

He woke up to the dawning sun, a stiff mountain breeze, and the fresh scent of a new kill.

"Eat."

He blinked and sat up to the stern face of a woman. She wore her black tresses tied back from an angular face of a harsh beauty above the curves of a scaly armored body suit, probably the Ra'Lof he had seen last night. At her feet lay the bloody remains of a carcass.

Je'Kaoron was no longer near him, but a white tiger sat facing the sunrise while licking its coat.

"You sleep too long, and you stink," the woman said.

Je'Rol curled his lip back in a slight snarl, the beast rumbling defiance in his throat. The woman gave no reaction, where a human would have backed away in fear of upsetting him. Instead, she gave him a dark look and walked away.

The dried blood on his clothes did stink. He'd tried not to notice and had almost forgotten. Almost. At the first chance, he'd wash it off; before then, they'd offered fresh kill. He didn't have to worry about soiling his clothes if they were already crusted with blood.

Je'Rol ate less than he'd expected, but he recalled the images of attacking a horse the day before and a feeling of fullness upon waking from the beast's control. It had fed yesterday, but at least it hadn't been on Nadia.

As Je'Rol finished, Je'Kaoron blurred and transformed. His robes were clean like the first time Je'Rol had met him in the company of a variety of demonlords representing different clans, except for a faint pink on the sleeves. He turned from the sliver of sunlight cresting the mountains but said nothing.

"They grow impatient," the voice warned him. *"I would not displease them. Ra'Soria has a nasty temper."*

With a low growl of frustration, Je'Rol wiped his mouth on his sleeve and joined the Je'Gri ambassador.

"Your friend is not far behind. What should become of her?"

Did the demonlord honestly seek his answer or was this part of his game? Whatever the outcome, Je'Rol had no intention of giving Nadia another chance, but part of him despaired at the thought of them hurting her.

"Leave her."

White eyebrows lifted on a face of measured curiosity. "You wish her to interfere with your search?"

"No. But I don't want your kind hurting her."

A reproachful frown melted away the curiosity. "I would not hurt her."

"What about them?" Je'Rol motioned his chin towards two of the demonlords standing ready nearby.

"They respect the Adepts of Te'Mea and the Li'Ador who protect the humans from natters; but they know the stakes of our mission aren't worth sacrificing for one demon hunter's revenge."

"You didn't answer my question," he growled. Claws extended with his impatience.

"They would do all they could to deter her without bringing harm."

Je'Rol looked at one of the women in leggings and a blouse of a deep green with brushes of blue and purple and hints of brown throughout and a man with his white front darkening to brown on the back of his robes and matching hair tied up in a tail. Dark eyes met Je'Rol's with warning scowls.

He didn't trust them, but his word probably meant nothing, coming as it did from a half-blood. "Leave her…Let's go." He started down the plateau to the road along the mountainside.

The demonlords surrounded him once more, while they trekked through the day towards a wall of mountain ahead. The road wound down to a valley floor, where it all but disappeared among the foliage. The mist of a tall waterfall cast ephemeral rainbows into the air against the mountainside ahead, the roar only a faded whisper to his ears from the far end but growing louder as they approached.

They crossed the stream at a narrow point after bending down to drink. One of the men insisted Je'Rol submerge himself to bathe. He begrudged them because he also couldn't stand the reminder of his last blood rage. He handed his cloak to Je'Kaoron, who carried it along a narrow foot bridge to the other side with his group of myriad demonlords. The little blood staining it could be scrubbed later. He'd want it dry when he stepped out into the chilly air.

The last time he'd bathed had been to clean dried natter guts off. This time, the cleaning wasn't so bad, except for where he'd wiped blood from his face, and most of that was on a corner of his cloak.

He shivered in the stream but submerged his body and scrubbed rigorously to remove the dried blood. Shivering and nearly blue, he stepped from the water soaked from head to toe and took his cloak from Je'Kaoron. After securing it again, he walked back to the water to clean that corner.

"Now you wish to wash your cloak? Have you not wet yourself enough?"

"Blood."

Je'Kaoron followed him, his steps crunching on the grass. "The blood is tolerable, even preferable. The stink of human after some time is not."

The stink of human...not the answer he expected. They preyed upon humans and lesser animals without washing them. Yet they couldn't stand the smell of live humans after a few days of sweat and filth? He would have expected the dried blood to bother them more, or maybe that was him, a result of his guilt of the blood rage. He noticed the stench of sweaty, dirty humans and disliked it too. How much of that had been him, his human side?

He smelled human to them, as other half-bloods had smelled not quite human to him. The demonlord scent was light in their human forms, usually fragrant, but if they remained in their natural forms, the scent was altered. He guessed it had something to do with their transformation, a work of the magic that was the demonlords, but he would never know.

"Leave the cloak. Your friend is near."

Je'Rol sniffed the breeze blowing from the southwest. The faint hint of dirty human carried to him now that he wasn't overwhelmed by the odor of blood.

"Time to move." Je'Kaoron motioned ahead.

Two of the demonlords transformed—one into the canine form with bony spikes along its back and a shoulder nearly level with Je'Rol's and the other into a snakelike reptile with four legs on which it moved surprisingly fast. The pair disappeared over the river and into the foliage.

Alarm awoke the beast to fight the demonlords, but Je'Rol held it in check, the claws only extending a little.

"They won't touch the hunters, only spook their horses to slow their progress. Come now." Je'Kaoron spoke with a firm, commanding voice.

After a moment of staring after where the demonlords had vanished, Je'Rol followed. He shouldn't care for Nadia anymore, not now that she was a demon hunter determined to see him dead, but he wouldn't sacrifice her to the demonlords.

"They better leave her alone," he grumbled next to Je'Kaoron, who said nothing.

The anger subsided as they walked and the roar of the waterfall grew louder, drowning out all but the highest whoop or trill of a bird. A cool mist permanently hung in the air at the base, where a bridge crossed the pond it formed before diverting into the river.

But they weren't crossing. Rather, along the steep cliff, a staircase only accessible on foot angled up with wide landings on ledges along the zigzagging climb.

The demonlords led him up the stairs hewn from the rock, stopping to rest on the first landing. From there, Je'Rol overlooked the trees and spotted movement to the southwest. The water crashing on the ledge, which extended across its path, drowned out all sounds.

At the third ledge, they stopped and gathered along the rocky wall. Ra'Soria traced her finger along the rock in a pattern of curved and straight lines looping over each other into a complex circle. The moment she finished, the pattern glowed and the ground vibrated under their feet.

Je'Rol waited, expecting the demonlords knew what they were doing and not bringing the mountain tumbling down on him. One looked out over the valley and the mountains around it. He followed the man's eyes and caught the movement of something dark, but they were too high to see clearly whether it was Nadia in her black cloak or the Li'Ador in their black and silver uniforms. One was as bad as the other.

The grinding of stone over the crashing of water snapped his attention back to the rock, which disappeared into darkness. A doorway! Then Je'Dron wasn't *at* Mount Serako, but *inside* it.

"A new world awaits within," Je'Kaoron said with his arm extended towards the darkness.

* * *

The rock reappeared as if nothing had happened. Nadia wouldn't have believed it if she hadn't seen it. Not even the sorcerers could make solid rock disappear like that.

"Interesting," Je'Mika said.

Nadia looked down from her horse at the armored woman. "More than that."

The rider bearing Skar rode up on her other side. They'd been rotating several times a day to relieve each man of the burden and the discomfort of the extra rider in his saddle. "He's been yanking on my arm and pointing the whole time." Lieutenant Molinar itched his grizzly chin. "I think the goblin knows something."

Skar blinked behind his glasses, his mouth open as if to speak, but nothing came out.

The tigresses. They were too close, but so were other demonlords.

She wanted to know what this little demon had to say about the mountain and the strange light that had glowed briefly before the rock disappeared. The tigresses had to go, at least for a while.

"Lady Je'Raoni."

The tigress blurred and transformed to an armored guard. "Yes, Huntress."

"Would you both scout for spies? We don't need any more trouble." The two demonlords who had spooked the horses had been enough trouble for one day.

The tigresses nodded to each other and transformed without a word.

"Bring the goblin. Captain!"

The jingle of metal accompanied the squeak of leather and the soft thump of hooves on the ground. Captain Karik reined his horse next to her.

"Split your men into two groups. Send one around each side to see where they might come out. With luck, I'll meet you on the other side, or back here."

His dark beard shifted with the movement of his jaw, until a shrug seemed to loosen any hesitations. "If they came out somewhere."

"If not, someone will be here when they return—me."

"You're staying here alone?"

She glanced aside at the goblin and the man crammed into the saddle. "I'll have company. Have your men ride around and signal if they see any sign of Je'Rol."

"Yes, Huntress." He motioned to the men around them and called out orders. They galloped away through trees and brush.

Their last two horses danced to join the others, but she reined her horse closer to the remaining soldier and it calmed.

Je'Rol was hers to recapture and she wanted to know why Je'Kaoron had taken him here, likely to Je'Dron. Although she preferred that Je'Dron not fall for his brother's plan, High Lord Je'Rekun would be furious that his plan had gone awry. She couldn't return to him empty handed and risk her reputation, especially if he reported her to the *Kodre Noctir du Te'Mea*, the elder Adepts who governed both sects, and this was her only option for recovering Je'Rol to finish her task.

"Tell me, Skar, what you know."

He opened his mouth and nothing came out. Damn it! There might be too many demonlords around for him to speak.

"Then we wait." She wasn't giving up this hunt.

24

The moment the crash of the waterfall cut off from the door resealing itself, lights blinked on along smooth walls, illuminating a corridor, but not one Je'Rol would have expected. No natters had been here, but with the door sealed, he wouldn't expect them to unless they burrowed into the mountain.

Je'Kaoron took a scepter from the tunnel wall like the one Je'Sikar had carried in their escape through the catacombs beneath the palace. "No doubt you have questions." Despite lowering his voice, it cracked the stifling silence.

Around a bend in the corridor, the tunnel widened, until a cavern opened like the mouth of a hungry demonlord, sprouting teeth from the ceiling in rocky formations far above. Through the center rose a single round pillar supporting a globe from which a light radiated like a false sun or a million of the light scepters. The pillar stood out as artificial from the natural beauty of the cave, like the stone city at its base.

Je'Rol stared in awe, his breath stuck in his throat. From where he stood far outside the city, he saw demonlords representing all the clans whose domains he had searched in his travels moving about. A dammed lake of water stood on the outskirts of the city, whose buildings rose higher near the center pillar.

"Welcome to Mount Serako." Je'Kaoron motioned to two of those behind him and they blurred for a moment in the transformation to their natural forms before running off towards the city. "Most of this was here when we found it."

"*'We'* found it?"

"Yes. I was with my lord Je'Dron. We returned from successfully defending the northern border from the Dai'Kowa with three thousand soldiers and set up camp at the base of Mount Serako's north face. He called me aside to speak about Je'Rekun's ambition, but on our walk, we noticed a rock that seemed to be there one moment and gone the next, a faulty magic. We had discovered a back entrance, which has been sealed since, I assure you."

On return from defending the northern border, and discussing Je'Rekun's ambition…Something didn't fit. Why would Je'Dron be entrusting Je'Kaoron with his concerns about his brother when Je'Kaoron served that brother? Had Je'Rekun learned of this secret fortress from Je'Kaoron?

A bemused smile touched the demonlord's lips as he set the darkened scepter in a holder on the wall. "And I assure you that I have never betrayed Je'Dron in any way he has not allowed. Your capture was advantageous, if a little premature, for completing our plans to defeat Je'Rekun. My position allowed me privileges to serve our needs, including the meeting in Dev Nadir, where I learned how far many of the domain leaders are willing to go and the real danger threatening us."

By real danger, did he mean the Adepts or the other demonlords?

No. That issue was a moot point in Je'Rol's eyes. Anger writhed around the beast, stirring it from the calm and wonder inspired by the cavern. Claws extended and muscles tensed. Je'Rol whirled on his host and slammed the demonlord against the rock. "You let them torture me!"

"Would you risk losing yourself to the blood rage for the last time?" Je'Kaoron quietly asked, a hint of threat in his tone.

Although Je'Rol wanted to give in for all he had suffered, the demonlord was correct. Each time could be the last. His time ran out and he couldn't afford to let it happen again. Je'Rol let the claws shrink, containing the beast and backing off, and Je'Kaoron regained his composure with an adjustment of his shoulders.

"I'm sure Je'Sikar suffered far worse than you."

"How do you—" No! The answer stared him in the face. "You?"

"Yes, I arranged for Je'Sikar to free you. I'm not the only Je'Gri feigning loyalty to Je'Rekun. Others who believed in him once, because Je'Dron let you live and by so doing betrayed our most sacred laws, have begun to dissent to his heavy hand and ambition. He has gained allies but they influence Je'Gri power and more are seeing that, and his actions have stirred the nest of the Adepts of Te'Mea.

"The revelation of the *am'taerad* in the sorceress's hands confirmed what we've suspected for some time—that the sorcerers, if not all Adept sects, are seeking and finding the lost treasures of the Master Race, likely to eliminate all demonlords. Je'Rekun's plans have only made them more wary of us, and with good reason. In fear, they will act, and they will force their own destruction. We have no desire to cause harm, but we will defend ourselves."

"You only want to keep your power," Je'Rol growled.

"You misunderstand, but that will change. Come." Je'Kaoron started towards the city but paused when Je'Rol didn't follow. "You cannot leave without the key."

"So I'm your prisoner?" He should have known the demonlords would trap him.

"You're free to leave, if you wish, but your questions would go unanswered. Have you come all this way to sacrifice that knowledge?" The pale blue eyes of the royal Je'Gri gazed with the same gentle patience he'd come to expect whenever Je'Rol wanted him to fight back.

Unable to come up with a good reason to deny his curiosity, Je'Rol let out a heavy sigh and adjusted the hood of his cloak over his white and black hair, the mark of his own royal lineage he denied. "No."

They crossed the smooth floor to the nearest streets between the buildings, some of which rose three floors high with windows merely cut out as holes. Without natters to fear or weather, they could afford such openness.

They walked among demonlords in the streets, and a different but familiar scent took him by surprise. "There are humans here."

"Yes. Very few; only those welcome. I expected you to notice."

From ahead, a slender figure rushed towards them, her white and black hair pulled back from her face in twists, her gown a simple but elegant cut of green with gold braiding at the collar and wrists with an open robe of ebony and white over it. "Lord Je'Kaoron!"

He stopped and met her eyes. The girl slowed her steps until she stopped a few strides away, her eyes darting to Je'Rol and back to Je'Kaoron, whose eyes never left her.

"I…heard you returned…I'm sorry." She dipped in a quick bow, the grace of her movements every bit matching what he'd come to expect of the demonlord she appeared to be. After another glance at Je'Rol, she strode forward more slowly to meet them, her eyes on the demonlord. "I understand."

Je'Kaoron's concentration broke with his smile as she met him with an eagerness barely restrained by decorum.

"Lady Je'Surana." He spoke in a tender voice and took her hands in his, keeping her distant when she looked ready to rush into an embrace.

Her eyes shimmered with the pale blue of the Je'Gri, but the tears never flowed. She was young yet, a woman of mature beauty but with the slenderness of a human woman never having borne children. Female demonlords were known to be cold and aloof, but this woman waited on baited breath for Je'Kaoron. Odd that her clothes, normally a transfiguration of the demonlord's covering bearing their color, weren't the royal Je'Gri white with black like her hair. They looked tailored by hand.

The answer came in her scent—half-blood. Je'Kaoron kept a half-blood lover, or teased the poor girl. It fit that only a demonlord might conquer the beast, or survive its savagery.

Je'Kaoron caught his eyes on them, but Je'Rol felt nothing. Although the presence of a half-blood surprised him, the business of the demonlord's wasn't his. Je'Kaoron could have his pleasure if it suited him. At least it left a human from the trouble such relationships caused. "I assume you've already noticed. Je'Surana is like you…" His eyes lit up on her. "My dear, would you show Je'Rol the city? I must speak with Lord

Je'Dron."

"Yes, my lord." Disappointment lowered her voice, which contained more of the telltale growl in that moment than it had in her greeting.

"We'll have more time later. I promise." He kissed her forehead and released her hands to rush off. After a blurry moment in the transformation, the tiger ran away through the streets.

Je'Surana's smile faded somewhat. "He said you were coming. It's an honor to meet you...Lord Je'Rol."

"Just Je'Rol." The title of Lord made him shift with discomfort.

"Je'Rol. But aren't you High Lord Je'Dron's son?"

"It doesn't matter. I'm a half-blood, a fugitive. Everyone wants me dead. I'm lord of nothing."

Her eyes widened with horror but she let out her breath and relaxed. "I'm sorry. I didn't realize— I've never been outside, but my father warned me. He said I should never go out without guards. He's very protective." She rubbed one hand up and down her opposite arm, her eyes following the street Je'Kaoron had taken.

Her father didn't protect her enough if he allowed a demonlord like Je'Kaoron to seduce her. Je'Rol scoffed and looked around, noticing the scowls directed his way from some of the demonlords. The girl was accepted while he was not.

Her hand around his triggered a warmth that rose to his face; she assumed far too much familiarity. She was Je'Kaoron's lover, wasn't she? "Let's go. Not all of them are sympathetic to us."

Us? Half-bloods. Yes, Je'Surana was like him. Although she lived among demonlords and humans, apparently she had not been accepted by them all as he had first assumed.

He pulled his fingers away but followed her from the busy street to the quieter spaces between clusters of buildings. She might display the beauty of a demonlord, but she was Je'Kaoron's prize. He had no intention of incurring a demonlord's wrath for even the smallest mistake.

"It's nice to meet another Je'Gri half-blood," she said.

"Aren't there others?"

"Half-bloods? Yes. Je'Gri, no. I've been...alone, except for the tigresses. I can't do anything without them watching over my every move, except when my father returns. He ordered them to protect me when he's gone, but it feels like he doesn't trust me."

As young as she was, he understood that sentiment. She couldn't have been more than twenty by his estimation.

Odd that he saw no tigresses with her if they guarded her every move. Her father must have been present somewhere.

Her pouting dissipated with the brightening of her expression. "I've only seen the land outside the mountain, but my father says you've been to other domains across the sea. How marvelous it must be!"

Her enthusiasm begged for explanation. No one had ever asked him for the story of his wanderings, but they weren't pleasant memories to be described. "Not…so much. I'm hunted. Half-bloods are feared by humans and despised by demonlords. The world is dangerous for us."

Disappointment dragged at her features. "But you've seen wonders…"

The girl wanted to hear of good things, not the dangers her father must have warned her about to keep her locked up in that mountain, where she was protected from the threats that would confront her beyond those walls. He could give her that much, leaving out the harsh realities that would spoil the beauty he had seen.

"Nothing like this place, I assure you." He walked beside her among the homes, avoiding the gazes of the demonlords when he could and telling her about the canyons and deserts and oceans and other natural phenomena he had seen. Recalling sights he'd hardly noticed for their moments of magnificence and beauty erased the fighting, the killing, the blood, and the blood rages for a while. He'd visited every continent of Derandria and never really appreciated the wonders he had beheld at the time, until then. Always it had been with a critical eye of searching for the peace he desired, but maybe it had been there in moments, fleeting as they may have been.

"I wish I could see it myself! It sounds spectacular."

A smile played at his lips. The girl contained the innocence that the blood rage had stolen from him long ago. It was as if she had never suffered. "My lady, how do you contain it?"

"Contain it?"

"The beast. The demon side. Have you never suffered the blood rage?" Was she so protected that no one dared push her emotions? Or was there some secret she might impart?

Her eyes dropped with her smile. "Once. I was barely a woman when it happened…I argued with my father to let me outside the mountain, like I'd done before. But this time was different; I felt it like a snap inside me and remember nothing until I woke to my father's arms crushing me…He was bloody and his clothes torn, but…he'd held me throughout the whole ordeal." She shook her head and rolled a fold of her robe sleeve between her fingers. "It was the second time I'd ever seen tears in his eyes, and then I cried, because I saw what I'd done…He never…never let go or fought back, and…he never blamed me."

She forced a smile and wiped her eyes. "He's a very gentle man, Lord…Je'Rol."

"What about your mother? Where is she?" Why wasn't she there if this demonlord father cared for her so much? When did demonlords care for their half-human offspring?

Je'Surana sniffed and wiped her eyes again. "She died almost ten years ago. He still goes to visit the ashes where they burned the body; he didn't want the natters to get her. It was the only other time I've seen him in tears. The demonlords claim they don't feel emotions like humans, but…it's not true. He loved my mother."

Her smile returned and she pointed him to a bench in an open plaza. "I'll never forget the story she told me. She was a sorceress—"

"Sorceress?" A demonlord and an Adept? But they despised each other, and the sorcerers and their dark ways…impossible.

"Yes. He was assigned by High Lord Je'Rekun—" She said the name with a level of derision he wouldn't have expected. "To keep a watch on the activities of *Serae* Surika, who was reported to have settled in the territory overseen by my father. He watched her tend her garden and serve the villagers, and she called him out for it. He was suspicious, but she assured him she only wanted to relax the rest of her days.

"He *didn't* know that she suffered a painful disease in bouts that could last several days; so when she didn't tend her garden for three days, he entered the house suspecting she'd secretly moved or that natters had…ahm…eaten her. He found her in bed curled up in pain and felt sorry for her, so he took care of her until it passed. That changed things, and he would check in on her and help her through the episodes of pain. She said he'd often lie as a tiger next to her and the softness of his coat would make her forget the pain enough to rest." Je'Surana smiled wistfully, her gaze distant as if she could see the story take shape as she told it.

"She said she only became a sorceress in the hopes that she could find a way to treat herself; she hid the pain so well that no one in the sects knew she was ill. She didn't like the training, though, and wouldn't talk about it. She always changed the subject…But she loved talking about *him*. She loved him more than anything.

"A lot of time passed and my father never did anything but hold her and be there for her. She finally said something about it to him, she told me, on one of her good days—the bouts of pain came more frequently over time. She said she knew he loved her when he told her that he didn't want her to suffer…because of what happens to most half-blood children."

Je'Surana shuddered and looked at him for confirmation, but he could only swallow. She must have been told of the demon hunters and the majority of demonlords' disdain for such offspring, and then there were the captured half-bloods forced to fight in the Dao Larashi tournaments. He almost felt shame for cutting off her enthusiasm, when she wanted to not think of the warnings her father must have given her.

They both should have been dead by the customs of demonlords, but both their fathers had spared them. And her father apparently had Je'Rekun's trust while also working with Je'Dron. Suspicions almost stopped his breath, but he waited for her to finish. If she told him, he wouldn't have to make false accusations, if they were false.

"He told me he started feeling something when he cared for her that first time, maybe before then, which was why he took care of her. But she seduced him when he was content to see her healthy. She said the pleasure he gave her when she was healthy sustained her through the painful days…And then he disappeared for a long time, during which she felt the quickening inside her. He returned from convincing Je'Dron to allow her in the mountain like the others. He told me he knew she conceived by the subtle change of her scent, and that it wasn't unexpected.

"What *was* unexpected was that while she was pregnant, she suffered no painful bouts of her illness. She made the journey with my father, who had begged and slept little while convincing the others to allow an Adept in the mountain. Any other human lover would have been welcome, but because she was a sorceress, who might later run to reveal the secrets to her sect, they debated against it. Je'Dron finally relented…after recognizing in my father much the same that he had suffered for Amia, and because she was sick and would likely go nowhere."

A shot of mixed emotions jolted Je'Rol to his feet at the mention of his mother's name. Anger, frustration, betrayal, sorrow, guilt, and love blended into that moment. He'd loved his mother but had left to protect her from the anger of others that she protected a half-blood son whose father had sent him away. Yet Je'Dron allowed the half-blood of another to stay with her family.

Claws extended, ready to rip the demonlords to shreds at the beast's command for such hypocrisy.

Je'Surana slid away, her manner demure. "I'm sorry. I shouldn't have said her name. He just…Je'Dron told me what happened when my father came back, and…he seemed scared but so hopeful, Je'Rol. He's anxious to meet you, and sorry too."

Je'Surana's touch on his hand was like water on fire, calming the beast. "Please. You must regain control." Her pale blue eyes fixed on his with an unwavering determination. He recognized that look; she used her *dispirit* abilities on him. As with Arak, he gave in, grateful not to lose control in the presence of an innocent child.

The beast quieted, but the emotions tangled within him, ready to tempt it again. Her presence soothed him, despite his knowing—or maybe because of his knowing—of her abilities to quell the rise of the demon side, and he followed her to one of the taller central structures. "It's hard for me too. I know how to control the demon side and have lived in this mountain all my life, so I don't know what horrors you've seen; but I know what it's like to lose someone I love. And I fear every time my father is gone that

Je'Rekun will discover his lies and execute him, that each time he leaves will be the last time I see him." Her throat flashed with a swallow as she again looked down the road Je'Kaoron had taken.

Guilt ate at Je'Rol's heart, although he shouldn't have cared. The political games of the demonlords weren't his to worry about, but when they involved a lovely young woman like Je'Surana, a part of him cared. He pitied her for the potential to lose her one ally. Her innocence in the face of what was almost an affliction should be protected. He hoped she never came to know the same hardships he'd experienced, but she had the benefit of the *dispirit* ability, something which panged him with a touch of jealousy.

"I'm sorry. I'm not being a good escort. Come. There's more to see." She started towards the central pillar as a white tiger trotted to meet them.

Je'Surana halted and waited. A few steps away, the tiger blurred into a man in a white tunic and trousers with black accents, his long hair pulled out of his face with the rest down.

"My lord." Je'Surana bowed her head.

A hint of a smile touched his lips. "Je'Surana. Would you excuse us, please?"

"Of course." Her eyes went to Je'Rol with a warm smile. "It's been a pleasure speaking with you. I would like to hear more when you have time."

"No, you wouldn't."

The smile wavered, but she held it and hurried away.

"She's a sweet child," the demonlord said. "Your words were cruel."

"The world is a harsh place," Je'Rol growled, his patience lost at the intrusion of the demonlord. "The sooner she understands, the better off she'll be." He wished for her sake that she never experienced the realities outside the mountain.

The demonlord stood silent, his critical gaze giving Je'Rol an uneasy feeling. "Your life is not a measure of hers."

"Who are you to judge?"

After a moment, the hard stare softened into something more understanding with the demonlord's nod. "Come with me."

"Where?" He'd had enough chasing around and being told what to do. The girl had been a sweet distraction, but no demonlord would command him without his consent.

"Je'Dron awaits."

"Where's Je'Kaoron?"

"He has…other affairs to tend upon his return." His eyes shifted to the parting girl.

Je'Rol would bet he did, like the girl and her mother's ashes. The thought cut through him in its sharpness of emotions, dulling his with a certain pity for her and envy that she would be so protected here among those who respected her, unlike the life he'd been forced to endure.

"Come."

Begrudgingly, Je'Rol joined the royal tiger demonlord through the streets.

"You're a quiet man. Haven't you questions after seeing all this?"

"I've learned it's better to say nothing."

The demonlord huffed in amusement. "Would you rather always be alone?"

No, but he wasn't about to tell that to an unnamed demonlord.

After an awkward silence, the demonlord asked, "Why did you come?"

"Did I have a choice? Eight demonlords when I'm no match for one?" Je'Rol balled his fingers into fists and relaxed them again to ease the struggle with the beast. Now wasn't the time to argue. This escort made it sound like he had a choice. Whether the demonlords would have given him the opportunity to leave or not, the fact that he needed the favor of Je'Dron to continue his search negated that issue.

"So you have no reason for being here except that Je'Kaoron and the others frightened you?"

The beast rumbled in protest. "I'm not afraid, but I'm not stupid."

"I see," the demonlord said in a quiet voice as they passed a man in the orange and black armor; the helmeted Je'Gri guard gave a slight bow to them. "Then maybe it's best if you leave."

"I'd have no objections." Except he needed Je'Dron's cooperation. That thought tainted the purity of hope that arose with the suggestion that he leave. "But not until I see him myself." The words ground out through clenched teeth to restrain the anger extending claws beneath his cloak.

The demonlord slowed to a stop, his cheek shifting with the tightening of his jaw. "Je'Dron is busy. In two days he leaves to meet his brother at the Nik'Terek Gate."

No! Je'Rol's blood ran cold. "He can't. Je'Rekun will have a trap to eliminate him."

One silvery white eyebrow lifted. "I didn't know you cared."

He didn't, but he did, if only for his own interests of needing Je'Dron to win this battle.

Je'Rol growled low in his throat out of frustration and a lack of words to express it.

"It doesn't matter. The Nik'Terek Gate is one of the few remaining wonders of the Master Race. The resources in this mountain have revealed many secrets, Je'Rol. One of those is the portal. They used the gate to remove their mistakes from this world. Je'Dron will use it to remove his."

"Me?" Was he such a mistake that his father had turned him away while allowing other half-bloods to join his little movement to change the world?

"No." The demonlord's face hardened. "Je'Dron made the mistake of trusting Je'Rekun with the leadership of the Je'Gri domain while he put his life in harm's way to defend it from invaders. He had no idea the traitor converted or replaced key positions in the hierarchy."

Pale blue eyes softened when they met his. "Your birth was the catalyst for his plan. Je'Dron was prepared to end your life himself soon after your birth, but Amia begged him not to. She was his greatest weakness, but holding his own son...*his* son, not one of a litter of cubs but a human-borne son, gave him a new perspective. He knew all half-bloods should be killed, but he couldn't do it, and...he gave Amia and Je'Rol his adoration, to the degree that he deafened himself to the warnings of those still loyal to him. It was almost too late when he sent you away with your mother. The tigresses obviously protected your escape."

He leaned closer and lowered his voice. "Don't make him regret letting you live."

Fire and acid flowed through Je'Rol in a torrent of emotions, launching his hands at the demonlord's throat. Je'Dron never cared about Amia. The demonlord was a fool to think he would believe that. "You lie. Demonlords don't care about anyone but themselves."

Like Je'Kaoron when he attacked him, this one made no move to stop him but grunted when Je'Rol slammed him against the wall of the nearest building, his throat moving beneath Je'Rol's grip. "You're wrong. Je'Surana is proof of that, as are you."

The clatter of feet surrounded him, and Je'Rol glanced aside at the circle of orange and black armor around him. The demonlord raised a hand and they stayed their ground. Unwilling to release the beast, Je'Rol instead released the demonlord. Anger would serve no purpose but to erase his existence further, but he wasn't playing games. "Who are you? Why do you know so much?"

"You know the truth, Je'Rol." He motioned with his hands and the guards departed. "In here." With a hand towards the doorway of one of the taller structures, the demonlord guided Je'Rol into an empty room lit by a crystal above.

"You're no one's fool. Fighting for the amusement of men and to satisfy the dinner tables of the clans, escaping a sorceress, tortured by Je'Rekun and his demon hunter, tormented by the shadows of loss that haunt you, the life you can never have that you seek through the promise of an artifact that cannot be found. You've lived longer than most half-bloods and endured tragedy I wouldn't wish on anyone. If you can survive all that, you should know the answer to your question."

Certainty rang clear, stirring the beast. Claws extended and the struggle renewed inside him. Je'Rol growled and, in a split second, slammed the demonlord against the wall. "You should have killed me when you had the chance!"

"I should have sent you here, but I wasn't sure it was safe for you. I'm sorry...my son." Regret and disappointment pulled down the expression on Je'Dron's face. "I wronged you in many ways and can never atone for my mistakes or the suffering my actions caused you and Amia. It was never my intention, but good intentions do not equate noble deeds. Perhaps…"

The truth trembled through him. Je'Rol loosened his hold, his thoughts and emotions scrambled. This was his father, the demonlord who sired him, yet it wasn't. All his life, he'd imagined someone who despised him and wanted him out of his life, not a royal Je'Gri who swore his affections for a human lover and her half-blood child. His mother hadn't said much about his father, leaving him to form his own image.

"Perhaps it would have been easier to end your life then, but I couldn't risk losing what I had found." A bemused smile returned to his face as Je'Rol released him, and Je'Dron straightened his tunic with a light shake of his shoulders. "In some ways we envy humans for their passionate emotions, something we don't feel; but in those moments, we taste—if you will—the sweetness, so fleeting but desirable. It's unfortunate that that which we seek you must contain. Such is the curse on half-bloods. Our addiction is your bane.

"One which you seek to contain, to experience the benefits of both worlds…"

Je'Rol blinked in confusion. How did Je'Dron know?

"Yes, I know about your search. Lord Je'Kaoron told me all he learned—you seek the obelisk of Mai'Kari to control the demon side, but will that be enough? What do you really want, Je'Rol? More than anything else, what is it you truly seek? What will you do with this obelisk once you obtain it? Will you destroy it? Will you keep it so that you may live without restraint? Or will you use it as others did in the past, to gain control of all demons?"

The lift of his brow suggested the third question was the one he suspected held the greatest appeal, and with good reason.

"It's not your concern," Je'Rol grumbled. Je'Dron's truth tainted his desires by spilling them out for him to face in their horrific nakedness.

"Not my concern that you would seek to control us all?" His clothes shimmered and rearranged into a long robe. "Su'Tari was right to free you but wrong to trust you. I don't think you have any intention of destroying the obelisk, and I doubt you would use it only to control yourself. The temptation would be too great to abuse such power, which is why I've made arrangements that the obelisk is never found."

Je'Rol's blood ran cold at the implications in those last words. He must have heard wrong.

Je'Dron adjusted his furry robe. "And if you would not, someone else would steal it from you for the power. No, it's not you I don't trust, Je'Rol. It's everyone else, especially the Adepts of Te'Mea. The obelisk will disappear…forever."

He *did* have it! "Where is it?"

Je'Dron gazed at him in what seemed a look of pity. "*I* do not even know that. Only one does, one I trust with my life, because that is what the obelisk controls. No one else knows it exists."

And he'd likely never say who had it, even if Je'Rol never knew who it was. Lies upon lies.

"Je'Rekun and those who believe as he does must never be allowed to gain that kind of power; nor should the Adepts. There is a war coming, but it will not be at this time. I won't allow them to return us to the darkness of the times when we hunted humans like any animal. We have shaped them into something greater than we could ever be. That scares some clans, and the possibilities frighten me. But with the right molding, we can shape this world into something better."

"So make something better, but leave me the obelisk." Je'Rol adjusted his hood to cover his face and crossed his arms. Je'Dron was a dreamer and a fool, giving his power away too easily by entrusting others with it, including those like Je'Rekun who hungered for more. He wanted nothing of his father's ideals, only a small piece of freedom from the demon side.

"I can't do that."

Then he was done with this conversation. The obelisk was there, though, and he had only to find it. The sooner he started searching, the sooner he'd find his peace. Je'Dron couldn't hide it permanently.

He didn't intend to *hide* it; he intended to destroy it! Je'Dron said he'd made arrangements so that it would never be found. Destroying it was the only way. How did one destroy an object rumored to contain such magic? Why hadn't he already destroyed it?

He couldn't, but he must have known a way that he could.

There was something not fitting together yet, but Je'Rol had a feeling the answer was more obvious than he was seeing.

For the moment, he'd listened to enough talk. The time for action had come. He had to find that obelisk before Je'Dron succeeded in destroying it.

Je'Rol passed the High Lord on his way to the door behind him. "We're done."

"I am sorry…my son."

Je'Rol whirled on the demonlord, barely containing the monster lusting to shred the man for abandoning him and his mother to a world that wanted him dead. "You don't own me. I am not *your* son!"

"Very well…Je'Rol."

Better. He huffed out the anger, quelling the beast into a low rumble of ill temper. He marched from the home to the outskirts of the cavern and the dam holding the reservoir of water. The stones fit tightly together, sealed from leaking and more than wide enough to walk across with raised edges along the walkway overlooking the city and its artificial sun.

Alone on the dam, Je'Rol turned from the city to the reservoir. The fall of drops made light plinks into the pool, the only disturbance of the surface other than a whorl above a section where a cylinder on the dry side ran down and towards the city. He lifted his eyes to the ceiling, where jagged teeth of rock cried their tears.

The rock could do all the crying for all he cared. He didn't cry. He wouldn't cry.

Je'Dron was nothing like what he had expected, not the terrible human rapist he'd imagined and he doubted that had been an act. His mother had never talked about Je'Dron, but now he could see it—the tears of pain not because of being raped but because she had lost the man she loved. Still, Je'Dron had no right sending her away while allowing others to keep their families.

Worse, he'd had the obelisk all along, but where would it be? Who would be keeping it? And how would he destroy it?

The answer was before him. It squirmed just out of reach in his mind, teasing him into chasing it.

In frustration, Je'Rol looked back at the city around the pillar. Tigers occupied most of it, but other demonlords walked the streets also. A few humans lived there, and a few half-bloods. Families, or as close to it as demonlords allowed.

He could have lived there with his mother, grown up among the demonlords as Je'Surana had, accepted or as close to it as they came here.

Guilt gnawed at his conscious for what he'd said. He hated seeing how they cared for her, when he had been pursued and chased all his life. She deserved to know how scary the world outside was, but she wasn't all naïve. She'd understood. A beautiful but dangerous woman, she could control the demon side with a gift he'd been denied—the gift of *dispirit*. She lived as he wished he could.

In all that she had, he envied her.

But he wouldn't wish any of his suffering on her. As unfair as his life had been compared to hers, it had made him what he was—a survivor. The world hated him and would hate her, but he'd learned to survive among hardship and pain.

He couldn't blame her for what she was. Her demonlord father had protected her, maybe even loved her.

Je'Rol lifted his eyes to the glowing mass at the top of the tower, a constant sun in the darkness of the cavern. No, he didn't envy the girl. This place was her prison. He'd lived, experienced what the world had to offer, both its wonders and its sufferings. That could never be taken away, but he could appreciate the peace of a life without it after enduring.

He let out a heavy sigh and laid back on a rocky incline. Je'Dron would soon leave to meet Je'Rekun at the Nik'Terek Gate, a portal, as he called it.

A portal …

To what? Destruction? Disappearance?

The nagging sense of what Je'Dron meant by the obelisk never being found blossomed into understanding with a sharp intake of air. He said the Master Race used the gate to eliminate their mistakes.

Je'Dron was taking the obelisk to the gate! It had to be.

If he was right, Je'Rol would have to join them to have his chance of obtaining the obelisk, or solve the mystery of who had it. Chances are they wouldn't talk about it, much less to him.

In two days, he would have the obelisk and his freedom.

And he would end that madness.

25

Night came and with it, the rustle of movement in the bushes, but whatever it was stayed out of the light of the fire crackling in their clearing. Two of the Li'Ador had returned to Nadia with a report that they found no obvious exits from the mountain and that Karik had organized them into two other camps. They had the mountain surrounded, but that might not be enough.

It would have to suffice. She didn't have a whole army.

Je'Rekun did.

This wasn't his fight. Je'Rol was hers. Besides, she wanted Je'Rekun out of power. He would ruin the hopes of the Adepts. Je'Dron had to be stopped from going, if he still intended that now that he had Je'Rol, or at least she assumed he was in there, or wherever they had taken Je'Rol.

She had to tell him what Je'Rekun planned, but she didn't know where they went, and if they were inside the mountain, she couldn't get in.

Or could she?

Skar said he studied the knowledge of the 'Old Ones'. Could this magic be the work of those same Old Ones? Would he understand? Is that what he'd been trying to tell her?

Nadia looked aside at the goblin with his hands and feet tied to prevent escape. His glasses sat askew on that long nose, his dark eyes enlarged behind the round lenses.

"Can you speak yet?"

He opened his mouth but nothing came out. He closed it and shook his head. The demonlords were too close, but it wasn't likely the tigresses. No surprise that the residents of the mountain probably watched her and her entourage, and listened. Would they respond to her?

The bigger question was whether they would take her to Je'Dron. The goblin was her only way to know that they were near. He had proven useful, if only because he couldn't say anything.

One of the men threw another piece of wood into the fire.

Animals called through the night, singing with the rustle of leaves in the breeze.

Nadia stood up and listened past the whistles of birds and the chirrup of insects. Something else called with a regular howl. The three men with her sat in perfect quietude, listening. The demonlords were close. She would never know what Skar wanted to tell her, but she could speak with them.

"Come on out!" she called. "Show yourselves!"

The howling ceased, but the roar of a large cat silenced all.

Her heart pounded in her chest. Now would be a good time to shut up, but the desire to know overrode her sense of caution. "I know we're surrounded! I—I want to talk!"

Only the hush of the wind answered.

Movement rustled in the brush. The men gathered their weapons and stood in a circle with her.

Something snuffled behind them.

Nadia whirled and swallowed the strong desire to flee. These were demonlords, reasonable beings, and she could *dispirit* natters. Fear was a part of her job. She'd be dead without it. "Show yourselves. I wish to speak to Je'Dron. I bear a warning."

The soft growl of a predator came from her left.

She stood ready with the three Li'Ador, although what good the four of them had against any demonlord she couldn't guess. They could put up a fair fight, but they couldn't hope to win.

The shadows of the night shifted as tall figures materialized from the darkness to surround them.

Five orange and black armored Je'Gri stepped into the firelight with one white and black robed woman with a severe look upon her face. This was more than Nadia had expected.

"I am Lady Je'Mara. You will give me your message for Je'Dron and leave." The lady's scolding eyes shifted to Skar and back. "None of your kinds are welcome here."

"My message can only be delivered in person."

Je'Mara paused. "Such as you say, but your word holds no sway, demon hunter."

"There's a traitor with him. I know who it is." She couldn't let Je'Kaoron carry out Je'Rekun's orders, but she wasn't about to give up this shaky leverage against getting in to see Je'Dron.

One fine white eyebrow arched up. "Give me the name."

She had to think fast now to keep her advantage. "How do I know I can trust you? You may be with the traitor. I'll only tell Je'Dron; it's his life that's threatened."

Je'Mara's gaze was hard and probing, almost as if she sought to pry the answer from her soul, but Nadia refused to give in to the intimidation.

"Very well. You may come…alone." Je'Mara motioned to the guards, who closed in around her. "Bring her."

"Huntress—"

Nadia shook her head in response to the unspoken question from the Li'Ador. If she couldn't trust the demonlords with her life, she was dead anyway; they all were. This way, she might get into the mountain, and she would find Je'Rol.

The demonlord led her into the dark of night. While the Je'Gri didn't have any trouble, Nadia tripped a few times on underbrush and rocks. The lady led her to the waterfall, where she started up the stairs that Je'Kaoron and the others had taken with Je'Rol.

The higher they climbed, the greater Nadia's anxiety about slipping on wet stone with a long drop a misstep away. Perhaps coming in the dark wasn't such a bright idea. She should have waited until morning, but the need to know refused to let her rest.

Several landings up, they stopped, the guards closing in.

Nadia saw only a flick of the lady's wrist in the wan light when strong arms grabbed hers and her cloak flipped over her head and was tied off.

"Let go of me! What are you doing?" She struggled to free her arms, but the strength of those holding her didn't budge.

The demonlords said nothing but held her steadfast.

A few seconds later, the crash of the waterfall was replaced by a rumble of stone and she was shoved forward.

Her feet touched a perfectly flat surface, which vibrated with the return of the rumble of stone. In seconds, quiet fell over them.

"Where are we?" Nadia could see nothing with her cloak secured over her head, and she couldn't remove it with the demonlords holding her arms.

"You'll see Je'Dron when the time is right."

They led her through the tunnel, their steps echoing for a while. She had a sense of it opening from the quality of the sound changing. Instead of bouncing back from close in, the sounds came from a distance, what she thought were gurgles of water and a steady hum of something she'd never heard before. The cloak muffled it slightly and made breathing difficult, but it didn't cut off the outside completely.

Her feet crunched over loose rock, and the demonlords said nothing but guided her for a length of a gentle slope. She saw nothing but darkness, nor could she catch herself if she tripped, but the demonlord guards supported her.

They led her to level ground and along its gravelly surface for a ways before the scrape with the faint hint of hinges warned her of a door. There, they pulled her through sideways with the guards still holding her and continued across a smooth floor. They were inside somewhere she guessed was a fairly large room by the number of steps until a click and the scrape of another door, which warned her before they shoved her through and released her.

Her free hands shot up to her cloak, which she hadn't realized needed washing until having it wrapped around her face so she couldn't escape the odors.

Upon pulling it off her face, she inhaled deeply and turned to the tigress standing beyond the door.

The corner of Je'Mara's lips twitched up in a coy smile. "Sleep now, Huntress. High Lord Je'Dron will listen to your warning in the morning."

The door slammed, sealing her in a dark room, except for the faint line of light at the bottom of the door. That faint light outlined the shape of a mat on the floor and two blankets folded next to it.

She was in, and she didn't have to worry about natters for a night with demonlords on guard, but what would happen in the morning?

["No one gets in or out."] Je'Mara's muffled voice came to her through the door. ["You know the stakes."]

["Yes, my lady."] Several voices replied.

What were they hiding?

She wasn't going to find that answer anytime soon, and she was tired.

But at least she was inside. That was a start. She had only to figure out what came next.

* * *

Morning came soon and with it, a plate of food and a scepter of light in a holder near the door.

As she finished the simple breakfast, a familiar demonlord stepped inside in white and black tunic and trousers belted at the waist with a sash. She nearly choked on a bite of cooked poultry, barely swallowing it before falling to one knee with her head lowered. Every hair on her neck stood up with the sense of caution that shot through her. "Lord Je'Kaoron."

"Rise, Huntress."

She obeyed, wary of the tone he used.

Je'Kaoron bent down for the plate on the floor and handed it to one of the guards in the open doorway. ["Bring the High Lord."]

["Yes, my lord."] The guard retreated and closed the door behind him, sealing her in the room with the one demonlord she had hoped not to see.

She swallowed the rising anxiety. *Calm. They don't know we know the Lexic.* She should look attentive at best, confused at worst.

Je'Kaoron's gaze fixed on her, his hands clasped loosely before him. "You're persistent. I'll give you that. What is it…Je'Rol?" He froze and the expression on his face brightened. "Ah, no. They said you had a warning for Lord Je'Dron."

Warmth rose from under her collar. This wasn't how it was supposed to be, but she didn't know Je'Kaoron was so high ranked in Je'Dron's order. *Think!*

Amusement softened the lines of his face and he distracted himself with the scepter in its holding sconce on the wall. "You think I'm betraying one against the other."

Panic swept through her but she took a deep breath and let it out slowly.

"Partially correct. I would never betray High Lord Je'Dron. Only his brother believes otherwise. Yes, I was aware of you in the garden, Huntress. What I wasn't certain was what you understood. Our Lexic is commonly spoken around humans. I expect many understand. We are not ignorant." He returned from the scepter after a touch brightened the stone.

"I…never thought you were ignorant."

He stepped close so his warm breath hinting of raw meat made her nauseous, but she choked down the reflex.

"You do well to remember that." His quiet words carried a hint of menace, but those eyes never hardened, and his voice returned to the easy tone he started with. "I've lived long enough to know humans who understood. You're no exception. You wouldn't know that Je'Dron might be in danger if you hadn't understood…My purposes are not yours to know." As if the threat had been nothing, he stepped away with a casual grace.

"Now the question is what do you have to gain by coming?"

She caught her breath and reorganized her thoughts with the revelations he'd given her to return to her purpose—finishing Je'Rol.

"You're no threat to us. Your mandate is to eliminate half-bloods, like Je'Rol. But High Lord Je'Dron would not allow that."

She didn't think he would, but as long as she was there, she would be close to Je'Rol. When the time was right, she would act, giving up her life if that's what it took to gain the satisfaction of finishing her task.

Je'Kaoron could think all he wanted about her and demon hunters, even Adepts, but she wasn't going to give in to him. Still, this visit felt less like an interrogation and more like a test. He already knew everything. If that's the way he wanted it, he could figure it out for himself.

Je'Kaoron's pale blue eyes met hers with a knowing smile. "And I doubt you really want that."

Hot and cold raced through her like the conflicting emotions his statement aroused. Je'Rol had ruined her life. "He deserves to die."

"So you say, but what do you feel?" Those eyes burned through her, and she looked away while trying not to fidget from the confusion inside her since seeing Je'Rol again after all those years. The light press of a finger beneath her chin tipped her head up to the soft lines of his face. "I see a woman who has never moved past the pain of love lost. Why are you really here, my lady?"

His words hit too close to the mark, but she couldn't give up her mandate to eliminate half-bloods. Je'Rol deserved to die; she meant it when she said it. He'd killed innocent people and would kill more. She'd almost been added to that list days ago when the blood rage took over; he'd seen that. It had all happened so quickly, and that proved the threat he posed. Obviously, Je'Kaoron had known a way to bring him out of it, but at some point, that would no longer be possible and Je'Rol would live like a predator whose hunger was never sated.

She knew her answer and jerked away from his touch. "To finish my task."

Je'Kaoron sighed and shook his head. "Je'Dron will never allow it."

"I'll hear it from him." Je'Kaoron only delayed her. And she would tell Je'Dron of his betrayal. Despite his smooth explanation, he would betray Je'Dron, and that would endanger the Adepts. She couldn't allow it.

"I see." He stepped to the door and pulled it open. A demonlord stood in the doorway in white and black robes similar to Je'Rekun's the day he had called her to escort Je'Kaoron with the fugitive Je'Rol to the palace. It had to be Je'Dron.

Once again, she fell to one knee. "My lord."

"You heard?" Je'Kaoron asked.

"Yes."

Her blood ran cold. If he heard everything she had said, they had no reason to trust her. What would Je'Dron do knowing she was really after Je'Rol? Was he attached to his son? Impossible. He had sent Je'Rol away. He was a demonlord. They didn't care about their offspring. Je'Rekun had only been guessing.

"I can assure you, Huntress," Je'Dron said, "That I knew my brother's moves before Lord Je'Kaoron returned. I knew this time would come and am prepared to face my brother to regain my rightful place. Lord Je'Kaoron is no traitor to me. I go to meet Je'Rekun at the Nik'Terek Gate fully prepared for the confrontation he brings..."

No "Lord" before his brother's name. Especially since Je'Rekun was *High Lord*, he should have. If she understood right, he didn't recognize Je'Rekun as leader of their clan.

"It was my suggestion, planted by Lord Je'Kaoron in my brother's ear." He met Je'Kaoron's eyes for a few seconds and the latter gave a nod. "As for Je'Rol...he's free to choose his own way."

At a nod from the High Lord, Je'Kaoron left them, much to her relief.

Or maybe not. Alone with the rightful High Lord of the Je'Gri, she noticed a change. Je'Dron's expression darkened, making her step back into the wall to escape, but she had nowhere to go.

"You will *not* pursue him any longer. He was and is *my* son." His words ground out in a growl as he pressed close on her. Where Je'Kaoron had merely sought to intimidate her but didn't have the presence for it, High Lord Je'Dron held nothing back, his imposing presence shattering her determination and pounding it to dust to leave her cowering. "Lord Je'Kaoron may favor you, but I would have no trouble feasting on you or any Adept who touches Je'Rol. Do you understand?"

Her heart raced to escape but she could go nowhere and her powers wouldn't work on the demonlord to save her. Only one answer would. "Y—Yes, my lord."

He eased back, giving her space to catch her breath and chase out the fear. Je'Dron hadn't been High Lord of the Je'Gri for hundreds of years for nothing. He might grant humans more freedom than other demonlord rulers, but he was a leader with all the presence of someone used to others obeying him.

Perhaps the Adepts would be no better off under his rule than Je'Rekun's.

"This is not a matter I take lightly, Huntress."

She didn't doubt that. But why would he even care about a half-blood son? Demonlords didn't care. Or was it possible? Morana said the father of her child had returned to console her while Nadia was gone to retrieve Je'Rol. And before her stood a noble Je'Gri in human form declaring his protection for a half-human offspring.

Such emotions were not the place of demonlords, or so she had been taught. It made them almost—*almost*—human. They were still predators with greater power than any race on Derandria.

"You will leave here as you came and forget Je'Rol."

"What about Je'Rekun?"

White eyebrows lifted in a curious expression. "My brother will not claim the title High Lord for long…I didn't know it concerned you." He paused, staring as if through her for a few seconds before focusing on her again. "Perhaps you can be of some use. I'll have a message for all the sects when this is finished. With you here, I won't have to send another. Make yourself comfortable, Huntress. You'll be staying another day. Tomorrow, we ride to the Nik'Terek Gate."

Her insides twisted to make her grimace. What could Je'Dron want to say to the sects? What did he have planned for Je'Rekun?

The demonlord opened the door and hesitated. "You may have saved me some trouble." He left, closing her inside the room with her thoughts.

Through the door, his muffled voice reached her: ["Keep the demon hunter in that room until we make ready to depart."]

["Yes, my lord."]

That settled it. She was stuck there, and without any signs of Je'Rol. Where was he?

26

Je'Rol squatted on a ledge outside and above the city, watching the activity in and out of the city to the open areas beyond.

Demonlords filled the cavern, making preparations to leave. The vast majority were Je'Gri—a good two-thirds he estimated. He wouldn't have believed so many lived there if he hadn't seen it from above. From what he saw now, he would guess a couple thousand, but from down there, among them, he thought a fraction of that. Je'Dron had a good-sized army ready to go. Maybe he could face Je'Rekun and win.

The ledge had provided a means to observe alone. Je'Surana had hunted him yesterday, pursuing him with questions about his travels. Her curiosity would be cute on a young child, like Arak—part of him wondered if the boy would train to be a demon hunter— but coming from an attractive young woman, the persistent harassment came off as desperation for something else, something he couldn't give her.

That part of him had died learning that Nadia hated him.

He had loved her, but she was determined to kill him. He had hurt her in an effort to protect her, but it wasn't good enough. He could never make it right.

One day he would have peace like he had known in her presence a lifetime ago, but without the power of an Adept.

But would it be enough? Je'Kaoron's and Je'Dron's words had hit him as if with a knife to the chest. They knew he would never be content to let demonlords continue their reign. Worse, others would come to steal his treasure, the one thing he knew could give him the life he wanted, or used to want.

What did he want? After searching for so long, would he be content to make a home, or even to fall in love again? He'd learned to rely on himself and to prefer the loneliness of his travels. What would he do with the obelisk of Mai'Kari?

If the sorcerers took it from him, they would control him, as Liandra had.

A growl rumbled low in his throat at the memories of what she had forced on him for nothing more than entertainment with the purpose of gaining a political advantage for her client. He would not be used like that again, but he would have no control if they possessed the obelisk, nor would any demonlord. Demons and half-bloods would be forced to obey the will of the humans, who wouldn't be affected by the power, which worked almost like *dispirit*.

Je'Rol stood up, the claws extending with the tension hardening his body. *Dispirit.* The legend of the obelisk of Mai'Kari. The *am'taerad* control stones. They only worked on demons.

Something connected them all, something he felt with certainty inside was connected to whatever Skar knew about the 'Old Ones'. The goblin had been knowledgeable in reading the ancient texts and at least a little about many other things.

And he, Je'Rol, determined to not waste time searching for the obelisk, had forsaken the opportunity that had been right before him. He'd given up a real treasure in the form of information, because he thought he could do better alone.

But the little demon couldn't even show him the maps he'd found. The goblins guarded them.

Someone called a name above the din of voices from below, but it barely distracted him from the race of ideas catching up in his head, circling around the reality of Skar's purpose.

"Goblins!" He breathed the word in a hush of air. They were cursed—never to give up the secrets of the Old Ones, the Master Race, to the demonlords. They knew the history, the connections, the darkest secrets sought by demonlords and Adepts. A small race of relatively weak demons, but more powerful than any would know. They hid their secrets, keeping alive the knowledge of their masters for thousands of years.

They were the true masters.

Laughter arose from within him at the irony and escaped in a chuckle that relaxed him into leaning on the wall of the cavern. "They'll never know." And he wouldn't be the one to tell the demonlords or the Adepts. Now he knew why the goblins stayed close to the demonlords—Adepts couldn't force them to talk with that curse in effect.

It didn't help him in his quest, but he would get that obelisk and stop the madness. Once he did, he could order the goblins to give up their ultimate knowledge. That would give him the advantage he needed, and perhaps real peace from his demon half.

A long figure climbed a stairway at his end of the cavern. He'd leapt up from the tunnel at the top of those stairs to avoid any traffic. A few tigers had gone that way earlier and not yet returned. He could only guess what lay beyond, as he hadn't been inclined to explore the tunnels and lose himself and his chance to join Je'Dron's forces to confront Je'Rekun's.

From the moderate blue of the gown billowing behind and the contrast of white and black hair mixed together, it could only be Je'Surana. As he'd learned, demonlords did occasionally wear tailored clothes, but most often they preferred the ease of transforming their hides into and out of what they needed. Je'Surana was the only woman he'd seen in tailored clothes contrasting the stark white and black of her demonlord side. The figure growing in definition could only be her.

If she came to pester him, he was leaving.

Je'Rol had nowhere to hide on his ledge and waited with his arms crossed for the inevitable.

Instead, she reached the tunnel opening, gave him a cursory glance, and grabbed a scepter that brightened at her touch and disappeared into the tunnel.

Odd.

His curiosity piqued. Where would she go without her guards who had accompanied her yesterday?

More interesting was where the tunnel led. He hadn't explored that one, but he hadn't wanted to get lost in the dark and had no idea how to use the scepters. She'd be easy to follow with the light, as long as she didn't get too far ahead. Her father wouldn't leave her behind without protection, though. He'd search for her if she didn't return.

What was at the end of the tunnel?

Having nothing better to do than stare at Je'Dron's army, Je'Rol leapt down to the landing of the tunnel, the light only a blur ahead. Seeing what Je'Surana did would break the monotony. She moved quickly, but he could too.

On light feet, he hurried to keep the light within his sight. Fresh air trickled from ahead, blowing away the dank, stale air of the tunnel around a few turns. Ahead, the light steadied and fresh air brushed his face, the breeze billowing his cloak. Without a doubt, she had found an exit, or opened one.

If this one was like where they had brought him in, it wouldn't stay.

Je'Rol raced ahead, but the rock never closed.

The muted light of a cloudy day made him blink after the darkness of the tunnel. He halted and gazed out at the ominous rises of mountains around a shallow valley.

On a wide, grassy ledge before him, Je'Surana laid her head on a white tiger lying among the grass and flowers. The tiger licked its paw near fresh earth upturned with gouges that could only have come from its claws.

"Why are you here?" Her voice admonished and her blue eyes glimmered with unshed tears.

It took him aback, and Je'Rol fumbled for the right words. "I—" What could he say? She was obviously safe and didn't want him.

"You're not welcome here."

At that, the tiger rose to his feet and licked her cheek. She sniffed and nodded her head, but embraced the demonlord as if afraid he might vanish, burying her face in his coat along with her tears. Her body trembled.

Je'Rol stepped back, ready to leave the two to their private moment, but a whimper from her made him pause. Something inside sympathized with the young woman for whatever had happened in those seconds before he arrived. The tiger wasn't hurt, was it?

He shouldn't care, but something inside him couldn't leave her like that.

"Yes, my lord." Je'Surana sniffed and stood back.

The tiger blurred and transformed into a man with his back to Je'Rol and dressed in white leggings and a tunic belted at his waist with a shimmering vest bearing jagged and curved black lines like the tiger.

Je'Surana flung her arms around the demonlord, her sobs muffled in his chest.

In an act of clear affection, the demonlord embraced her and rubbed her back.

A couple seconds later, she peered around the demonlord's shoulder with red eyes swollen from tears, the menace gone and the gentleness of the young woman returned. "What do you want?"

The demonlord turned, his expression as calm as Je'Rol had come to expect of the man, yet that face still sent a shiver through him in its familiarity. Seeing Je'Kaoron in the young woman's arms made him doubt his eyes.

"I—" What had he wanted? To know the way out. No. Not just that. He wanted to see where she went alone during so much activity when normally she went nowhere without the Je'Gri guards. "I was concerned."

A smile alighted on Je'Kaoron's face, but Je'Surana closed her eyes and pressed against him. He brushed away the hair sticking to her cheeks and gently pushed her away. "Don't take too much time," he said and kissed her forehead.

She sniffed and nodded and let him go, her lips pressed together.

Je'Kaoron stepped away and stopped next to Je'Rol. "Come." His tone gave no indication of anger. "She needs her time alone."

After a glance back at the girl, who kneeled down to the flowers, Je'Rol joined the demonlord in the tunnel, where Je'Kaoron grabbed one of two scepters filling five sconces in the wall.

"It's the one place she's safe alone, the only place I'll leave her alone," Je'Kaoron said with a glance back. With her blue gown out around her, Je'Surana could have been one of the flowers.

"The flowers never die on that ledge. I can only guess..." Je'Kaoron paused and cleared his throat. "It was Surika's last miracle. Her ashes coat that ledge, and are scattered across the valley by the wind, but the bones are buried beneath, making that her burial place. Surika always took Je'Surana there to play, away from the others."

Guilt snaked through Je'Rol. He'd interrupted a private moment for the girl when he'd had no right. "I'm sorry."

A brief smile flashed across the demonlord's face. "She is not the one to pity...You are. You know nothing of Je'Dron's anguish after sending away you and your mother. I never understood and tried to console the High Lord that he'd done the right thing for us all. I told him Amia was just a human and her son merely a half-blood." He let out a heavy sigh, his gaze distant. "I was wrong."

Emotion weighed down the demonlord's voice, human emotion unlike anything Je'Rol would have expected. "I never loved like that before, but I'm reminded every day of what Surika gave me…"

What Surika gave him…Je'Rol's suspicions were correct.

Je'Kaoron took a deep breath that seemed to lift him again to the noble poise with which he normally carried himself. "I understand now what the others fear, why there is such a split among our kind. They are afraid of becoming…human."

Je'Kaoron couldn't expect him to believe they would give up their power for mortality. Was it even possible? Or was this simply a metaphor for something else?

"Or maybe the humans are rising to challenge us. The Adepts may become a threat, but we have the chance to delay the madness. Je'Rekun would lead all demonlords into a war with the Adepts and humanity, which would ruin this world. Je'Dron won't allow it. We need time to understand, and maybe to adapt."

He'd bet they did. A low growl rose from the beast. "So you can keep them enslaved."

"No. Je'Dron wouldn't allow that. Five hundred years ago, maybe, but things have changed, *are* changing quickly. The Adepts have learned tricks we were never aware of, or we've forgotten. The stone used to control you was only one of those. There are others, like the obelisk. We can't allow them to gain that power."

"You're afraid." Je'Rol had never noticed it before, but the demonlords gave nothing away. They showed no emotion; as Je'Dron had said, they didn't feel emotions as humans did. They were the immortal rulers of the world, but they could be killed by their own kind, or perhaps by a higher power. That's what they feared.

Je'Kaoron's cheek twitched with shadows for a moment. "I'll do whatever I can to protect her. If the Adepts of Te'Mea gain power over demonlords, they gain power over me. If that happens, I can no longer protect Je'Surana, and I can't allow that. Fleeting as her life may be, she deserves the chance for happiness, perhaps more so than anyone, because the life of half-bloods is shorter than humans and every moment is precious." His voice faltered at the end, trailing off until he cleared his throat.

The emotional appeal wouldn't work. Je'Kaoron wouldn't manipulate him. Je'Rol had endured too much pain and suffering in his life to let others use him.

Je'Rol stared down the tunnel, as much to avoid the sorrow on the demonlord's face as to watch where he walked.

"She deserves the life you would have had, had Je'Rekun not gathered the support of those opposed to Je'Dron's change of policies regarding humans."

Twisted opinions. Now he saw what Je'Kaoron was getting at. The beast growled in defiance, ready to tear the demonlord apart to end the conflict rising within. "You blame me for this."

"Yes and no. You were merely the catalyst, but you were not the beginning. This started over one thousand years ago, when the first Adepts were recognized by Te'Mea, although we suspect humans had the power far longer. She tested them but they weren't a threat to demonlords, so she taught them to develop the gift we call *dispirit*. It was considered beneficial to protect the primary food source from natters. The Adepts she trained kept the pests away and humans bred and lived longer in communities protected by her Adepts, so she traveled the world to find others and trained them.

"The clans welcomed the chance to cut back their herding duties."

Herding humans. A demonlord would describe it that way. Despite the sickening thought, Je'Rol said nothing.

"Humans were able to manage their own herds. They were unique, being both predator and prey, a position many clans object to."

Ah! Not herding humans, but herding livestock prey. That realization cooled the sore spot of demonlords hunting humans and considering them nothing more than prey creatures.

"The Adepts soon organized their own formal training. Te'Mea is said to have died in battle serving her High Lady of the Te'Kuri, but her legacy lives on in something that now threatens our existence."

Such an irony almost made Je'Rol laugh. A demonlord—as he had expected by the name—had started the training of Adepts, and now the demonlords were the ones defending themselves against a beast of their own making. He'd never heard the history, but he hadn't cared. His only concern had been avoiding the Adepts and their *dispirit* powers. He could blame the demonlords for part of that too.

"What was thought to be a benefit to the clans has twisted into a problem for us. All the major predators are demons, except humans. They are immune to the power they possess; thus, the problem they present to us—competition without outside control, except the clans. By controlling all demons, they eliminate the controls on their own species. They would become the new Master Race."

The light of the pillar in the center of the cavern brightened ahead as Je'Kaoron's revelation brightened before him. In his mind, he recalled the image of the building where he had found Skar, the human figures of the pillars and the statue the goblin had called the 'Old Ones'. Were they human? Were humans somehow the product of the Master Race or something else?

With this news, a part of him pitied the demonlords. They had initiated their own downfall and now struggled to prevent it through two opposing opinions; one wanted to eliminate all Adepts and erase one thousand years of sliding power, while the other sought to make peace but destroy the tools that immediately threatened them. Whether Je'Dron's policies would eliminate the threat or delay the inevitable could not be foreseen, but neither could Je'Rekun's desire to annihilate those who threatened them and, therefore, their lifestyle made easy by the labor of humans.

At the top of the stairs to the floor of the cavern, Je'Kaoron stopped, the scepter dark in his hand. "Now do you understand?"

Yes, he did. All this time, Je'Rol had searched for his own peace, but he could never have it as long as one side sought to eliminate the other.

Su'Tari was right; the obelisk must be destroyed, but so too must the *am'taerad* and any other nefarious devices left by the Master Race. But the demonlords needed to remain in check also, and the answer to that was with the Adepts. Neither could be allowed total power over the other if both hoped to survive.

Humbled by the epiphany, Je'Rol pushed back his hood, exposing the white and black hair of his demonlord heritage. He would never have peace as long as the obelisk existed. "It must be destroyed," he grumbled, and the best way was to send it into the Nik'Terek Gate.

Je'Kaoron replaced the scepter in one of the sconces in the wall of the tunnel and rejoined him. "I know it's not an easy choice, but you would never have true peace. They would all hunt you, more fiercely than ever."

The beast growled its defiance of the truth in those words. "I said it must be destroyed, not that I would help you."

Concern hardened the demonlord's expression. "You would not stop us?"

Je'Rol's fingers clenched and unclenched in his struggle between desire and reality, until the truth won. "No."

Without a word, Je'Kaoron descended the stairs.

After a glance at the dark tunnel behind him and a brief concern for the half-blood daughter Je'Kaoron had left on the ledge, Je'Rol followed. If the demonlord as a protective father was confident in her security, he would trust that.

But the army prepared to leave.

At the bottom of the stone stairway, Je'Kaoron stopped. "Your friend will be joining us."

"Friend?"

"The demon hunter."

Every vein in Je'Rol's body ran cold. Nadia! What had they done to her? When had she been brought in?

"She hinted of a past relation, but I suppose that's changed."

Je'Rol said nothing, his jaw clenched on the betrayal and anger strangling the fondness he once had for her. She didn't deserve his mercy, but he wouldn't let the demonlords hurt her.

"Calm, Je'Rol. She asked to be brought inside and has been treated fairly, but we couldn't allow her to learn anything about Mount Serako. She'll be taken out blindfolded until the doorway is sealed."

Then she was unhurt; he didn't doubt Je'Kaoron's words. She knew about the mountain, but at least she wouldn't learn its secrets, and neither would the sects of Adepts.

"We leave soon." Je'Kaoron started forward again. What must have been a couple thousand demonlords gathered on the outskirts of the city, along one side of the reservoir.

"What of Je'Surana?"

Je'Kaoron continued towards the growing group of demonlords in natural and human forms. "I'm touched that you care, but give her no more thought. She'll be safe." A moment later, the man blurred into the form of a tiger and ran away, leaving Je'Rol to wonder.

He looked back at the dark tunnel. For a moment, he thought he saw a shape in the shadows, but it disappeared. And among the flurry of scents stirred by the activity, he didn't detect hers.

Even if she stayed, he wouldn't. Je'Dron intended to destroy the obelisk by sending it into the Nik'Terek Gate. His chance to stop the madness would be lost.

27

They shuffled her through a commotion of voices and the press of bodies, her hands secured behind her, which, along with a demonlord at each arm, kept her from removing the blindfold over her eyes. Nadia listened for clues about what was going on but heard only orders to carry supplies and move out. It was as if they moved an army, a very large army.

From what she'd overheard through the door of the room where they'd kept her and had been told by Je'Dron and Je'Kaoron, the only demonlords to give her any information, they did move out an army from the mountain. An army they felt was capable of matching High Lord Je'Rekun's.

They departed to face him at the appointed place and time.

"Move along," a gruff voice said. Strong hands on her arms dragged her onward, giving her no chance to keep up and almost tripping her on her own feet, as if the uneven ground wasn't bad enough. The flap of wings echoed in the cavern above her in multitudes.

Fresh air brushed her face, blowing away the stagnant air. Still, they nearly carried her forward, demonlords on each arm catching her from the ridges and bumps on the ground her feet struck.

The creak of wood and grinding of wheels over rock blended with the clop of hooves. They had horses, which they must have hidden somewhere she hadn't seen. It surprised her that they would use horses, but by the creaks and grinding like wheels on gravel, it sounded like they were used to pull wagons, likely supplies, like food.

A dismal thought made her shudder, but this was Je'Dron's army. Surely he wouldn't allow them to turn her into their next meal.

He might if she didn't cooperate. He'd said so himself.

She struck her toe on a jut of rock, sending a spear of pain through her foot. Damn her and her imagination! That's just the kind of fear Je'Dron hoped to inspire in her. Yet, she didn't doubt he meant it. Je'Dron might favor peace with the Adepts, but that didn't mean he would allow them total freedom.

She was surrounded by demonlords and little better than a snack for them.

The demonlords on her arms tightened their grips and nearly lifted her off her feet.

Faint light reached her eyes through the blindfold made from a strip cut from the bottom of her cloak. They continued on, the rock giving way to tufts of tall grass brushing her calves in reassurance, except the uneven ground threatened to crunch more toes if she didn't pick up her feet.

They were outside the mountain, yet they kept her blindfolded. How much longer would she have to stay like that? Hopefully not the whole journey.

The ground beneath her trembled and forceful hands yanked off the blindfold.

At the sudden light of day, she blinked, until her eyes adjusted, and scanned around her. Behind her, a great maw in the mountain was replaced by the face of the stone reappearing. Around her, a sea of tigers and myriad other demonlords flowed in one direction, led by a group of riders on horseback and surrounding a few carriages and several wagons loaded with supplies. Overhead flew a few dragons and raptors of various sizes. The demonlords went to battle, and they took her with them.

At least now she could see where she stepped; small consolation to the toe she had already jammed.

A demonlord came up behind her and freed her hands, much to her relief. Her wrists ached from the tight wrap they'd used, and her shoulders ached from the awkward position of her hands secured behind her back for so long.

Was she free to leave? Was Captain Karik still waiting, or had the demonlords seen to dispose of him and his company or send them away? Je'Dron had said he wanted a messenger after he won, *if* he won the battle.

That thought disheartened her, although staying with the demonlords and out of the battle could work to her advantage, no matter who won. Whatever news she carried back to the temple would bear importance to Adepts everywhere, as the sorcerers had indicated.

More of the demonlords blurred and transformed into their natural forms, most of them lower than her eye level, although a few clans were larger in their natural forms. Luckily, most of those around her were tigers; how ironic that she should consider that luck.

As the armored guards and royals went down on four paws, she had a clearer view of the mass of bodies around her. They included one with the white and black hair of a royal pulled back into a tight tail at the nape of his neck who wore clothes that weren't the natural color pattern of a tiger.

Je'Rol. He left his hood off for once and walked next to one of the carriages. Seeing him triggered only a whimper of frustration—so close yet out of her reach. She dared not try. Je'Dron's threat dampened her determination to capture him again.

Or was it?

Seeing Je'Rol in the blood rage had scared her more than any other half-blood had in the years since she started hunting them. She had focused all her power on controlling Je'Rol but barely connected to him somewhere inside. The Je'Rol she had known long ago had never let that side of him show in her presence. He said he'd left to protect her. Although she appreciated his concern for her safety, it wasn't an excuse for not returning to explain himself and tell her the truth. He should have been honest with her from the beginning and said he was a half-blood rather than let her believe he was a full demonlord.

He'd taken advantage of her naïveté.

Still, after seeing him in the blood rage, she couldn't help but feel relieved it hadn't happened then, before she knew how to control him. A part of her had never wanted to believe he was a half-blood with the danger that came with it, or at least that he could ever hurt her. He'd been gentle and quiet then with a sorrow that had slowly lifted with time, not the monster she'd seen a few days ago.

Life had been easier before she learned the truth.

Nadia shook the thought away, cursing herself for letting the fantasies of the young girl replay in her mind. She hated him for leaving her, and he deserved to die, before he killed anyone else in the blood rage. He had proven to her that he was a threat.

One way or another, she would kill him.

First, she had to survive the coming battle.

Before that, she had to survive the travel. The least they could have done was allowed her on a carriage or cart. Her only consolation came in the fact that Je'Rol walked, but he was used to it. She was used to riding, and these demonlords kept up a fair pace.

If she could weave through them to the carriages…

Three tigers stopped and growled at her, cutting her off only two steps towards the carriages.

"All right. I understand." Je'Dron had probably left orders to keep her away from Je'Rol, lest she *dispirit* him or attempt to kill him, although the demonlords could interrupt her power. With so many between her and Je'Rol, she had no chance of influencing him. Even up close, she doubted she would have any control, unless the demonlords allowed it, but they wouldn't.

No. She was stuck walking alone among a sea of creatures who could decide she was dinner.

Nadia let out a huff and resigned to walking. Along the journey, she rested when they allowed and ate when they did.

At the midday break, she looked up from her loaf and fruits as the door of one of the carriages opened. A woman stepped out in a flowing blue gown, her white and black hair pulled away from the lovely face of a demonlord. Two tigresses stood by in human form, white royals but in armor rather than the elegant robes they most often preferred, and accompanied the young woman to where she disappeared around the other side. Another tiger blurred in the transformation to human form and closed the door of the carriage. He stood with his back to the door and caught her eyes with a frown on that calm visage.

She looked away from the confident eyes of Je'Kaoron, but his eyes burned through her back.

Resigned to her little hole among the demonlords around the fresh kills many of them had dragged back—she hadn't realized how many more belonged to the group since so many had been out hunting all morning—Nadia chewed her food and choked it down. If not for her hunger, the reek of dead animals would have stolen her appetite. She sucked water from the canteen they had provided. The rough shape of a ball hung in a leather pouch with a stopper in it, like the one she'd had on her saddle.

Her saddle. The horses ridden by the Li'Ador…

Nadia scanned the area around her. Je'Dron's army had stopped on a grassy hill surrounded by the mountains, a narrow river flowing serenely along the valley to the south. The Li'Ador should have seen them leave, if the demonlords hadn't warned them off. Captain Karik and his men might be out there, but she didn't see anything. Rather, the jagged lines of mountain broke the skyline around them with Mount Serako towering over all the land behind them. Nothing but brush and boulders littered the landscape her eyes could trace.

The crunch of bone made her stomach knot. Its mouth and paws bloody like the three others sharing the same deer carcass, an orange tiger nearby looked up with bits of bone in its mouth and a low growl rumbling from its throat. It met her eyes and flicked its tail as if daring her to cross it.

Trying to forget being surrounded by tigers and other creatures ready to crunch through her the same way they did that deer, Nadia focused on her food.

While she tried to forget the carnage around her, her mind wandered to what Je'Kaoron guarded in the carriage and the identity of the woman who had left it.

Something was off about the woman; she was different, special. Why did the tigresses accompany her?

Too many questions! Just eat. She'd need her strength for the latter half of the day.

Still, Nadia watched for the woman. Most of the demonlords, having cleaned the carcasses, stretched out to clean themselves and relax.

The woman returned soon after with the tigresses. After they disappeared into the carriage, a handsome boy in green clothes with an almost metallic sheen took the feed bags from the horses and returned to the driver's seat with the driver, a demonlord of similar coloring. Je'Kaoron stayed at the door of the carriage until the others rose from their midday breaks, when he walked to where a group of young girls held a few horses ready for their riders. He took the reins of one and mounted.

So, he had been riding, and she'd bet he stayed with Je'Dron. Why did he take such an interest in the carriage of the young woman? What was he planning?

She'd keep a watch on him.

He did nothing out of the ordinary the rest of the day, nor during the night, when he ate and lay down outside the carriage where the young woman rested. With him guarding the carriage so closely, she would never get close enough to ask a name much less satisfy her curiosity.

Tired from a long day of travel and secure for her safety surrounded by demonlords filled on fresh kill again that evening, she fell asleep easily. Her last thoughts drifted to Je'Rol and where he might have gone.

* * *

The next day repeated much of the same, except Nadia's feet ached and Je'Rol acknowledged her, although with no more than a lingering glance and only once. He never made any attempt to speak with her, but she hadn't exactly given him a reason to want to be near her.

From a small corner of her heart rose a whimper, faint but there. He hated her now, and a part of her ached to consider it, as it had when he disappeared. She shouldn't care, but a small part of her still did.

Damn him! She didn't want to care.

Did he?

When she talked to him in the chamber of the palace where they held him in chains, he had sounded like he cared, or had cared. Whether he did now or not didn't matter. Nadia had a job to finish.

Before midday, the demonlords broke to rest in a small valley, this time without food. Hunting had been scarce, so they loaded one of the less full carts with the carcasses they had found. Besides, they had eaten well yesterday. Demonlords didn't need food as often as humans, but they needed rest.

So did she.

Nadia sat with her back to a tree, her knees thanking her for bending and her back grateful for the chance to rest.

The tigers around her sprawled out in the sun.

She closed her eyes to wait for them to doze off with the security of believing she had also.

After some time, before her own fatigue overcame her desire to stay awake, she opened her eyes. Quiet pervaded the valley now littered with demonlords.

This might be her chance to reach the carriages or Je'Rol, but she'd have to step lightly.

Nadia stood and stretched. So far, none of the demonlords lifted a head from the grass. And Je'Kaoron was nowhere near the carriages or carts, nor the horses tended by the younger demonlords, if he wasn't in tiger form.

That could be a problem—she couldn't tell him apart from Je'Dron in tiger form—but if she wanted answers, she'd have to take the chance. What's the worst they would do?

Eat her…maybe. Most likely just keep extra close watch on her.

Her feet stayed planted as if nailed to the ground with doubts, but after a deep breath, she lifted a foot and set it down in the space between two tigers. They didn't move.

Encouraged, she took another step and another, her eyes scanning the sleeping bodies around her, senses alert to trouble. They couldn't have slept through her movements, but maybe they didn't care.

Halfway between the carriage and her previous location, she halted, feet spread wide to avoid a couple of tails.

A white tiger emerged from the other side of one of the loaded carts and stopped.

Its eyes caught hers and stopped her breath. The woman who emerged from around the cart behind it broke the moment of panic.

But the demonlord was not amused. The tiger pinned its ears back at Nadia and hunched down as if ready to pounce, its tail whipping in agitation. Lips curled back in a terrible snarl directed at her, then, in an odd change, it twisted around to the woman and growled at her in the same threatening manner.

Unmoved by the behavior, the woman merely dropped her eyes to the tiger, her smile vanishing. "Yes, my lord," she conceded and disappeared again behind the cart.

The tiger took a step towards Nadia and growled again in warning, teeth bared and ears back. A couple seconds later, it followed the woman.

Nadia got the hint—back off and don't come near the woman. Who was she? Few demonlords wore anything but their hides transformed to clothes, yet this one wore what obviously was a tailored gown and hadn't transformed like the rest. Where were the tigresses that guarded her? Why did they guard her?

The woman wasn't a half-blood, was she? Fully grown and guarded by the demonlords?

Impossible, yet Je'Dron had allowed Je'Rol to live. Had he sired another or allowed another demonlord's child to live among them? Why would she be with them now?

Too many questions going unanswered! Nadia wanted to know, but they didn't trust her.

And now, she stood amid the resting demonlords.

Another step towards the carriage was as far as she got without one of the orange tigers sitting up in her way. Point made—they obeyed the noble's warning. She retreated and returned to the tree to rest.

Not long after, they resumed their journey along a winding road through the valleys and along steep cliffs. Resting for the night brought much the same as the rest break earlier. She slept among the tigers on the hard ground and remembered dreaming and thinking she woke up at one point to someone standing over her, but the images blurred and merged with odd dreams.

The next day saw a change of events.

28

At Je'Kaoron's insistence, Je'Rol had avoided Nadia, but the tigers between them had kept her back. After meeting her eyes one time, he'd passed to the opposite side of the carriages, where she couldn't see him and he didn't have to see her. She would have no power over him.

Je'Kaoron had said she had been taken into custody, but he didn't warn him that she would be accompanying them on the journey to the Nik'Terek Gate. Of all the demonlords, he would have thought Je'Kaoron the most vocal in opposition to a demon hunter joining them. But Je'Rol also wondered why he'd allowed Je'Surana along, putting her in danger from Je'Rekun's forces. The demonlord placed far too much faith in Je'Dron's plan.

Perhaps that's what the two discussed while riding side by side on the horses near the front of the group. Or they spoke not at all. He'd never seen their lips move, but if Je'Kaoron could speak in his mind, then other demonlords must have had the same ability, one which no one spoke about. If that was true, then the possibility of Je'Kaoron and Je'Dron speaking without anyone overhearing wasn't farfetched.

Je'Rol glanced back at the carriage where Je'Surana sat with the two tigress bodyguards. Why had Je'Kaoron brought her? Was he afraid to leave her behind?

Had they left anyone behind?

Someone must have been left guarding the mountain.

It wouldn't matter if Je'Dron failed in his mission, so perhaps they had all come to see it through. The obelisk was there somewhere with an individual Je'Dron trusted with his life. Who would that be—Je'Kaoron? That would be too obvious. It had to be someone else.

Just because the demonlord trusted the keeper of the obelisk didn't mean Je'Rol did. He should have it, to use it the right way.

A formation of winged demonlords flew from over the peak of a mountain ahead, their wings rising and falling steadily. The caravan continued without stopping, until the V formation grew in size to where he recognized a few Val'Tiro and a couple of a clan he'd seen long ago but never identified.

The demonlords on horseback stopped, halting the procession, and the raptors leveled above the ground and transformed.

Je'Rol rushed to the front past the tigers and a couple bears, a few representatives of the wolflike Cas'Lu clan, and a handful of others of clans he'd always avoided. They waited in silence, leaving only the wind rushing through the grass and rustling leaves of trees. Still, he heard nothing, even as close as behind and to the right of the horses ridden by Je'Dron and Je'Kaoron.

The woman facing them in her colorful robes bowed with the other five women and men to the two Je'Gri royals and led her group away to transform and return to the sky.

Je'Dron turned to Je'Kaoron with a grim frown. After a few minutes, Je'Kaoron gave a nod. The High Lord's eyes slid away to Je'Rol for a moment. Just as Je'Kaoron had spoken in his head where no one else could hear, the others did amongst themselves, keeping any news private.

A low growl of dissatisfaction rumbled in his throat. Apparently he was still an outsider, whether he agreed with them or not about the fate of the obelisk.

Je'Dron met Je'Kaoron's gaze again. "You have your orders."

"Yes, my lord." Je'Kaoron dismounted and handed his reins to one of the boys who had changed to his human form. He stepped around the horse and, on passing, met Je'Rol's eyes but said nothing. A moment later, he transformed and ran off among the other tigers.

"Je'Rol."

He looked up to Je'Dron.

"You know how to ride?"

Not well, but he'd appreciate the chance to rest his legs. They hadn't allowed him to ride, but neither did they give that courtesy to Nadia. She wasn't so high and mighty when forced to walk. That gave him some satisfaction.

Je'Rol took the reins from the boy and flipped them over the head of the dark bay, who chewed the bit a little before quieting down and sniffing him. A moment later, the horse acted as if nothing had changed, and Je'Rol put his foot in the stirrup and swung his other across the saddle. Not the most comfortable way to travel, but at least he had a chance to rest.

"Where's Je'Kaoron—"

An admonishing look from Je'Dron corrected his mistake of the lack of respect. Apparently only other demonlords could speak without titles of others.

He fought off a snarl and asked, "Where's Lord Je'Kaoron going?"

Je'Dron relaxed and his horse moved off. Without a cue from Je'Rol, the dark bay stayed beside them. Je'Rol grasped the pommel on the front and regained his balance.

This wasn't as easy as everyone made it look.

"His mission will ensure the success of our plan."

Whatever that meant. Je'Rol didn't like being kept in the dark, but he'd promised himself he wasn't leaving until he saw the obelisk destroyed with his own eyes. His lifetime quest for peace would soon be gone.

Then what would he do? Where would he go? His search would be over.

Maybe he could rest. Would the demonlords allow it? Why not—they allowed Je'Surana to live among them. That represented a great shift in old ways.

What had Je'Kaoron called it?

The *caer sekiya numa*. He'd claimed the law gave the right to the clan to judge their own half-bloods along with the offending demonlord. The judgment was death, as Je'Rol understood, but Je'Dron had ignored the old law of the demonlords and Je'Kaoron wasn't likely to obey it either. They'd both be dead according to the old laws.

"It'll be over soon." Je'Dron looked out over the valley through the mountains and the shallow river winding along the dips of the hills. "You'll be free to stay at the palace, Je'Rol."

Free? The realization sent a breath of fresh air through him.

But the couple of dozen orange and white tigers running off through the valley stalled that sentiment.

"No more Adepts after you; I'll see to that. You've had a difficult life, but the rest of it can be free of hardship." Je'Dron stared ahead as if afraid to catch his eyes. "You'll have whatever you desire."

He'd like that, except for one thing. Such promises usually came with a price, a thought that spurred suspicions to rise up and irritate the beast. "Why?"

Je'Dron turned aside to him. "Because I could not do less. No matter where you were or what you did, I was not there as I should have been."

"So you want to keep watch on me?"

"No. Not like that. More…" He looked up at the formation of raptors in the sky. "More like a…atonement."

"Atone to the woman you seduced," Je'Rol growled. "For the suffering you caused her." She had awakened him many nights with her crying and had suffered to raise him in a world in which people, once they discovered what he was, ostracized her and refused to barter for the least amount of food. He and his mother had spent many days hungry, eating only what he could hunt.

Je'Dron's cheek twitched and his fingers shifted on the reins. "She is happy again with a man who loves her as much as I did. That's all I could hope, as should you."

How did Je'Dron know? Or was this a lie to appeal to his emotions?

It wouldn't work. Je'Rol refused to fall for any games.

"I sent a message to her to join me, but after thirty years, a long time by human lifespans, I doubted she was still alive. I was relieved to receive her message. She's an old woman now, living her remaining days in peace with a man who loves her, but she expressed her sorrow in not knowing about you." The last part came out with a strong hint of reprimand in his voice.

Je'Dron could think as he wished, or so Je'Rol tried to tell himself. He'd left his mother without a word that fateful day that the beast had taken over and killed his first love. Too afraid to admit that he'd lost control, he instead had fled. Shame had followed him, and now caught up.

He said nothing, but rode next to the man who had sired him as if a boy caught misbehaving and scolded by an adult. In retrospect, he should have risked a quick visit or sent a note to tell his mother saying he was sorry for the pain he'd caused, but he'd been frightened, as much of himself as of the demon hunters he knew would be on his trail.

"Amia is happy, but what about you? The obelisk you've sought all these years will be gone. The least I can offer is a chance at the peace you so desperately seek." Je'Dron took a deep breath and hesitated, his eyes on the mountain looming over them, around which their destination lied. "No one will provoke you or challenge you. I'll see to that. No more blood rage, no more running from demon hunters."

He paused and glanced aside.

Je'Rol met the eyes of a man who regretted his actions. That much he read on the demonlord's human face. The offer tempted him, but how long could it last?

"Lord Je'Kaoron said he saw you in the blood rage. The transformation was nearly complete. The next time could be your last."

Silence fell between them, as if they existed in a bubble separate from the world. Je'Dron watched the road ahead, and Je'Rol watched him while considering his words. The time was coming; he knew too well, but he'd always come out of it. That wouldn't be true much longer and his life as Je'Rol would be over.

But if he had peace, if the beast was never taunted into taking over, he might know the true peace he sought. Only one problem remained. "And if the others don't accept it?"

"I'll make them." A slight growl accompanied Je'Dron's words, but he calmed himself. "You are…my son, whether you accept it or not. They will respect that."

The ferocity of his last statement caught Je'Rol by surprise. The rightful High Lord was determined to make his offer stand with the others, and from the rage he'd demonstrated, that argument must have been made many times. Je'Dron meant what he said. His offer was good.

But was it the life Je'Rol could live? One place. No more traveling. No more wandering. A peaceful life where no one would question his right to live. But only as long as he stayed there.

He'd wandered for so long in his quest that settling down seemed like a rest long overdue. But because he'd spent all his life traveling, would settling down be enough for him to enjoy the rest of it, however long that may be?

The arguments rang through his mind. Part of him desired the rest promised but part of him was forever restless and wanting to travel. He'd enjoyed it, as his discussion with Je'Surana had revealed to him. The places he'd seen and the excitement he'd experienced could never be replaced. He had been fortunate in that.

Too many factors to consider. He couldn't decide yet. "I'll think about it."

A smile flashed across Je'Dron's face and the demonlord said nothing more about it.

They rode through a valley, past a small cluster of homes and livestock. It all seemed serene and calm and so easy to choose, but they passed among the homes unhindered and without sight of the human tenants.

Beyond the farms, they rode over a high hill and emerged to a sight that sent a shiver down Je'Rol's spine. They had only referred to the Nik'Terek Gate as if it was some dangerous magic, so what he saw was unexpected.

A decayed city of stone rose at levels cut from a mountain whose peak seemed to have been hewn away to form a wide plateau. The city started in the valley and climbed magnificent sheer walls. A waterfall at each end sprayed the lower ruins of the ancient city in rainbows, flowing from caverns within the walls into the valley. There, the water flowed from the pools to join as the river they had been following.

A road wound up along the various steps of the city, zigzagging across and inward with each narrowing level to the top. A few structures remained mostly intact, their roof tiles only partially missing or in a few piles alongside cracked walls. Staggered as they were, the levels appeared to step along the plateau. Most of the city stood on top of that plateau, as grand in its decay as *Acropa Je'Gri* was in its newness, with flowers budding along vines wrapped like lovers around pillars and posts and the flowering trees twisted into languid poses accentuating the balance and harmony of the city's layout.

Je'Dron halted his horse on the hilltop with a view of the idyllic city. "The Nik'Terek left this place over eight hundred years ago, abandoning the last great work of the Master Race, which is rumored to have been brought from another domain. Lord Je'Kaoron could tell you about them someday."

That explained the name, Nik'Terek Gate. But why "gate"? Why not something more ominous if it was meant to destroy? Where was this lethal device?

Je'Dron stared ahead as if searching.

For a moment, Je'Rol thought he caught movement among the moss-covered pillars ringing an area of one of the mid-levels. But it appeared again higher up. No, to the left.

And he realized what he saw—tigers moving in and out of the buildings. Were these Je'Rekun's forces or Je'Dron's advance party led by Je'Kaoron?

He would soon learn.

Je'Dron reined his horse around to face the mass of demonlords behind them, while Je'Rol turned his horse with less skill. There must have been thousands covering the valley behind them. Their place at the crest of the hill gave him a view that took his breath away. From the ground, he'd seen an undulating sea of orange and white broken by the occasional outsider, but nothing like this. They covered the valley, surrounding the carriages and supply wagons so the vehicles looked like boats on the ocean.

Tails lashed and ears flicked attentively but with an eagerness that infected Je'Rol. They were ready for battle.

Je'Dron made a hand motion and a group of tigers ran off towards the city. Another signal sent a second group of tigers elsewhere. A whistle from the demonlord was returned from the air in a shriek that shriveled Je'Rol's spine worse than the goblin's voice had.

In the quiet of thickening expectation, Je'Dron waited, those pale blue eyes studying the massive army.

Je'Rol glanced back and spied the tigers making their way up the city, some of them climbing the angled mountainside attached to the plateau.

The click of a door in the quiet pulled his attention to the carriages. From the second carriage stepped Je'Surana in her blue gown, a pair of tigresses in orange and black armor at her side this time.

Je'Rol clenched the pommel of his saddle and bit his tongue on the urge to command her back from the danger. What was Je'Kaoron thinking by bringing her? She wasn't fit to face this.

And from near the back of the line of carriages and wagons came Nadia. For a change, the tigers and other demonlords let her pass. Conflict roared up, stirring the beast within him to growl for release. Je'Rol's instincts to protect Je'Surana were strong, even against a former lover.

"Calm yourself," Je'Dron said in a soothing voice.

Easy for him to say.

Nevertheless, Je'Rol did as commanded, or as much as he could under the circumstances.

The demonlords parted before Je'Surana, clearing a path directly to Je'Dron.

A few strides before she reached them, Je'Dron dismounted. Immediately, a young boy appeared to take his reins. Je'Rol did the same, glad to be off the horse and curious what brought Je'Surana forward.

Amid the road-weary predators, they met on the hill.

Je'Surana stopped before Je'Dron and gave him a graceful bow. "My lord."

"Lady Je'Surana." Je'Dron smiled and extended a hand to her, but she stepped towards Je'Rol instead.

Je'Dron dropped his hand, a frown creasing his forehead in a sign of a possible argument, but he gave a nod, seeming to accept her decision. "Very well." He motioned to a few others, who transformed to accompany them as the orange and black guards, and gave Je'Rol only a passing glance before his eyes settled again on the young woman. "Come."

Je'Surana looked up hopefully at Je'Rol. "Thank you."

Uncertain what to say, he held his tongue but stayed with her when she followed the demonlord, his insides twisting with doubts uplifted by hope and the presence of the young woman. He considered leading her away, but she focused ahead with purpose in each step.

The scent of human fear came from her, but she continued without hesitation. Her courage surprised him coming from one who seemed so innocent. Perhaps he had been wrong about the daughter of Je'Kaoron; she bore an inner strength he admired. While it could have been her *dispirit* power, he would still have admired her dedication to serving Je'Dron.

Along the sheer side of the plateau, several tigers ran down the zigzagging road while others materialized from shadows along the cliffs and structures of the city. A few goblins bobbled along among them in their dark colored robes, reminding Je'Rol of Skar and the secrets the goblins bore.

Still, his eyes beheld nothing extraordinary. "Where is the gate?"

"There." Je'Dron extended an arm and a finger towards a formation among the rocks near the base of one of the waterfalls. From the silver mist and rainbow behind it emerged an innocuous doorway. Like the statue of rings in the ancient building, carvings of people stood on each side with slumped shoulders bearing a burden—a bow supporting a globe. The Nik'Terek Gate was indeed a work of art of the Master Race.

From the opposite side, a large force of tigers emerged from the misty rainbows of the city, led by royals already on the floor of the valley.

From their side, Je'Dron's forces followed behind him and formed an arc around their half of the area.

In the center, the gate stood on its circular pedestal like the piece of art it was, drawing one's eyes to the anguish of the faces frozen in time to bear their burden. The pathway under the arch stood clear, inviting one to pass through, but Je'Rol had seen enough in his travels to know looks could be deceiving. If the gate was a doorway of destruction, he wasn't about to test it. He'd leave that to the demonlords.

The game board had been set. Je'Rekun had lured Je'Dron there, but it had been Je'Dron's idea through his agent, Je'Kaoron. Je'Rol had played his part and suffered for it, but no one else would. When Je'Dron revealed the obelisk, he would gain control and end the bloodshed, and then he would destroy it. He would protect Je'Surana and find his peace, and not Nadia nor Je'Dron nor Je'Rekun nor Je'Kaoron nor any other Adept or demonlord would stop him.

Beneath the cloak, his fingers tightened into fists and legs tensed to make the spring for the obelisk when Je'Dron's trusted bearer revealed himself.

Je'Dron stopped at the base of the pedestal. Je'Surana stopped a few strides behind him with Je'Rol at her side determined to protect her.

Two of the lead tigers broke from the other group, which fanned out into an arch opposite the one made up of Je'Dron's forces. Growls and snarls accompanied tails lashing and ears pinned from the larger group. More than one swiped a claw through the air in threat, but so far, none dared ignite a bloody confrontation.

Je'Rol stepped closer to Je'Surana as the two tigers transformed into the robed figure of a scowling Je'Rekun and the white and black breeches, shirt, and vest worn with the calm neutrality of Je'Kaoron. Or was that a hint of a smile?

Je'Kaoron with Je'Rekun. Did Je'Rekun even suspect his duplicity?

The two demonlords stopped on the opposite side of the gateway. The two armies quieted behind them, giving the crash of the waterfall the only voice for what seemed an eternity, while the two brothers stared at one another.

"The message said you sought peace," Je'Dron said.

Smugness crept up Je'Rekun's face. "Then you misinterpreted. My message said to meet me here, on this day, to discuss *ending this feud*. Peace with you was never my intention."

"As I expected." Je'Dron stepped aside, giving Je'Surana a clear exposure to what stood beyond, including Je'Kaoron, who bobbed his head in a brief nod. "You could never be trusted, so I came prepared."

Next to Je'Rol, the woman took a deep breath. What part did she have in this? Did they intend her to test the gate?

Je'Surana lifted the bottom of her gown. What was she doing? How could Je'Kaoron allow her to expose herself like this? She was too innocent to allow herself to be used, or had they groomed her for this part all this time?

"What are you doing?"

"Quiet, Je'Rol!" She continued to expose her leg up to her thigh and a harness of some kind with a strap that went up further, likely to her waist. Secured within the leather was an object the length of her forearm, and about the same width, which ended in a point. Gold gleamed in the sunlight, blurring the markings covering it.

Je'Rol's heart stopped for a second with the realization as she untied the strings holding it to the front of her leg. No! Her? All this time? "*You* had it!"

Je'Dron had said the obelisk was with one he trusted not to use it. After all the years Je'Rol had spent searching, it was there before him, on the leg of another half-blood.

One with the power of an Adept. That thought turned his blood cold, yet it made perfect sense. No demonlord would strap anything to their bodies, which would be awkward when they transformed. They could hide nothing. Half-bloods couldn't transform but had to wear tailored clothing like humans. It was easier for Je'Surana to bear the obelisk, and more convenient under her gown, than for any demonlord.

"What is it?" Je'Rekun demanded.

Je'Surana finished untying the straps holding the obelisk in place and lifted it away as her gown dropped back into place to hide her legs and the harness.

Je'Rol's heart pounded in his chest, the debate raging inside of what action to take. He wanted it; his search would be over.

But it wouldn't. They would take it from him.

They would be powerless against him.

If he figured out how to use it. And Nadia…If she took it, all hope would be lost. Even if he was able to use it, he would never be free of those hoping to claim it for themselves, and there were far worse and far more powerful individuals who could wrest it from his hands.

"You haven't heard of it." Je'Dron made no move to take it, as Je'Rol would have expected after speaking with the demonlord. "The obelisk of Mai'Kari, able to control all demons, now in the hands of a half-blood. Like the legends that said a half-blood had destroyed it, that will now bear truth."

Je'Rekun's face contorted in rage and fear. "You're lying!"

"Am I?" Je'Dron gave Je'Surana a questioning look. She clutched the obelisk close to her and nodded.

The urge to take it exploded inside Je'Rol, calling forth the beast, but the truth of Je'Kaoron's words tightened his fingers into fists at his sides to stop his hands.

Je'Kaoron was right.

Je'Rol's job now was to see it destroyed. No one would control him again, nor would they control Je'Surana or any other half-blood. Except the Adepts didn't need the obelisk to control them; they needed it to control the demonlords.

He glanced back and caught Nadia's eyes not far away among the tigers. She could command Je'Surana or him to give it up, but if he destroyed it, the Adepts would lose one tool they sought for domination of the world. Nadia would take this information back to them, though. They would learn that Je'Dron had destroyed the obelisk.

For the best. It would be one less means for the Adepts to take over the world.

Next to him, Je'Surana closed her eyes, the golden artifact pressed against her. He couldn't think of a safer keeper for it than the innocent young woman raised by demonlords yet with the power of an Adept. She had the power but never used it. Very clever of them to entrust her with it.

"Well?" Je'Rekun crossed his arms, a smug grin on his face, while worry crept into Je'Kaoron's face.

"Are you all right?" Je'Rol whispered aside to her.

"Ssh!"

He watched her, each second raising his concern as her face pinched tighter and her fingers paled around the obelisk.

"Enough!" Je'Rekun's roar seemed to silence even the waterfall for a moment. "You're a fool, and you will die with the rest." He signaled to the growing army behind him.

"No," Je'Surana whimpered, her eyes on her father.

"Take them out!" Je'Rekun called.

Tigers growled and roared, closing in on them from both sides.

The snarling and thrashing of tigers around them drowned out the crash of the waterfall.

Je'Rol closed in on Je'Surana to protect her, but a slash across his back stung and snagged his cloak to yank him off balance backwards and away from her. He stumbled back, but a heartbeat later, panic crept into his heart at the sight of Je'Surana curled up with the obelisk. He ran a tongue across sharp teeth while claws extended and yanked the cloak from the tiger's claw.

An orange mass of tiger knocked him to his back.

The scream of fear from Je'Surana sent a cold shudder through him, calling on the beast's hunger to fight. He struggled against it; transforming would put her in worse danger.

While the other tigers engaged each other in bloodshed, one of the tigers snarled and bit at him. He barely avoided those teeth, but claws dug deep into his shoulder, drawing the stench of blood craved by the beast within. The scent called to it, taunted it. Je'Rol struggled to restrain it, but the strength of the demonlord threatened his life, drawing the beast out in defense. He couldn't concentrate on fighting the tiger and the beast within.

If Je'Dron could stop this, he might be saved. Already the beast growled as Je'Rol dug his claws into the neck of the tiger to hold back those jaws.

* * *

It happened in a blur, the mesh of tigers, and she was in the thick of it; but they weren't interested in her. Nadia dodged and avoided the snarling, clawing melee of bloody bodies to reach the woman. That artifact was the key to the survival of her kind. If they could control the demonlords with it, humans would be free of their tyranny and she could stop the battle to save herself.

One of the white tigers stopped before her and snarled, its tail lashing.

Her heart pounded and her breath froze in her lungs. She had no business there and no favor among the demonlords, especially Je'Rekun's forces. Another tiger leapt at it and sank its jaws in the neck of the first.

She caught her breath and hurried towards the woman with the obelisk. Skar had been right or, rather, Je'Rol had been right. It did exist. If she could get her hands on it—

Something else jumped in her way, something neither tiger nor man. Ripped clothes and flesh hung from his body. The ears of a tiger had replaced a man's among the frayed white and black locks tied back in a tail. Black lips curled away from sharp teeth and he hunched on claws, not a man's hands.

"Je'Rol?" Her heart whimpered at the sight before her.

He growled, those pale blue eyes fixed on her and his posture that of an animal ready to strike.

She swallowed her hesitations and focused on her power. "Calm yourself, Je'Rol." He shouldn't be that way. He had to return to himself. *Had* to. She never wanted this to happen to him.

"Listen to me." It took all her concentration to make him step back. "You're a man. You're Je'Rol. You want to be human."

He hesitated and she caught her breath. The blood rage had taken him, but something of the man still remained. There was hope.

Behind him, a pair of orange tigers thrashed at a royal, but one of the wolf-like Cas'Lu twice their size snarled and bore down on them. They jumped onto its sides, but it took them from the bleeding white tiger.

Je'Rol's ear twitched back, half his attention on her and the other on the events behind him. Now was her chance to regain control and pull, or hope to pull, him from the blood rage.

A tiger snarled behind her. *Not now!* She couldn't afford to take her eyes off Je'Rol, but the threat surrounded her. If she survived, she would count herself lucky.

Behind Je'Rol, the young woman fell to her knees next to the bleeding white tiger as if to protect it from the chaos, while Je'Dron gazed at the obelisk standing on his palm. His eyes caught hers for a moment with a scowl, before he threw it towards the gate, where it disintegrated at the threshold.

No! It was gone in a blink. Rather than use it to stop the madness, Je'Dron had destroyed it.

Idiot! He could have ended this.

But it would have started again with the destruction of the obelisk anyway.

A heavy weight threw her forward to the ground, knocking the wind from her and sending pain through her chest. Spikes like daggers pierced her shoulders. In that second, she took her last breath, expecting a quick bite to end her life.

But something else knocked the points of claws from her, relieving her of the tiger's weight. She lay in the grass, her ribs aching with the struggle to breathe, and caught sight of a bloody Je'Rol breaking away from an orange tiger. He was more tiger now, his body positioned strongly over four legs and his face extended with a flattened nose.

The orange tiger snarled, its tail thrashing as it hunched down.

A white blur landed on the orange tiger, its jaws sinking into the neck of the orange with a sickening crunch.

She hardly had time to think as Je'Rol's cold eyes snapped back on her with his snarl.

Nadia pushed herself up from the ground, the ache of her chest disrupting her concentration on controlling him. Nevertheless, he stayed back, those gleaming teeth exposed and ready to rip her to shreds if she wavered in the slightest.

The obelisk was gone, but her life wasn't. And neither was his.

"Let me help you," she pleaded. The girl from that old life called to him as she had then. As he had saved her from the natters then, he had saved her from a demonlord now, except in the blood rage. Something of the Je'Rol she loved was still there. He wasn't gone.

She could help him.

She didn't want to kill him.

Nadia rose on her hands and knees and hesitated to wipe the cool wetness from her cheek. Faced with the decision now, she couldn't do it. Je'Rol wasn't a murderer. Even in the blood rage, he still had some control. He chose not to hurt her but to save her. He had stopped short of attacking her when they caught up to him on the hunt too. Something in him still cared. Maybe....

Maybe half-bloods weren't the threat they thought. Maybe they could be trained—

Je'Rol took a calculating step forward, his eyes never wavering from her.

Maybe not. Her heart sank in disappointment. She wiped her eyes and stood up slowly, as much as to avoid a quick attack from him as to avoid the pain that made her wince with each movement. She backed away, aware of the threat all around her. If he attacked, she would never escape.

Despite her lapse of focus, he still hesitated, but it couldn't last forever.

Nadia slipped her hand to her waist and grasped the dagger sheathed on her belt. She didn't want to use it, but he wasn't the only threat around her.

The grip of the leather-wrapped dagger handle in her palm brought a sense of security. Her fingers clutched it tight.

Je'Rol sprang at her—

A white blur knocked her down. The air of its passing brushed against her face.

Je'Rol clawed at the tiger wrestling him down, squirming and growling while struggling to escape. He twisted and contorted his body, still the size of a man and with much of the shape. Somehow he freed himself of the tiger while slashing at it and leaving bloody marks, but the tiger never attempted to kill him.

The bloody man-tiger backed away, his ears flattened back at the white tiger now standing between him and Nadia.

The white tiger backed towards her, growling in warning at him.

Nadia glanced aside, but the other demonlords were all engaged. The young woman lay still over the body of the white tiger near the gate, and Nadia saw no signs of either Je'Dron or Je'Rekun.

It had all exploded into chaos in a blink.

In a blur, the white tiger transformed. With red streaks staining the white and black tunic and trousers he now wore, Je'Dron stood between her and Je'Rol, his eyes never leaving the creature threatening her.

He backed towards her and leaned close. "He's frightened and hungry. The blood rage has consumed him wholly."

"No. He saved me. There must be a way to save him." This couldn't be the end of the Je'Rol she knew. She had to try to bring him around.

From the corner of her eyes, she saw nothing on the demonlord's face to give her hope, only the tightening of his jaw and a slow nod.

"You may be the only one."

Her? But demonlords possessed far greater powers. "I've been trying."

"And he was hesitant until you gave in to other thoughts, like killing." He glanced at the dagger in her hand.

Je'Rol paced warily, unconcerned by the melee around them. His attention focused on her and Je'Dron.

Nadia looked down at the dagger. Had that been it? An instinct to protect himself?

Why didn't he attack the tigers around him, or was it because part of him knew he had no chance of surviving a direct confrontation? That indicated reasoning, not the blind rage assumed of half-bloods in his state. There might be hope yet.

"Put it down," Je'Dron said in a steady tone.

She glanced down at the dagger in her hands, giving the handle a squeeze of reassurance. Without it, she was helpless.

Except she had a demonlord protecting her.

"Do it!"

She squatted down and set the dagger on the ground, her mind focused on *dispiriting* the demon side now fixed on her. *Please come back, Je'Rol.* "Easy, Je'Rol," she said in a calming tone amid the growling, snarling, barking, squawking mass of bloody predators battling across the valley.

He snarled, those black-tipped ears flat back to his head.

She swallowed her fear, focusing on bending his will to hers. She wanted the man who had loved her, the one who had protected her from this side of himself.

"Come back to me, Je'Rol. This isn't you. You're a gentle man, not a monster."

His lips twitched in a snarl but he hesitated and closed them over sharp teeth.

Encouraged by her success, Nadia took a small step forward. "It's all right. I'm here. I'm…No more hunting, Je'Rol. I promise." Tears blurred her vision with the strength of the emotions she dug up on which to draw her power. "I never wanted to hurt you either. I'm sorry. I didn't know."

Je'Rol stood on legs and arms quietly, his ears forward, listening.

Something knocked her off her feet from the side. In that motion, she caught the blur of Je'Dron's transformation as another tiger sought to sink its teeth into his head.

A heartbeat later, Je'Rol snarled and launched himself. On instinct, she grabbed the dagger from the ground and brought it up to defend herself as she rolled up to her knees.

It all happened so fast, she didn't know which one the knife sank into as their weight came down on her. Not until he landed on her and rolled off, gasping and reaching for the dagger did her heart stop.

"Je'Rol!"

He fell to his knees, blood pouring from the wound in his chest. She caught him as the dagger fell from his hands.

In the second it took her to reach him and grab his shoulders to keep him from hitting the ground, his appearance changed.

He looked up at her with the face of a man, gasping as if he couldn't breathe. "Nadia." Bloody hands grasped at her clothes.

"I'm sorry," she cried. Why him? It shouldn't have been him. Damn him! Why couldn't he have stayed away? He'd been so close to coming back to her.

"I…lo—loved you." He coughed up blood and gasped and struggled as if choking.

"No. Je'Rol." Sobs shook through her from watching him suffering and being helpless to save him, and she held him in those final seconds of his struggle. He'd never survive that injury.

Her only consolation came in holding his limp body seconds later. But the tears refused to stop. She held him close to her, burying her tears in his hair and not caring about the wet warmth of his blood soaking into her uniform. "I loved you too," she whispered and meant it.

She hardly noticed the battle dying down around her, leaving bodies strewn upon the bloody valley around the gate. Even after some time, when gentle hands rested on her to separate her from the lifeless body, she refused to let go. They pried her away amid her protests while she watched them take Je'Rol from her.

29

Nadia stared at the tigresses seated across from her in the carriage but saw nothing except the final moments when Je'Rol leapt, as if time slowed so each fraction of movement replayed in her mind. He hadn't leapt for her directly. He had reacted to the fighting and her break of control in that moment.

She should never have reached for the dagger. Every second she cursed herself for not trusting him.

Amid the dreary rain of mourning, they arrived at *Acropa Je'Gri* and ushered her into a room where the tigresses went through the motions of bathing her and dressing her in a fresh gown while she sat listless, the pain of her loss immobilizing her with regrets. They left nothing behind that she could use to hurt herself, nor did they leave the balcony doors unlocked.

She lay in bed, wishing the pain would leave her. He had been a half-blood and deserved to die.

But he had loved her, or else he would have killed her sooner, and she had never stopped loving him. The pain of thinking he had betrayed her was proof of that.

The Adepts were wrong about half-bloods. Even in that last blood rage, something of the true Je'Rol had lingered, stopping him from attacking her without reason.

She wiped the tears sliding across her nose before burying her face in the pillow beneath her head.

From somewhere close, a bell resounded into the silence, its solemn, mourning toll aching through her heart.

When it ended, a new sound arose—singing. She listened to the lamenting of life and the relief of death sung in the beauty of the demonlord *Lexic*. There was no anguish but a peaceful surrender to the words and the harmony which echoed with surreal grace through the palace.

After some time, it died away, leaving her lighter and her tears dried. She closed her eyes and slept.

A soft voice and a gentle touch roused her from dreams she didn't want to wake from, dreams of escape to another land where she was young and in love with a man who held her close, but she never saw his face.

She rolled over, seeking the solace of the dreams as long as they would take her. Her ribs ached but the pain faded as she lay still.

A short time later, the snick of the door broke the spell. She opened her eyes to the sun slanting across the floor from the balcony doors. The scent of food surrounded her in an aroma that should have stirred her hunger after seven days of almost no appetite, but it did nothing more than draw her eyes to the plate of food and glass of water on the chest of drawers nearby.

She stared at it for a long time, until the slant of the sun climbed up the bottom corner of the bed. It crept along towards her bare feet. For a few seconds, she contemplated pulling away, as if the sun itself was a poison, but decided against it.

Despite the ache in her sides, Nadia rose and slid off the bed. A few nibbles of the small loaf and downing the glass of water satisfied her insides. In her gown and with her hair long over her shoulders, she walked into the sunlight shining through the glass doors of the balcony. It cast the gardens below in a radiant glow. Pink blossoms spread upon the vines climbing the palace walls. Outside, the world went on without her. Life went on as if Je'Rol's death meant nothing, as if nothing had happened seven days ago.

She gazed out there, separated from the world by remorse, until her legs trembled in weakness and she had to sit. With her head against the warm glass, she reached for the world beyond, which had weakened into a delicate fragility with the revelations that had come. It was smooth, not the rough texture it appeared to be. She ran her finger along it, waiting for the truth to reveal itself in rough edges that would prick.

Everything she had believed had been proven wrong. The Adepts had trained her to despise demonlords and to hate half-bloods. And it had come so easy after Je'Rol had left her that night to protect her from the blood rage. She couldn't have controlled him then. He had made the hard decision to leave rather than risk killing her. He never wanted to kill but had run to avoid persecution and the threats to his life which brought on the blood rage.

And Je'Dron, who could have controlled all demons including his own kind, had forsaken that power and destroyed the obelisk. What did it all mean? What did he want?

What did she want? Why was she there?

Her training had taken her many places to kill demons and half-bloods, many at birth. Yet the demonlords who spawned them seemed to care. Maybe Morana had been right and the demonlord had loved her. Was it possible? She'd been trained to believe they didn't care about anyone or anything but their own satisfaction. Je'Dron had sworn to avenge any attempts on Je'Rol's life by taking the life of the one who killed him.

Except he had let her live. She almost wished he had upheld his vow.

The world was changing, but not all for the better. The Adepts sought power, hungered for it enough to risk annihilation by the demonlords.

Where did she fit? Why had she lived?

A soft knock on the door faded into the background of her thoughts, until a voice interrupted.

"You need to eat, my lady."

She recognized that voice, and only one demonlord had ever addressed her as an equal.

Nadia looked up at the gentle face of a man in a fur robe bearing the markings of his true nature. He squatted down next to her, the sun on his face casting it in the glow of something beautiful and ethereal. Was she dreaming yet?

"Your injuries cannot heal if you're weak."

She turned away from Je'Kaoron and stared outside. "I'm not hungry."

He said nothing for a long while, nor did he leave her.

The world outside drew her attention from him, helping her to forget the company, until he spoke again.

"Je'Dron places no blame on you for acting in self-defense."

Although she had realized she wouldn't be alive if Je'Dron had been angry, his words relieved her and opened a doorway inside to let out some of the misery. "What happened? What went wrong?"

He shook his head, his expression sullen with regrets. "I should never have involved Je'Surana. It was my fault. I thought she had mastered the obelisk, but her practice with me was insufficient to prepare her for the pressure of facing Je'Rekun and the others."

He took a deep breath. "I had to do something. The moment Je'Rekun signaled his forces to attack, I took the opportunity of his distraction to throw him at the gate. He reacted quicker than I expected and transformed and turned the attack on me. We fought and, had I not contacted those in his forces still loyal to Je'Dron immediately before we met with him, I would have disappeared. It was a split second decision that saved my life. In that we lost one of our own in the gate with Je'Rekun, but it's nothing compared to the deaths of the battle. Je'Dron finished the task by destroying the obelisk. Now, no one may use it."

It had all happened within minutes, sending the field into chaos and blood.

"In a way, Je'Rol's death is my fault, not yours." His voice was gentle and quiet, soothing some of the blame she had taken, yet...No. He was wrong.

Tears stung her eyes and choked her on the horrible truth. She swallowed it but her voice trembled. "*I* stabbed him. It was my hand that bore the dagger." If she never saw that dagger again, she would still regret it. It was lost, she hoped.

Or not. Je'Kaoron reached inside his sleeve and pulled the accursed weapon out.

He turned it over lengthwise between his hands. "A powerful weapon but very dark magic," he said.

She pulled her legs tighter to her beneath the gown and pressed away from it and the accusations it stabbed at her.

"It grows more powerful with each spirit it takes." Je'Kaoron offered the handle to her. "But not Je'Rol's."

She refused to look at it, but found some comfort that it hadn't taken Je'Rol's spirit. The last one had been Morana's child, a half-blood Je'Gri. She didn't want that reminder and what it represented.

Je'Kaoron set the dagger on the floor between them. "You must be a strong Adept to wield such a weapon."

Nadia gazed at it but pressed into the glass of the balcony door to escape. It might not have taken Je'Rol's spirit, but it had taken part of hers when it ended Je'Rol's life. She couldn't touch it; not yet.

A soft caress brushed away the hair from her face, tracing a line around her jaw to her chin. The pressure lifted her face and her eyes to the concern on his face.

"You need to eat, my lady. Bread and water are not enough." His hands went to hers and pulled her up with him so the knife lay at her bare feet. "Come. You need your strength."

She hesitated but took a step over the knife. In that moment, a wave of dizziness threatened to darken the world around her.

The next thing she knew, soft fur surrounded her. A demonlord held her, and not just any, but Lord Je'Kaoron.

Warmth flooded up through her. This wasn't what she wanted. It should have been Je'Rol, but she had killed him. Tears welled up with the sobs that returned and soaked into the fur.

"We can only envy humans and their capacity to care so profoundly for someone that it could cause such deep pain. That is a power we will never possess but for fleeting moments so precious and few."

Never? Then they didn't feel regret or sorrow?

Nadia sniffed and pushed away. Did he feel anything? Or was there something he wanted from her?

"You honor Je'Dron and his son with your tears. Such remorse cannot be faked…High Lord Je'Dron is sorry for your loss." He turned so that one arm supported her next to him and helped her walk to the bed, where he sat her down. "Eat, my lady. You will need your strength for the journey ahead of you."

"My journey?"

"The message High Lord Je'Dron wishes you to carry to the Adepts in their temples." He moved as if to leave her, but she held onto his robe. The softness brushing through her fingers provided some small comfort she hadn't expected.

A part of her didn't want to be left alone, and his presence had brought some peace to her world. "Why me?" She sought his face for an answer, but only confusion furrowed his brow.

"Why you…what?"

He didn't get it, and it wasn't worth explaining. Nadia let go and shifted her gaze to the plate of food likely cold after setting so long. It had been hot that morning, but the morning had passed on.

"Eat and heal, my lady." His gentle voice drew her eyes to follow his back receding from the room. Lord Je'Kaoron wasn't like the others, nor was Je'Dron. In many ways, he seemed more human than not. How many other demonlords had changed similarly?

Did the Adepts plan to eliminate them?

Nadia stared after the door closed behind Lord Je'Kaoron. What would happen if they vanished from the world?

What would happen if Adepts were eliminated?

She shuddered. Je'Rekun hadn't been the only demonlord aware of something planned by the sects, but what was going on? She had to know. If Je'Rekun was willing to go to war, he must have sensed a new threat emerging. Traveling as she did kept her away from the temple, even the sects. The sorcerers who visited her at the palace had known something but hadn't shared it.

What were they hiding?

Nadia eyed the food, her stomach aching with a renewed interest.

The time had come to return.

About the Author

M. A. Nilles is the darker side of Melanie Nilles. She currently resides in central North Dakota with her family, cats, and her horse. Her published works under the name Melanie Nilles include the *Starfire Angels* series and the *Legend of the White Dragon* epic. *Tiger Born* is her first book as M. A. Nilles. More can be found at www.melanienilles.com.